SPIES IN

— OUR —

MIDST

To Fred —
It was such a pleasure
meeting you. Enjoy!

A NOVEL

LM REYNOLDS

LM Reynolds

Published in the United States of America by Mirage Books

ISBN 978-0-9862327-1-8

Cover design by Damonza
Cover photographs: Yeko Photo Studio, rasoul ali, Adisa, Ints, Studio37, STILLFX, Eky Studio/Bigstock.com

For Joe

An extraordinary man, an extraordinary life.

"You have zero privacy anyway. Get over it."

—Scott McNealy
CEO Sun Microsystems, 1999,
at an event launching a new technology
for his company

Prologue

July, present day
Marblehead, Massachusetts

I drove by the house today. It looked as if somebody had finally moved in, judging by the newly mown grass and the open windows on the second floor. I wondered briefly if they knew. How could you keep it a secret, even from some outsider? Maybe the new owner intended a tourist attraction. I could even visualize the sign: "This is where it happened. Full tour $10. Video $25."

The property had been seized by the government several months earlier, put up for auction, purchased by a property investment company, rebuilt, and finally offered for sale. There are currently a number of lawsuits working their way through the tangle of the judicial system. The lawyers are having a field day and pundits argue various points via the media, but legal scholars are quick to declare that the case follows no known precedent.

I doubt that the courts will ever truly figure it out, given that 90 percent of the details are being withheld in the interest of national security. If you attempt to research the case, you'll find a considerable amount of speculation out on the World Wide Web. There are all manner of sites offering theories and media reenactments, and discussion threads are rife with accusations of conspiracy and the usual off-the-wall opinions on the "facts" of the case. If you access the government sites, however, you'll find nothing of value because the government maintains, and I'm quoting the head of the FBI here, "The FBI had no involvement in the incident on Harboredge Way, but we are continuing to investigate the circumstances surrounding the events that took place there."

But the bottom line is that five months ago two people died, and somebody in some alphabet-soup agency knows the truth. So do I ... I just can't prove it.

PART ONE

Lindsey

February, five months ago
Friday through Wednesday

Chapter 1

Friday night
Marblehead, Massachusetts

It was almost midnight when my cell phone chirped its annoying electronic tones. They're the sounds that come with the phone and will automatically cause at least twenty people in the vicinity to check their own phones for an incoming call. I tried changing the ringtone once, but changed it back. I had become so accustomed to the standard tune that every time the new one rang, I assumed the call was for someone else. Did I mention that I'm a creature of habit?

The display showed that it was a blocked number, and I was tempted to dismiss it. I was enjoying an evening with friends, and we'd done an admirable job of polishing off multiple bottles of a fairly decent Cabernet purchased earlier that day.

The chirp continued. Jason, never one to hold back his opinions on any matter, rolled his eyes. "Tell the client that Friday nights are sacrosanct, particularly at this hour." The assumption, of course, was that some critical application on some computer, somewhere, had gone awry and someone wanted it fixed, pronto. This wouldn't be good, considering my present condition.

I run a business that provides website design and integration with internal business systems, as well as networking and security architecture. If you've ever visited the Colonial Airways website, then you've seen our work. Of course, Colonial isn't exactly a major airline, so it may not be on your radar screen. Basically, we'll provide similar services for whoever wants to pay our asking price. Well, there are exceptions. We won't work with people we dislike. I can usually ferret them out in fifteen minutes of conversation. I just politely inform them that we really don't have the resources to accommodate them right now, offer them a few names of others in the business, and thank them for the call. Fortunately, there are fewer of these Napoleons out there than you might imagine. Otherwise, we'd be flipping burgers at a local fast-food joint just to make ends meet.

We all make a comfortable living, and have learned to take time to smell the flowers along the way. There are only six of us in our little company: the four of us here tonight and two part-time staffers. It's a great team, and we're also good friends. We've remained stable and sane during a time when so many of the bigger companies have undergone cutbacks and layoffs. And we still enjoy our work, which really says something. The downside of this business is that occasionally problems arise at the most inopportune times. This was one of them.

I hit the button. "Lindsey here."

"Miss Carlisle?" I didn't recognize the voice. Polite, businesslike ... a touch of, perhaps, Texas? I noticed that he used Miss—not Ms., not Mrs. Who did that anymore?

"Speaking."

"This is Special Agent Adrian Santori of the FBI. There's been an incident, and we would like to talk with you as soon as possible."

Right. An FBI agent who knew my cell number. "Ha ha," I said flatly. "Bye now."

A nanosecond after I ended the call, it chirped again. This was irritating.

"Get a life, or lose my number. Bye."

"Please don't hang up." He said it fast, hoping to get the words out before I terminated the connection.

I paused for a moment. "Who is this?" I was buying a little time, thinking it must be a rather stupid practical joke, trying to place the voice, mentally sorting through the audio files stored up there in my fuzzy gray matter.

"Special Agent Adrian Santori of the FBI."

"You said that before. I don't know anybody in the FBI. I don't even know anybody who does. If you think this is funny, your sense of humor needs an adjustment."

The buzz of conversation in the room ceased abruptly as the faces around me stared wide-eyed.

"I assure you that this is no joke," the caller continued. "We have a serious situation here. Where are you?"

The pleasant buzz from the wine was instantly replaced by a shot of adrenaline as fear kicked in. I'd been stalked a couple of years ago. That period in my life had robbed me of more than sleep; it had changed me. There was no way in hell I was telling some stranger where I was.

I was talking louder now. "I don't understand why you're calling me. What do you want? What's happened?"

Jason, previously sprawled in front of the fireplace, was now standing over me, hands on hips, concern marking his face, eyebrows raised in question. Jason was my best friend, business partner, and self-appointed protector. We'd known each other since the diaper age, and I relied on him completely. He was a shade over six feet, with straight, light-brown hair pulled back in a shoulder-length ponytail, and had a black belt in tae kwon do, a genius IQ, a sense of humor that just knocked me over, and a steady calm that made me feel safe. He was also gay. I kept my eyes fixed on him while I listened.

Agent Santori, if that's who he really was, responded, "Ma'am, I cannot provide details over the phone. Where are you?" More formal now, he knew he had my attention—and wanted control.

I wasn't going to give it to him—maybe I've just dealt with too many telemarketers. I said the only thing that popped into my head: "Name and badge number. I'm calling the FBI office in Boston."

I frantically mimed to Jason for pen and paper as I heard a long sigh, followed by a few muffled sounds. "Adrian" must have covered the mouthpiece, either to mask a stream of obscenities or a conversation with some other participant in this little drama. I was vaguely aware of hands digging in purses and feet running for the desk. A pen and notebook were in my hands before he spoke again.

"Special Agent Adrian Santori." He spelled it for me, making sure I understood that it was Adrian with an I-A-N and Santori with an R-I. "89484. I'll call you back in five minutes."

He even gave me the number for the Bureau. I copied it down, but didn't intend to use it. I'd get it myself. God help him if he was an imposter, since I'd report him in a heartbeat for impersonating a federal officer. I was pretty sure they'd be able to trace the caller, blocked number notwithstanding.

I clicked off and stared at the group. I started to dial information, and noticed that my hands were shaking. I'm usually reasonably composed under pressure, but being contacted by the FBI was a little beyond my limit. I was beginning to understand why television and the movies always show people getting nervous in this kind of situation. I'd always thought it was a bit absurd. After all, if you haven't done anything, what's the big deal? But what if he wasn't FBI, but was instead some lunatic who wanted to hurt me? And if this guy really was FBI, didn't they have ways of tracking cell-phone locations? TV showed cops using all those electronics that triangulate the suspect's position. I was becoming irrational, but at least I recognized the problem before I dialed; I needed someone who was a little more in control. Wordlessly, I handed the phone and the information to Jason.

As he handled the details of contacting the FBI to verify the identity of "Agent Santori," I wondered about the reasons for the call to me, figuring that if the call was legit, then it had to be related to one of my clients. I mentally paged though them, but came up blank. None of them seemed a likely candidate for an FBI investigation.

Jason hung up the phone and took a deep breath. "He's legit. They said he's out of the DC office and verified that he's working a case in the Boston area. They wouldn't tell me anything else, other than to say we should ask for his identification when we meet him and what to look for on the ID. I don't get it. If it's one of our clients they're after, what are they doing in Marblehead in the middle of the night?"

I hadn't even considered that part of the equation. I was so accustomed to calls at strange hours that it hadn't seemed abnormal. But Jason was right. A couple of our clients lived up here, but their offices were out on Route 128, a major highway that was home to dozens of high-tech companies. It didn't make sense.

My friends engaged themselves in conjuring up possible scenarios, from the plausible to the ridiculous. Within a few minutes we were all laughing, having convinced ourselves that whatever was going on had nothing to do with us—we were just a follow-up call from a business card they'd found somewhere with my cell number scribbled on the back. But I was still disquieted. Why would the FBI call at this hour? What could be so urgent?

Agent Santori's five minutes stretched into more than ten by the time the cell rang again. I saw the blocked-number text and hit the button to talk. "Lindsey here."

"Miss Carlisle, I assume that you've verified my identity, and that you will now tell me where you are." There was that bossy tone again, with no pretense of amicability, no pleasantries. He just cut straight to the chase.

Evidently we were going to have a face-to-face, whether I

liked it or not. But I didn't care for his tone, and I don't like to relinquish control that easily. This was my town, my turf, and my time. I decided to draw a line in the sand. "Could we do this tomorrow? It's very late; I'm enjoying my evening, and discussing business isn't on my agenda tonight."

There was a long pause at the other end. When I was a kid, I could always tell when I had stepped over the line with my mother. Instead of yelling, which only resulted in a shouting match, she would become very quiet. Those silences were so discomforting that I would actually experience a kind of anxiety attack. I had that same sensation now: my pulse was racing, and it felt as if the temperature in the room had gone up twenty degrees. It was time to call a truce.

"Look," I said, "I'm sorry. This whole thing has caught me off guard." I looked around at the others in the room, gave them a resigned shrug, and recited Jason's address on Gregory Street. Jason exchanged my glass of wine for a mug of coffee. Marblehead is not a big town. If the feds were already in Marblehead, they would be on the doorstep in less than ten minutes.

I stepped outside, the frigid air relieving the heat in my cheeks. The deck overlooked the shimmering waters of the harbor and the spit of land that the natives called the Neck. In summer, the place was so packed with boats that you could almost hopscotch from here to the yacht club, directly across the way. Launch services from the five clubs in town picked up and delivered boaters, and weekend evenings would echo with beckoning horn blasts. In winter, however, the nights were calm and serene, punctuated by the gentle slap of the waves caressing the docks and the occasional clanging of the bell on a buoy. If there was peace to be found on this earth, this was it.

Jason cracked the door open and mouthed through a fog of vapor, "They're here."

Chapter 2

I had conjured up a mental image of Adrian Santori, relying heavily on the last name to create the look of a mob-
ster-cum-supercop. I'd pictured him with dark hair and
olive skin, in his fifties, somewhat on the chubby side, moderately short, wearing the requisite rumpled white shirt and dark
tie. Watching him enter the room, I discovered that I'd pegged
the hair color, and that was it. The flesh-and-blood person was
probably late thirties, stood a solid six-three or four, and there
wasn't an ounce of chubby anywhere. Smartly attired in a
taupe shirt and olive drab khakis that accented dazzling green
eyes, he had a tanned and rugged look that suggested an out-
doorsman. While not exactly movie-marquee material, he was
still eye candy in a hardy sort of way. I couldn't help myself,
and glanced at his left hand even before the introductions.
Damn. The good ones are always taken.

He waited until his two companions were inside the room and
took positions behind him. I almost giggled at the cast of characters: one Caucasian male, one African American female, and one
Hispanic male. Could this be any more politically correct?

"Miss Carlisle?"

I nodded. "Call me Lindsey. I assume you're Mr. Santori. I guess since I made such a big deal of it, I'd better see the IDs. Sorry."

There was no hesitation as all three passed their credentials to me. Jason, who'd been the recipient of instructions on ID verification, peered over my shoulder and pronounced, "Looks good to me."

As I introduced all those present, prompting handshakes everywhere, I forced what I hoped was a charming smile. It wasn't that hard to do, considering the target. I was taken aback when he didn't reciprocate. This guy was all business.

"Miss Carlisle—Lindsey—it might be better if we had this conversation in private."

It felt like a script out of a TV show. This was where the poor shmuck always asked, "Am I in trouble?" If you were smart, you just called your lawyer. Obviously I wasn't, because I hadn't, and instead just blurted my thoughts on the matter. "These are my best friends and we work together. They should hear whatever you have to say about our clients." I registered the heads bobbing in agreement.

"Actually, this doesn't have anything to do with your business." He paused and looked directly into my eyes. Instead of the cold professionalism I'd been anticipating, his features softened, and he looked very human. For all his insistence that we meet, he suddenly looked as if he would prefer having a tooth extracted. I was completely confused.

"There's been an explosion and fire at your sister's house. I'm very sorry, but it appears that your sister and her husband were both killed."

I'd never completely grasped the meaning of the expression "time stood still" until that moment. For an instant, the world froze. For several moments afterward, I felt as if I were underwater, so distorted were the sounds reaching my consciousness. I must have just stood there gaping, because I gradually became aware of voices raised in concern. When my brain finally turned itself back on, I heard the female agent—I think she'd called herself Angela—issuing instructions to the others. I found myself guided to the sofa, a blanket draped over my shoulders, and a glass of liquor put in my grasp.

"Drink it," someone ordered. I'm not usually a hard-liquor kind of girl, but tossed it back in one swallow. While it was crucial to be clearheaded, it was also absolutely essential to dull my senses. Faced with the paradox, I held out the glass for another shot.

"How are you doing?" This from Santori, sitting in the wingback chair next to me.

I opened my mouth, but no words came out. I just stared at him, trying to come to grips with what he had said. It was completely irrational and obviously a horrific mistake of some kind. There was no way my sister was dead. There was no way her house exploded. There was no way the FBI would have been there. I've studied enough psychology to be familiar with the five stages of grief. I was firmly in the first stage: absolute denial.

"Look, I know this is terrible news for you and I honestly don't mean to be callous or insensitive, but we really need to ask you a couple of questions. Do you think you could do that?" It was Santori again.

The second shot was in my hand. Fight or flight? I set the full glass on the table. Fight. "Okay," I nodded. "But first I want to know exactly what happened."

"Fair enough. I can't give you all the details, so I'll just give you the *Reader's Digest* version. The DEA had been monitoring some drug activity on the North Shore. Since a lot of drug money eventually gets funneled to terrorist organizations, we cooperated and set up an operation to assess the situation and see if we could find a money trail. It led to your sister. We ran surveillance, and we've had her phone tapped for about a month; that's why we had your cell phone number. We had federal indictments for your sister and her husband. Tonight, we were supposed to meet a couple of blocks away from her house and go in with the warrants. We were just approaching her house when we saw the flames, and then there was an explosion. By the time the fire trucks arrived, the east wing of the house was pretty much destroyed. That's where we found the bodies."

I just couldn't believe what I was hearing. My sister complicit with funding terrorists? I looked at him blankly and held up my hands. "Whoa! What are you talking about?"

"I know this is a shock to you. We've reasonably determined that you had no prior knowledge of her activities."

"A shock? I am completely and totally stunned. I don't understand. First you tell me that my sister's dead, and then you tell me she's giving money to terrorists? It's just not even possible." My voice had gone up at least an octave.

"I'm sorry, Lindsey, but—"

I didn't let him finish. "You're wrong. You've got the wrong people." It took a minute for his words to register, something about them knowing I wasn't involved. I frowned as the realization came to me. "And are you saying that you investigated me, too?"

The eye contact didn't waver, but his head dropped in a slight nod. "You were a peripheral investigation."

I'd never heard a more asinine story. Denial was losing ground and was rapidly giving way to the anger stage. I knew I was going to lose my temper, but I kept trying to hold it in check because there were a couple of questions that needed to be answered first. I tried to focus on the story he'd given me. The east side of the house was basically the activity center: kitchen, office, TV room, deck, hot tub. If they'd been awake, it stood to reason they'd have been in that part of the house.

"How do you know it's my sister?"

"We don't have positive identification yet. That's one of the things we need your help with. But based on the fact that it's their house and there are two victims that appear to be a male and female ... uh ... sorry, it's just that they were pretty badly burned ... uh ... anyhow, we're making the preliminary assessment that they are the victims."

"What caused the fire?"

"We won't know for sure until the investigators can get out there in daylight, but it appears that a spark from the fireplace may have started the original fire. We think that the explosion occurred because of a leak in the propane tank for the hot tub."

"Wait a minute. If they were in the east part of the house,

then they weren't asleep." The bedrooms were at the other end.

"Well, they could have been in bed. It's possible that the smoke detector woke them up and they went to see what was wrong."

"Still, it doesn't make sense. It's not like this is a fifty-story building and there's nowhere to go. They have a two-story house built on a slope. The top floor opens onto the lawn in front and a deck in back. The bottom floor opens onto the back lawn. There are sliding doors everywhere. You just step outside. And wouldn't they have smelled the propane? How could they have died? I don't understand."

"We're thinking that maybe they were trying to fight the fire and were overcome by smoke. That happens more often than you care to think."

My thoughts were jumbled. I wasn't trying to argue the point so much as figure out how my sister, who was terrified of fire, could have succumbed to one. I tried to imagine the circumstances under which she would have gone toward the smoke and flames rather than away from them. It just wasn't computing.

"But she wouldn't have ..." I lost the rest of whatever I was going to say.

"We'll have more answers for you tomorrow. I'm so sorry, but I have to ask if you know their dentist. We'll need the records. We also want to know if you're aware of any safe deposit boxes they might have kept, any storage units, offshore accounts, things like that."

"I beg your pardon?" My face was hot again; I could feel

the blood surging through my temples. The alcohol may have contributed, but mostly I was becoming incensed by the responses I was getting. I briefly thought about how my sister would have handled this situation. I could picture her: calm, firm, not allowing anything to rile her, negotiating like a pro. But then she'd had some training in these matters. And that raised a rather important point. These jerks didn't seem to know who she was. Something wasn't right here.

I'm reasonably tolerant and fairly patient, but I have an incredibly short fuse when it comes to dealing with incompetence, bureaucratic bullshit, or lying in any form. Those who know me well will tell you that I'm not pleasant when I'm angry. They're also familiar with the signs of an impending eruption, particularly the tattoo that my right pinkie plays on the table. I've been known to throw things. Not that I ever actually aimed at anyone, but Jason's worried look told me he feared the worst.

The feds, not having a clue, remained comfortably seated. Agent Santori was probably just doing his job, while making an effort to be kind and solicitous at the same time. I didn't know his level of involvement, and I couldn't imagine that he would have been the one calling all the shots. Unfortunately, however, he was the one bearing the news, the one with answers that weren't answers at all. I was now pissed off. That made him my target in a classic case of shoot the messenger.

While I'm not usually prone to use profanity, it does have a way of surfacing when I lose control. Firmly embracing the anger stage, I lost it. "You are out of your minds. I don't give a flying goose liver what you think you heard or saw in whatever half-assed operation you had going up here. There is no fucking way. My sister *loved this* country. She was a patriot and you've got your wires crossed. I thought that after 9-11 all of you supposedly *intelligent*"—wiggling my index fingers to mime quotation marks—"intelligence people were supposed to have started talking to one another. As far as tomorrow goes, you need to know that I'm a detail person. I will have questions, and I will want to know who, what, when, where, how, to what extent, and why. You can skip the *Reader's Digest* version and save it for some dolt who doesn't have a clue. The dentist is Dwight Richards, in Swampscott. What time tomorrow, and where?"

I would suppose that most FBI agents aren't easily shocked; they're well-trained. But I guess they weren't quite prepared for the thing I'd just done, which probably had them making comparisons to the possessed girl in *The Exorcist*. All three were wide-eyed, and Angela—or whoever she was—actually had her mouth hanging open. Maybe they expected my head to do a 360-degree rotation. I give credit to Santori: he blanched but recovered quickly, and he didn't strike back.

"I'm sure we can use the local police station. I'll set it up for"—glancing at his watch—"ten in the morning. You know where it is?"

"Gerry Street. If you came into town from Boston, you must have gone by it." Like I said, Marblehead's a small town. It would be pretty hard to miss.

"Yeah, I remember. Here's a number where you can reach me, in case there's a problem." He scribbled a number on the back of his business card and handed it to me. "I am truly sorry for your loss."

For the first time, my eyes started to fill with tears. I just nodded and turned my head away. The three of them got up and awkwardly performed their farewells, Jason escorting them to the door. He stood in the window overlooking the street to make sure they left.

Chapter 3

A surreal quiet enveloped the room. Jason, brave soul, was the first to make a move, putting his arms around me and tucking my head into his shoulder. The human touch was all it took. I let go, sobbing for my sister and her husband, Tom. I was grief-stricken, angry, and confused. None of it made any sense, and it was so contrary to all that I knew and believed. Of course my first reaction had been to defend my sister, but if I subjected that reaction to analysis, it came from my heart and not because I could factually attest to her innocence.

As close as we were, I still didn't know exactly what my sister did or who she worked for. What was more distressing was that the FBI didn't seem to know either. If you follow the news at all, you're probably aware that there are at least a dozen federal agencies trying to keep the bad guys at bay, each of which claims its own turf and doesn't allow any other agency to play there. So I shouldn't have been surprised that they didn't have a clue that she was ultimately on the same team. I was aware that she'd been, shall we say, "involved" in a number of incidents over the years. There had been vague references to Washington and government and secrecy and national interests, but questions had always been discouraged. I'd been on the receiving end of the "I'm not at liberty to say" phrase more times than I could count, and after a while, you just get tired of asking. The assumption, the intimation, had always been that she was on the side of the good guys. Given our rally-round-the-flag upbringing, I couldn't imagine otherwise.

My sister, Cat, was actually my half-sister: same father, different mother. When Cat's Italian-born mother had died some thirty-five years ago, Dad created a scandal by remarrying within six months of the funeral. It didn't help that he chose a woman more than twenty years his junior. Their union was solid, though, and had lasted until my mom died a little over five years ago. Dad passed away two years later. Other than Cat and Tom, my only close family consisted of an aunt and uncle who lived in the Midwest and visited Marblehead each summer.

Cat had already graduated from college when I was born, and we weren't close until I was about twelve. I guess I'd finally reached the age where I was worth the interest, and I became her project. From the time I turned fourteen, we would take two trips each summer: one to two weeks motoring around the United States, and then four to six weeks traveling in some other corner of the world. She became the one person with whom I could share my most private thoughts. She gave me the confidence I needed to get through so many of my teenage issues, and became the guiding force behind my career path and relocation from the heartland to New England.

For the first time since my father's passing, I was relieved that he was no longer around. I couldn't even fathom how I would have broken the news to him. He loved both Cat and me, but deep down, I think Cat was his favorite. It dawned on me that I would need to make arrangements for her funeral, and I had no idea what those should be. I was just beginning to realize how many things needed to be done; there wasn't enough time to wallow in self-pity.

I wiped my eyes with the heels of my hands and blew my nose into a proffered tissue. Scanning the faces of my friends, I realized that they probably wished they could make an escape from their current surroundings. Jason had propped himself against the windowsill, arms folded over his chest. Gabe leaned back in the rocker and twirled his wineglass. Annita sipped her water and stared at the floor. She sat close to her husband, Jerome, who held her hand and likewise stared at the floor. It had to be awkward for them, struggling to find the right things to do and say. But I was grateful that I had such close friends to support and comfort me. My hands were trembling, and so was my voice.

"Hey, you guys. Thanks for being here. I don't know what to say. You all know my sister. It's got to be a mistake." I bent my head into my hands and pressed my fingers into my forehead, trying to find the words.

"I want to try to get to the bottom of this, but I probably can't do it alone. And I'm not really thinking straight anyhow. So I'm going to need your help. Can you help me make a list of all the things I've got to take care of tonight and tomorrow? After that, I'll take it a day at a time."

Surprisingly, it was Gabe who spoke first. A nerd in the truest sense of the word, Gabe was an introvert, who was more comfortable listening to a conversation than participating in it. "Look, we've been friends for a long time, so I'll help in just about any way I can. I didn't spend a lot of time with Cat, but I'm having trouble believing she was involved with a bunch of terrorists. The big question I have is whether or not Big Brother's been watching us like they were watching Cat. And if they were, how far did they go?" He was obviously wondering if our computer system had been compromised. Well-known as a hacker during his adolescent years, Gabe had gone righteous and now used his talents to sniff out other people's malicious little intrusions into the systems of our clients. His skills were legendary.

There were some mutterings, and Annita threw in her thoughts. "But that's the point, isn't it? We don't know. I have to tell you that the possibility alone has some pretty far-reaching implications. They must have had a ton of evidence to be up here arresting people in the middle of the night, and I can't imagine that the DEA and the FBI conspired to manufacture a case against some obscure middle-aged WASP chick living on the North Shore. On the other hand, I can't imagine Cat being involved. But something's going on, so whatever we do, we'd better make sure that we protect ourselves. I don't want to end up on some government blacklist." Inherently more conservative than the others, Jerome nodded vigorously in support of his wife.

Gabe didn't mince words as he glared at them. "You afraid to get into a pissing contest with the feds? To hell with them. When they stomp on people's rights, the people should stomp back." Gabe was one of the most independent-minded people I'd ever met. It was a quality that had not endeared him to his former employers in corporate America, who seemed to prefer conformity over individuality. Personally, I like mavericks. And now I liked him even more.

I could feel the tension as my friends wrestled with their private thoughts. Although we'd done nothing wrong, guilt by association could easily tarnish our reputations. We may have been good friends, but ultimately people look out for their own best interests. There was a potential rift developing, but they were going to stick together and with me, at least for the moment. I knew, however, that if the going got tough, who'd be going.

Taking command, Jason broke in. "Hey! We have plenty of time to dissect this. But right now, let's concentrate on what we need to do to get Lindsey through the next couple of days. Let's just be careful for the time being, until we figure it all out."

Numbly providing answers when a question was posed to me, I otherwise allowed myself to be swept along as they settled into the task of organizing my life. As the office manager, Annita inherited most of the business issues. Gabe and Jason would simply handle whatever I needed them to do. When they finished about half an hour later, they had assembled a list of about twenty items, with three calls to be made that fairly screamed priority. The first was to my aunt and uncle; the second was to find an attorney. While we had a lawyer who handled our business dealings, issues involving terrorism and the FBI were far out of his league.

Gabe, ever the logician, clarified the second point. "Actually, you've got a lot of legal stuff going on here. But first and foremost, I think you need a criminal attorney. Anybody know one?"

We picked our brains for several minutes before Annita pulled a name out of her hat. "Evelyn Wainwright. Isn't that her name?"

Evelyn was a high-profile defense attorney, and a friend of Cat. I'd met her once or twice, and we were passing acquaintances. I knew of her reputation somewhat through conversations at the dinner table, and primarily because she had been at Cat's side during one of those past "incidents." The nature of her client list made her unpopular politically, but there was no doubt that she was well-respected—and feared. Better still, I was fairly sure she would remember my name and take my call.

The Ambassador would be call number three. Paul Marshfield was a former ambassador, and rumored to be on the newly-elected president's short list for a Cabinet position. He was an unusual man, having advanced to an ambassadorial position through a career in the US Foreign Service. To our surprise, he had stepped out of the State Department and into what I perceived as a more political role. He was temporarily residing in Berlin. My understanding was that he was currently tasked to mend the rift with Germany and some of our other European allies.

Ambassador Marshfield was also Cat's best friend, and I

had always thought of him and his wife Maggie as my aunt and uncle. The media were going to make his life miserable—there was that guilt-by-association thing again—and I needed to warn him right away. Looking at my watch and considering the time difference, I moved him up to the first position in the call list.

Tracking down Paul Marshfield proved to be easier than I would have guessed. I had his phone numbers at home on my computer, but that didn't do much good here. Jason got on the web and hit the site for the State Department, locating the number for the embassy in Berlin. After explaining the emergency nature of my call, I was passed to his secretary. While we'd never met, she knew my sister from Cat's frequent visits with Paul and Maggie. She explained that Paul was at a breakfast meeting in Dusseldorf, but promised to reach him immediately. Three minutes later—you had to love the man—I was sobbing the story over thousands of miles of phone line. He had the gift of an effective communicator: a man who listens as well as he speaks. And while he may have been a diplomat and politician, I never doubted his sincerity or integrity, or the depth of his friendship with Cat. This situation could be devastating to his career. I was relieved when he told me that he would clear his schedule and fly into Boston on Monday.

I glanced at my watch and debated whether to call Aunt Holly and Uncle Pete now, or wait for a more civilized hour. At two thirty in the morning their time, they would be asleep. On the one hand, they weren't as close to Cat as they were to me. On the other hand, I had no way of knowing if this would attract media attention, and the last thing I wanted was for them to learn about it from CNN. My uncle had always been a bit of a mystery to me. I liked him, but never understood exactly who paid him to do what. He was certainly successful, and as far as I knew, legit. But the authorities could show up with a warrant, or I could find out that he'd just been nominated as the chairman of the Federal Reserve. Neither would surprise me.

I punched in my uncle's number, letting it ring five times before hanging up and trying again. Unlike me, he could sleep through anything. On the fourth shot, I caught an irritated "Hello?" in the speaker.

"Uncle Pete? It's Lindsey."

"What's the matter?" At the sound of my voice, he was instantly alert, and worried. Friends of mine with teenage drivers tell me that phone calls at this hour are among the things they dread most. They always bring bad news.

My intent had been to break it gently, but that evaporated like spit on a hot skillet. It came out in a rush, a condensed version of the condensed version that the FBI had presented.

"Uncle Pete?" I could hear him breathing, but no other sound on the line. "Are you okay?"

He assured me that he was fine, but shocked, and proceeded to pepper me with questions for which I had few answers. Like me, he was outraged at the accusations and supportive. I told him that I would do everything in my power to determine the truth and restore Cat's good name, although at the moment, I had no idea how I was going to accomplish this. I let him know that I would look into arrangements for a funeral or memorial service or whatever, and would call as soon as I knew more.

The final call was to Evelyn Wainwright's answering service. It was, by necessity, an even shorter version of tonight's events. I mentioned the meeting at 10:00 a.m., a scant six hours from now, in the vague hope that I wouldn't have to attend without legal representation.

Chapter 4

Saturday
Marblehead, Massachusetts

I t was fast coming up on four o'clock by the time everyone left. Rather than go home, I decided to bunk on Jason's sofa. Part of my strategy for remaining sane over the next few days was to minimize my time alone. There was also a topic that I needed to discuss with just him. In case we were bugged, I passed him a note as I requested a cup of tea.

About a month ago, Cat had been having trouble with her laptop. After spending hours trying to determine the source of the problem, she'd asked Jason to take a look at it. It was a friend-to-friend request, with no business record of the transaction. Jason had swapped out the hard drive and power supply, performed several security scans, and killed a couple of suspicious programs that were lurking in the file system. He'd also made a complete backup of the drive's data. I wanted to know if he still had it.

After a moment of uncertainty, Jason's eyes popped wide

with comprehension, and he gave me a thumbs-up signal. I had no idea what we'd find when we had time to examine the data, but it certainly warranted a look-see. As we grinned at one another, I couldn't help but think that this kind of activity was exactly what Annita had wanted to avoid.

I downed a couple of aspirin with the tea, wished Jason a good night, slipped under a blanket, folded myself into the fetal position, and closed my eyes. Sleep did not come easily.

Evidently I dozed off, because the next thing I remember was struggling to locate the source of whatever was ringing. There is a primitive function deep in my brain that forces me to respond to any sort of ring: doorbells, phones, alarm clocks, microwaves, you name it. I'm as predictable as Pavlov's dog. When the instrument is a phone, I will answer it and start talking while still asleep. The cell had been on the table next to the sofa, and I must have already answered, because the voice on the other end was talking back.

"Lindsey? Is that you? This is Evelyn Wainwright."

"Evelyn," I croaked, "thank you for calling me back. I'm dead asleep, so bear with me while I try to wake up." I pulled myself to my feet in an attempt to jump-start my brain cells.

"Absolutely. You have a meeting with the FBI?"

"Yeah, at the police station. At ten."

"Which station? Marblehead?"

"Sorry, I'm not coherent yet. Yes, Marblehead."

"Good, I was hoping that would be the case because I'm on

my way up there now. I'm just coming into Swampscott, and I'd like to spend some time with you before the meeting. Are you home?"

I looked around, trying to orient myself. I've spent so many nights in hotels that I sometimes wake up and have no idea where I am. The light seeping through the window shades provided enough illumination that I finally placed my location.

"No. I'm at Jason Bigby's place on Gregory Street." I gave her the house number and told her where to park. "What time is it?"

"Eight o'clock. I'll stop at Starbucks and pick us up a latte and some scones or something. Is Jason there as well? Shall I make it three?"

"Great idea. He's here, and we're both going to need the caffeine. Thanks."

"No problem. I'll be there shortly."

I hung up, trying to clear my head. Last night hadn't been some ghoulish nightmare. Cat and Tom were dead, the lawyer was on her way here, and I felt like hell. Could a new day begin more badly? I pounded on Jason's door to ensure he'd share the agony of this early meeting, before heading for the shower and a toothbrush.

Chapter 5

There is something distasteful about taking a shower and then putting on yesterday's clothes. It just always makes me feel scummy. I had even washed out my underwear, but didn't have an opportunity to dry them—or my hair—before the doorbell sounded. Slipping into the soggy bikini briefs didn't improve my mood. Glancing at my reflection in the mirror only made it worse ... no makeup, drip-dry hair, wet underwear. About the only positive aspect of the morning was the new toothbrush that had been graciously placed next to the sink. Lathering up your index finger for a swipe at morning mouth was about as effective as using toilet paper to scrub dishes.

Evelyn passed me a venti latte, which I gratefully accepted. It occurred to me that Starbucks should make an even bigger version, something like a double-grande-venti, for heavy-duty occasions. And then I realized that she'd brought two for each of us, as well as an assortment of scones and muffins. At that moment, I considered the woman a saint.

She was in her mid-fifties and had obviously long ago given up any aspirations of winning a beauty pageant. She was probably about five-six and a good forty pounds over the limit for good health. Her makeup was carelessly applied, with little to show for the effort other than a smear of plum-colored lipstick. She had mousy brown-going-gray hair, cut short—probably by a lawn mower—and sticking out at odd angles, and her navy suit was early frumpy. While not exactly appearing to be a candidate for a homeless shelter, she nevertheless wouldn't strike you as being one of the most powerful attorneys in New England. It was no wonder that her name was often bandied about in various publications, but was seldom accompanied by a photograph. I deduced that her accomplishments were achieved through arduous work, and not by sleeping her way to the top.

My thoughts must have betrayed themselves on my face, because she smiled at me and said, "It's part of the strategy. The pundits are right about dressing for success, but not quite in the way they'd have you believe. Dressing down causes your opponents to underestimate you and juries to view you as someone to whom they can relate. Works like a charm. So tell me exactly what happened."

Evelyn waited expectantly as Jason, appearing none the worse for wear, grabbed an unclaimed latte and stuffed a chunk of scone into his mouth as he took a place at the table. One could have said that he was actually chipper. Of course, he had a closet full of clean clothes and dry shorts, never wore makeup, hadn't lost a sister, and wasn't being plagued by the FBI. In comparison to my demeanor, anyone would have seemed cheerful.

Following suit, Evelyn and I seated ourselves. She pulled a tiny recorder from her briefcase and placed it in the center of the table. "I take notes, but this is my backup for those niggling details that escape the pen and paper version."

The recorder roused my previous anxiety about bugging devices, so I thought it best to apprise her of my concern. "Before we start, you need to know that Cat was under surveillance. Her phones were tapped. They were also looking at me, and I don't know to what extent. I'm worried that they may have planted a bug somewhere along the way, or even last night when they were here. What do you think?"

Two deep creases appeared between her eyebrows, and her eyes narrowed. It was evident that this twist was more than a passing annoyance.

"Well, it certainly wouldn't be the first time that the government has overstepped its bounds. It will be interesting to see exactly what warrants they have obtained. The content of our conversation is privileged and cannot be used in a court of law. However, that doesn't necessarily preclude someone from using it to their advantage in other pursuits. So I'm going to bring in an investigator I keep on retainer, a security specialist, to check for any devices. I think it would be best to sweep your house, Jason's house, and your offices. He can probably be here within half an hour or so. I'd like for you to meet him so that you will recognize him in the future. And just so you know, he works alone. If he can't take care of a job, he'll call me and I'll arrange a replacement, and I'll notify you. He'll never send someone else. Okay?"

Jason and I both nodded our assent. She made a very short call with a couple of pleasantries and the address. For the briefest moment, I felt sorry for the man at the other end of the line. It had to be rather degrading to be on a short leash, subject to the master's beck and call—but then I realized that my relationship with our clients was exactly the same. That was certainly food for thought.

Wanting to get started but concerned about bugs, we bundled up and huddled together outside on the deck. I laid out the story, providing as many details as I could recall, with Jason interjecting his perceptions. Evelyn listened carefully, took a mountain of notes, and rarely interrupted. I certainly didn't introduce the subject of a certain hard drive backup that was in our possession; we needed to discuss that in a place where we could be more assured of privacy. I had no intention of letting anyone else know of its existence.

When I concluded, Evelyn stood and leaned against the railing, gathering her thoughts. "Okay. You haven't been charged, at least not that we know of."

My eyes must have registered alarm, because she continued quickly, "I don't think they're after you; otherwise they would have stayed longer and really questioned you. As I said, I'm going to take a very close look at their warrants and any indictments that have been issued. I already have a couple of people researching that. When we go to this meeting, I want you to be seen as cooperative. I must ask you, though, were you in any way aware of any illegal conduct on Cat's or Tom's part?"

Jason and I both gave a forceful "No."

"So, that being the case, it doesn't seem that there's much

to gain from interrogating you … unless you know more than you realize, or they want your help in uncovering something that you might know about. As I said, I want you to appear cooperative. So here's what I want you to do. Whenever they ask a question, look at me before you answer. I'm left-handed. Glance at my right hand. If it's on the table, answer the question. If it's anywhere else, I'd like for you to evade somewhat. I don't want you to lie, ever. My strategy is to get them to reveal information without us asking them directly. So look puzzled, ask them what they mean, anything that gets them to provide more details. If you can't evade an answer, then be truthful, and we'll deal with it later. If, at any time, I tell you not to answer a question, then don't."

She paused for a moment, measuring her words. "Lindsey, you run your own business, and you're probably used to being in control. This is important. Just as I would never presume to tell you how to write computer code, you should never presume that you know more than I do about this kind of situation. You're an expert in your field, and I'm an expert in mine. Trust me. Just follow my lead at all times, and you'll get through this just fine."

I knew she was right on both counts. I liked being in control and was not one to relinquish it. I'd have to stifle my impulses and put myself into someone else's care.

Knowing it would be a difficult task, I nonetheless nodded my agreement. "That's a tall order, but I'll try." What choice did I have?

She also nixed the idea of Jason appearing at the meeting.

"Every indication is that they want to talk to Lindsey. I

wouldn't think that Jason would be directly involved in any investigation. Let's not give them any more than what they request. I don't want to seem adversarial, but you've got to look at them as potential courtroom opponents."

I got her point. We did agree that she would act as counsel for Jason, as needed, since we had no way of knowing whether or not he would become involved.

My next request of Evelyn was advice about who should actually represent Cat. Although she was deceased, there were still certain rights assigned to her and Tom, and to their estate. I knew the name of the attorney Cat had used for purchasing the property, since I'd been there for the closing, but had no idea if the man was still her attorney of record. This was another point that would require further investigation.

I was surprised and intrigued when Evelyn revealed that she had a copy of Cat and Tom's will and a page of instructions to be carried out in the event of their deaths. Cat had always been extremely organized, and I could see that she might have taken steps to ensure that no one would be burdened with her death. But it still struck me as morbid. My own will, which I'd finalized only about a year ago, was self-prepared and tucked in my safe deposit box at the bank. I certainly hadn't involved a lawyer. Cat's action did, however, give me something to think about. If I were to die, how would anyone even know about the last will and testament of Lindsey Carlisle? I put the thought aside for future consideration as Evelyn informed me that Cat's will stipulated a private service and cremation. Her ashes, as well as Tom's, were to be scattered at sea. According to Evelyn's records, Cat had made and paid for the arrangements about a month ago.

I asked for the name of the funeral home that Cat had specified, assuming that it would be one of the two in town, and was dumbfounded to learn that she had selected a place in Gloucester. Gloucester was almost an hour's drive, and I couldn't imagine why she would have made that choice. There wasn't anything to be done about it now, however. In the morning, I'd have to make the arrangements.

The doorbell was a startling intrusion, given our concerns. I'd almost forgotten that we were expecting Evelyn's security expert to arrive. Jason opened the door to face a red-haired, freckled man in his mid- to late forties. He stuck out his hand. "Donnie Kirkpatrick. Ms. Wainwright called me."

Evelyn made the introductions and further explained our potential security problem. He asked for the keys and alarm codes for my house and the office, as well as Jason's home. As we supplied him with the information, I focused on his face to ensure that I would recognize him should he appear on my doorstep later.

He looked around briefly. "If it's all the same to you, I'll start here. Is that okay?"

Since it was Jason's house, it was his call. "I'm cool," he said. "Go for it."

Heading for the door, Evelyn thanked Donnie for his quick response and Jason for his assistance. She beckoned to me and swept her coat from the sofa. "Let's take my car," she suggested.

Chapter 6

The Marblehead Police Department occupies a newly renovated granite and glass structure at the corner of Gerry Street and Atlantic Avenue.

Atlantic Avenue, or simply "The Avenue," is the primary means of entering town when driving up from Boston. Marblehead sits on a spit of a peninsula, connected at its base to Swampscott and Salem, and with water in every other direction. The Avenue's initial path into town is bordered by pretty New England cape homes, often dressed in red, white, and blue banners to underscore the town's patriotic connection to the American Revolution and its historical significance as the birthplace of the American navy. Approaching the center of town, the sidewalks are dotted with quaint shops, small eateries, and other mom-and-pop establishments. Marblehead is fiercely protective of its image and its native commerce, and is disinclined to admit chain stores of any ilk. There are a couple of exceptions, but it is noteworthy that you won't find the golden arches here.

A fairly sizable chunk of property spanning both sides of the Avenue is owned by the Catholic Church. The church has become woven into the fabric of the community and is perhaps less a religious artifact than a comfort zone for the residents. The parking lot for the police station borders the south side of the church. There were five or six police cars and a few other vehicles in the lot when we parked. I fished a brush and elastic band out of my bag and forced my still-damp hair into a scraggly ponytail. I didn't dare look in the mirror. I shrugged at Evelyn, "Might as well get this over with."

I've lived in town for years and had never been inside the station. I hadn't done anything wrong, yet I felt uncomfortable under the scrutiny of the bodies milling around the desk of the officer on duty. After Evelyn stated our business, we were directed to the conference room upstairs.

As we entered the room, Agent Santori rose from his seat and circled around the table to shake hands with me and introduce himself to Evelyn. He gave me an appraising look. "You probably didn't get much sleep. It must be very difficult for you, and I'm sorry that we have to do this now, but we do. Please take a seat. Can we get you some coffee or water or anything?"

Agent Santori was definitely showing us his good side. The funny thing was, it felt honest, and he seemed like such a nice guy. If Evelyn hadn't been there to rein me in, I feel certain that I would have gladly given him any information he wanted, and then some. The ability to exude such charm and appeal was probably in every successful interrogator's arsenal of tricks, and it was hard to resist. It also didn't hurt that the cold light of day hadn't diminished his good looks one iota. I made a concerted effort to appear somewhat aloof as I acknowledged his comments and expressed a preference for water.

The two agents from last night's encounter were present, as were two unfamiliar faces. Both were older, and fitting my preconceived notion of the FBI dress code, both wore dark gray suits with white shirts and navy ties. There was also a woman setting up a machine of the type that court reporters use. This meeting was apparently going on the official record. There were eight chairs circling the round conference table, and we had a full house.

Agent Santori resumed his seat and initiated the introductions. The taller of the two suits was a Mr. Farrell, the Special Agent in Charge of the Boston office of the FBI. The man sitting to his right was his assistant, Mr. Wolanski. The female agent from last night was confirmed to be Angela, and the other agent was Roberto. The door popped open, and three other individuals entered the room. While one of the locals was summoned to find additional chairs, the three were introduced as members of a DEA task force: Celia, Wes, and Bernardo, no last names provided.

There is no question that I was intimidated, having lost my bravado from the night before. I glanced nervously at Evelyn, who seemed perfectly bored with the entire display. I silently thanked whatever supernatural being had led me to her door.

I snapped out of my reverie as I realized that the proceedings had begun. The date and the names of those present—minus a few surnames—were read into officialdom. It appeared that Agent Santori was to be the master of ceremonies, so to speak.

"Miss Carlisle," he began, "you are the half-sister of Catherine Ames Powell. Is that correct?"

I nodded before realizing that a verbal answer would be required. "Yes," I confirmed.

"She did not use the name Carlisle?"

"No. After college, she began using her middle name instead. Ames was her mother's maiden name."

"Why? Why not keep Carlisle?"

"I never asked specifically, but I think it was out of love and respect for her mother. They were very close."

There were a number of other questions to verify my identity and relationship with Cat. I suppose that in the investigative business, it's crucial to dot all the *i*'s and cross the *t*'s. But it was deadly dull stuff. It was all so mundane that I was caught off guard when he began to ask about Cat's business dealings.

"Your sister seemed to be quite the philanthropist. Can you name some of the institutions to which she donated money?"

I had lapsed into complacency and had been forgetting to check for Evelyn's signal. I glanced over at her, to see her hand on the table. So far, so good, it seemed.

"Well, I know she was a pretty big supporter of Brigham and Women's Hospital and the Science Museum. And she did a lot of work for the historical society here in town."

"Any other causes that you know of?"

Evelyn's hand had fallen to her lap. Appearing perplexed didn't require much effort as I asked, "What do you mean by causes? Like was she a Democrat or Republican, or what?"

"Have you ever heard her talking about fund-raising or contributions to groups abroad?"

Evelyn's hand was still in her lap. "Well, I believe she donated money to the International Red Cross after a few large-scale disasters, and she was a regular contributor to UNICEF. Is that what you mean?"

"Actually, we were wondering if you'd ever heard her mention the Foundation for the Preservation of Ancient Artifacts."

Evelyn hadn't moved a muscle. "I don't know. She liked visiting ancient ruins, and so I guess she appreciated archaeology. I think she may have had a membership at the Smithsonian. Is that one of their projects?"

There was a long sigh from someone in the room. I was obviously trying their patience. I could have given the simple "No, I don't have a clue" response, and we would have been out of there. But Evelyn had indicated that it was important to milk the meeting for all it was worth. So I settled into playing the ditz while he ran through the names of several other innocuous-sounding organizations. It wasn't much of a stretch, considering I had no idea what he was talking about. Evelyn relaxed her hand on the table.

"The American Education Foundation?"

"No."

"How about the Institute for Islamic Women?"

Actually, I'd heard her mention it. "Yes," I stated.

"Would you please provide the details?"

Evelyn's hand came off the table as I asked, "What do you

mean?"

"When was this, where were you when she talked about it, who was with you, and what was said?"

"I'm not exactly sure I remember all of that. Uh, it may have been within the last few months. As I recall, she made some comment about some women who were trying to express their independence by forming a 'Burn the Burka' movement. Sort of like the 'Burn the Bra' thing back in the sixties."

I heard a snort, and someone muttered, "Figures. She was good at that."

I looked around, but couldn't identify the source. Agent Santori, however, was shooting a disgusted look toward the DEA representatives. Evelyn apparently took a very dim view of the outburst. "Excuse me. I would like to know exactly what the gentleman meant by that comment," she said.

There was an extended silence. It appeared that no one was eager to respond.

"Well, perhaps we can enlighten you somewhat." Surprisingly, this comment came from Mr. Farrell, the SAIC, who until this moment had not uttered a word.

"Please do."

"Back in the seventies, when she was Catherine Ames Carlisle, she had a number of close friends affiliated with various antiwar and antinuclear groups." He tilted his head back, and with his thumb and forefinger, moved his glasses a bit lower on his nose. Whether it was to adjust the focus or was simply habitual, I couldn't say. Regardless, the gesture resulted in the appearance that he was looking down his nose at us.

Evelyn didn't even blink; she had obviously mastered the

art of maintaining a poker face. I caught her eye and gave a quick shake of my head to indicate that this information was news to me.

Her response was curt. "Even assuming that what you say is correct—and I am frankly dubious about its accuracy—it appears you have no evidence to support your implied accusations. Indeed, I fail to see how the activities of a teenager's friends all those years ago would be relevant to this conversation."

Farrell responded smugly, "To the contrary, I believe it to be quite relevant. It demonstrates a history of antigovernment sentiment and involvement in terrorist activities."

To my amazement, Evelyn actually laughed. "That's quite a rationalization, Mr. Farrell, but we both know that it would never hold up to judicial scrutiny, particularly since J. Edgar and his successors had a file on nearly every college student who had the temerity to even hint about being opposed to the war in Vietnam, the building of nuclear power plants, the treatment of American Indians, or busing in Boston. It was an era of protest and unrest that fostered dramatic change in the way we now view our government's obligations to its citizenry. Shall we move on?"

Farrell conceded the point by holding up his hands in a suggestion of surrender. He turned his head to gaze out the window, signaling that Santori should continue.

"All right, Miss Carlisle, you mentioned some women who may have been involved with the Institute for Islamic Women. First, did you ever meet any of them, and second, do you recall their names?"

I looked him straight in the eye. "No."

"Well, then, I'm going to list some names for you. After each, please tell me if you have heard of the person, and if so, in what context."

"Okay, I'll try."

He ran through about a dozen names, all of which were unfamiliar. Unlike Cat, who was incredibly skilled at determining the origin of a name and its pronunciation, I was inept. At that moment, I represented the typical American, whose grasp of the world is defined by news bites on CNN. Most of the names sounded vaguely Arab, but could just as easily have been Indian, Pakistani, Korean, or Russian for all I knew. I shrugged hopelessly, declaring "No" after each. That is, until he recited the name Jalil Badakhshanian. I should have figured out that the name would eventually surface, and mentally kicked myself for not coming to the realization sooner. Of course they would know that I would know his name.

"Jalil Badakhshanian. Yes, I knew him." Evelyn's hand dropped to her side, warning me to approach this line of questioning with some care. I was happy to oblige, and thankful that I didn't have much information to share anyhow. "He is ... was ... whatever ... a sort of friend."

"A friend of yours or your sister, or both of you?"

"Well, I met him a few times growing up. His parents were good friends with Cat and Tom, so we all got together occasionally. When Jalil ended up at Harvard, I saw him more frequently. I was across the river, going to school at Boston University. Cat invited us to dinner quite a bit, and we both wanted some home cooking, I suppose. After graduation, I saw his parents a couple of times when they were visiting Cat and Tom, but I can't remember ever seeing him again."

Jalil had dropped out of my field of vision sometime after graduation, when I started working and could afford a decent meal without having to sponge off my sister. I'd always assumed that he'd followed a similar path to success. I certainly hadn't spent any time thinking about it, at least until five years ago, when his picture was splashed across every newspaper and television in the country. For whatever convoluted reason, he'd smuggled a small vial of anthrax spores into the country. Somehow, and the details were never released, he was flagged as he was driving out of Boston's Logan airport after arriving on a flight from Frankfurt. According to news reports, the police blocked his car on one of the exit ramps, and when he pulled out a gun, they fired. The hazmat team safely retrieved the vial, and we were all safe. Until the next time, I guess. At any rate, I'd been shocked, Cat was stunned, and Jalil's parents were completely devastated.

"So the last time you saw him was before he graduated?"

"I think so. It could have been after that; I don't really remember. I wasn't paying much attention to when and where."

"Wait a minute. Are you saying that you met him at places other than your sister's house?"

"No, no. Maybe. Maybe a movie, a drink somewhere, and I don't really remember if we even did that. I don't know ... we were sort of friends. Not great friends, but we could have met, and why would I even keep track of it, you know? Sheesh ... it was just an expression."

I rolled my eyes in frustration. The long interrogation and

lack of sleep were making me irritable. I was beginning to comprehend the reason why, after hours in the hot seat, a person would confess to a crime he or she didn't commit. I was ready to say anything to get out of here and go take a nap. I needed some fresh air.

"Do you mind if we take a break? I'm exhausted, and I just want to walk around for a few minutes."

On television, nobody ever gets to take a break. But this was real life, and half a minute later I was outside, breathing deeply of the frigid salt air. Evelyn stood silently at my side, watching the traffic zip up and down the avenue. I sensed her mood of reproach and apologized immediately.

"I'm so sorry. I should have expected that they'd bring up Jalil. Duh."

She gave me an appraising look, as if assessing my sincerity, then shrugged her shoulders. "No harm done. Actually, I'm the one who should apologize. I should have made the link myself, particularly since I was there with Cat when it all went down."

She shook her head in a gesture of remembered sadness and let out a deep sigh. We stood quietly for a few minutes, contemplating lives lost in events that we would probably never understand.

She tilted her head toward me. "I'm curious. Did they ever question you after Jalil was killed?"

"No. I always assumed that they would at least pay me a visit, but they never did. Is that important?"

Her brow was furrowed in puzzlement. "I don't really know. It's a bit strange, considering the feeding frenzy that went on around here." She paused briefly, giving me a piercing look. "Did Cat ever talk to you about her interrogation?"

I had the odd feeling that she was putting together pieces of a puzzle that I didn't even know existed. I felt my eyes widen in surprise.

"Well, no. As far as I know, they never interrogated her at all. I remember talking to her that night, about how horrible it was and how we couldn't comprehend Jalil being involved in anything like that. I also remember Cat saying that you'd practically dared the feds to get within a mile of her. Still, we both expected the FBI to come around, but they never did. We laughed about how it was just another example of government bureaucracy at its best, or that they were just scared of you. Either way, eventually I just stopped thinking about it. It's not like I had anything important to contribute, since I didn't know him that well. If I'd known something, I probably would have called them."

She gave me an odd sly smile, reminding me of the proverbial fox in the henhouse.

"Well, we probably won't get all of our questions answered today, and certainly not by this group." She tilted her head toward the station. "But I certainly have some fodder for my research staff. I'm not going to voice my suspicions just yet, but this could prove to be very interesting. I'm freezing. Let's get back in there and finish this off."

And with that, she put her hand at the small of my back and practically pushed me into the station.

I spent the next hour reviewing names I'd never heard and rejecting any knowledge of offshore accounts and large sums of cash at Cat's home. Since I was completely ignorant, the ordeal progressed reasonably quickly. Through it all, Evelyn continued to take copious notes, filling sheet after sheet in her legal-size notebook. I was grateful for her presence, and even more grateful that she was in charge. It was Evelyn who had the presence of mind to inquire about Cat's body.

The agent named Angela fielded the question. "We've sent the body to the Essex County Medical Examiner for autopsy. They should have the dental records by now. As long as there are no complicating factors, I expect that they'll be able to release the remains sometime tomorrow."

Evelyn gave her a withering stare. "Her name was Catherine, Catherine Powell. It would serve you well to consider those little details when in the presence of a family member."

Angela cringed and murmured a halfhearted apology, and I caught Agent Santori suppressing a grin. Unless I was mistaken, he seemed to be enjoying his fellow agent's discomfiture. *Strange.*

I wasn't prepared for Evelyn's next shot. "I'm sure that the FBI would not be content to have a mere county coroner perform the procedure. I'll wager a week's salary that you've got one of your own doing the honors, or at least supervising. Any takers?"

Mr. Farrell rubbed his forehead and gave Evelyn a defeated look. "Are you asking to have one of your people there?"

"Why, what a good idea." She pulled a business card out of her briefcase and handed it to Farrell, who passed it over to Santori. "Would you like me to call him and set it up, or would you prefer to conduct the arrangements?"

Agent Santori waved her off. "I'll take care of it. Anything else?"

"I have a couple of people that I'd like to send over to Cat's house, and I'd like for them to be given full access to the site and to whatever physical evidence you might have already retrieved from it. They're both fully credentialed and won't interfere in any way with the scene or with your investigators."

I detected some hesitation in Santori's response. "There may be national security considerations. I'll agree to provide access, as long as I can background your people and they agree to back off if told to do so. Are we clear?"

"Crystal. I'll make sure they understand. Here are the names." She handed him two more cards.

As he glanced at them, I noted his response to the names. Examining the last one, he closed his eyes and shook his head slowly. "You don't roll over easily, do you?"

"Nah. Wouldn't be any fun. We'll be in touch."

Chapter 7

It was after two when we left the Marblehead PD. I was famished, but the day was slipping away with nothing on my list having been accomplished. I could feel my blood pressure rising along with my anxiety level. I must have appeared overwrought, because Evelyn pulled to a spot in front of one of the local food and drink joints on the Avenue.

"You're starting to panic. I can see it. You need some food, something to drink, and to step back for a little while. You won't do anyone any good if you fall apart."

Evelyn wasn't easily dissuaded, so we spent the next hour relaxing over lobster rolls and mugs of beer. The last thing I wanted to do was rehash the interrogation, but I was puzzled about the business cards she'd passed to Santori.

"Who were the people on the business cards?" I inquired.

"Chief Medical Examiner for the city of Atlanta, the current Atlanta City Attorney, and a former assistant director of the Criminal Investigative Division of the FBI."

I gaped at her.

"Well, two of them are dear friends from Harvard Law. The third is my friend's husband. We get together two or three times a year. This is your lucky week." She grinned, really grinned, and actually winked at me.

I started to giggle, amazed and amused at the reach of Evelyn's network. I could only hope that Evelyn's friends found some redeeming evidence and that the agents who were so certain of Cat's guilt would get their comeuppance.

We otherwise avoided discussing the case, and I found Evelyn to be an engaging and perceptive conversationalist. Despite my fatigue and sorrow, I actually enjoyed the hour and the opportunity to put all my anxieties aside. I thanked her profusely for her kindness and picked up the tab.

When we pulled into Jason's driveway at a few minutes after three, he bounded down the steps, climbed into the backseat, and presented a large brown envelope to Evelyn.

"That's Donnie's report." Jason went on to explain that while his house was clean, Donnie had found electronic devices in the phones, alarm systems, and elsewhere in my home. He was planning to check the office later, after everyone had gone home. He'd made copies of my keys, so he didn't have to break in every night. This matter-of-fact statement implied that our locking mechanism wasn't as secure as we believed it to be. It was becoming impossible. Companies that supplied retinal scanning devices were beginning to sound like they'd be solid additions to my stock portfolio.

Donnie also suspected that they may have planted hidden files or devices in my computer to monitor my activities. If they had been clever, and I assumed that they were well beyond the casual user level, then they would have ensured themselves remote access. Like many computer professionals, I'd gone wireless. That meant that I could go anywhere in the house, and even outside on my deck, and communicate with my other machines and the Internet without being plugged in. Our office was wireless, as well.

We'd configured what most pros considered to be a fairly secure setup and our wireless setup was encrypted, but there was a basic rule stipulating that your network is only as secure as the people who have access to it. According to Donnie, our setup wouldn't present much of a barrier to a trained federal agent. And my house was an open invitation. I had locks on the doors, but that was it. I'd never given it much thought, considering that I live in an incredibly safe town and don't keep any client data of a confidential nature in my home.

Breaking into computers wasn't my primary area of expertise. Gabe was our critical resource for advising clients about such matters. I was, however, acutely aware that a stealth virus, implanted on my laptop, could replicate to a server in our office when I connected to it. In turn, the virus could replicate to any other computer that connected to it.

We were well-protected with firewalls and antivirus software, and Gabe felt that we were reasonably protected from viruses and worms and other malware. We didn't present much of a target for the hacking community either. There's very little glamour in hacking Lindsey Carlisle's servers, compared to something like the Pentagon. What did give me pause was the knowledge that the US government had created their own little arsenal of viruses. It's not widely known, but US

internet companies that create encryption keys are being compelled to supply the government with master keys that can be
used to decrypt whatever has been encoded. Likewise, clandestine viruses created by the government may be completely undetected by antivirus protection. Questions have even been
raised about whether some antivirus software is deliberately
programmed to ignore them.

I was incensed at the invasion of privacy, but not particularly surprised. Gabe was going to be busy.

Jason gave me a questioning look, and I realized that he
was trying to determine if I'd told Evelyn about our backup of
Cat's computer. I shook my head slightly.

Evelyn noticed the exchange. "Something more you'd like
to share?"

I nodded at Jason, who explained how we had come into
possession of Cat's computer files.

Evelyn, listening to the details, seemed unperturbed. In her
profession, she likely had abundant experience with omissions,
half-truths, and lies from her clients. "I will be better-
positioned to guide you through this legal tangle if you
promptly share relevant information with me. The more I
know, the more I will be able to anticipate and prepare. We'll
have greater success if we establish a relationship of mutual
trust. I will trust you to tell the truth, the whole truth, and
nothing but the truth, and you will trust me to take care of
you."

I knew she was right, and nodded meekly.

She went on, "I'll just add that the feds never inquired
about any files that might be in your possession. Nor did they

ask you to report back if you encountered any information about the topics discussed today. Rather an oversight, I think. So until they do, I would say that you're free to explore those files. Keep me apprised. I'll call you tomorrow." She shook her finger in my face and astonished me with a quick hug before slipping out the door.

While I'd been undergoing a grilling by the FBI, Jason had been exploring the contents of Cat's file system. He was eager to share the fruits of his labors, but I had to put him off.

"I just can't look at it now. I've got to call my aunt and uncle; I can't put it off any longer. They're probably furious with me for not getting back to them sooner. And where's that list we made?"

He reached in his jeans pocket and, looking hurt, handed me the list. I immediately regretted my brevity. The strain had frayed my nerves.

"Sorry. It's been a long day, and I'm maxed out. I've just got to go home and take care of a few things first. Want to tag along, so we can talk?

He paused to consider the invitation. "I'm worried that somebody could do to me what they did to you. I'm almost afraid to leave the house."

"You could be right," I said. "But by now they must know that we're onto them. Donnie's going to check things out every day. It seems to me it would be pointless for them to dump more bugs in, only to have us kill them every night."

Resignation setting in, he pulled his coat out of the closet and started for the door. Reaching for the knob, he stopped and suddenly headed for the bedroom. "Wait a sec."

When he returned, he had a hairbrush in his hand and was pulling a long hair from the tangle. Using his thumbs and index fingers, he pulled it straight, then carefully wound it around the two handles of the French doors leading to the deck.

I rolled my eyes. "Been studying a secret agent manual? Spycraft 101?"

"I know it's dumb. But just in case someone breaks in, I'll know."

"And what about all the windows?"

"I'll figure something out tonight."

I went outside to my car, leaving him to determine a method of booby-trapping the front door. Sitting in the car while the engine warmed up, it occurred to me that they could have bugged my car as well. It was getting out of hand. I was becoming a paranoid lunatic.

Chapter 8

I didn't think about taking the detour until we got to Five Corners, one of those quirky New England intersections where multiple streets converge in a confused web of pedestrian walkways, stop signs, and no signs. You can easily identify the out-of-towners. First, they actually stop—primarily because they have no idea where to go, given the complete absence of street or directional signs. Second, you can see their heads whipping back and forth as they try to figure out how to navigate the morass without being the victim of, or cause of, vehicular homicide. Locals, on the other hand, just blast through.

I was a local, faking a stop at the bottom of the hill and whipping a right. I zipped straight across the next intersection. To reach my home on Abbot Street, I would have made the next left. Instead, I took a right, followed by a quick left. Jason, following in his car, got caught in traffic. But I didn't have to tell him that I was headed to Cat's.

Harboredge Way is one of the few unpaved roads left in

town. Before Cat and Tom bought their little acre of heaven, the road's only function was to provide access to a children's park and playground, as well as to the dock and small rocky beach that fronted Salem Harbor. Given that any view of the harbor is marred by the smokestacks of the Salem power plant, it isn't the most favored real estate. But unlike the area around Jason's home and the entire length of Marblehead Harbor, this side of town is quiet and comparatively uncongested. The city's Parks and Recreation department offered sailing lessons here, and the single ancient house at the end of the road was used for their equipment storage. Cat and Tom had built their dream home across from the park and had loved the serenity.

There was a small gravel lot beside the park, and there was rarely more than one car to be found there. Today, however, the lot was overflowing, as was Cat's driveway. Like many streets in town, Harboredge Way is one lane. I pulled up next to the end of the driveway, with my right wheels at the end of the drive and the body of the car basically in the middle of the road. I turned off the ignition, effectively blocking everyone. Jason pulled up directly behind me.

The cop at the head of the driveway began a purposeful strut toward my car. As he came closer, I realized that he must be new to the force because I didn't recognize him at all. If you lived in this town long enough, you became familiar with the names and faces of those in the public trust, as they became familiar with the residents and their eccentricities.

He took an aggressive stance, legs apart and hands on hips. "Ma'am, this is private property, and your vehicle is blocking a public roadway. You'll have to move your car."

I wasn't in the mood to be particularly tolerant. I got out of the car and looked at him squarely. "This *is* my property."

He appeared momentarily confused, eyebrows knitting together in suspicion. "No, ma'am, I don't think so." Then, hesitating, "What is your name?"

"Lindsey Carlisle."

Apparently recognizing the name, he shifted his stance and dropped his arms. "I'm sorry, Ms. Carlisle. But since this is your sister's house, we can't legally allow you in here yet."

Glancing past his shoulder, I saw Agent Santori heading down the drive to join our little drama. The man was everywhere. I waited until he was within earshot before making my point.

"Actually, I am an owner of this house and have every right to be here."

This was something else I'd neglected to mention to Evelyn, and I knew that she wouldn't be amused at the omission. I hadn't deliberately withheld the information, but with all that was going on, it hadn't bubbled into my consciousness until I was driving through the intersection at Five Corners.

When Cat and Tom bought the land and financed the building, they had convinced me to throw in some money as an investment. I'd done so, and we held the mortgage as tenants by entirety. This type of arrangement was typically set up for two unmarried people who were enjoying a committed relationship, be it of the same or opposite sex. Effecting the same result as spousal rights, it ensured that, upon one's demise, the property would pass, in its entirety, to the surviving significant other. In our case, we'd done it primarily to avoid the issue of inheritance tax. Cat and Tom were considerably older, and the assumption had always been that they would be gone long before me. Tom's parents were deceased, and he was an only child with no children resulting from either of his two marriages. Their will had made some allowances for charity, but I was essentially their sole heir. Having my name affixed to the property made the title issue quite clear and saved me from paying the Commonwealth of Massachusetts for the privilege of having a family member die. Tit for tat, we'd arranged an identical setup for my house. And it was all perfectly legal.

Agent Santori's lips tightened into a straight line, hardening his expression. I didn't expect him to be startled by the revelation, given the extent to which they'd supposedly examined Cat's financial dealings. The property's ownership was, after all, on the public record and easily determined. But judging by his reaction, this bit of information had caught him unaware. He started to say something, but stopped when he heard the shouts.

"Miss Carlisle! Miss Carlisle!" Reporters were on me like jackals on a carcass.

I tried multiple "No Comment" statements, but to no avail. They pushed microphones in my face and shone lights in my eyes, shouted questions, and shoved against me in a crush of revolting animal behavior. I was disgusted and sickened by their disregard for my privacy and their sordid interest in my misery. Agent Santori tried to hold them at bay, but finally grabbed my arm and steered me back to the car. He directed me into the passenger seat, took my keys, and drove farther down the road and onto the back lawn.

"Quick." We jumped out of the car, and he pulled me under a ribbon of yellow crime-scene tape, knowing that the media would respect the barrier. "If we stay out of their sight for an hour or so, they'll give up and crawl back in their holes."

"Thank you for rescuing me. I wasn't prepared for that."

"No one's ever prepared for an invasion of cockroaches."

For the first time, I looked up at the house. If you looked at it from a certain angle, you'd never know anything was awry. The west side and middle looked mostly untouched, with only a few broken windows. But walking a few steps forward, I could see what little was left of the east part. If you've never been to the aftermath of a fire, then it's difficult to imagine its assault on the senses. First, your brain can't comprehend what you're seeing because whatever was once familiar is now almost unrecognizable. Rooms that formerly had walls and ceilings are now open to the sky because the roof is gone. With everything burned or coated in ash, the environment is devoid of color—a charcoal rendering in shades of black and gray. The materials that remained were saturated with water from the fire hoses. What were once hardwood floors and oriental carpets were now pools of leaden slush. With temperatures in the twenties last night, the scene was now a bizarre rendering of carbon-veined ice dripping rhythmically under the relative heat of the sun. Everywhere I looked, I caught a glint from the sun reflecting off thousands of shards of broken glass. After a fire, the smell becomes infused in the charred remnants of the building's construction materials and content, and drifts upon the air. It's not the pleasant smell of a log in the fireplace; rather, it's an acrid smell that brings tears to your eyes and bile to your throat. I tried to hold back my nausea.

We were standing just outside what had once been the wall-to-wall expanse of glass doors that had opened onto the back lawn. Splinters and ashes were the only remnants of the deck that had previously sheltered the lower entry. As I felt the tears welling in my eyes, I wondered why in the hell I was there.

"The damage was pretty well confined to this side of the house. You want to take a look at the rest?" Agent Santori was offering me a chance to explore the undamaged areas of Cat's house.

I'd lost track of Jason when we'd been confronted by the media. I was a little surprised to see him only a few feet away, inspecting shards of what might once have been the hot tub. "May I tag along?"

"Sure. Just be careful where you step, and don't touch anything," Agent Santori said.

We walked across the lawn to the other side of the house and entered through the door leading to the master bedroom suite. The door itself was hanging loosely in its frame, the victim of a forced entry.

As if reading my thoughts, Santori commented on the damage. "We had to break down the door. We've posted a guard to prevent any looting, in case you're worried about that."

Actually, it hadn't even entered my mind. I was concentrating on the serenity of this area of the house, where everything was in its place and the only hint of something amiss was the awful smell permeating the air. When you read articles about fires, they often mention smoke damage. I was getting a firsthand education in the concept and wondered if there could possibly be anything salvageable.

As we walked past the master bath, I noticed Cat's robe hanging over the corner of the door. It was a beautiful Japanese yukata decorated with origami-like cranes in deep blue. It was so personal—I could see her wearing it, sitting in the kitchen in the morning, sipping a cup of tea, reading the newspaper. In Japan, the crane is believed to be a bearer of good luck, and Cat had enjoyed the symbolism. I stood staring at it for some time before Jason and Santori realized I wasn't responding to them.

"Are you okay?" This from Jason.

"Yeah. Just remembering."

We wandered down the hall to the central area of the house, where the living and dining rooms were located. There were several people milling about, poking and pointing and commenting. In a display of technology meeting human resistance, some had microphones clipped to their chests and were recording impressions into tiny digital recorders, while others were jotting notes into old-fashioned wire-bound notepads. We drew a few sidelong glances, but accompanied by Santori, we were mostly ignored. Here, too, things looked untouched. Aside from the smell, one would hardly know that a tragedy had occurred here. There were some stains visible on the walls and ceiling, which I assumed to be from water.

It wasn't until we moved into the wide hall leading to the kitchen that the fire's ravages became apparent. It was actually rather confounding, because my brain was telling me that the destruction wasn't as extensive as it should have been. How does one section of a house sustain such major damage and the rest remain intact? And why weren't Cat and Tom able to escape?

Agent Santori pointed in the direction of the office. "We found them in there."

I couldn't stand it anymore. I turned and nearly ran back through the house to the door by which we'd entered. I bolted outside, gulping the clean air, grateful to be away from the stench.

Jason and Santori followed me out, eyeing me with some concern. I was a little embarrassed at having panicked so easily. "Sorry, I just had to get out of there."

"It's perfectly understandable. It's not easy. Why don't we take a walk and get you away from here."

Agent Santori's suggestion sounded like a good idea. I motioned to Jason to come along.

"No, I want to look around for a minute. Yell at me when you get back."

We walked down the length of the back lawn toward the strip of rocky land that represented the beach. What had originally seemed a needed escape now felt somewhat uncomfortable. I was, after all, in the company of an FBI agent. What did he want? He was very quiet, not saying a word, even after we'd reached the water and stood staring at the line of buildings that was Salem. I kept trying to figure out what to say to fill the void, but the lack of conversation didn't seem to disturb him at all. I sat down on a rock and pulled my coat tighter to block the wind coming off the water. He set one foot on a boulder and leaned both arms against his knee, facing the harbor, content in the silence.

After a few minutes, the fragmented thoughts that had been stewing in my brain finally took shape. "Why didn't the fire spread?"

He inclined his head slightly in my direction, but kept his gaze focused on some distant point. "There was a double masonry wall between the office area and the rest of the house—a firewall like they use with attached buildings, and very unusual for a single family home. The wall for the center of the house stayed up when the east section collapsed. And the whole area around the master bedroom was constructed like a fortress ... or a very large safe room. At least that's what the experts are saying." He paused. "Your people, the ones that Ms. Wainwright sent over, already know this, so I might as well tell you ..." He sucked in some air, and his nostrils flared slightly. "We know that the propane was a contributor, but we also found traces of plastic explosive. Speculation has it that it was a shaped charge, designed to inflict maximum damage in one area." He turned to me, awaiting my reaction.

It was a long time coming. I sat there, stunned, digesting what he had just told me. My voice, when I found it, was barely a whisper. "Agent Santori, are you telling me that the explosion wasn't accidental? That someone intentionally ..." I didn't finish the question, but the meaning was clear enough.

"That's exactly what I'm saying."

"But who ...?"

"There's the question. We don't know yet if they set it themselves, or if it was someone else."

"You think they wanted to kill themselves?" I was aghast at

the idea.

"Maybe they just screwed up and got caught in the blast. Maybe they were murdered. I don't know. We're examining the evidence, trying to figure it out."

This was a nightmare that kept getting worse. I wanted to ask more questions, but I really didn't want any more answers. I was beginning to unravel. "Whatever. I'm going home. I'm going to make phone calls, pour myself a glass of wine, and sleep in my own bed. And when I wake up tomorrow, I hope that I'll be in some alternate reality, because I can't deal with this one." I stood up abruptly.

Agent Santori dangled my keys in his hand. "I'll take you home, but I need a minute. I'll meet you at your car." And with that, he sprinted up the hill toward what was left of Cat's house.

Chapter 9

I don't know what the protocol is for inviting federal agents into your home for a glass of wine. It's probably not done. But the invitation slipped out of my mouth automatically when we pulled up in front of my place on Abbot Street. It was merely an expression—"Thanks for the ride. Would you like a glass of wine?" I wasn't expecting him to accept, just as when you greet someone by asking "How are you?" you don't really expect them to elaborate.

I flipped on the lights and pointed the way to the kitchen while Jason hung the coats. Having people in the house was comforting because I didn't really want to be alone, but I wasn't sure how I felt about Agent Santori being there. He seemed like a decent guy, despite the grilling he'd given me a few hours before, but I was grateful that Jason was there.

Excusing myself, I stepped into the spare room that I use as a home office and sank tiredly into the desk chair. Swiveling toward the window, I dialed my uncle. He answered on the second ring, and I instantly regretted not having called earlier.

He was irate and let me know it. My uncle and I usually got along well, but we approached the world differently. I resisted the urge to snap at him and tried to calmly explain the events of the day. He settled down when he realized that his life wasn't the only one turned upside-down by Cat's death and the circumstances surrounding it. He, in turn, related to me that the media had also descended on their house and had camped out for most of the day, until finally realizing that there was nothing to be gained by staying there. I didn't share what I'd just learned about the fire. It would only produce another barrage of questions to which I had no answers.

Uncle Pete had made flight arrangements, and he and Aunt Holly would arrive in Boston tomorrow at about noon. Ordinarily I would have picked them up at the airport, but I suggested that they rent a car instead. I also told him where to find the hidden house key in case I wasn't home when they arrived.

I looked at my watch, deciding to go ahead and call the other four people on Cat's list of notifications. I'd already talked to the first person on the list, Paul Marshfield. I managed to reach all but one, imparting the bad news in a monotone that provided no room for further inquiry and left no doubt that the service would be brief and private. I gave each the name of the funeral home and said that it would probably be Tuesday, but to verify before making the drive.

Finally setting the phone in its cradle, I stretched and let my gaze settle on the blinking red light of the answering machine. I'd been avoiding it, not wanting to deal with a bunch of sympathetic "I'm so sorry" messages. Reluctantly, I hit the Play button and winced at the electronic voice. "You have twenty-seven new messages." "Lindsey, I'm so sorry ..." Erase. "Ms. Carlisle ..." Erase. And so it went until I heard Evelyn's command, "Lindsey, call me. Tonight."

I dialed the number, hitting the speaker button out of habit. It went to voice mail, and I was leaving a message when she picked up. I told her what I'd learned about the explosion, and she confirmed that it meshed with what her friends had found.

"Lindsey, that's not all. They did the autopsies late this afternoon. The dental records match, but—are you sitting down?"

"Yeah, but I'm not sure I need any more surprises today."

"Well, you're going to have to deal with one more. I got this twinge today when we were talking about Jalil. So I asked for hair and tissue samples, and I had a lab run the DNA."

I was confused. "Whose DNA? What for?"

"You left your hairbrush in my car, so they were able to compare your hair to the samples. We could only do the test for Cat. It's not ideal, given that you only have one parent in common, but it's enough to establish probability. It's not her."

I'd been hoping for an alternate universe, but not exactly the one to which I'd just been transported. I couldn't mask my disbelief. "What are you talking about? How—"

I jumped at the sound of footsteps behind me. I turned to find Agent Santori striding toward the desk, speaking brusquely in the direction of the phone. "Ms. Wainwright, don't say another word. Go to the FBI office in the One Center Plaza building, sixth floor. We'll meet you there in forty-five minutes." As an afterthought, he added, "Please." But it wasn't a request. Then to me, "Please hang up."

I couldn't believe he'd invaded my privacy. And nobody tells me what to do in my house. "Excuse me? Who in the hell do you think you are?"

He reached over and clicked the phone off before setting a wineglass on the desk. His voice was steady, but his eyes blazed angrily. "I think," he answered, "that I'm an employee of the federal government engaged in an ongoing investigation of a potential terrorist threat involving your sister. Would you please get our coats."

I don't know why I obeyed when my normal reaction would have been to tell him to go to hell—perhaps I was so stunned at the turn of events that my brain stopped functioning. He prodded me forcefully toward the door, telling a bewildered Jason to remain there until we got back and not to speak with anyone. I started to tell Jason about Evelyn's call, but stopped short under Santori's warning glare and the "Bad idea" he forced from under his breath. There was a moment when I actually wondered if he might shoot me.

Chapter 10

Saturday night
Boston, Massachusetts

How his car had ended up parked by my house, I had no idea. At least I was assuming that it was his car, considering that we were now shooting down the road toward Boston in a black BMW with Virginia plates. He'd made two calls to cohorts in the Bureau, telling them to meet us at Government Center. He hadn't said a word to me, and I wasn't exactly disposed to making idle chitchat. I'm not sure which one of us was angrier.

I finally gave in. "Do you always listen in on people's private conversations?"

He ignored me.

"Do you make it a habit to barge into people's offices uninvited?"

He pursed his lips, making an effort to control his words. "You were gone quite a while. I thought you might appreciate a glass of wine. Your door was open."

I couldn't hide my skepticism. "Right. At exactly the same time as I was talking to Evelyn."

He rolled his eyes upward. "Believe whatever you want. I don't care."

I don't remember ever feeling quite so miserable and sorry for myself. I should have been elated to find out that Cat wasn't killed, but her disappearance only compounded the problem. And now I was going to be subjected to another round with the FBI. I bit my lip and tried to hold back the tears, to no avail. I turned my head toward the window to hide my face, not wanting to display weakness in front of this man.

He noticed anyhow. "Sorry. I do care. I was bringing you the wine; I heard the conversation. It was a coincidence."

I still couldn't look at him. "So how long have you known that it wasn't my sister?"

"I didn't."

That got my attention and explained his anger. The FBI had relied on the dental records, and Evelyn had trumped them. He probably felt like an idiot.

All I could manage was, "Oh." Lost in our own thoughts, we didn't talk for the remainder of the drive. I stared out the passenger window as we sped past the airport, through the tunnel under the harbor, and into the maze of streets that was downtown Boston.

The FBI's Boston field office is on the sixth floor of One Center Plaza, in the heart of Government Center. The area, as the name implies, is a repository of city, state, and federal offices. The brass from the morning's meeting, Mr. Farrell, was waiting for us when we got off the elevator.

Evelyn stormed in a few minutes later, obviously not pleased at the summons. "You are not earning any brownie points this evening, Agent Santori."

After we were ushered to a small conference room, Agent Santori directed his questions to Evelyn. "I inadvertently overheard part of your phone conversation with Lindsey. With her permission, I'd like you to repeat what you told her, and provide the details."

Funny how he was now asking permission, as if I'd had a choice about being there. I nodded wearily at Evelyn.

She briefly explained about the DNA testing and the results she'd obtained, concluding with, "So we obviously have a problem of some magnitude."

"Indeed we do. I'm curious. What prompted you to order the test in the first place?" This from Farrell.

"Something Lindsey said earlier when we were talking about Jalil Badakhshanian. She told me that Cat had never been questioned. There have been some hinky things going on since 9/11, and it was just a hunch."

"Strong hunch. You should play the lottery this week." Farrell scrunched his face. "Are you sure the results are accurate?"

Evelyn handed him a copy of the report, which he passed to Santori for interpretation.

"They used nuclear DNA for the comparison," Santori explained. "They had Miss Carlisle's hairbrush. It was easy enough to find some strands with the root attached, and some of those may have had follicular tissue—you know, from the hair follicle. Nuclear DNA inherits characteristics from both parents. So even though Miss Carlisle and her sister had different mothers, there would still be some commonality because of the father. According to the report, there are no common markers. So yeah, it's accurate."

Farrell accepted the news with all the professionalism he could muster. "I still want our own lab on it, just to confirm. And we need to run it through CODIS."

I'd heard of CODIS on TV, but Agent Santori explained the acronym. "It stands for Combined DNA Index System. Basically, it's a huge database of DNA profiles that have been collected from both crime scenes and felons in all fifty states and Puerto Rico. The people that we thought were Tom and Cat may be in there. If they're not, we'll add them."

Evelyn eyed them keenly. "I presume that you now believe that Cat and Tom are alive and have fled indictment?"

Santori's answer surprised us all. "Actually, I don't know what to think."

Evelyn's eyebrows shot up in an exaggerated arch. "So why are we here?"

"I'm not quite sure of that either. Give us a few minutes." He signaled to Farrell and exited the room, leaving Evelyn and me to twiddle our thumbs.

Evelyn began to scribble on her notepad and gestured for me to move closer. "I've looked at the charges against Cat and Tom and want to discuss that with you, but privately. Also, you're obviously going to have a problem with the insurance. First, the fire and explosion were deliberate. Second, Cat and Tom weren't the victims, so the presumption may well be that they were the perpetrators of the arson. Bottom line, the insurance company isn't going to pay a dime."

I hadn't even considered the issue, and I inhaled sharply. "Wow. What do I do about the house?" Whatever was coming, it would be expensive.

"You'll have to hire a contractor. Right now, the premises are guarded because it's an active crime scene. When they release it, someone has to secure the rest of the house. They may have to board it up."

I was trying to remember the balance in my checking account as she added, "But before doing anything, let's verify that the government isn't considering confiscating the house."

It took a moment for her comment to register. "You mean like they do with drug money?"

"Exactly. It's not always drugs; it can be any property deemed to be the proceeds of illegal activity. Given their appearance at the police station this morning, the DEA is invested in this operation—and they can move swiftly. I'll see what I can find out."

The door to the room popped open, and Evelyn transitioned the conversation without skipping a beat. "And then there's the matter of canceling any funeral arrangements you've made."

Santori held up his hand. "Actually, we'd rather that you didn't. We've just been discussing that."

I felt a surge of irritation. "I beg your pardon?"

He continued, "I'm not trying to be melodramatic, but there are potential national security issues at stake here. I can't tell you any more than that. But until we learn more about what happened and who those bodies actually are, we want you to carry on as if Cat and Tom really died in the fire. Whatever is said in this room tonight goes no further. Not to your friends, and not to your family.

"We're the FBI. We don't play well with others, and my boss wasn't exactly pleased when I told him what I was going to do. But this is critical, and none of the evidence that we have makes sense. I can understand that you want to protect Cat, and we may be prosecuting her. That means that we're not exactly on the same side. But I've got two things on my mind here: preventing a catastrophe, and getting at the truth. If we work together, rather than as adversaries, maybe we can find the truth and avert a disaster at the same time. That's what I'm asking."

This was why Agent Santori had been so insistent upon having Evelyn present at this meeting. The ball was in her court.

"Mr. Santori, you've invited me to play a role to which I am not accustomed: that of being joined at the hip to a law enforcement agency. My inclination is to avoid you like the plague."

I broke in. "But Evelyn, I know Cat hasn't done anything criminal. She's not a terrorist, and I want the truth too."

Evelyn let out a long sigh. "Well, Lindsey, it's easy to be taken in by what we perceive to be the noble intentions of federal agents, but let me awaken you to the reality. Nobody cares about the truth. All anyone cares about is what they can make a jury believe."

Agent Santori raised his eyebrows. "That's pretty cynical, Ms. Wainwright."

"Just years of experience. That having been said, I will admit that I, too, am impressed ... and intrigued. So with some reservation, we will agree."

He pulled two documents out of a folder and asked each of us to sign one. In my business, I've signed many contracts and nondisclosure agreements. Nothing in my professional experience, however, had prepared me for the oath of secrecy that lay on the table. The declaration had a lifetime of twenty years and prohibited disclosure to any unauthorized persons under penalty of imprisonment. I actually had a physical reaction upon reading the terms—my pulse quickened, my hands got clammy, and a chill ran down my back. I finally realized that this was way over my head. I pushed my chair back from the table.

I must have looked like a deer caught in the headlights, because Evelyn seemed to sense my panic. She whispered a few words of encouragement, telling me that she was certain I had the integrity to maintain the agreement. Her strategy didn't work. Being entrusted with confidential client information was one thing, but being privy to secrets involving national security was a different affair. I am accustomed to speaking my mind when I encounter situations that upset my moral compass. What if we disagreed about the nature of the information and whether it should be made public?

Seeing my hesitation, Agent Santori put forth his opinion. "We do have the very best interests of the country at heart."

I signed the form.

Evelyn had more to say. "I do have a stipulation. No more bugging Lindsey's house, or anyone's house, for that matter, and no more sending little viruses into their computers. They run a legitimate business that could suffer irreparable harm if you continue to attack them in this manner."

Caught off guard, Santori's jaw went slack. "Computer viruses? Ms. Wainwright, if there was any such monitoring of Miss Carlisle or her business associates, I can assure you that the FBI wasn't aware of it."

"Well, that's certainly enlightening. To use your analogy about playing with others, Mr. Santori, it would seem that someone else has been playing in your sandbox. Whoever it is may not share your sense of honor. Tread carefully."

Agent Santori managed to recompose his expression, though his skin was now drained of color and his eyes were grim. "Would you happen to have samples of that handiwork?"

Evelyn nodded without hesitation. "I'll have the micro-devices here within the hour. The viruses present a different challenge. We suspect them, but haven't found them. Given the level of sophistication required to pull off that feat, we may never have proof of their existence."

Farrell and Santori made eye contact, and the wordless exchange clearly conveyed that they had read each other's thoughts.

Our little rendezvous broke up as quickly as it had begun, and we retraced our steps to the car. As we were pulling out of the parking garage, I leaned back against the headrest and closed my eyes. That was all I could remember, and we were now parked in front of my house.

"Have a nice nap?" He was grinning.

I was immediately embarrassed, thinking that I must have

been snoring or drooling with my mouth hanging open. "I guess so. I must be tired."

We were halfway up the walk when the porch light came on. Jason was still awake. He'd been the subject of a heated debate about whether or not to include him in the agreement. The FBI folks were reluctant but finally agreed, with the stipulation that he sign the oath as well. After we gave him a brief summary of the events, he signed without hesitation.

As he was putting on his coat to leave, Santori asked, "I know you have things to take care of, but do you think the three of us could meet for a couple of hours in the morning?"

I looked at my watch—it was almost midnight. "Sure. What time?" I was hoping he'd make it late.

"Eight okay with you? Or eight thirty?"

My eyes crossed. "Yuk."

"Hey, at least you don't have to drive back to the city, and then back here."

I was dismayed to realize that he must be staying at a hotel in Boston. With the exception of a few B&Bs, there wasn't much around here. "You know, this may be entirely out of line, but you're welcome to stay here. That little sofa in the office is a futon." While I had a spare bedroom for guests, the gesture of hospitality to a stranger only extended so far. The futon served to maintain a respectable distance in the invitation.

I could see that he was considering the offer.

"I have an extra toothbrush and razor, and maybe a couple of shirts and sweaters that would fit." I'd had male guests before. A couple had even moved in for a while; sometimes they left things behind.

"You know what? It's too late and it's too far to drive and I've already broken about a thousand other rules today. So yeah, I accept. And under the circumstances, I think you should call me Adrian."

Behind him, Jason was waving and gesturing toward his ring finger. I rolled my eyes, guided him to the door, and whispered in his ear, "I know he's married. Everything is not about sex. Sometimes being nice is just being nice. Sleep well." I gave him a kiss on the cheek and sent him on his way.

After giving Adrian—switching to his first name took some getting used to—a quick rundown on the eccentricities of the faucets in the bathroom, I handed him towels and sheets and headed for the comfort of my pillow.

Chapter 11

I slept fitfully and was awake before the alarm went off at six. I threw on some sweats and a hat, grabbed a couple of oranges, and drove over to Devereux Beach. From there, I had a regular three-mile jogging route across the causeway and around Marblehead Neck. The run always energized me, both physically and mentally. It was also a good opportunity to think things through.

I tried to connect the dots. There were two unidentified bodies in the house, and Cat and Tom were missing. Someone had started the fire, molded the plastique, and ultimately detonated it. It seemed that the explosion had been calculated to inflict a minimum of damage to the house and a maximum to the two corpses. Whoever set this up probably assumed that the dental records would suffice for identification, at least initially. What was also becoming apparent, at least to me, was that this had been planned for some time. The will and the arrangements with the mortuary had been taken care of within the last month, and the funeral was to take place in Gloucester— a location that wouldn't attract nearly the same attention as Marblehead. By the time I'd circled back to the car, I'd reached an unsettling conclusion. Whatever was going on, Cat and Tom were in it up to their necks.

Opening the door to my house, I was greeted by the aroma of fresh coffee and momentarily unnerved until remembering that there was a guest afoot. I pulled off my hat and headed for the kitchen, where Adrian handed me a mug. He'd showered and shaved and donned a navy crew neck sweater, along with yesterday's olive drab khaki pants.

I thanked him for the coffee, inserting a dose of sarcasm as I added, "Nice color combination."

He grinned. "Just making a fashion statement. Enjoy your run?"

"Yeah. Helps clear my head." I leaned against the counter and cast my eyes downward. "They're really in trouble, aren't they?"

A few seconds passed before he responded, "Yes." He looked at me grimly. "Listen, I know this is hard as hell for you, and for that I'm sorry. It's just that—" He didn't finish the thought. "Why don't you go take a shower while I make a couple of calls? Then we can talk more about what we're going to do to help each other."

Thirty minutes later, I felt almost human. Appraising myself in the mirror, I could see the effects of the stress on my face, and wondered if it was as noticeable to others as it was to me. No one had ever described me as beautiful, although occasionally someone would say I was pretty. Actually, I wasn't. I had decent bone structure, large light brown eyes, and a nose that wasn't overly prominent. Any inclination to comment favorably on my appearance was merely the result of skillfully applied makeup and a decent head of hair. An old boyfriend had once said that the color reminded him of buttered whole wheat toast: a little light brown, a little dark brown, a little blonde. Under the skilled hands of my stylist, it had become my best feature. Take away the hair, and I was quite ordinary.

I slipped into a turtleneck, jeans, and a pair of boots and returned to the kitchen for a refill of coffee. Adrian was still on his cell, so I decided to phone the mortuary. It gave me the oddest feeling to discuss my sister's wishes with the woman who took my call, knowing that it would be someone else's body. I did experience a moment of anxiety when she mentioned the cremation, wondering if we were really going to incinerate those two unknown people. The woman on the other end of the line was suitably reverent and accommodating, and after considering rush hour and travel time, set the service for 11:00 a.m. on Tuesday. When I inquired about a nearby florist, she offered to handle that as well, asking if I had any specific requests. I deferred to her judgment, telling her only to stay away from pink. I didn't know about the preferences of the two people in the morgue, but Cat hated it.

Jason let himself in at a little after nine, cornering me immediately. It wasn't much of a leap to figure out that he'd been up all night. His eyes were red, he hadn't shaved, and he was wearing yesterday's clothes. He pulled me close and whispered, "Wait until you hear what Gabe found in Cat's files."

This presented a dilemma. If we and the FBI were supposed to be working together, then we should share whatever Jason had uncovered. On the other hand, it might be incriminating to Cat. Evelyn was right. I do have integrity. But I was out of my league in this game and quickly came to the conclusion that this was probably a decision better left to lawyers. I inclined my head toward the kitchen. "Later."

I was trying to think of an excuse to get Adrian out of the house when I heard him coming down the hall. He tilted his head toward Jason and nodded a quick greeting before facing me. "Listen, I know we're supposed to chat, but I've got an urgent meeting and I have to run. I'll call your cell in an hour or so, if that's okay?"

"Sure. No problem." I flashed a smile, and he was out the door at a half-run. I beckoned Jason into the office and punched in Evelyn's number on the speakerphone. Hearing her voice mail, I had started to leave a message when she picked up. She obviously screened all her calls with a little more scrutiny than just relying on caller ID. "Evelyn, we've found something in Cat's files."

"It's worm code," Jason interjected.

Thinking that some explanation might be needed, I explained, "A worm is sort of like a virus. Most viruses get shipped with attachments in e-mail. When you click on the attachment, it starts the virus code. A worm, on the other hand, has the capability of breaking into another computer all by itself, and then doing whatever it is that it was programmed to do. Sometimes these things don't do much, but some of them will destroy your files. Either way, it's code that's not supposed to be there."

"No, no." Jason was shaking his head. "Cat wasn't infected. It's her code! She was using this puppy to infect others."

Evelyn was perplexed. "Excuse me? So what?"

I got it immediately. "Hang in there a minute, Evelyn. Okay, Jason, so what does it do?"

"Actually, she's got a setup that compiles the worm with a spreadsheet file. If she e-mails the file and the user opens it, the worm code detaches. From there, the worm operates on its own. The user would never know it was there."

Jason was growing more excited. "It's how this worm propagates that's really interesting. Like Lindsey said, worms break into other computers. The code contains a mathematical model, called a 'spread algorithm,' that dictates how to find the next computer to infect. You know how sometimes you'll see numbers in your browser like *10.25.11.1*? That's an IP address, sort of like a phone number for a computer. If your computer is attached to the Internet, it's got an IP address. So let's say that in my worm code, I just specified one IP address in there. Then the worm would only try to find that one computer. But what most of these worms do is to keep generating additional numbers, so it can attack one computer after another. It's called 'random scanning' and can spread the worm all over the Internet."

I could almost see Evelyn's eyes glazing over. I was pretty sure that geek-speak wasn't her cup of tea, and the impatience in her next question confirmed it. "And this is relevant how?"

"Well, that's the cool thing about this little guy from Cat's machine. He only cares about what you actually connect to. So he's not trying to spread it all over the place; he's being specific. It's called 'topological scanning,' and it's pretty rare and exceptionally hard to detect."

"All right. So it's targeting specific computers. What's it doing when it gets there?"

"We haven't got it all figured out. We need to poke around more, maybe experiment a little. From just a quick scan, it looks like it's trying to capture data."

Cat had written some code in her day, but this struck me as well beyond her capabilities. "This isn't Cat's work. Where did it come from?"

"You're right. It took us all night just to figure out the little I've told you. Whoever wrote it is top-drawer; it's a very sophisticated piece of work."

Evelyn asked the question I hadn't thought of. "Was there anything else on the computer of interest, or just this 'worm' thing?"

Jason shrugged. "I don't think I'm the right person to make that assessment. I'm not sure I'd know what's important and what's not. We did find a folder called *Whale Watch Lindsey* with a few thousand images in it. We haven't looked at them yet—haven't had time—but that's a lot of pictures for a three-hour cruise with a pod of humpbacks. There might be something in there."

My eyes almost popped out of their sockets. "What did you say?"

He started to repeat the folder name, "Whale—"

I jumped in, anxious to steer the conversation elsewhere. "Never mind. She had a thing for whales. So we have a problem and need your advice, Evelyn. Do I have to turn the files over?"

The question hung in the air for what seemed like several minutes. When she answered, the pitch of her voice was lower and her diction precise. "Let me ask you: is there any legitimate reason why she'd have this worm thing on her computer?"

In my world, I couldn't think of a single one. In Cat's world, whatever that was, I had no idea. I hesitated. "Evelyn, how well do you know Cat?"

There was a long pause while she considered a response. "For the most part, I think I know her quite well."

"And the other part?"

"I think we both know the answer to that."

My entire core of belief in myself and others is based on integrity and trust. While I couldn't provide a single detail about whom Cat worked for or what she did in the course of that work, I trusted her with every fiber of my being.

"She would never betray her country. I don't know what's going on, but I trust her."

"Then what do you think you should do? What would Cat expect you to do?"

I was momentarily irritated. I was the client, I was asking for an answer, and all I got was another question. The pique wore off quickly when I finally figured out that this was some kind of litmus test. With the kind of cases she normally accepted, she probably took the measure of each client while working out the strategy. I have a long-standing history of being true to myself. While I had already been somewhat concerned about withholding the existence of the files, that guilt had been tempered by loyalty to my sister. After adding the hidden worm code into the mix, things didn't balance as well. I'd been brought up to do the right thing and taught that truth should always prevail. Cat knew that, too.

I let out a sigh. "Turn them over."

Evelyn laughed. "See? You do have integrity." Then, softly, "Look, I know you're worried about whether this might be bad for Cat. But—"

"Yeah, I know. The greater good."

"Exactly. But I also think that it doesn't hurt for you guys to keep working on it. Jason, can you make a copy to work with?"

Evelyn couldn't see it, but Jason looked smug. "Already done."

We discussed the whys and hows for a bit before agreeing that Evelyn would contact Adrian directly and confess our transgressions. Desperately needing a few minutes of solitude, I shooed Jason out of the house, thumbed my cell phone to silent, unplugged the office phone, poured another cup of java, and sank into the oversize upholstered chair in the corner of my office.

I stared vacantly into space for several minutes, willing the dull throbbing in my head and the tension in my neck to vanish. For me, relaxation techniques have always been exercises in futility. I leaned back into the cushions and let my eyes wander over the collection of photos on the opposite wall. Most of them were from trips I'd taken with Cat, and I gradually focused on the small one in the middle. I'd been what, twelve or thirteen? It had been my first solo visit to the Boston area, when Cat had introduced me to some of the wonders of the city that lay considerably off the well-trodden tourist path.

Chapter 12

When I was a child, visits to Boston had been a family affair: Mom, Dad, me, and Cat and Tom. We had a structured routine, with the New England Aquarium always the first adventure of the day. Growing up in the Midwest, I'd had little exposure to the wonders of the ocean. The three-story tank, with its hammerhead sharks and moray eels, was an amazing sight. I'd linger for what seemed hours, watching as the fish circled round and round in their slow dance, seemingly unaware of the predators in their midst. The visits to the aquarium had been the primary impetus behind my quest for a scuba certification a few years later. We'd also catch the show with the sea lions, where I'd giggle at the creatures' antics, then stroll the short distance to Quincy Market for lunch.

The market was like a foreign land, so different from the sterility of the supermarket where we shopped at home. The crush of people, the cacophony of languages unknown, and the wafting smells of a hundred foods were a delight to my senses.

The adults would select some exotic fare, while I would predictably insist on a meatball sub. Then we'd amble through Faneuil Hall, Mom oohing and aahing over the myriad shops and boutiques that offered an assortment of wares so different from home.

The afternoon was invariably devoted to educating us on an aspect of the city's history, with walks along the Freedom Trail, tours of the Massachusetts State House, or admiring the architecture on Commonwealth Avenue. Most children would have been bored out of their minds, clamoring to go home, but I was invariably mesmerized. Cat was a fountain of knowledge, offering insights into the past that probably escaped the vast majority of both visitors and residents. She brought these places to life with stories of intrigue and seduction, tales that are never told in classroom textbooks.

In the summer of 1992, my birthday present was an airline ticket to Boston, just for me, unencumbered by parents. From the moment I stepped off the plane at Logan airport, I'd been shown sights that don't make the brochures. We'd driven past the meshwork of banks and office buildings that make up the downtown area, and crawled through the traffic on the Southeast Expressway, or "Distressway" in local parlance. We took an exit that led us to the heart of what I would later learn was Roxbury. Cat admonished me to keep my windows up and doors locked, and to avoid staring at any of the people there. The first request was not a problem, since I knew instinctively that this was not a safe place to be. The second, to keep from staring, wasn't as simple. I gaped at the colorless tenements, rotting buildings, broken windows, graffiti-laden walls, and knots of tough-looking black men who returned my gaze with a coldness that made me shiver. Two white females in a BMW sedan could not pass through those streets unnoticed.

We'd gone about four or five blocks when one of those groups stepped in front of the car. I remember being paralyzed, cemented to my seat, and unable to utter even the slightest sound. And then Cat did the unthinkable—she rolled down her window and leaned her head out. My heartbeat accelerated into a crescendo of pounding that I was sure could be heard for miles. She uttered a single word, "Jones," in a deep voice that expressed neither fear nor intimidation, and rolled up the window. God, I was scared. But in the next instant, it was as if Moses himself had parted the sea of men. We nosed into the channel they'd created.

I'd watched enough television to anticipate the worst, and I think I fully expected them to box us in and bash the car before setting it afire and roasting us in the front seat. Instead, we rolled unimpeded for another half block before a solitary figure stepped off the curb. He was built like a mountain, taller than any man I'd ever met and with shoulders the width of a bulldozer. His skin was very dark, almost ebony, and was a startling contrast to the whites of his eyes. I sank lower into the seat, willing myself to be invisible to this ominous giant of a man. Rolling down the window once more, Cat silently waited for him to approach the car.

He bent down, his face not six inches from hers, and said, "Hey, Ellis." I wasn't sure I'd heard it right, but couldn't come up with another word in my vocabulary that matched. I'd considered that maybe he was Mexican, since it came out more

"Ay-lis," and thought it might be a greeting in Spanish. The first few moments of their conversation dispelled that notion, however. There was no trace of an accent. His voice was deep, surprisingly gentle, and most astonishing, educated. When they lowered their voices to an indistinct murmur, I strained to hear what was being said, but couldn't make out the words.

He was leaning on the doorframe, arms crossed at the wrist, his huge ring-adorned hands dangling inside the car. I'd never seen a man wear so much jewelry—one on each finger, eight in all. Only his thumbs were bare. I studied the heavy gold-colored rings and wondered if they were the real thing. If I hadn't been so fixated on his hands, I would have never noticed the action. In a move so surreptitious that I almost missed it, he pulled a small box from the sleeve of his parka and dropped it inside the car. This was followed by the much more obvious gesture of pulling a plastic baggie of white powder from his right jeans pocket and handing it to Cat. She, in turn, passed him a stack of money. What he thought of me being a witness to all of this I'll never know, but he gave me a wink and said "Happy Birthday, Lindsey" before turning away. I sat mute until we were back on the expressway, and even then, it was Cat who spoke first.

"Don't ever forget what you saw there. Life for a lot of people doesn't even remotely resemble the life you lead. Boston is a great city, but it has its underside that most outsiders never encounter. Places like that are always simmering in discontent, and it doesn't take much to push them over the edge; you never know what's going to happen." She shook her head in frustration. "I don't know how we'll ever fix it."

I was still struggling with what I'd seen, still withdrawing from the adrenalin that had surged through my system during our encounter in the street. My voice was very small when I asked her, "Do you do drugs?" It was a child's question, far from the "grown-up" girl who'd climbed off an airplane just an hour or so ago.

She glanced quickly at me before returning her eyes to the road. "No."

I started to ask another question, but she interrupted me. "No. I know what it looked like to you, but drugs aren't involved at all."

She pulled the baggie from her bag and gave it to me. "Taste."

I wasn't at all sure that this was the smart thing to do, but this was my sister. She'd never do anything to harm me, would she? I opened the bag and tentatively poked my index finger into the powder, then put it on my tongue.

"It's a mixture of sugar and baking soda. It won't fool anyone close-up, and certainly not if they taste it, but from a distance it looks like powdered cocaine."

She continued, "I know you have questions and someday I might be able to answer them, but right now I can't. You need to remember what you saw today, for many reasons, and you need to remember Jones." She'd looked at me with the most serious expression I'd ever seen her wear. "And you can never tell a soul, under any circumstances, ever. It's our secret."

At one point, I'd leaned in close to her and whispered, "What does 'Ellis' mean?"

She'd given me a puzzled look. "Ellis?"

"Yeah, remember? When he first came up to the car, he said, 'Hey, Ellis.'"

Her eyes glinted with amusement. "Ah, Ellis. Well, it's a nickname of sorts, I guess. He probably says that to all the girls."

And with that, she'd whisked me to the North End, to some tiny hole-in-the-wall Italian place, and introduced me to osso buco, cannoli, and espresso. In a span of less than three hours, I'd gone from being a naive and sheltered little Midwestern smarty-pants to becoming the confidante of my adult sister. No more meatball subs for me.

The next day, she woke me up before six and shepherded me to the car—a surprise, I was told. We maneuvered through Salem and Beverly before turning east on Route 128—destination: Gloucester. We stopped briefly at the Dunkin' Donuts, where she sipped black coffee while I inhaled two French crullers. The pink and white box at my side contained four more crullers and an assortment of doughnuts. "For later," she'd said.

Guiding the car closer to the harbor, she seemed to know exactly where she was going and pulled into a parking area adjacent to a sign marked "Captain Andy's Whale Watch." I was beaming from ear to ear as she led me toward the pier.

A man with sun-bleached strawberry-blond hair, a somewhat florid face, a bulbous nose, and intensely blue eyes detached himself from the crowd and waved a greeting.

"That's Smith," she said. "He's an expert on whales, and I asked him to join us for the trip. Is that okay?"

"Oh yeah, that's way cool!" I couldn't contain my excitement.

Smith stopped about five feet in front of us and made a courtly bow. "Miz Lindsah, ah presume. A very happy birthday to you."

I giggled at the deep southern accent and made a self-conscious attempt at a curtsy. "Thank you, Mr. Smith."

"Now ya'll can just call me Smith." And with a wink at Cat, he took my hand and ushered me onto the boat.

It was one of the most exciting adventures in my young life. The seas were like glass, the sun dazzling, and we must have seen twenty-five or thirty humpbacks that morning. Smith's animated lecture about the humpback whale, punctuated with greetings to some of the creatures, entertained all within earshot. I remember being almost deliriously happy.

Afterward, we'd gone to the Fisherman's Memorial. The bronze figure of a man in foul-weather oilskins, grasping a boat wheel and staring intently ahead, is as haunting as the inscription at its base: "They that go down to the sea in ships." Smith explained that since the early 1600s, Gloucester had lost nearly five thousand of its citizens to the whims of the Atlantic. Cat put her arm over my shoulder as we stood solemnly contemplating that so many men from this small town had perished that way.

Although I wasn't aware of it at the time, Smith must have snapped a picture. About a month after my return home, it came in the mail. Framed in bronze, the photograph captured the two of us, faces upturned to the "Man at the Wheel," with my right arm wrapped around Cat's waist and the other holding tight to the pink and white box of doughnuts.

The folder on Cat's laptop may have been called "Whale

Watch Lindsey," but she hadn't taken a single photo that day. She hadn't even taken a camera.

Chapter 13

I hadn't really thought about that trip for a number of years, and now the flood of memories hit me with an unexpected force. I wiped my cheeks with the back of my hands and considered the past from more than twenty years later and the perspective of an adult. Although there were several times during my teenage years when I'd wanted to impress one friend or another with tales of my excursion to Roxbury, I'd kept my word and never breathed a word of it to anyone. But I'd always wondered about the package that Jones had slipped to Cat, and now there was the curiosity of a funeral in Gloucester and a folder full of images that probably had nothing at all to do with whales.

I sat up with a jolt as the irony washed over me like a tsunami. Smith and Jones. I'd thought that Jones had called Cat "Ellis." But that wasn't quite it, was it? It was more like "Aylis." Not Ellis at all. Not Aylis either. He'd said "Alias," as in *Alias Smith and Jones*. In all these years, I'd never once considered that Jones and Smith were phony names derived from an old television show. Who in the hell were these people?

I booted the computer and plugged *www.bostonglobe.com* into the browser. As a subscriber, I had free access to the archives, so I brought up the search page, entered *Jones Roxbury Drugs*, and selected a twenty-five-year span beginning in 1988. I reasoned that even if he didn't actually deal drugs, he certainly did play the role, and that he must have lived there for some time before I met him and perhaps for some time afterward. In some room miles away and full of servers, one of the machines churned through the database and spit out 7,523 links. With so little information, I had no idea how I could refine the search further. Initially, I concentrated on the titles, hoping that one of them would spark recognition.

I quickly discovered that many of the references were obituaries, which, given Roxbury's penchant for violence, didn't surprise me. Figuring that Jones could easily be among them, I opened each, hoping for a picture or some other means of elimination. How old had he been? At twelve, I'd been a terrible judge of age, since just about every adult looked old. I mentally compared him to the men I know now, finally reaching the conclusion that he was probably in his late twenties at the time, but that a few years either way was entirely conceivable. I eliminated females and any male under twenty or over forty. I'd been at it for over an hour, with nothing to show for my efforts, and had probably covered fewer than 10 percent of the search results. At this rate, it was going to take all day.

Idly wondering why it was so quiet, I finally realized that I'd never turned the cell back on. I considered the ramifications and decided that I was rather enjoying the blissful silence.

If I missed a call, so be it.

I spent another hour looking at faces of people long dead, reading about brutal murders, drug deals gone bad, arson, rape, and other nasty events that seemed to happen all too frequently in that seamy part of town. It was incredibly depressing, and I'd gone from 1988 to 1993 with no more answers than when I'd started. On a whim, or perhaps hoping that somehow Roxbury had managed to improve its lot in life in later years, I decided to move to the end of the list and work backward. While the number of violent crimes had declined significantly, my wishful thinking about the state of the area was ill-founded. Cat had said that day that she didn't know how we'd ever fix it. *Maybe never*, I thought.

It was midway through 2009 when I struck the jackpot. The article was written the day after Jalil Badakhshanian, carrying the insidious vial of anthrax, had been killed in the shoot-out with police outside Logan airport. The *Roxbury* hit in the search occurred because, at the time of his death, Jalil had apparently been living there. How he'd traveled the downward path from Harvard graduate and son of a prominent physician to Roxbury ghetto radical was beyond my comprehension.

The *Jones* actually referred to Lt. George Jones, a spokesman for the Boston PD. The tiny black and white, passport-size photo showed a Caucasian in his mid-forties, obviously not the person I was looking for. But it was the color photograph taken at the scene that took my breath away. There, beside Jalil's white Acura and encircled by the ribbons of yellow tape marking the crime scene, stood a giant black man with his body in profile to the camera. The photo's caption read, "*Authorities examine a vehicle involved in a shootout at Logan airport. Jalil Badakhshanian, suspected of smuggling anthrax into the country, was killed.*" The man's face was partially obscured by the massive hand pressing a cell phone to his ear, but I knew intuitively that it was Jones. I just knew. That revelation led me to another conclusion: he wasn't a drug dealer at all—he was some sort of cop.

Stepping into the kitchen for yet another caffeine fix, I tried to work out the puzzle of how these seemingly random people and events fit together. Coincidence is often just that, but I simply couldn't dismiss the possibility that they weren't random at all—that there was a thread tying it all together.

Deep in thought, I never heard the key turn in the lock. When the front door opened, I nearly jumped out of my skin, hands flying into the air in a classic startle reflex. The mug crashed to the floor, spraying shards of glass and coffee for five feet in every direction.

I turned and saw the drawn, weary faces, mouths agape in astonishment. My aunt and uncle had arrived.

Chapter 14

Absorbed in searching through the *Globe* archives, I had completely forgotten they were flying in today, and hadn't given the first thought to how I was going to handle the situation. Making an effort to appear solemn, I embraced them both, ducking my head into my uncle's shoulder in an attempt to hide my face.

"I'm sorry," I murmured into the soft fabric of his sport coat. "I didn't sleep well, my mind was a thousand miles away, and you just startled me." I needed a moment to compose myself, to appear as grief-stricken as I knew they were.

I pulled back and examined their faces carefully. Aunt Holly's eyes were red and slightly puffy, but Uncle Pete's were clear and focused. I should have known; he was a disciplined man, a master at managing emotion. I'd only seen him cry once, at Mom's funeral, and even then he had quickly regained his composure. But he wasn't the hard-nosed persona that he presented to others. In his private moments, he probably shed enough tears for all of us.

"There's coffee in the kitchen. Let me just clean this up." I needed to buy a little time. I was probably going to have to conjure up enough lies that it would make the American political landscape seem like child's play. The mess in the hallway afforded me the perfect opportunity to think.

Grabbing a sponge, paper towels, and the wastebasket, I forced my physical being to the task while my brain worked elsewhere. The rules were clear. I couldn't tell them Cat was alive; I couldn't tell them about Jones or Smith or the hidden files on Cat's computer. What could I tell them? Realistically, nothing more than what they'd already heard. But I'd had hours to find out more details, so surely they'd expect more than the meager crumbs of information that I'd related previously. What is it they say about being successful at deceit? Stick as close to the truth as possible, avoiding any embellishment that might trip you up later. And divert attention from the core issue by concentrating your remarks on related, but irrelevant, events. I took a deep breath, closed my eyes, and composed a mantra: *You can do this, you can do this, you can do this.*

The next forty-five minutes were agonizing as I related details about the fire, the FBI investigation, my contact with a lawyer, and arrangements for the service. A knowledgeable observer would have noted the glaring omissions, but the performance, while far from Oscar-worthy, appeared to have satisfied its intended audience. I answered their questions as succinctly and as truthfully as possible without stepping beyond the limits of what I could reveal. I'd ask forgiveness later.

I glanced at my watch, stunned to realize that it was almost two o'clock. My brain was buzzing with questions of my own, questions that demanded answers. To get answers, I would need to make phone calls, and that would require privacy. It quickly became apparent that I would have to get them out of the house. Fortuitously, Uncle Pete provided the perfect excuse.

"You look like hell, Lindsey. Are you okay?"

Slumping my shoulders in a gesture of fatigue, I nodded numbly.

"Yeah, I'm fine, I guess. What I'd really like to do is soak in a hot tub of water and take a nap. I'm exhausted." In a flash of brilliance, I added, "You're both probably starved. I'll bet you haven't had anything to eat except a power breakfast of pretzels on the plane. And I don't think there's anything in the fridge except two-week-old Chinese. Maybe you could go get some lunch and stop by the store while I try to make myself human again?"

It wasn't so much a request as a plea. *Just go away.*

They gave me an appraising look, and finally nodded their assent. They weren't entirely familiar with the area, so I directed them to a small, intimate tavern where I knew the service would be gracious, but slow.

Uncle Pete slipped on his parka and pulled me close in a familial embrace. He was no fool. "It's okay," he whispered. "Do what you have to do and tell us about it when you can."

Chapter 15

Fairly sprinting into my office, I grabbed my laptop and cell and closeted myself in the bedroom. I turned the tap in the tub to a slow trickle of hot water and squeezed a glob of shower gel into the puddle. The thought of a drowsy soak was enormously appealing and it would help relax me, but time for frivolities was limited. I stepped into the tub, reclined in the steamy water, and retrieved my voice mail.

Surprisingly, there were only five messages: Evelyn, to tell me that she'd been unsuccessful in reaching Agent Santori and had left a message to call her. *Delete*. The funeral home to advise that a car would pick us up at 9:00 a.m. on Tuesday. *Delete*. A call from Ambassador Marshfield's secretary, advising that he had reservations at the Westin and would call after his arrival at Logan at four thirty in the afternoon on Monday. *Delete*. Pete, to let me know they'd landed. *Delete*. Tom's cousin, Arnie, to offer condolences. *Delete*.

My brow furrowed, I contemplated the absence of the one call I'd fully expected: the one from Adrian Santori. While on the one hand relieved, I also felt a stab of disappointment. I actually liked the guy. *Stop it. He's married. He's out to crucify Cat.* I pushed aside all thoughts of the absent agent, set the phone on the shelf, and closed my eyes.

I woke, startled and disoriented, to the ring of my phone and the sensation of water lapping at my neck. Stepping out of the tub, I grabbed the phone, saw the missed call from Jason, and hit the redial.

He picked up on the second ring. "Lindsey, sorry I didn't call earlier, but this code has us tearing our hair out."

"What's the problem?"

"From what we can figure out so far, it's primarily scanning numerical data. It appears to concentrate on financial stuff, but it also grabs other data, like phone numbers and IP addresses. Wait a minute ..."

"Jason? What's going on?" I could hear Gabe in the background, hollering, and waited for someone to return to the phone.

A few moments later, Jason said, "Damn! We just ran a test on a backup drive of files from my machine. You're not going to believe what happened. Are you ready for this?"

"So tell me, already." I was growing impatient, in no mood to play Twenty Questions.

"Okay. In about a nanosecond, the worm whipped through my files, grabbed every spreadsheet in the system, took my entire address book, and snagged all the cookies, as well as the history of every website I've visited in the last week."

The scope of the worm's capabilities was breathtaking. "How did you determine what it accessed, and what does it do with it?"

"Well, the answer lies in your second question. We found an encoded string of several IP addresses that it tries to connect to, and it sends to the first one available. Then it disconnects and erases any evidence of what it's done. It's so fast and so buried that, unless you're a whiz from MIT, you'd never know. Gabe set up another machine as an imposter with one of those addresses, isolated them both, installed the worm on one, and voilà—it tried to connect, and we were able to extract the file it compiled. The real problem is the authentication. The code sends a 128-bit encryption key."

I thought about encryption keys and how they work. When encrypting a file, the user employs a piece of code, a "key," to scramble the data. If the user sends it to someone else, that someone needs the same key to unlock it. Without the key, the file is just gibberish. In much the same way, when two secure computers connect to each other, one method of verifying the authenticity of another computer involves comparing its key to that on the other machine. In basic terms, if the keys match, then they're authenticated and are allowed to send or receive information. It's sort of like two people giving each other a secret handshake, but considerably more complex. And that's just one method.

Cracking a sophisticated encryption key can take years longer than I'll be on this planet. Chances of winning the Powerball lottery are about one in 146 million, and that's just picking five one or two-digit numbers from one to fifty-five in any order, plus one out of forty-nine to match the Powerball number. 128-bit encryption employs a huge number of combinations, as in numbers with sixty-six zeroes. If I started counting now, one number per second, in eighty years I'd only be up to about two and a half trillion and wouldn't have scratched the surface. Numbers that big make my brain hurt.

"Okay," I said flatly. "That's clearly impossible. Any idea where it's trying to send the info?"

"That, my dear friend, is the million-dollar question. Gabe is a tad reluctant to try and access it directly. Given his history, can't say that I blame him. But he did run a WHOIS on the IP. It's not registered."

"Not registered?" My voice went up an octave or six. This was highly unusual. The WHOIS directory out on the net tells you who the address is assigned to, akin to a reverse lookup for your phone number. *Government. It had to be government.* "What's Gabe's best guess? Federal? Military?"

Little splashing sounds intruded into my consciousness. The tub was overflowing.

"Wait—I'll be right back."

The floor in the bathroom was quickly morphing into a small lake. I sloshed to the tub, turned off the faucet, and tossed several towels on the floor.

I put the phone to my ear. "I'm back. So, what does he think?"

"Considering the complexity of the code itself, it's definitely not the Department of Agriculture. It could be military—but it's doubtful; more likely, one of our sainted intelligence agencies—FBI, CIA, NSA, or somebody we've never heard of. Who knows?"

The silence on the line was deafening as we considered the ramifications. Jason voiced his concern first.

"Lindsey ..." he started, then paused. "This is actually quite—well, in a word—scary."

All my internal alarms were blaring, the voice inside my head practically screaming. *Back off! Back off!*

I obeyed the voice. There was no way I was going to put Gabe and Jason in jeopardy. "Shut it down. Now."

"You sure?"

He was attempting to be solicitous, but the panic in his voice was palpable.

"Yes. Shut it down. I'm going to make a list of what I want you to do." Despite knowing that Donnie had swept the house for bugs, I was nevertheless paranoid about the possibility that something might have escaped his examination. General e-mail wasn't secure either, but I had an ace in my pocket.

I went back to my office to retrieve a red flash drive I kept in the middle drawer. Its primary treasure was the product of one of Gabe's special little talents—a highly sophisticated, private encryption key created from an algorithm that he'd developed. It was perfect for my immediate needs.

I typed the instructions:

1. Do these things right now.
2. Get five flash drives and put copies of the worm file and the "Whale Watch" folder on each.
3. Reformat the drive on the "imposter" machine.
4. Reformat the backup hard drive.
5. Toss both drives in the fire and make sure they burn.

6. Burn any and all copies of this encryption key.

7. Bring the flash drives to me in the morning.

After encrypting the file and attaching it to the e-mail, I removed the flash drive and shut down the laptop. With a calm that belied the situation, I strode into the living room, stacked a few logs in the fireplace, struck a match, and lit the newspaper beneath. When the wood started to burn, I tossed in the flash drive.

I'd formulated the plan at the moment Jason uttered the letters NSA. The National Security Agency undoubtedly possessed the finest tools in the arsenal of electronic intelligence. At the precise moment that Gabe had tried the WHOIS lookup, the alarms probably went off. A microsecond later, they would have had the identity of the computer making the request—and that machine belonged to us.

I'd debated about when to deliver the files, and decided to spend the evening with my family and take care of business on Monday. I'd go into the city early in the afternoon and deliver the first flash drive to the FBI office in Boston. If the NSA came knocking at my door, I'd be able to state in all honesty that I'd given it to the feds.

The second copy would go to Evelyn for safekeeping. The third and fourth copies were mine. I'd deposit one in some obscure place in the house, perhaps taped behind the toilet. When the feds found it, the effort would smack of an amateur and would hopefully stroke their smarter-than-everyone-else egos. The other was destined for a hiding place that no one would ever consider. And the fifth copy, well, that was for Cat.

Chapter 16

A fter accompanying my aunt and uncle to a quaint eatery in town for a light lunch, I suggested that they spend the afternoon wandering through the shops and galleries in town while I took care of some business at home. I sent a quick text to Jason and suggested that he come to the house in about an hour, allowing me enough time to walk home and get dressed for the trip into Boston.

I applied the requisite facial makeup while pondering the appropriate attire. I was headed into the city for the purpose of delivering the flash drives, but hoped to meet with Paul Marshfield as well. I had no idea what Paul Marshfield's plans might be, or if I might be included, but I was determined to corner a few minutes of his time. With an uncertain schedule, I needed to wear something that could work for dinner and anytime before or after. I raked through the closet and chose a calf-length, sleeveless black cashmere dress with a turtleneck, and struggled into a pair of skin-hugging glove-leather boots. I appraised the ensemble in the mirror and judged it to be simple enough for casual, elegant enough for dinner. Done.

I penned a brief note to my aunt and uncle, explaining that there was an emergency with a client that demanded my personal attention. I apologized for the inopportune timing and closed by saying that I'd return as soon as possible. I propped the note on the kitchen counter and gulped yet another cup of coffee.

Another ten minutes passed before Jason appeared at my door, Gabe directly behind him. While they'd followed my instructions to the letter, both were clearly agitated and wanting to determine if I'd finally reached the boundary of my sanity.

"Why do you need five copies? This is not smart. What on earth are you planning to do with them?" Jason's words were laced with concern.

It had become increasingly apparent to me that the best course of action involved terminating their involvement in this maelstrom, at least in the short term. I chose my words with care.

"I'm going down to the FBI office right now. Afterward, I'm meeting with Evelyn. I'm taking the flash drives to them." Not a lie. I was going to do just that. I merely omitted the part about keeping the other three.

Gabe's dark eyes were riveted on mine. "Lindsey, I know you too well. You're leaving something out."

Much more than you know. "Look, I haven't slept in two days, my family's here, the Ambassador's flying in, the service is tomorrow—in Gloucester, for God's sake—and I've got the

FBI hounding me. I'm not crazy; I'm whipped. I just want it all to be over."

They both studied me for a moment before Jason made his offer. "We'll go with you."

Jesus. "Thank you, but no. I need some time to myself." I had an inspiration. "But you could do me a huge favor by hanging around here for a while. Make my aunt and uncle comfortable—keep them occupied. I left a note saying I had to meet with a client. You can't tell them where I've gone. Okay?"

After a slight hesitation, Jason nodded, but Gabe countered with another question. "Lindsey, why did you use that old encryption key on the file with the instructions about the flash drives?"

That stopped me in my tracks. "I just thought it would be a good precaution. Why?"

"Once upon a time, maybe," Gabe answered, "but I surrendered that master encryption key to the government long ago. If you really want to be secure, don't use e-mail."

I gaped at him, adding yet another worry to my growing list of concerns. Would the government decrypt my e-mail? *Nonsense. They have bigger fish to fry.* I grabbed my coat and gloves, slipped the flash drives into my purse, and walked out, leaving Jason and Gabe to babysit my family.

By road, Marblehead is slightly over sixteen miles northeast of Boston. Even in light traffic it takes about forty-five minutes, but during rush hour it can be a lengthy commute. There's no easy dash to an interstate; it's thirty miles per hour snaking through residential and light commercial zones here, then the neighboring town of Swampscott, and past the waterfront homes and condos of Lynn. From there, you swing onto the Lynnway, where the speed increases to fifty. Lined with car dealerships and assorted discount warehouses, the road eventually transforms into Revere Beach Parkway and intersects with Route 1-A at Bell Circle. Its benign name belies the morass of roads that twine around and through one of New England's more notorious rotaries. Strategically placed stoplights now help somewhat in controlling the chaos, but Cat told me about the days before their installation, when you put on your blinders, bullied your way in, and prayed to come out alive on the other side.

For a short distance, 1-A parallels the Chelsea River. The river spills into Boston Harbor and is home to more than a half-dozen petroleum storage facilities. In total, there must be at least one hundred aboveground tanks to hold the millions of gallons of gasoline, kerosene, diesel, and fuel oil products disgorged there annually. Together, they supply almost 70 percent of the region's demand for jet fuel, gasoline, and heating oil, including all the fuel for nearby Logan airport. After slipping by the airport on the left, you are then sucked into the Sumner Tunnel and carried beneath the harbor before being spat out the other side and into the city proper.

At this time of the afternoon, I'd be going against the outflow from the city for most of the trip. Once through Bell Circle, however, it was almost guaranteed to be bumper-to-bumper the remainder of the way.

The alternative was to take the subway—the T. I could park my car at the Wonderland Station, not far from the hellacious Bell Circle, and ride the Blue Line all the way to State

Street, where Evelyn's office is located, walk the short distance to the FBI in Government Center, and finally catch the Green Line from there to the Westin in Copley Plaza. The fare was only $2.50, I wouldn't have to find parking, it ran until after midnight, and the ride would be mundane. I staged an internal debate relating to navigating the subway in my high-heel boots, and reached the conclusion that it was a no-brainer. If I fell down the stairs and killed myself, so be it.

I was just pulling into the garage at Wonderland when my headset chirped.

"Lindsey here."

The distinguished, yet subdued, voice of Paul Marshfield resonated in my ear.

"Lindsey, this is such a terrible way to become reacquainted after all this time. I'm so sorry. How are you doing?"

I tried to match his tone with a suitable imitation of being grief-stricken.

"I'm all right, I suppose, as well as can be expected. It's just very difficult to absorb."

"It must be extremely painful for you. I can't begin to imagine how you must feel."

Like someone dropped a boulder on my head. "The last couple of days haven't been easy."

"I'm sure they haven't." A pause. "What are the plans for the service?"

"Tomorrow morning at eleven, in Gloucester. It'll take you at least an hour to get there from the city. But I'd really like to talk with you before that."

"Of course. I can leave here as early as you'd like."

"Actually, I was hoping that you might have some time this evening." I crossed my fingers and hoped that he hadn't made other plans. His duties kept him incredibly busy, and I assumed that he would combine business with the necessity of attending a funeral.

"As a matter of fact, I was rather hoping for the same. Once the press gets wind of the fact that I've attended Cat's funeral, they'll be all over me. Tonight, however, should be relatively quiet. Why don't you meet me at the hotel? I'm in room ..."—I heard the rustle of papers—"1523."

I explained that I was just boarding the T, had to stop by my lawyer's office, and should be at the Westin by about five. I didn't mention the feds.

Chapter 17

The subway car was crowded with a typical cross section of urban America. Hispanic, African American, Asian, and Caucasian workers, university students, youngsters, and the elderly; tall, short, wiry, stocky, most were on their way home from work or school, or headed to the evening shift at the airport. Most would disembark long before reaching my stop. Like an elevator, a crowded subway presents an interesting study in human behavior, with each rider attempting to ignore the others and achieve some personal space in the shoulder-to-shoulder proximity of strangers. Some entertained themselves by reading the latest celebrity tabloid, a few were immersed in textbooks, and there were several souls who dismissed the ride with a catnap. The remainder of the denizens, however, stared blankly at each other as the train rolled jerkily toward the city. Somewhere between the third and fourth stop, in an area where the space between residences approximated that between the train's riders, the intricate dance disassembled.

It happened so fast that I still can't recollect the exact sequence of events, but someone yelled "Bomb!" and pulled the emergency cord. There was a terrific screech of metal against metal as the emergency braking system automatically engaged, throwing standees to the floor and thrusting seated passengers into seat backs and each other. An instant later, they were scrambling over each other, smashing the arms, legs, and faces of their fellow travelers as they pounded open the doors and emergency windows in a panicked and desperate attempt to flee.

Crushed in a tight knot of screaming bodies, I was propelled forward until the force of my bag being ripped from my shoulder disrupted the balance and sent me tumbling to my knees. I caught a brief glimpse of a man in a navy blue parka and black watch cap. He was cradling my bag like a football as he struggled to pummel his way through the detritus in the car.

I screamed louder than I'd known I was capable, "Stop him! He stole my purse!"

How my voice carried above it all, I'll never know. What happened next was the stuff of urban legends. A husky guy—with a buzz cut that had nearly denuded his scalp of his flaming red hair—launched his body forward, caught the thief in a flying tackle, and managed to wrest the bag away from the thief. The man in the watch cap, however, vanished into the warren of streets and buildings pressing against both sides of the tracks.

The bomb threat, of course, was a hoax. We were detained for nearly two hours as various law enforcement personnel ushered us off the tracks and out of harm's way, then searched the train, and our belongings, in an ultimately futile effort to find the device. They took statements from every person who hadn't bolted.

As I listened to the descriptions being given by the "witnesses," I almost burst out laughing. At this rate, the resultant composite would be for an elderly guy in his early twenties, medium height, about six foot five, really heavy, weighing 130 pounds, with sandy-blond and black hair. Any faith I'd had in eyewitness accounts was permanently snuffed—not that I was any better. I'd been so focused on the sight of my purse tucked under his arm that all I remembered was the parka and the watch cap. I couldn't have told them whether he was black, white, green, or purple.

It wasn't until my savior, an Army lieutenant home on leave, told them about the attempted purse snatching that their attention to me became considerably more focused. These people are experts at interpreting criminal intent, and the interrogatory evolved into two separate, and possibly related, investigations: finding the person or persons who instigated the threat, and finding the person or persons who attempted the robbery.

Sgt. Irene Sanders, from the Revere PD, a cherry-cheeked diminutive woman whose demeanor probably instilled fear in her male counterparts, took me aside. "Do you need a doctor?"

I shook my head.

"Is there anything missing from your purse?"

I shook my head again. "No, there's not much in there anyhow ... just some lipstick, a couple of credit cards, car keys, and about forty dollars. And my cell phone."

"Pretty big purse for so little. Doesn't quite match your outfit, does it?"

I winced inwardly. I'd selected the larger bag because of its inner pocket, where I'd deposited the flash drives. The drives were now secreted in the deep inner pocket of my coat, where they'd be a little more difficult to snatch.

"It's just the one I carry most often. Habit."

"Uh-huh. Why don't we make sure everything's there?"

I knelt down and emptied the contents onto the sidewalk.

She looked at me steadily. "And there's nothing missing?"

"No, ma'am."

"A bit strange, don't you think? Most perps would wait for the train to stop before making their move. Easy to get lost in the crowd when people are getting off the train."

Perps? I held her eyes. "I don't know. I've never even thought about it." But you can bet your Smith and Wesson that I'm thinking about it now.

She gave me another long look before shrugging her shoulders and directing me toward the exit.

Chapter 18

I could have walked a few blocks to the next station, but the sun had set and I was feeling vulnerable after the attack on the train. I breathed a sigh of relief when I saw three taxis parked on the street. Rationalizing that the "perp" probably hadn't commandeered one of them, I was nevertheless becoming a bit paranoid. I slowed my pace and let a young couple forge ahead to the first cab.

I slid into the backseat of the second taxi. "Exchange Place, please."

My wallet contained enough cash to get downtown, but forty dollars wasn't going to get me there *and* back to my car. Thank God for credit cards in taxicabs; the probability that I would make the return trip on the Blue Line was exactly zero.

The driver, a pleasant young Pakistani, tried to engage me in conversation, so I excused myself by saying that I needed to make a couple of calls. I'd already called Evelyn, and left a message at the Westin, while waiting for the police to process the scene. But I wasn't in the mood for chatting with the driver, so I pretended to dial and chatted dully with myself all the way into the city.

The forty stories of the blue-glassed Exchange Place loomed above as I stepped to the State Street entrance. While some describe its architecture as sleek, I personally find it rather uninspired. The arrogant posture of the security guard did nothing to alter my opinion. In the world of post 9-11, post-marathon-bombing Boston, there's not a high-rise in town that will admit you without first signing over your firstborn child. At night, the resistance doubles. I provided the guard with my name. He checked his computer and placed a call, appearing rather disappointed that I was expected. After supplying a visitor's badge, he directed me to the electronic turnstile, where I passed through without incident. I offered the guard a perfunctory thank you, but he turned back to his post without responding. Ya gotta love the kindness of strangers.

Evelyn's office is on the thirty-ninth floor, offering a commanding view of the city below. It's beautiful during the day; by night it's spectacular.

"My God!" she exclaimed. "What happened?"

Shaken to the core by the incident on the T, I never considered what I must look like. She took me by the shoulders and nudged me into the ladies room. The full-length mirror reflected the image of someone I hardly knew. My face was scratched in several places, clotted blood was smeared on my forehead like a child's finger painting, and my right cheek was swollen and turning blue. The cashmere dress was torn at the knees, exposing skin that was similarly shredded, and my hair was a tangled mess. It's no wonder the guard had been reluctant to let me in the building.

She eased me onto the chaise lounge and, with a warm towel, gently wiped my face.

"Stay right here. I'm going to get you some tea. You're shaking like a leaf."

I hadn't noticed, but she was right. I could see my hands quivering as I raised them to wipe away the tears streaming silently down my cheeks.

She returned carrying a large mug of hot chocolate.

"I decided this would be better. Hot milk will help you relax. I've ordered some antiseptic and bandages from an all-night pharmacy. They're going to bring it here. Now tell me what happened."

I related the story in a monotone, covering every detail from the time of the phone call about the worm file to my arrival in her office. Well, not exactly everything. I told her I had two copies, not five.

I pulled one of the flash drives from my coat and handed it to her. "Whatever this is about, you need to put this in an extremely safe place."

"Not a problem. We've got a safe here that Houdini himself couldn't open."

She continued, "Now, here's what's going to happen. I'm going to patch you up, although I'd prefer that you go to the hospital. I sense, however, that you won't even consider it. But before I do that, I'm going to call our FBI friends down the street and tell them to hustle their little asses over here yesterday. You're going to give them the file. Then I'm going to relate to them what you've related to me, while one of our drivers takes you over to the Westin. You'll be escorted to the Ambassador's room, and the driver will wait until you're ready to leave. By that time, I'll have arranged one or two more for your protection detail. Give me the keys to your car. They'll want to inspect it before going back to Marblehead."

I started to object. "But—"

"No buts. I'm a criminal attorney—a good one—and I've had enough experiences with these situations to last a lifetime. Trust me on this."

I obeyed, giving her the keys and describing where I'd parked the car at the station.

Fifteen minutes later, an irate and storm-faced Mr. Farrell himself strode into the offices of Wainwright, Johnson, and Kendall, LLC, carrying a bag with a CVS pharmacy logo. Cocooned in a large chair in the corner, I was still as a stone. I don't think he even realized I was there as he directed his fury at Evelyn.

"What in the hell is going on that you order me over here like that? And you expect me to be your delivery boy as well?"

He threw the bag on the desk. I must have jerked slightly, his peripheral vision catching the movement.

"What in the hell?" His eyes were round as saucers as he took in my appearance.

Evelyn moved between us, crossed her arms in a gesture of defiance, and glared at him.

"You and I are going to have a conversation. But first, Ms. Carlisle has something to give to you."

She gave an assenting nod, and I held out the flash drive.

"What is this?" He gave me a quizzical look, then reached over and took it from my hand.

Pandora's box.

Evelyn deterred any further interruptions from the increasingly impatient Mr. Farrell, and he finally took a chair and watched mutely as she attended to me. Evelyn Wainwright, champion Doberman of the Boston Bar Association, had a carefully hidden weakness: she cared about people. I succumbed to her ministrations, sitting numbly while she deftly applied antibiotic cream and bandages to my knees.

She escorted me down the elevator. I assumed there'd been a shift change, as the previous guard was nowhere in sight. His replacement eyed us carefully as we paused to return the visitor's pass, and watched as Evelyn led me through the lobby and out to the street.

I was mildly taken aback when the driver turned out to be a woman. I mentally admonished myself for the stereotype as she introduced herself as Michelle and offered a firm, confident handshake. She was tall, five ten or eleven I guessed, and approximately my age. She was slim and moved with an easy grace that suggested an athlete. *Runner.*

Before placing me under Michelle's care, Evelyn gave me a reassuring hug. And in a manner that reminded me of my mother, she whispered, "It's going to be all right, honey. Don't you worry about a thing."

Michelle opened the right rear passenger door of the Mercedes, and I slipped into the car. Five minutes later we glided to the entrance of the Westin Hotel.

Chapter 19

K nocking on the door of room 1523, I saw a shadow briefly obscure the small peephole. Paul Marshfield swung the door open, shock written on his face.

"Lindsey! Are you all right? What happened?"

He glanced questioningly over my shoulder at Michelle, who offered a respectful nod of recognition. "Good evening, Mr. Ambassador. I'm assigned as Miss Carlisle's driver for the evening." Then to me, "Take as long as you like and call the concierge desk when you're ready to leave. I'll come up and get you. If you're going to have dinner, I suggest that you remain in the hotel. Please don't go anywhere without notifying me."

Paul Marshfield studied her back as she walked to the elevator, and then welcomed me into his room.

It was a small suite, and he gestured toward the sofa that backed up to the window. "Would you like something to drink? You look like you could use it."

I spied the bottle of Grey Goose on the desk and nodded gratefully. He was right. I needed it.

Watching him pour a hefty measure for each of us, then artfully twist the lemon garnish, I noted how he'd changed over the years. Once the classic embodiment of the blond and darkly tanned California surfer, he now sported fastidiously groomed and starkly white hair that contrasted sharply against his lightly bronzed skin. He was a shade over six feet and carried himself with dignity. He appeared to still be in good shape, though there was a softening around his chin that spoke of too many nights being wined and dined.

He handed me the drink and looked at me with concern. "How about something to eat? I made reservations for dinner, but it appears that idea isn't going to fly. So perhaps room service is in order?"

I tried to remember the last time I'd eaten. *Yesterday?* I was suddenly starved. "Please. I'm really hungry."

We perused the menu, and he placed the order. Sitting in the chair directly opposite the sofa, he set his glass on the table, leaned forward, clasped his hands, and gave me his full attention. "Now, what happened?"

Paul Marshfield was a powerful man, with connections not only in the White House and around the globe, but also in the Pentagon and any number of intelligence agencies. His security clearance was most assuredly way up there. As such, there was every possibility that he already knew more than I did. But he was a man of honesty and integrity, someone Cat had trusted forever. Any reservations I had about discussing the events of the last two days simply didn't apply here.

He listened intently as I told him everything, interrupting only when he needed to clarify a point. I told him about Roxbury, the photograph of Jones by Jalil Badakhshanian's car, the fire at Cat's house, the DNA results, the worm file we'd found, the events on the train—everything. I didn't finish until after the food had been delivered, and then I handed him the flash drive. There wasn't any doubt in my mind that he'd know best what to do with it.

He accepted it with a wry smile. "Well, dear Lindsey, I'd say you've opened quite the can of worms, so to speak."

He set the drive beside his plate and ate quietly for a few minutes. I couldn't read his face; whatever he was thinking was well-masked. Finally, he put his fork down and shoved his plate to the side, then stood to pour us another drink. I felt that he'd made a decision of some sort, and waited expectantly.

"I've never known the entire story on Cat," he said. "Some of it, of course. We've been very close friends for a long time. But she's generally very tight-lipped about her work. I've had ideas, naturally, and some of what you've told me tonight fills in a few of the blanks."

He looked at me carefully.

"As her sister, you've probably always thought that you knew her well, but it's been rather a one-dimensional view. To really appreciate who she is, it's important to have a little history. You understand that I can't tell you everything I know, and that pains me terribly. But I do hope you understand."

It wasn't exactly what I wanted to hear, but I nodded. I'd had high expectations for this meeting, but perhaps not realistic ones.

His eyes took on a faraway look as he began, "I first met Cat—before you were born—in October 1978, in Tehran."

Chapter 20

As a newly minted member of the US Foreign Service, Paul's first posting was the American embassy in Kuwait City. He'd been there for less than a year, working with the staff to develop contacts in the area, including a number of local and expatriate journalists and academics who had their fingers firmly on the pulse of current political sentiment and any undercurrent that could affect the stability of the Middle East. During his tenure, concern about the state of affairs in Iran had been escalating exponentially.

Under the rule of Mohammad Reza Pahlavi, the shah of Iran, the country experienced two decades of strong economic growth that helped transform it into the preeminent power in the region. The capital, Tehran, had evolved into a cosmopolitan city that rivaled its European and American counterparts. These efforts to modernize and educate the country, including extending voting rights to women, were accomplished in no small measure through strong ties to the shah's primary backer, the US government.

While these policies of change generated self-satisfied nods of approval from the West, they inflamed the sensibilities of the Islamic clergy. To counter the dissidence and silence those critical of his reforms, the autocratic shah established a unit of secret police, SAVAK. Translated to English, SAVAK was an acronym for the National Organization for Information and Security, and it quickly established a reputation for brutality that has been likened to the GRU in the Soviet Union and the dreaded Stasi in East Germany. Their tactics, and the despotic manner in which the shah ruled the country, far from quelling the opposition, only served to further anger and alienate the clerics and solidify their position. In January 1978, a newspaper article critical of the Ayatollah Khomeini, an exiled fundamentalist Islamic cleric, sparked violent demonstrations in his native city of Qom, and the situation worsened daily. To counter the mounting unrest, the shah imposed martial law. As conditions deteriorated, fearful foreigners—and more than a few well-to-do influential Iranians—left the country in droves.

Bordered by the Soviet Union and Caspian Sea to the north, Iraq and Turkey to the west, Afghanistan and Pakistan to the east, and the Persian Gulf and Arabian Sea to the south, Iran occupied a strategic geographic position. When combined with its prominence as one of the globe's leading suppliers of petroleum, the country's stability was considered vital to American interests. The growing unease caused various US agencies with a presence in the Middle East to dispatch personnel to Iran to quietly evaluate the situation and measure the opinions of its citizenry. Paul was on his third weeklong visit in fewer than four months.

The disparity between the haves and the have-nots further inflamed the passions of the insurgents. The sight of a well-appointed automobile or tailored suit could spawn a dangerous confrontation. After a particularly harrowing day, Paul had gratefully accepted the invitation to Tom Powell's weekly Friday-night rooftop barbeque.

As the director of Mideast operations for a large multinational engineering and construction firm, Tom maintained a close association with many local industrialists and government officials. Being responsible for the welfare of hundreds of American employees in the region, he had also made it a point to foster a relationship with key personnel from the American Embassy. His kind and amiable nature, combined with an enviable sense of humor, generally attracted a broad range of people to the weekend ritual; many attended regularly.

It also helped that, as the cousin of one of the operations managers for Pan American Airways, Tom had ready access to a commodity that most did not: quality booze. Protective of its economy, Iran encouraged the purchase of domestic products by establishing high tariffs on foreign goods. The cost of even a mediocre imported scotch was prohibitively expensive, and over-the-counter sales of premium brands demanded a king's ransom. While local brands of liquor were readily available, their taste was not exactly manna to the more discriminating palate. The result was a thriving black market, where a quart of decent scotch could bring a tidy profit to its seller. It was also an effective bartering tool, and Paul had slipped more than a few bottles to locals with information to share.

Paul was tense as he stepped onto Shah Reza Avenue and walked the mile to Tom's home. Bands of armed malcontents roamed the streets of Tehran with regularity, rousting Westerners and anyone else who might appear disdainful of their agenda. Careful to avoid drawing attention to himself and more mindful of his surroundings than in previous visits, he found himself wondering about the anonymous beings who inhabited this obviously well-to-do area of walled residences and tastefully styled apartment buildings. What would their lives become if the shah were overthrown? The possibilities were chilling.

Nearly two hours late by the time he arrived, Paul expected the party to be well-underway, with the attendees somewhat juiced. While the size of the gathering had diminished in direct proportion to the number of people who had fled the country, its stature had been elevated to that of necessity. There was no other place so conducive to the exchange of ideas and information. The main room was filled with people and a thick haze of cigarette smoke, and was uncomfortably warm. Most of the guests were inside because, as one well-lubricated Brit put it, "I'd rather not be about when one of those bloody jerks offers a few bullets to Allah. Obviously never grasped Newton ... what goes up bloody well kills people coming down."

Paul recognized a number of faces from various functions he'd attended, and circulated among the various conversations, shaking proffered hands and introducing himself as necessary without offering a lengthy explanation of the true nature of his visit. He sought out the host, finding him in a cozy study at the rear of the house and removed from the main gathering. Tom was engaged in a quiet discussion with four others, a man and woman who were undoubtedly Iranian nationals, another man who was probably American, and a striking brunette female in her early twenties, who might have been Italian.

"Sorry, I didn't mean to intrude. I just wanted to thank you for inviting me."

"Paul!" Tom stood and offered his hand. "How good of you to come; I'm so glad you could make it. We were just having a little discussion about the current state of affairs and were about to pull out the Ouija board to predict the future. Let me make the introductions."

Doctors Reza and Simin Badakhshanian appeared to be in their late twenties and were distinguished, charmingly polite, and if one were to make judgments based on appearance, quite well-off. The doctor was a scientist and frequent lecturer at Tehran University, and his wife a practicing psychologist.

The American was Tom's cousin, Arnie. Both Tom and Arnie were tall and muscular, but the genetic similarities ended there. With his sandy-blond hair and fair skin, Tom's coloring was the opposite of Arnie's dark curly hair and swarthy complexion. A few years younger than Tom, Arnie had been lured into the airline business by the promises of adventure and travel to exotic destinations. After a year learning the ropes at Kennedy airport in New York, he'd seen a posting for an operations position in Tehran and jumped at the opportunity. He'd been in Iran for two years and was, as he phrased it in his letters to home, "living the dream."

The brunette was Catherine. She turned out to be an American, and when Paul remarked that he'd thought her Italian, she confirmed that her mother was originally from Florence.

He chatted politely for several minutes before excusing himself. Threading his way through the knots of people, he went up to the roof for a breath of fresh air. He sipped his scotch, letting the smooth flavor linger on his tongue, and gazed thoughtfully at the glittering lights of the city spread out below.

"Penny for your thoughts."

The sultry voice was startlingly close, and he turned to find himself in the company of the brunette, her hazel eyes sparkling and her lips up-curled in a playful smile.

"Catherine Ames—we met downstairs," she said. "But my friends just call me Cat."

"Paul Marshfield. And my friends call me Paul," he responded with a grin.

Cat proved to be an astute and engaging conversationalist, speaking knowledgeably about a diverse range of topics. When the talk turned to skiing, Cat admitted that while she wasn't a skier herself, she had often accompanied others who were quite accomplished in the sport. Paul found himself enjoying her company.

She was an accountant by profession, she said, but found the work maddeningly dull and had given up her job, packed a suitcase, and begun to travel. She'd visited friends in Tehran and had met Tom Powell a year ago. Revealing that they had been involved in an on-again, off-again long-distance affair, she'd come back a few months ago to determine if there was any true substance to their relationship. She'd recently returned to the States to attend to a business matter and had arrived back in Tehran only that evening.

After a brief discussion about the travails of air travel, the talk transitioned to the topic of Iranian politics. Flattered by the attentions of this charismatic woman, Paul found himself openly expressing his opinions of the current situation.

"It's like standing in the middle of a tectonic subduction zone. You feel the tremors, and every second you wonder if this is going to be the big one. With all the volatile forces currently at work here, I just can't escape the feeling that the country's on the verge of a major rift."

"Wow! Do you really believe that the fanatics could take over?"

"I do. Not everyone shares the same sentiment, you understand, but I'm of the firm belief that it's going to happen ... and sooner rather than later."

Having sent a number of forceful communiqués to that effect to his superiors at the embassy in Kuwait, Paul had sometimes wondered if they were as attentive to the danger signs as they should be. Privately, he'd been concerned that his memos might be dismissed as the histrionics of an inexperienced observer. He tempered his initial indignation by admitting to himself that there was every possibility that he was overreacting; he was, after all, a mere novice in the heavy-stakes game that was international diplomacy.

She listened solicitously for a time, then stifling a yawn

and admitting to a bad case of jet lag, expressed her pleasure at meeting him and excused herself.

Paul had little expectation that he'd ever run into Catherine Ames again, so when he returned to Tehran in December, he didn't give it a fleeting thought. It was with considerable surprise, then, that he saw her emerge from a taxi not four feet away as he was leaving a meeting at the posh Intercontinental Hotel.

"Why, Paul," she exclaimed, "as I live and breathe. I was just thinking of you. Could you spare some time for lunch? My best friend's here, and we'd enjoy your company."

He had nearly declined, but in a quirk of fate, altered his plans and accompanied her. Walking into the hotel, she radiantly explained that she'd quit her job and was now living full-time with Tom. The friend, Maggie, was a perky, petite, red-headed stewardess for Pan Am. Polished and worldly, she nonetheless exuded a warmth and friendliness that he found enchanting and irresistible. Within an hour, he knew he was hooked. He'd found his soul mate.

Chapter 21

I n marked contrast to the regimen of a typical Monday to
Friday nine-to-five worker, international stewardesses
could be gone for days at a time, followed by a lengthy
stretch of days off. The unique work schedule, combined with
the benefit of free travel, afforded them an opportunity to live
anywhere in the world, as long as they met their obligation to
show up for assigned flights. Nearly 30 percent of those assigned to the crew base at JFK airport chose to live elsewhere.
Maggie Kendall, however, lived in a tiny studio apartment in
midtown Manhattan, sharing the cramped space with a fellow
crewmember. Their rotating schedules allowed a modicum of
privacy, as they were rarely home at the same time.

After meeting Paul, Maggie began a daily routine of listening to the taped recordings of open flight positions with
scheduled layovers in Tehran, the Pan Am destination nearest
to Kuwait. Harried crew schedulers, frequently amused by the

far-flung romances of their globe-trotting wards, were generally amenable to accommodating personal requests that fell within the confines of the union contract. In short order, she finessed two additional flights to Tehran during the month of December.

In return, however, there was an expectation that these same stewardesses would be equally accommodating when there was a shortage of available personnel. Such was the case in mid-January, when an unexpected blizzard in Boston prevented over thirty commuters from reporting for duty as scheduled. One of the resulting open slots was to Frankfurt, and from there, to Tehran. She made a quick phone call to Cat.

Chapter 22

Romancing a young lady from a distance of several thousand miles was difficult at best. Paul set aside an hour each evening to put his thoughts on paper and shipped the letter out the next day in the embassy's diplomatic mail pouch. She responded in kind, but since it usually required five days for the note to be delivered to her apartment, and another five days for the reply to arrive back in Kuwait, much of the time it felt as if he were carrying on a one-sided conversation. Telephone calls were by necessity brief, and ridiculously expensive. So when Cat called with news that Maggie was arriving in Tehran on Tuesday, and despite the fact that she'd only be there for one night, Paul sacrificed his next paycheck and wasted no time in booking a flight.

Thus, on the morning of January 16, Paul caught a Kuwait Air 707, arriving in Tehran shortly before nine. The Pan Am flight from Frankfurt wouldn't arrive until that evening, and he was anticipating a restful day at the hotel before spending a long and lively night with Maggie. With his black diplomatic passport firmly in hand, he was waved quickly through the customs formalities and was ready to hail a cab and be on his way. Instead, he found Cat, and Tom's cousin Arnie, waiting expectantly.

"As long as we're all here, I thought you might enjoy having brunch with us," she said. "And there's something we want you to see. Arnie's car is just outside."

The airport restaurant was on the second floor of a building about two miles distant from the international terminal. In addition to housing the offices of airlines serving Tehran, the edifice also contained the offices for civil aviation and the weather bureau, as well as a large room, dubbed "The Royal Pavilion," that was used by VIPs arriving or departing by private aircraft.

Nearing the building, they encountered a barrier of stern-faced guards, who refused to let them pass. With tremendous patience, Arnie produced his airline identification and explained that his office was in the building. After an extended exchange, permission was granted. Arnie inclined his chin toward a large jet with the Farsi characters of the word *Shahin* stenciled forward of the wing. The gleaming aircraft, liveried in white and royal blue, was parked on the tarmac about two hundred yards away. He spoke quietly. "Iran only has one privately owned 707, and it belongs to the shah. Rumors are running rampant that he's leaving the country."

While the restaurant's food was passable, its view of the airport was the primary attraction. Seated by the window, they had the best seats in the house for watching whatever was about to occur. Over the next hour, the military presence grew steadily, surrounding the airplane and restricting entry to the area.

Shortly before eleven in the morning, the shah emerged from the building, surrounded by loyalists, many of whom were weeping openly. Paul watched in awe as the shah mounted the steps of the rollup stairway and boarded the plane. Strapping himself into the cockpit's left seat, Mohammad Reza Pahlavi took the controls of the 707 and departed Tehran.

Stunned by what they had witnessed and trying to absorb the implications, no one spoke for several minutes. Cat broke the silence by excusing herself for a visit to the ladies' room. After ten minutes, Paul began to worry—she might have run afoul of the security forces in the building, slipped on wet tile in the bathroom, or any number of possibilities that catapulted into his imagination—and set out to find her.

Approaching the suite of Pan Am offices, he heard her muffled, but obviously angry, voice carry into the hallway. The door was slightly ajar, permitting the conversation to be barely audible. It wasn't his intent to eavesdrop, but—hand on the knob—he stopped in his tracks at the import of what she was saying.

"Frank, I know that you and I don't always agree, and it's been inherently apparent that you have little regard for my field reports. But would you put your damn ego aside for a moment, pull your head out of your butt, and get on the damn horn to Langley? I am telling you that he's gone. I just saw him get on the damn plane, for God's sake."

As quietly as possible, he turned away from the door. As he walked back to the restaurant, he conducted a mental review of every conversation he'd had with Cat over the past few months, searching for some small detail about her activities that might have escaped his notice.

It was not at all unusual for the US government to have clandestine agents conducting intelligence-gathering activities in a foreign domain. In fact, most countries did the same thing. Some of these agents performed their duties under the guise of an official job, such as consular officer or a similar job function, while others worked beneath the radar without benefit of diplomatic cover. It was also not unusual for the expatriate community to enliven their gatherings by playing "Spot the Spook," in which they made often hilarious attempts at guessing who was really who. But the agents with official cover would merely be deported if the true nature of their activities were discovered by the host country; those without official cover could face far more serious consequences. It could be an exceedingly dangerous job.

Given the sensitive nature of such operations, there was an established protocol to be followed. Embassy officials, juggling the intricacies of diplomatic relations, depended on having prior knowledge that would enable them to handle a delicate situation in the event that something went awry. An ambassador would be privy to this information, as would his or her deputy chief of mission and probably the political officer. Public servants who were lower on the totem pole, like Paul, would not. Langley, Virginia, was headquarters for the US Central Intelligence Agency. Paul could think of only one reason that

Cat would be browbeating someone to send a flash message there. She was CIA, and he hadn't had a clue.

Chapter 23

With the shah's departure, all semblance of order evaporated. As competing factions fought for control of the government, the groundswell of revolutionary fervor erupted into a firestorm, throwing Iran into turmoil and causing the thousands of remaining expatriates to seriously question their decision to stay. Representatives from American, British, and other Western companies hastily put their heads together and drew up plans to move their employees out of the area should the situation become untenable.

It was with equal concern that one company devised a covert scheme to extricate two of its American employees. The men, who had been arrested and sentenced on charges of conducting illegal business practices, were inmates at the notorious Evin Prison. The crux of the company's problem was twofold: they would have to stage a breakout from the prison stronghold, and then somehow slip the escapees out of the country. To accomplish the latter, it was their initial hope that they could enlist the assistance of a cooperative Pan Am employee who might enjoy a significant boost to the balance of his bank account. To that end, they offered Arnie six figures. And to their wide-eyed dismay, he refused.

On February 11, Tom, Arnie, and a number of other interested parties met at the Hyatt Hotel for another round of discussion and planning. Unbeknown to those present at the meeting, a mob of insurgents had stormed the gates at Evin and released those imprisoned there. Realizing too late that they had also released the Americans, the mob set its sights on places where the two might have sought refuge, and headed for the nearby Hyatt.

Cloistered in a suite on an upper floor of the hotel, those inside were blissfully unaware that anything was amiss until hearing shouts in the hallway, and they were quite unprepared for the volley of gunfire that ripped through the door. One of the wayward bullets punched a walnut-sized hole in the wall where Tom was standing, missing his right ear by less than an inch. The concussive impact deafened him for the rest of the day.

For those present, the event was cathartic. While Cat previously had a soft spot of empathy for those who had endured some of the shah's more repressive activities, and some very private thoughts of embarrassment at her country's role in installing him to power, this incident indicated a dangerous rift in the country's infrastructure.

The US Department of State requested that Pan Am evacuate thousands of Americans from Iran. As well, the Iranian Revolutionary Government strongly recommended that Pan Am evacuate a number of Israelis. Processing for the passengers was conducted at both the embassy and the Hilton Hotel, where rooms were requisitioned. The workload demanded the services of many embassy staffers, both local and American, and Paul was drafted from Kuwait to assist.

Chaos reigned as the revolutionaries, relishing their new role as final determinants of who would be allowed passage, spent hours examining the passports and luggage of the nervous would-be travelers. The first flight, a 707, carried all but one of the airline's employees, a number of its subcontractors, the staff of the Intercontinental Hotel (which was owned by the airline), and a number of Israelis. Over the next six days, Pan Am 747s rumbled into Tehran's Mehrabad airport, loaded the grateful evacuees into every available seat and much of the floor space, and flew them to safety.

On the morning of the last flight, Paul had been originally assigned to remain at the embassy, but was called to the Hilton when another official fell ill. Paul was tired, irritable, and ill-inclined to personalize the interactions. Thus, he didn't even look at the next group to approach his desk, and instead merely moved one set of documents to the side as the next was slipped in front of him. In this instance, his state of fatigue and the bureaucratic behavior played in his favor. As he looked at the documentation for Mr. and Mrs. Ali Amani and their five-month-old son—Mr. Amani an American employee of Tom Powell's engineering firm—he nearly choked. The pictures on the US passports were those of the Iranian couple he'd met in Tom's house, Doctors Reza and Simin Badakhshanian.

Afraid that his face would betray him, he kept his eyes locked on the documents and examined them as normally as possible. He considered the possibilities. If the passports were forged, and he suspected that they were, they were very well done. Either way, the names didn't match what he'd been given earlier. The CIA's fingerprints were all over this deception, and he experienced a momentary flash of anger at the jeopardy into which Cat and her cohorts had placed them all. They would have some explaining to do.

Slowly, deliberately, heart racing, he raised his head and looked into Simin's pleading and desperate eyes. Praying that his voice would remain steady, he adopted the most bored tone he could manage and said, "Thank you, Mr. Amani. Have a good journey home."

With passengers aware that this was Pan Am's final scheduled evacuation flight, the atmosphere at the airport was tense—everyone concerned that some infraction might bump them from boarding. Arnie worked both the terminal and the tarmac, trying to keep the situation calm.

Maggie, despite having been warned by Paul to keep away from Iran, had immediately requested a position on one of the all-volunteer crews and was consequently aboard the airplane. With no word from Cat or Tom to indicate that they'd already left the country, she fully expected to see them in the swarm of boarding passengers. As the final few approached the aircraft, she spotted Arnie.

"Where's Cat?" she cried out.

"Cat and Tom are staying behind, at least for the time being. He wants to make sure that all of his people are really out, and he wants to gather as many of the company's records as he can before leaving. He can't convince Cat to go without him. They've been arguing about it for days."

Maggie was horrified, unable to imagine any need more crucial than getting out of harm's way by the fastest means possible.

"What about Paul? Do you know where he is?"

Arnie nodded sympathetically. "He's at the Hilton; it's been just a little busy over there, and they drafted him to help out. Did he know you were coming?"

"No," she admitted. "I didn't have time to call."

"If I see him, I'll let him know you were here. He'll probably be ticked off that you came." He shrugged his shoulders and added, "But I'll bet that, deep down, he'll be proud that you did."

He tilted his chin toward the group of stragglers and, leaning closer to Maggie, whispered, "See the couple with the boy?"

"Yes."

"Take good care of them. They're very special friends of Cat."

"Sure. I'll see that they're well taken care of." She frowned in consternation. "But what about you? You're coming with us, right?"

Arnie smiled resignedly as he shook his head. "No. We're going to give it a couple more weeks and see if it stabilizes before deciding if we're going to resume scheduled flights in here. The company asked if somebody would stay, and I volunteered."

Maggie studied him for a moment. "Will you be okay?"

"Yeah, I keep a low profile, and I know enough Farsi to keep me out of trouble. I know some of the guards here reasonably well. They've been escorting me between my apartment and the airport; it helps that I give them a couple of shots of scotch every night for their trouble."

He escorted her to the aircraft door, and she gave him a quick hug. "Be safe," she said.

"I will. You have a safe flight," he replied, and closing the aircraft door, gave it a fond double-pat in farewell. After snapping a salute to the cockpit as the aircraft began to roll, he lingered on the tarmac and watched the gigantic bird gracefully lift its nose to the darkening sky, remaining until the spotlighted blue globe logo on the 747's tail was no longer visible.

Chapter 24

October–November 1979
Tehran, Iran

P an Am resumed scheduled service to Tehran several
days after the evacuations, but the planes now stopped
only long enough to let off the passengers destined
there, before taking off again with those fortunate enough to
be allowed to depart. Many were Iranians who left on con-
trived business trips, vacations, or for medical consultations,
always promising to return. Most never did. In an ironic twist
after his departure from Iran in January, the shah had been denied asylum in the United States. The government that had
helped install him in power—now more concerned with diplomatic fallout—proved to be a fair-weather friend.

The modernizations put in place under the shah quickly
fell victim to the fundamentalist regime led by the Ayatollah
Khomeini. Many of the few remaining Westerners banded together in havens of relative safety and tried to remain as unobtrusive as possible. Behind closed doors, they shredded

documents and pictures that might indicate any ties to the shah or his loyal followers.

Tom and Cat moved into Arnie's apartment not far from the airport. Attempting to establish some normalcy in a time when there was none, the three quietly and carefully went about their business. Arnie exchanged frequent calls with the US Embassy, providing updates about events at the airport and passing along information gleaned from conversations overheard. A few of the locals with whom he came in contact knew that he spoke a few ill-pronounced perfunctory words of Farsi. None of them knew he was fluent; it was a charade he managed well.

The accuracy of Paul's predictions regarding Iran's destabilization significantly elevated his stature within the US diplomatic community in the Middle East. Perceived as an effective analyst, albeit somewhat inexperienced and overly prone to speaking his mind, he was temporarily posted to Tehran to conduct ongoing assessment of conditions within the country. Paul's grasp of Farsi was limited, so he was assigned a trusted Iranian on the embassy's payroll to act as his driver and translator. During the day, the driver transported him to various areas of the city, where they conversed with the locals and Paul attempted to gauge the overall mood of the citizenry. At night, he slept securely within the walls of the embassy compound. He saw little of Cat and Tom, and nothing of Maggie—the daily letters and infrequent telephone calls becoming their only thread of contact.

On October 22, the former shah of Iran was admitted to the United States for treatment of non-Hodgkin's lymphoma. Incensed by the turn of events and suspecting that the story was a ruse for allowing him to seek asylum there, the Iranian population responded with a vengeance, staging demonstrations and demanding that he be returned to Iran for trial. The American community, anticipating trouble, raised its state of alert.

On November 4, Paul left early for an appointment in the northwest section of the city. As a security precaution instituted by the embassy, Paul was required to regularly notify them with regard to his whereabouts. To that end, all official vehicles were equipped with two-way radios that allowed instant communication between the car's occupants and the embassy. Midmorning, he picked up the handset and pressed the button. "Post One, come in."

There was no response.

Thinking that the radio had somehow malfunctioned, he tightened his grip, pressed the button firmly, and tried again. "Post One, come in, please."

There was no answer.

He ordered the driver to pull to the side of the road, stripped off his suit coat and tie, and asked for the driver's woven red and brown plaid sweater. Hands shaking, he slipped it over his head, thinking that if he were somewhat more casually dressed, he'd be less conspicuous.

"Take the car and get out of here," he commanded, stepping out of the car. "And be safe."

The driver stared at him for a split second, wide-eyed, before stepping on the accelerator and peeling away from the curb in a cloud of dust and gravel. With its diplomatic plates, the black sedan was instantly recognizable and a magnet for trouble. He would be safer without it. Paul was sure that the driver would take the car a couple of blocks and abandon it, no more willing than Paul to take the risk.

The instructions to diplomatic staff had been clear. In the event of an emergency, you were to make your way to the nearest friendly embassy and ask for sanctuary. Paul contemplated his situation. The nearest "friendly" embassy was miles away, and he was on foot. Cut off from any means of communication, there was no way to know what had transpired and what might be encountered if he tried to go there. He needed shelter and a place where he could obtain information. Arnie's apartment was less than a mile away. It was an easy decision.

Arnie was in his office at the airport, awaiting the radio call from the 747 inbound from New Delhi, when one of the employees informed him that the US Embassy had been overrun by militant students and that hostages had been taken.

Oh shit. While the airline had codes for these situations, he'd hoped never to use one. Minutes later, the radio jumped to life.

"PanOp, Clipper One," the pilot intoned.

Arnie spoke into the microphone. "Clipper One, PanOp.

Divert redbrick instructions."

No further communication was needed. With those simple words, the aircraft made a southwest turn toward the most feasible alternate, Bahrain.

Arnie wasn't overly worried. Revolutionaries had briefly seized the embassy in February, but only for a few hours. He placed a call to headquarters in New York, alerting them to cancel all flights to Tehran until further notice. As a precaution, however, he secured three tickets on a Gulf Air flight to Bahrain five days later.

Chapter 25

November 1979
Tehran, Iran

The unexpected knock on the door sent a shiver of dread down Cat's spine. Half-expecting a cadre of police, she tentatively opened the door and was shocked to see Paul. She grabbed his arm and quickly drew him into the apartment.

"My God, Paul! What are you doing here?"

"I tried to call the embassy, but nobody answered, so I ditched the car. I was less than a mile from here, and this seemed like the best option. What the hell happened?"

Cat quickly related what little she knew. "A mob of students took over the embassy, and they've taken everyone hostage. I don't know if anybody got out; I don't know if anybody's hurt. This is a nightmare."

He looked at her intently. "What about the chief of station?"

If Cat was startled by his question, she gave no indication.

Chief of station is the title given to the ranking CIA official within a given country.

"I beg your pardon?"

Paul held her eyes. "I know," he said quietly. "I overheard you the day the shah left."

Cat sighed in resignation. "Well, I guess the cat's out of the bag, isn't it?"

He chuckled at the pun. "So, what do you really know?"

"Honestly, no more than I've told you. I haven't been able to reach anyone. Maybe Tom or Arnie will have something." She glanced at her watch. "We'll just have to wait."

She offered him a beer. "We're down to a six-pack. Consider yourself honored."

Paul accepted it gratefully, savoring the German brew. While alcohol was still available within the sovereign walls of the embassy compound, the Ayatollah and his followers had successfully purged it from the rest of the country. What little was left was either a vestige of former times or smuggled in.

"So, exactly who is Reza Badakhshanian? Or should I say Ali Amani?" He'd been waiting months to ask the question.

"Ah, I wondered when you'd bring that up." She sat across from him, wrapped her arms around her knees, and explained.

Dr. Badakhshanian's resume contained a great deal more than university lecturer. He was a nuclear physicist and had been a member of the team developing the reactor at Bushehr prior to the revolution. While this in itself did not tilt the tables in favor of spiriting him out of the country, his father's position within the Ministry of Justice held greater sway. While many men in similar positions of influence had fled months earlier, Dr. Badakhshanian's father was a true patriot to his country and would not abandon it. During the months leading up to the revolution, at great risk, he had voiced his opposition to the extremist Ayatollah Khomeini and lent his support to those with more moderate views.

His dedication notwithstanding, when the Ayatollah gained control, the elder Mr. Badakhshanian had quietly approached a US official and requested asylum for his family. In return, he would remain in Iran and supply the US intelligence agencies with any and all information to which he had access, and would continue to do so for as long as the Americans required. The deal was struck, the only hitch occurring when his family had refused to leave without him. He had prevailed over his son and his son's wife, but his own wife would not budge. Thus, the Doctors Badakhshanian and their young son were now living in the United States.

"You could have warned me," Paul said. "I'm still not sure exactly how I managed not to spill the beans."

"That was a bit of a screwup, wasn't it? You weren't on the need-to-know list. You weren't scheduled to be there, remember? That, by the way, was intentional. You're a bit of an uncharted territory, and there were some concerns about your reaction if you saw them. From what I understand, several of our people were holding their collective breath."

"I'm a bit amazed that you've told me as much as you have. This isn't one of those 'I can tell you, but then I'll have to kill you' scenarios, is it?"

Cat sighed deeply. "Unfortunately, it's all moot now. About a month after we got his son out, the elder Mr. Badakhshanian and several others were murdered by the revolutionary guards. There were so many assassinations going on that the name probably didn't ping your radar."

"Terrible. This is going to sound wrong, but I hope whatever he gave you was worth it."

"That," she replied, "I'm not at liberty to say."

Upon Tom and Arnie's return to the apartment, they hashed over the information they'd gleaned about the embassy's fall. Throughout the evening and into the wee hours of the morning, the four huddled near the radio and awaited news that the crisis had been resolved. By midmorning of the next day, they learned that the Ayatollah had lent his support to the takeover and that negotiations had thus far failed.

For the next three days, Arnie was the only one to venture out. Driving to and from the airport, he tried to assess the chances of slipping Paul past the unpredictable security checkpoints and into an embassy compound. At the airport, he scrutinized the methods used for passenger processing, seeking a weak link that could be exploited to get Paul on an airplane.

He reported his discouraging findings to the others.

"The checkpoints are completely unpredictable. They just pop up anytime, anywhere. Sometimes they just wave you through; sometimes they don't. When they do, I just talk to them in German, and they let me go. The airport is impossible. If Paul had a regular passport, I could get him out, no problem. The guards aren't so much anti-American as they are anti-US government. With his diplomatic passport, there's no way."

Cat chewed on her lower lip for a moment, then looked at Paul.

"So, the airport is out. Our flight leaves day after tomorrow, and we can't leave you here—you'd be completely on your own. We could try to take you overland, I suppose, but the only reasonable option is Turkey, with six hundred miles of bad road between here and the border. And the area north of Tabriz? It's completely lawless. Never mind that your only documentation is your dip passport. We'd need help, and I don't have any way to arrange it now. We're out of options. We simply have to get you to an embassy—tomorrow. Do you have a preference?"

Paul was pensive. "Okay. The Brits would be first on my list, I think. They've dealt with this kind of thing before. There are the Swiss, French, and Germans, but I doubt any of them would be terribly pleased to have me knocking at the door— it's very risky for them. The Canadians might be an idea."

Cat's eyes widened appreciatively. "Now that's a thought. They're low-profile. The others could very well be inaccessible. I like it. Now, let's figure out the timing. I think daytime would be best. Any Westerner with a grain of sense stays inside at night, so to be out and about would be suspicious. During the day, there's much more activity, and that might seem threatening, but it's really much easier to blend in with the crowd."

Juggling the possibilities, Paul finally turned to Cat. Unsure of how much Tom and Arnie knew of her clandestine activities, he chose his words carefully. "No matter what we think, you seem to have the best handle on this. What's your opinion?"

Cat caught his eye and offered him a quick wink of appreciation. "It seems to me that morning would be the best choice—right around the time the embassy opens. People are still trying to wake up, trying to get organized, and they're not as alert. You'll want to wear something very ordinary—nothing that might attract undue attention.

Tom offered to drive, and when Cat stated that she'd be the one driving, he expressed his irritation. "Sheesh, Cat, that's crazy."

She patiently explained her reasoning. "Look, I appreciate that you're worried about me, but I can pass for Iranian a lot more easily than you. My skin and hair are the right color, and I'll wear the chador." She reached out and patted Tom's arm, smiling affectionately. "Plus, my Farsi is almost as good as yours. But we will need your car."

Chapter 26

The following morning, Paul marveled at Cat's transformation. Clad in a black chador, the traditional garment for Muslim women, and with her eyes dramatically outlined in black eyeliner, she looked for all the world like any other Iranian woman, albeit a very pretty one.

Paul was wearing the driver's plaid sweater, and well-worn khakis and everyday shoes that Arnie had pulled from his closet.

Cat appraised him and nodded her approval. "You look fine. Now, I've given this a lot of thought. If we're stopped, I'll just say that you've been very ill, and I'm taking you to a doctor. Armish Maag Hospital is only a stone's throw from the Canadians. It'll make sense—just let me do the talking."

Paul frowned. "But I don't look sick."

She placed a small cellophane bag in his hand. "If you see that we're going to be stopped, tear off a small piece of this and rub it on your face. Then eat it. It'll make your skin break out in a rash, and I guarantee that after you swallow it, you'll definitely look sick."

Paul warily studied the round, deep-red fruit in the bag. "What is it? It looks like a weird cherry."

Cat snickered. "Hardly. It's a filfil-i-hind pepper. They're very hot; don't get it anywhere near your eyes. If you have to use it, wash your face and hands as soon as you can. It won't be pleasant, but it will help the illusion."

Tom's car was a perfectly ordinary white four-door Paykan, manufactured in Iran. There were thousands of these vehicles choking the streets of Tehran. Paul scrunched down to minimize his profile, leaning his head against the bottom of the passenger-door window.

Heading east on Vanak Parkway, Cat drove aggressively. Concealed only by the illusion of normal behavior, she jockeyed for position in the snarls of traffic and no one paid them the slightest attention. She explained her intentions. "I don't see any roadblocks yet. I'm going to take the exit onto Pahlavi; it's very near the Hilton."

"How far from there?"

"Not far, a mile, maybe a little less. Just cross your fingers and hope."

"I've been doing that since we left."

Cat smiled. "Nice to see you still have a sense of humor. Here we go."

She breathed deeply as they turned off the freeway and onto the broad avenue that ran through the heavily congested residential area. The road was clear. Making another turn, she steered into the Elahieh district. Veering onto Bustan, she was driving directly toward the hospital when traffic came to an abrupt halt. Peering through the windshield, she could see about half a dozen guards in the road.

"Paul! Use the pepper!"

Paul didn't hesitate as the adrenaline rush kicked in. He tore off about a third of the pepper, rubbed it hard on his face, and popped it in his mouth. Within seconds, his face and hands were stinging painfully, and his mouth turned to fire. He choked violently and clutched his hands to his throat, tears and mucous streaming down his face.

When the guard motioned her to stop, Cat rolled down her window and started shouting before he could utter a word. "My husband is very sick. He can't breathe. Can't you see that? I'm taking him to the hospital!" Her Farsi came out as fluently as if she were a native.

The guard, taken aback, took a cursory glance at Paul, who was in obvious distress, and waved them through instantly. Cat stepped on the gas, sped toward the hospital, and made a left onto the entry road. She wheeled through the parking area before leaving the hospital the way she'd come in, another anonymous white Paykan among many.

She made a right turn off Bustan and glanced toward Paul, concerned. "Are you all right?"

He responded with what he hoped was a gesture that indicated *Yes*, but honestly wasn't sure. He was gasping for breath. He'd never tasted anything so hot in his life.

"There it is." The Canadian Embassy was directly ahead, and there were no visible signs of disturbance.

She pulled to the side of the road directly in front of the entrance, then reached over and pushed open the passenger door.

"Hurry!" she whispered, and as he stepped out of the car, added, "Godspeed, Paul."

Paul strode quickly to the gate, where a uniformed member of the Canadian Military Police intercepted him. "We're closed, sir."

"For God's sake, I'm an American." He lifted his sweater slightly to show the black passport tucked into his waistband, and the gate swung open. He was safe. When he turned to wave at Cat, she was gone.

Chapter 27

Monday night
Boston, Massachusetts

The ice in my glass had long since melted, the drink forgotten, as I listened spellbound to the tale. Cat had plied her trade on the stage of international intrigue, and this evening I was the beneficiary of a backstage visit.

Ambassador Marshfield shook his head at the memory and chuckled. "I haven't eaten a hot pepper since. I tell everyone I'm allergic, but the fact of the matter is that they scare me to death—I never imagined anything could be so hot."

"So what happened? Obviously you got out."

"Oh, yes. Cat, Tom, and Arnie flew out without any trouble, but had to leave everything they owned behind. One suitcase was all they were allowed to take. Not that they were unique; it happened to everybody. I'm sure that someone over there enjoyed the plunder. Arnie told me later that he'd poured a bag of sugar in his car's gas tank before he left. Retribution, I suppose. I would have loved to have been a fly on the wall when the engine seized up on whoever took it.

"I, on the other hand," he continued, "spent one night with the Canadians. It turned out that they already had a full house of six other US staffers who had slipped out when the embassy was taken. They gave me the original passport of a guy who'd reported his stolen the previous week. He'd left it at a hotel restaurant, and someone found it and sent it over to the embassy—a stroke of fortune that it hadn't yet been destroyed. We had dinner together, they dyed my hair and took a photo, and I was on a flight to Istanbul the following day."

"What happened to the other people?"

"They eventually left on a SwissAir flight, posing as a Canadian film crew. It was quite the caper at the time, headlines in the newspapers, that sort of thing. Of course, the Iranians weren't pleased. All these years later, it's an interesting and somewhat amusing historical footnote, but at the time the situation was quite tense. There was no guarantee that any one of us would be successful in exiting the country. If it hadn't been for the Canadians—and Cat—it could have turned out quite differently."

He grew more somber, his eyes distant. "You know, the Foreign Service is like an extended family ... some of the people you like, some you don't. The experiences that you share help forge the relationships. But only a few become really close friends, and Cat was one of my closest, even though we worked for different agencies. Did you know that we got married a week apart and spent our honeymoons together? Cat was Maggie's maid of honor, Maggie was Cat's. Same thing with Tom and me. We actually considered having a double ceremony. I miss her."

Maggie Marshfield had been killed in a horrific car accident just outside of Istanbul four years ago. "I was so sorry to hear about your wife. She was wonderful."

The pain was etched on his face. "Yes, she was."

I picked at the torn threads of my dress, uncomfortable in the sadness permeating the room, unsure what to say next, yet wanting to know more. Changing the subject, I probed further. "I'm sure you were both glad to be out of Iran."

Immersed in memories of sweeter times, Paul seemed startled by the words, as if he'd been unaware that I was still there. He cocked his head slightly, a deep furrow appearing between his eyebrows. "Were we glad to leave? Given the circumstances, yes, although I think we both had our share of regrets about Tehran. Right up until the end, until just before the embassy was seized, people were begging us for help. They were desperate, offering unfathomable sums of money for a passport. Cat, particularly, was besieged by friends and acquaintances who believed she had connections. One young woman, who had been in New Jersey on a student visa, was worried about her family and had come back to Tehran for a short visit. Instead, the revolutionaries confiscated her passport. It would have been just another hard-luck story, but the girl was pregnant. Unmarried, pregnant, Iranian, the father a fellow student back in the America ... no good was going to come out of that situation. But by that time our options were nonexistent; there was nothing we could do."

"What happened to her?"

"She was hanged."

I gasped. "What?"

"It was a lawless time, and the little control that did exist was religious fanaticism. The girl's death haunted Cat for a very long time."

I couldn't imagine the guilt she must have carried. She had assisted with safe passage for a nuclear physicist and his family, but couldn't do the same for a vulnerable college girl.

"So Dr. Badakhshanian—the family you helped—that was Jalil's father? Jalil was the little boy?"

"Yes, that was Jalil."

"I don't understand what happened to him. Good family, educated, and after all they went through, how did Jalil end up on the other side? I would have thought they would all be vehemently opposed to the extremist movement."

He raised his eyebrows slightly. "Appearances can be deceiving."

He was right, of course. Who knew what twisted ideology had led Jalil in that direction? I dismissed any further thoughts of Jalil as being irrelevant to the discussion. The goal was to learn all I could about my sister.

"Cat was in Saudi Arabia for a while, wasn't she?" I had vague recollections of chitchat about deserts and stifling heat, and oddly enough, fog at night. "Was she doing the same thing?"

"I assume so. Tom and Cat were there for about three years, as I recall. After the Tehran catastrophe, I spent a few months in DC, probably so the powers that be could make sure I was ready to go back into the field. I was one of the lucky ones; my experience was a cakewalk compared to the hostages.

I took a posting in Bahrain shortly thereafter. It's right next door to Saudi, but considerably less restrictive. We'd have several visits from Cat in quick succession, then wouldn't see her for months. Saudi was almost exclusively a male domain, but as Tom's wife, she was granted a resident's visa. I'm not sure how she managed the work, being female, but apparently she was effective—became quite the Arabist, actually. Spoke the language like a native, and with her coloring, well… I heard through the grapevine that she'd developed quite a reputation in certain circles. But I never knew the exact nature of her activities. Don't ask, don't tell."

"So then she went to Boston?"

"Well, eventually. There were other postings, but she returned to Boston after her 'skiing accident' in Switzerland." He wiggled four fingers in a double-quote gesture around the phrase.

"What do you mean? You don't think it was an accident?"

"Oh, she had an accident of some sort. But Cat didn't ski, at least that's what she told me when we first met."

I sat back and blinked in disbelief. The story I'd always heard was that she'd had a collision on the slopes, and that the injury to her leg forced her to give up the sport.

"I visited her in the hospital, you know," he continued. "Tom called and told me she was in the hospital at Landstuhl. I was getting ready to fly back to the States for vacation, so I stopped over in Germany on the way. Just the fact that she was there made me a bit suspicious. It's not the kind of place where one's ordinarily transferred for treatment of a skiing injury."

I'd heard Landstuhl mentioned on the news—as the place

where American war casualties receive urgent medical and psychiatric care.

"Maybe that was just the best place," I suggested.

He gave me the type of look a parent uses when dealing with recalcitrant children. "Hardly. I think she'd been shot, although she never admitted it to me."

This revelation really shouldn't have come as a shock, given what I now knew of her history, but I was flabbergasted. How had she managed to deceive me for so long? I was beginning to wonder if I knew her at all.

I struggled to regain my voice. "Where?"

He knew I wasn't asking about the location of the wound. "Best guess? Afghanistan. The Soviets had invaded the country; we were backing the mujahedin rebels. But that's based on a number of assumptions, and I could be wrong."

Jesus. I thought about the news clips I'd seen over the past few years—the inhospitable terrain, poverty, and its ranking as the world's leading exporter of opium. Visualizing her lurking around Tehran in a chador was difficult enough. To imagine the urbane Catherine Powell as a spy in Afghanistan was next to impossible.

"But how did she end up in Boston? Isn't the CIA confined to activities outside the United States?" I was recalling our excursion to Roxbury. *What was that about?*

"That question, Lindsey, points to the heart of our rather complex intelligence network, the ambiguity of the parameters under which they operate, and their obsessive focus on secrecy. They are instruments of the president, regardless of what their official role might be. Even then, I suspect that there have probably been more than a few operations of which even our chief executive was unaware. With lives at stake, and knowing that even well-vetted agents can be compromised, one can appreciate the need for tightly held information. The CIA is widely known, so it's often under the microscope, and that can be terribly inconvenient. Suffice it to say that there are other agencies operating so far under the radar that very few know of their existence. So while one might plausibly assume a person to be in the CIA's employ, it might not be the case at all."

I felt my eyes grow wide. "Are you saying she worked for one of those other agencies?"

He gave a slight shrug. "I'm merely making an observation." But his eyes held mine, and I knew.

He wasn't finished. "One of the problems with all this secrecy is that it can have unintended consequences, such as one agency unwittingly investigating people who are actually working covertly for another."

I sat still as a stone as I absorbed the import of his last statement. If I was reading him correctly, it was possible that the feds had inadvertently tumbled into Cat while she was engaged in something else.

"If you're saying what I think you're saying, why wouldn't someone have called off the FBI after the explosion? Why are they still involved?"

"Think about it, Lindsey. I don't know what she was working on, but they might have been afraid that if they disengaged the FBI, it could jeopardize the mission. Maybe they needed her to look guilty."

"So, what do we do?"

He stood and walked over to the window, deep in thought, rocking back and forth on his heels, thinking it through. "I'm not sure how much I can help you."

He turned to face me, his eyes grave. "It would be wise for you to stay out of it, you know. I'm not quite sure how to say this without sounding condescending, but you're way out of your league."

My throat went dry. If he was trying to scare me, he was definitely succeeding. To say I was out of my league was probably the understatement of the century. Revolutions, spies, electronic listening devices, muggings on trains ... I had no experience in dealing with the inherently dangerous shadow world to which Cat had bound herself. Maybe he was right. Maybe I should just walk away. Yet I could not escape the feeling that somehow I had a role to play, that Cat needed me.

I swallowed hard, trying to ignore the growing knot in my stomach. I attempted to answer with some conviction, but my voice trembled. "I don't think I can. Not yet, anyhow. There's something—I don't know, this little voice in my head—that's telling me she needs my help. I just don't know how or why."

He remained by the window, one hand on his hip and the other cradling his chin, as he contemplated my response. "The only other thing that I can tell you is that I last saw her about a month ago, when I was in Washington for a conference. She flew down, and we had dinner together. She seemed distracted, almost agitated, and that was very unlike her. When I asked what was going on, she expressed some concern that there might be someone who, to use her words, 'had his own agenda.' We were interrupted by a couple of senators and their wives, who ended up joining us, so she dropped the conversation. I assumed she was talking about someone she was working with, but she never mentioned it again. I don't know if it's relevant to what's happened."

If he didn't have any idea whether Cat's words were relevant, then I certainly didn't.

"I don't know what to do." The words emerged as a whine. I was stressed, scared, and beginning to ache all over from the beating I'd taken on the train. *Out of my league? Absolutely.*

"Well, from what you've told me, there seem to be two particular points of interest. The first, obviously, is the file you found; second is the connection to Jones and Smith. But don't get your hopes up. People in Cat's line of work are like ghosts. You'll only find them if they want you to."

He called the concierge desk to summon the driver, then picked up my coat and held it as I struggled to lift my painfully wrenched arm into the sleeve. When Michelle knocked, he escorted me to the door and gave me a brief hug, then took me firmly by the shoulders and handed me a card with a handwritten phone number. "Be very careful, and call if you need anything. I'll see you tomorrow."

Chapter 28

Tuesday
Gloucester, Massachusetts

T he morning's weather matched my mood: utterly foul. I sat in the back of the limousine with my aunt and uncle, staring numbly at the sleet spitting against the window as we rolled toward Gloucester, Michelle shadowing us in the Mercedes some fifty feet behind.

The limo was a hastily arranged substitute for the transportation offered by the funeral home. I'd been introduced to its driver, Arnold, last night after leaving the Westin. I had no idea of his background, but Arnold and Michelle were tasked with deterring any further encounters with purse snatchers or other assaults to my body.

I'd tried to camouflage the damage to my face with a slab of makeup, but nothing in my cabinet was meant to disguise the scratches and the sinister purple bruise that had developed on my cheek. My knees and shoulder were throbbing painfully, and even if the face had been perfect, the resulting limp would have given me away. It didn't help that my aunt and uncle had stayed awake until two, awaiting my return.

They'd peppered me with questions all morning. I'd brushed it off by telling them that I'd gone in to Boston to see Cat's lawyer, that there'd been a problem on the train, and that the emergency stop had sent me sprawling to the floor. It wasn't exactly a lie, but fell short of the full story. They'd finally given up, and were now sullenly silent, hurt, and confused by my abruptness. I'd ask forgiveness later. If they knew what really happened, they'd never leave me alone.

The Grimes & Babcock Funeral Home was an elongated two-story white clapboard affair, with a covered porch running its length. Set back from the road and unobtrusively nestled under the old-growth oaks dotting the property, it could have passed for the stately home of a local merchant. The only indications of its present function were an understated sign at the entrance to the circular drive and the nose of a hearse peeking discreetly from the back corner of the building. I wondered if the upstairs rooms had been conscripted as offices or if people actually lived there. *How do you take your coffee? Cream, sugar, embalming fluid?* Creepy.

Mr. Grimes was a short, portly man in his late fifties with an unctuous smile who, apart from murmuring his condolences, seemed to be more concerned with ensuring that our obscure little group didn't crash the well-attended gathering taking place down the hall.

"Samuel Hooker," he whispered reverently, inclining his head in the direction of the crowd.

Like I care. Masking my irritation, I arranged my expression to show that I was suitably impressed. *Just wait until the Ambassador shows up, you little snit.*

We'd arrived before nine, allowing two hours to finalize any unresolved issues associated with the service. Mr. Slime, as I dubbed the funeral director, ushered us into an office. When he tried to close the door, I was surprised to see Arnold step into view and hold up a hand. Mr. Slime frowned slightly before turning away, submitting to an open door. He returned to his desk and presented a sheath of documents for signature, to verify that the contracted services had been performed. He ran through the list perfunctorily, then sat back and steepled his fingers.

"We've left the coffin unsealed for the moment, as I believe that there was an item Mrs. Powell wished to accompany her on her final journey."

One of the stipulations in Cat's will was that I purchase a dozen French crullers from the Dunkin' Donuts and put them in her casket. Per her wishes, I had directed the limo to stop at the same place where Cat and I had gone so many years before. I felt a little foolish as I showed Mr. Slime the pink and white box. Mr. Hooker was probably being buried with his Rolls-Royce.

I forced a smile, inwardly wanting to stuff one of the pastries up his nose. "Memories," I said.

He held his hand out for the box. "I understand completely. We'll take good care of it."

I withdrew the box from his reach. "Actually, I believe that the instructions indicate that I am to put this into the coffin personally." My aunt gasped, and I felt my uncle's eyes boring into me.

Mr. Slime's eyes grew large. "Uh, although many of our bereaved do send mementos with the deceased, uh, under the circumstances it may not be, uh, comfortable for the family to do so personally."

I could certainly understand why few family members would want to view the remains of a loved one who could only be identified through dental records—I wasn't looking forward to the experience either—but this was what Cat had wanted, and I thought I knew why.

I looked at him coolly. "Nevertheless, it's my intent to follow her wishes."

At least the man had the good grace not to argue, and escorted me toward the rear of the building. Arnold positioned himself at my side. For a big guy, Arnold's movements were fluid and stealthy; I hadn't heard him come up beside me; I just found him there.

I desperately needed a few minutes of privacy, and found the pretense as we passed the ladies' room. I mumbled an excuse and hastily secluded myself in a stall. Lifting my blouse, I removed the plastic storage bag that I'd stuffed into my bra that morning—the flash drive inside had been burning a hole in my chest since we left the house—and slipped it beneath the paper in the bottom of the doughnut box.

I couldn't think of any logical reason why Cat would want me to put a box of doughnuts in her casket. Nostalgia was one thing, but our whale-watching trip was merely a blip in the landscape of our history together. There were countless other mementos from our time together that would have been more appropriate. The sheer idiocy of cremating a box of doughnuts had forced me to consider other, more meaningful intentions. Weighing a host of assumptions—all of which could be completely ill-founded—and including the fact that this had all been crafted a month ago, I could come up with only one explanation. My mission was to deliver Cat's files to her coffin.

I followed Mr. Slime down the hall, breathing deeply and making a supreme effort to appear calm. In fact, my palms were sweating, and my legs were unsteady. The thought of viewing a badly burned body had my insides churning.

The room was chilly and devoid of dead people, save the two pine coffins near the back exit, and a chemical odor lingered in the air. One of the coffins was open, awaiting the delivery of my gift. I willed myself to put one foot in front of the other, and was relieved to see that a sheet of muslin-like material was draped over the body. I gently laid the doughnut box in an indentation that might have been the crook of an arm, pushing down slightly to secure its position. I nearly jumped out of my skin at the resulting crunch and stumbled backward into the arms of Mr. Slime. The bile rose in my throat. I whirled, careened into Arnold, ran for the bathroom, and promptly gave up what little was in my stomach.

With a breath strip dissolving on my now-rancid tongue, I wobbled to the front porch and the reward of a cleansing brace of cold air. I found a perch on one of the benches, squeezing my eyes shut as I struggled to regain control. If I hadn't been sick, if I hadn't gone to the porch, if I hadn't selected that bench, if I hadn't opened my eyes at exactly the right moment, I would never have seen the van. Less than a hundred feet away, it rumbled down the street beside the funeral home, with a very large black man at the wheel, and in the passenger seat, a woman shrouded in a black scarf and dark sunglasses. Cat?

I bolted upright and ran for the steps as the van turned the corner. In that same instant, several people appeared out of nowhere and sprinted after the van. I heard a screech of tires and had just reached the bottom step when someone grabbed my elbow and jerked me backward. A uniformed officer pointed sternly at the door and insisted that I go back inside. Despite my protests, he didn't budge. I reluctantly obeyed.

Chapter 29

The service was sparsely attended. There were three of us representing the family of Catherine and Thomas Powell, and fewer than a dozen others who saw fit to honor their memory. A few of Tom and Cat's friends had come to offer condolences, as had Evelyn Wainwright, Jason, and Gabe. I thought it interesting that my office manager, Annita, was not present. While the weather and her pregnancy did provide a convenient excuse, friendship should have seen her husband, Jerome, attending in her stead. Our tight little group didn't feel quite so chummy anymore; I doubted I would ever forgive the slight. It certainly didn't bode well for the future of our business together.

In the normal course of events, the family would be seated while the mourners filed in, with social niceties reserved for afterward. In our case, there were so few in attendance that the protocol was abandoned before it could be implemented. In hushed tones, we gratefully welcomed those who had come.

Gabe touched my arm and nodded in the direction of the

door, where I spotted Paul Marshfield speaking with a cluster of people he seemed to know. I turned in his direction and was intercepted by a short, balding man wearing a priest's collar. He extended his hand in greeting and introduced himself as Claudio Poratti.

"I've known Catherine for many years and admired her greatly. I know her penchant for avoiding religion and am here only as a friend. I just wanted you to know what a special person she was."

I smiled graciously—while attempting to hide my amazement that one of Cat's friends was a Catholic priest—and thanked him for his kind words. We chatted briefly, and I inquired how he knew my sister. He clasped my hand. "It's a rather long story. Perhaps we'll have the opportunity to talk about it one day; I'd like for you to know of her courage." Immediately curious, I wanted to hear more, right now, and made a futile effort to engage him in further discussion. "We'll talk at another time," he assured me, and took a seat.

Mr. Slime had become considerably more attentive with the arrival of Paul Marshfield, the stature of our tiny gathering now competing on an equal scale with that of the late Mr. Hooker. A young woman I didn't recognize entered the room shortly after the ambassador, her spiky blonde-streaked hair and bare midriff attracting a number of curious looks. When I approached, certain she'd been misdirected, she introduced herself as Rhonda Miller and offered her condolences. I was about to inquire into her relationship to Cat or Tom when a large black man, accompanied by a woman who vaguely resembled Cat, appeared in the doorway. Losing all interest in

Rhonda, I started toward them just as Agent Santori stepped into view. I felt a stab of annoyance at the intrusion and, casting him a withering look, haughtily turned my back.

The funeral director orchestrated the memorial. Cat's words had been explicit: "No clergy." There was little point in having a minister recite meaningless platitudes about the lives and virtues of two people he'd never met. Instead, Cat had directed that whoever wished to say a few words should be allowed to do so. Paul Marshfield stepped forward, delivering a short and eloquent eulogy, and even managing a tear or two. *And the Oscar goes to,* I thought. Evelyn praised Cat and Tom's dedication to human rights and philanthropic commitment. A few shifted in their seats, uncomfortably reminded of the media accusations regarding some of those charitable causes. Even Jason managed a few carefully chosen words on their behalf.

I twisted to see if any other brave soul cared to speak, just in time to see the spike-haired woman slip out the door. She was immediately trailed by a man in his late fifties. I hadn't seen the man enter the room, but I knew him instantly. The strawberry-blond hair had yielded to stark white and his waistline had thickened with age, but he was the same person who'd thrilled me so long ago with stories of humpback whales.

It struck me as odd that Mr. Smith was leaving without speaking to me at all. My puzzled expression triggered an immediate reaction, as Adrian Santori skewered his head in the direction of the door and bounded after the mysterious Mr. Smith. I stood abruptly, startling everyone with this departure from established tradition, and attempted to ease past my uncle. He grabbed my arm, pulling me back into my seat, and whispered, "Don't worry. They'll find him."

Quicker than one can say "flash-bang," the place was crawling with law enforcement. To the astonishment of those attending the funeral of the blissfully unaware Mr. Hooker, identification lanyards and officially emblazoned windbreakers appeared in the crowd, as other official-looking personnel blocked the doors and denied egress to everyone trapped inside. I glimpsed a cluster of agents engaged in animated conversation with Mr. Smith. For the next ninety minutes, officials examined caskets and scoured every nook and cranny of the funeral home in an ultimately futile quest for whomever or whatever they were seeking. Those fortunate enough to have documentation at hand were released after careful scrutiny, while others were detained until their identities could be verified.

My uncle explained that while I'd been out the previous evening, a certain Agent Santori of the FBI had stopped by my house for a little chitchat. During the course of the interview, the agent had made it clear that I was not to be told of the visit, seemingly concerned that I might give away the planned presence of law enforcement at the funeral.

I actually found the whole affair to be quite entertaining, considering the circumstances. If nothing else, we'd certainly left an impression on the obsequious Mr. Grimes. I discovered later that even Rhonda Miller was caught in the net. She turned out to be a stringer for a local news service, with no other purpose than to fish for the names of North-Shore elite who were attending Mr. Hooker's final farewell. On a whim, she'd switched funereal allegiances upon seeing the names of the now infamous Tom and Cat Powell. Her firsthand account of the fiasco earned her a byline on the front page of the following day's *Boston Globe*.

What had it all been about? The thought came unexpectedly. I picked at the possibility, wondering when the authorities had actually taken their positions and why they were really there. At least one agent, Adrian Santori, knew that Cat was alive. Was it possible that they thought she would materialize at her own funeral? If so, why? I had no answers. There were too many secrets and too many lies.

The argument with my aunt and uncle started the moment we slid into the limo for the return to Marblehead. They wanted to know what was going on; I refused to confide. They wanted to help; I wouldn't allow it. They wanted to stay for a few days; I told them to go home. They finally lapsed into sullen silence. I felt like a traitor to what was left of my family.

As soon as we arrived at my house, I dropped my coat and stormed into the kitchen. While I had been frolicking around Boston the previous afternoon, Aunt Holly and Uncle Pete had thoughtfully found the market and stocked my refrigerator. Their kindness only served to annoy me further. Without a word, I found a box of frozen lasagna and shoved it in the oven, then attacked the French loaf with the biggest knife I owned. They shredded the salad greens and chopped the onions with equal fury. I flipped on the television to ease the tension.

The raid on the funeral home was the lead story on the local news, and as predicted, Ambassador Marshfield quickly became the focal point of the media's attention. The clip captured him moving through the lobby of the Westin, attempting to avoid and ignore the forest of microphones and shouting voices around him.

"Ambassador! Why were you at Mrs. Powell's funeral?"

"Mr. Marshfield! Why do you think she became a terrorist?"

"Mr. Marshfield! What do you say to reports that the FBI found a cache of military explosives at her house?"

One station's anchor, a well-respected veteran of broadcast journalism, used a more tactful approach, and was rewarded accordingly.

"Mr. Ambassador, Elaine Lieberman. Are you concerned that your association with Mrs. Powell might place your Cabinet nomination in jeopardy?"

He stopped and turned toward the distinctive voice. "Well, Ms. Lieberman, I can't answer that; I serve at the president's pleasure. All I know about the charges are what I've seen in the newspapers, and in this country, we abide by the principle of presumed innocence. Catherine Powell and I were close friends for over thirty-five years, and my primary concern right now is for her family."

Mine, too. I walked back into the kitchen and wrapped my arms around them.

Chapter 30

Aunt Holly and Uncle Pete left the following morning, embracing me tightly before getting into the car. As they pulled away, I locked eyes with my uncle. I knew he was worried about me, and I managed a firm thumbs-up and a determined smile. "I'll be fine," I declared.

I threw on my sweats and went for a run to clear my head, with Michelle tailing me in the car. The streets were a dirty mess of sand and slush, and I focused all my attention on avoiding the icy patches and spray from passing cars as I jogged toward the Neck. I'd gone about a half mile when I heard the steady thump of another jogger behind me—a man, I guessed, judging by the heaviness of his step. His pace was faster than mine, but slowed as he drew nearer. I heard the rev of the big Mercedes engine and, without looking back, shifted farther to the right to let the guy pass.

"You! Get away from the girl!" Michelle's voice boomed.

I froze, completely, totally, froze.

"Jesus! FBI! Put the damn gun away!"

My head jerked toward the voice of Agent Santori, who had jogged up behind me, then to the sight of Michelle, out of the car, forearms propped on the door, aiming the biggest damn gun I'd ever seen.

I fought to recover my senses, tried to breathe, tried to hear my voice over the pounding in my chest. "Well, this is fun. I needed some excitement in my life."

Santori, hands in the air, looked at me imploringly.

I flipped a wave at Michelle. "He's harmless, but maybe you should shoot him anyhow. Call it payment for scaring the hell out of me."

He lowered his arms and stepped toward me. "Lindsey, we need to talk."

Resuming my run, I called over my shoulder, "You talk. I'll listen. Maybe."

He fell in behind me and kept up for the next mile, his breathing becoming increasingly labored. He managed to follow me across the causeway to the Neck before breaking off. "Please stop."

I kept running, Michelle trailing in the car. I circled the Neck, past Castle Rock and the lighthouse and the yacht clubs facing the harbor. When I completed the loop, I found Adrian waiting at the causeway. He was hunched over, arms folded tight against his chest, stomping his feet in an effort to ward off the cold.

"D-d-damn it, L-L-Lindsey. P-P-Please, just st-st-stop." His chattering teeth caused the words to come out in a stutter.

I jogged in place, mute, staring him down.

He blinked first. "Give me a break. What's the problem? I'm freezing my butt off out here, and around you the temperature drops another twenty degrees."

Good. I kept staring.

He threw his arms in the air. "What do you want from me?"

Finally. "The truth," I breathed.

He threw up his arms in a gesture of defeated exasperation. "The truth? I wish it were that simple. I wish I could even figure out what the truth is."

I waited for more.

He stared back. "I need coffee."

I set a slower pace as we jogged back. As I opened my door, Michelle pressed the horn lightly and waved. I felt a pang of guilt at not having suggested that he ride in the car. Seeing his obvious discomfort, I hurriedly found a thick quilt, which he pulled over his head and body in a tight cocoon. I brought coffee, and his fingers brushed lightly against mine when I handed him the mug. They were startlingly cold, but the touch burned like a jolt of electricity. I withdrew my hand, and he grabbed my wrist.

"God, you feel warm." He gathered me into the quilt and held me for a long time, letting the heat from my body ebb into his. I stood still as a statue, an inner conflict raging.

When his shivering subsided, I pulled away and sat down in a chair opposite him, the coffee table between us acting as a deterrent to further physical contact. I was finding it difficult to breathe normally, but curled my legs under me and tried to appear relaxed.

"I'm sorry," he said in a soft voice. "I probably shouldn't have done that. But thank you. I've never been so cold in my life."

His head was bowed, contemplating some unseen object on the floor. I realized that he was actually embarrassed.

"Wimp," I replied gently.

"Sadist," he retorted. And with that, he looked up and smiled. He didn't speak for several minutes, and I waited patiently. He finally leaned forward, forearms resting on his knees and his hands loosely clasped. He took a deep breath before speaking.

"Cat showed up in my office in DC about three weeks ago. Ordinarily someone else would have talked to her, but she insisted on speaking to me. She knew my name."

"Why you?"

"That leads into another story that I can't talk about now. I'll tell you at some point, but this is not the right time."

"Okay." I drew out the "a" slowly. I let the subject pass.

"She looked like a bag lady. She had on a dirty coat, moth-eaten gloves, and her hair was ratty. I actually cringed when she walked in. I considered disinfecting after she left."

I choked in surprise. "Cat?" It was difficult to imagine my sister in such garb.

"I know now that she was in disguise, but I sure didn't know it then. We're supposed to take all of these reports—you never know—so I listened. She fed me some wild-ass story about clandestine assignments, terrorists, money trails, some big plot in the making, and that someone was after her. She was obviously well-educated, articulate, but I really thought she belonged in a psychiatric ward—you know, delusional, paranoid. It didn't help that she wouldn't tell me who she worked for or exactly what this big plot was, and wouldn't produce any identification. But when she told me to call Ambassador Marshfield, I seriously considered requesting a straitjacket."

I resisted the temptation to belittle his judgment; it's easy to be a Monday-morning quarterback. To be fair, I probably would have experienced the same reaction he did. And to his credit, I probably wouldn't have let her in the door in the first place.

"Did you call him?"

"Oh yeah, about three days later. Honestly, I assumed he'd chew me out for bothering him about some crackpot. Instead, he reamed me out for waiting so long to call. Jesus, I felt like an ass."

I laughed out loud, imagining the conversation. "He can be rather intimidating at times."

Adrian's voice rose an octave. "Intimidating? I received a summons from the director not five minutes later. He made me wait for almost half an hour. I thought I was going to lose my job."

"I guess that didn't happen."

"No. I did, however, get a fifteen-minute lecture on national security and interagency cooperation. After he calmed down, he gave me my orders. I'm not sure why he tagged me— I guess because Cat had sought me out personally. At any rate, this thing is so sensitive that he sent me here solo. I can call on resources if I need them, but the only ones who know the true nature of my assignment are the director, the SAIC here in Boston—you remember Mr. Farrell—and Ambassador Marshfield." He shrugged resignedly. "If it all goes to hell, I assume I'll be the scapegoat."

I almost felt sorry for him—almost—but I was also seething. "So why is it now okay to include me in this rarefied little circle? Why didn't you tell me this earlier instead of stringing me along?"

"Honestly?"

I nodded.

"We didn't want to involve you at all. You have no experience. Your face is completely transparent—you'd make a lousy poker player, by the way. You're naive. You live in a cute little house in a cute little town, and you feel safe and secure. You have no idea how dangerous the world can really be. Look at your town newspaper, Lindsey. What's in the police log? Hot news with global repercussions, like, 'A resident of Green Street reported a dead bird in the street.' Come on."

Defensively, I opened my mouth to argue, but he forged ahead. "That's not a criticism! It's the way it should be, and it's our job to protect that way of life and to make sure that your kids and your grandkids and their kids all get to live the same way, happy and free of fear. We had no idea you'd put yourself in the thick of things."

"It's not like I had a choice," I murmured.

"Sure you did. You signed an oath of secrecy. I was there, remember? You were supposed to tell us everything, but you decided that you wanted to play your own game. I'm sorry about what happened to you on the subway, but to some extent you brought it on yourself. And, Lindsey? While that might have scared you, it's hardly a blip when compared to what these people are capable of. Never mind the valuable time you've cost us."

I suddenly felt very small and very guilty. "I'm sorry," I whispered.

He let out a long sigh. "I know you want to help Cat, Lindsey. Believe me, I understand completely—I'd like to help her, too. But could you please just trust me?"

I curled up tighter in the chair and nodded mutely.

"That said," he continued, "I'll give you this—you've shown some chops. That was a neat trick with the doughnut box. You had us going there for a while."

"You knew?"

"Your uncle told me about the doughnut box; he thought it was a rather odd request. I liked him, by the way. He's a pretty astute old buzzard, and he's worried to death about you. I had to swear that I'd look after you personally … made me repeat it twice. He'll have my head on a post if anything happens to you, and I think Ambassador Marshfield would gleefully join him in the task. The Ambassador called me after you left the hotel. I put two and two together. I came up with about three and a half."

"Does my uncle know Cat's alive?"

"Not with any certainty, but like I said, he's pretty observant, and you're not exactly the most accomplished liar I've ever seen. I'm sure he has his suspicions."

"I didn't handle it very well with him. You're right. I'm not very good at this."

"Well, I'd say that was actually a good thing. I wouldn't like you nearly as much." He grinned, then became serious. "So, what was the deal with the doughnuts? I was sure you were going to put the flash drive in there."

My neck stiffened. "But I did. I put the flash drive in the box and left the box in the coffin."

His jaw dropped. "It wasn't in there."

"Well, of course not. I think that was the idea all along. I think Jones took it."

"What?"

He paced the room as I told him about the circumstances of my unplanned visit to the porch, the van that I'd seen, and my initial thoughts about the driver and passenger.

"You mean the big black guy? We stopped the van and questioned him. He knew Cat and was there for the funeral. You saw him inside."

"Yes, but when I saw that van, it was driving in the wrong direction, away from the funeral home. I'll bet that he wasn't even planning to attend the funeral until you guys intercepted him and he had no choice."

"Lindsey, there's no possibility this guy, Jones, took it. We had the place under surveillance before dawn. Nobody came in or out of that room other than the people who were supposed to be there. Jesus. Are you screwing with me?"

"Adrian, I swear to you—I put it in there."

"Okay, okay." He was talking fast now. "And the other guy—the one that spooked you at the end—that was Smith, right?"

"Yes. Older. His hair was different, white. But I believe so."

He ran an agitated hand through his hair. "I've missed something somewhere. Let's start over. Tell me everything that happened from the time you left here."

I ran through it: the limo to Gloucester, the stop at Dunkin' Donuts, my unease with Mr. Grimes, retrieving the flash drive from under my blouse, putting the box in the coffin, getting sick, seeing the van, wondering who Rhonda was, seeing Jones and the woman at the service, and finally seeing Mr. Smith at the end.

"That's all," I said.

"Nothing else?"

I shook my head. "That's it. Honestly."

He sat pensively, kneading his face with his hands, trying to work it out. I had nothing to contribute.

"We went over that place with a fine-tooth comb and found nothing. There were lots of people going into the funeral home, but only five who left before we put up the barricades: the driver from the funeral home, when he went to get you, and four florist vans. The mourners were friends and family, so they knew each other, except for that nosy reporter. The staff has worked there for years. The drivers are contract; yours started a month ago, but we ran a background on him. Regardless, he came back with you, dropped you off, and stuck around for the entire time. There was nothing out of the ordinary."

My eyes widened. "Wait—the guy who drove our limo—he didn't work for the funeral home."

Bug-eyed, Adrian yelled, "What?"

I explained about the protection detail Evelyn had arranged for me. "There's Michelle—you met her; she's the one who almost shot you this morning. The other one is Arnold. He's the one who drove the limo, and"—I swallowed hard—"he was in the room when I put the doughnut box in the coffin. He was there."

Adrian pressed his fists into his temples and squeezed his eyes shut. "A different driver? I can't believe it." He stood up and faced me. He looked shell-shocked.

"So, have I got this right? The limo driver, who's not a limo driver, takes you to the funeral home, sticks with you the entire time, including going into the back room, and then drives you home as pretty as you please? Unbelievable. I can't believe it."

He yanked the cell out of his pocket and thumbed a speed dial. "Angela, it's Adrian. Something stinks in Gloucester, and it's not the fish—it's the limo driver. Or rather the not-so-limo driver. Or both of them. Hell, I don't know." He rattled off the story.

"Find that lawyer, Evelyn Wainwright, right now. I don't care what legal mumbo jumbo she throws at you. I want to know everything about this guy, from what he's done for work to whether he wears boxers or briefs. She's the one who brought him into the middle of this. I want to know why. And put out an APB. It's a million to one that you'll find him, but do it anyhow."

Infuriated, he punched the button to disconnect and flung the phone onto the sofa. "Right under my nose. A limo brought you to Gloucester; a limo took you home. We weren't paying attention to the driver; he made himself part of the normal scenery and played us perfectly." He started pacing back and forth across the room, intense in thought. "But the bigger question is, what's so damn important about that flash drive that anyone would take the risk?"

PART TWO

Cat

February, five months ago
Friday through Tuesday

Chapter 31

Elizabeth McCarthy emerged from the shower, wrapped herself in a towel, and poured a cup of coffee. She moved to the side of the window and watched the street below through the veil of the yellowed lace curtain. The room was small but comfortably furnished, with a tiny kitchenette and a private bath. Even better, the monthly rental fee was half the rate it would be in summer. Gloucester has always been known as a fishing town by trade, but over the last two decades has seen its primary industry steadily diminished by economics and regulations purported to combat overfishing.

Tourism now ranks high on the list of contributors to the town's economic salvation, and visitors arrive in droves when the weather warms. They find the town quaint and historic—a great place to bring the kids and learn about the nation's seafaring past. Whale-watching cruises are a big draw, and the harbor churns with sail- and powerboats of every dimension.

In winter, however, the place turns deadly dull, and only the crews of the largest vessels brave the frigid waters. It is no wonder that those left behind turn to the waterfront pubs for solace.

Elizabeth watched her landlady cross the street and walk toward the small market three blocks away, a ritual the elderly woman seemed to follow daily. The landlady, in her early seventies, was the hardy and weathered widow of one of the men listed on the new bronze tablets fronting the Fisherman's Memorial. Her manner appealed to Elizabeth; she was observant without being nosy, and disinclined to gossip. She was also standoffish to strangers and wary of newcomers. Naturally, she hated tourist season, though she enjoyed the money it brought.

Initially suspicious when Elizabeth had stopped by to inquire about the room-for-let sign on the front door, she'd brightened at the sight of a thousand dollars in cash, and become suspicious again when Elizabeth asked her to tell no one about the rental. Elizabeth had persisted, letting slip a few well-chosen hints about her desperate circumstances and allowing the woman to draw her own conclusions. Upon deducing that Elizabeth was the victim of an abusive husband, the older woman had softened. It was the perfect ruse. The woman volunteered no information, and to those who raised questions about the stranger now living in her home, had responded that Elizabeth was her husband's illegitimate daughter, a product of his many flings down in Florida. The revelation invariably brought a halt to any further prodding. That she was, in effect, sullying the good name of her late husband seemed not to bother her at all. The lie, as she'd told Elizabeth more than once, was probably more truth than fiction.

Elizabeth placed the cup in the sink and returned to the bathroom. She tugged on the custom-made cap, to compress her own hair and prevent the odd strand from inadvertently escaping, before putting on the wig. The cap's textured surface helped ensure that the wig would never slip, but it also made it difficult to position. She then carefully applied the adhesive to the prosthetics and blended her makeup to complete the effect. The silicone nose and ears had been skillfully crafted and were nearly impossible to detect, even at close range. The eyebrows, thicker and more arched than her own, matched the wig perfectly.

She examined her appearance. It had taken days to adjust to the stranger reflected in the mirror. The human-hair wig was dark, almost black, and fell in soft waves to halfway between her chin and shoulder. The hair itself had been treated to dull the sheen slightly, and professionally cut to mimic the touch of a mediocre stylist. The color complemented her olive skin and was dramatically different from her own short, naturally curly brunette.

She perched the eyeglasses on her nose to complete the transformation. The frames were thick and rather masculine, and did nothing to enhance her features. Indeed, that was the idea. The ears, the frames, and the nose all contributed to not only presenting a different person to an observer, but also to defeating facial recognition software.

The various trips that she'd planted around the room told her that no one had ever entered in her absence, but she couldn't afford to overlook the possibility. Thus, she was careful to gather any brunette hairs and wrap them in a paper towel, which she put in her purse along with the adhesive and a backup set of prosthetics. The paper towel would be deposited in a street-side trash can when she was well away from the house.

The gun was another matter entirely. It was winter, fortunately, and bulky clothing facilitated one's ability to hide all manner of weapons. The slim cross-draw holster fit snugly inside the waistband of her jeans and, beneath the heavy knit sweater, did an admirable job of concealing the Walther PPK it carried.

Moving again to the window, she carefully studied the scene outside, looking for anything or anyone out of place. The automobiles were all familiar, and the street flowed with the normal amount of traffic. She put on her coat, and after making one final check in the mirror, left the house.

To her landlady, Elizabeth was a woman of modest income who maintained two jobs, one as a late-night attendant at a gas station in Salem, and the other as a daytime data entry clerk for a firm in Beverly. She left Gloucester late at night and returned late in the afternoon, driving back and forth in an old Ford.

In reality, Elizabeth's late-night activities involved driving from Gloucester to the commuter parking lot in Beverly and catching the 11:20 p.m. train for one hop to Salem. From there, she would walk to the Church Street garage, one of the few places in Salem that permitted overnight parking, and retrieve her regular car. Thus far, the subterfuge had gone well, and leaving the vehicle for the night hadn't been necessary. But

Elizabeth was a planner, and as she knew all too well, the devil was in the details.

Elizabeth left little to chance. Like many women, she carried a hand mirror in her purse. Hers, however, was far from typical. It had a carefully concealed telescoping handle that could be extended to allow an examination of a car's undercarriage. A car in an unsecured location was an invitation for disaster, and she had no intention of allowing herself to become a victim. After inspecting the exterior of the car, she would move some distance away before triggering the remote to open the door. Then she would inspect the car's interior with equal intensity. The task was slow and tedious, but as she well knew, absolutely necessary—she'd witnessed firsthand the damage that could be wrought from a tiny, but well-placed, device. Once satisfied, she would slide into the seat and close the door. Behind the obscurity of the heavily tinted windows, she would remove the disguise and drive home. Following a night's sleep in her own bed and a real day's work, she would reverse the process, returning to Gloucester late in the afternoon and starting the charade all over again.

The scheme was far from foolproof, but it was important to establish a presence elsewhere while at the same time going about her usual life. She'd been unable to detect anyone following her, but then again, anyone tasked to do so would be very proficient indeed. The additional danger lay in the security cameras at the garage, but that couldn't be helped. If they tracked her to Salem, they would eventually find her in Gloucester. She'd assessed the risk as slight, at least until she vanished. The real issue was timing.

Cat Powell had, over the years, used a number of identities in the course of her work. The requisite passports, driver's licenses, business cards, cash in various currencies, and other accoutrements of the trade were stashed in bank vaults, safe houses, and other secure locations around the globe, all of which were known, arranged, paid for, and managed by her employer.

Like any accomplished agent, she had developed a network of contacts—some known to her employer and some not—to whom she could turn when a situation turned dicey. Some of these contacts, when offered significant monetary incentive, would gladly accommodate additional requests. In the interest of self-preservation, Cat had no fewer than six current identities of which her employer was unaware. Her mentor, a veteran of Cold War espionage, had encouraged her to establish these safeguards. After all, one never knew when one might need to disappear.

Chapter 32

C at Powell had been in the spy business for more than thirty-five years and had been in more dangerous situations than she could count, including one particularly nasty incident in Afghanistan that had landed her in the hospital at Landstuhl. She'd taken a round from a Russian AK-47 before Jones had killed the bastard and dragged her to safety.

After years in the field, she had been increasingly called upon to aid in the planning of operations and management of other operatives. She had a gift for anticipating the unexpected and for mentoring those who were newer to fieldwork. Her talents were widely recognized by those in the agency.

Almost a year ago, she had been invited to a very private meeting with the directors of the CIA, FBI, and NSA. After acknowledging that cooperation and sharing of information among agencies had improved in the years since 9-11, they had expressed concern that sensitive information was still closely guarded and compartmentalized. Following a particularly

frustrating meeting at the White House, the three had conceptual-
ized the creation of a hybrid special intelligence unit. Initially
suggested in jest, the idea had taken root and been discussed at
length over the weeks that followed.

They envisioned a unit of carefully selected personnel
from the CIA, FBI, and NSA, with occasional recruiting from
civilian ranks to leverage perspective and diversity of thought.
The unit would function under a mixed mandate involving
both domestic and international operations and would be
granted broad access to information. The concept also proposed a very flat reporting and communication structure, helping to eliminate the type of barriers that plagued its larger
parent organizations. While the unit members would retain
their positions in the agencies they represented, their actual
work would fall under the all-embracing category of "special
project." This would allow them to maintain current relationships and information pipelines without raising undue suspicion about the actual nature of their work.

The reason for the meeting had become clear when they
asked Cat to lead the unit's operations. They sweetened the
deal by revealing that Paul Marshfield had accepted the role of
intelligence liaison for the project, contingent on Cat accepting the job. In any entity of this nature, it was critical to have a
polished senior professional to contribute planning and guidance for the team and to represent the unit's interests politically.
Paul's pedigree was perfect for the slot. She had taken several
days to consider the implications, and ultimately agreed.

In the months since, she and Paul had assembled a small
team from the CIA and NSA and were in the final stages of

reviewing a short list of candidates from the FBI. The unit had been shaping up nicely and had begun to reap promising intelligence.

Though rarely trusting anyone completely, Cat had always viewed the primary danger as originating from the outside. Both the agency and the new unit were, after all, careful about selecting those who were brought into the fold. Admittedly, bad seeds had sprouted. But in Cat's realm, there had been only one dirty agent of whom she was aware, and he'd been unceremoniously dispatched by a car bomb in Lebanon many years ago.

Everything had changed, however, a little over a month ago in a moment that was still imprinted in Cat's memory. It was a fluke really. She'd met with a contact in Cambridge late in the afternoon, before hopping on the subway at Porter Square to meet Tom for dinner in the North End. As the train approached the Harvard Square station, she'd suddenly remembered the invitation to a bridal shower the following evening. She got off the train and walked up the street to the glass-fronted home décor store in search of a gift.

She was on the second floor, standing next to one of the floor-to-ceiling windows, when she spotted Smith crossing the street below and entering a coffee bar just up the way. Her brow furrowed in puzzlement over the chance encounter.

There were currently five agents under her command who were assigned exclusively to work the hallowed halls of Harvard University: an associate professor, an administrative assistant, two posing as students, and one very enterprising computer technician. The two students lived in a small building just around the corner on Hilliard Street that had been purchased, at an astronomical price, for the unit's operations.

The small two-bedroom apartment was on the second floor directly above a local law firm. The apartment functioned as a convenient and unobtrusive place to meet and exchange information, and the common entry it shared with the law office afforded some protection from prying eyes. Cat had been there many times, posing as a mother to one of the students. The young woman was in the final year of a master's program and would graduate this spring, but her "kid brother" would be entering the program in the fall. The carefully orchestrated arrangement allowed the "brother" to become part of the fabric of campus life without arousing any unwanted curiosity.

The idea was to monitor the activities of a number of those who had entered the country on student visas, in hopes of uncovering any ulterior motives for their presence in the United States. The team's initial efforts had proved to be less than fruitful. The subjects generating the most interest were also the most difficult to get to know. Over a period of time, the team had gathered tidbits of information, but nothing substantive, and they had continued to revise their strategies in hopes of gleaning more useful intelligence.

It was the administrative assistant who had first proposed the idea of breaking into personal computers, but it was the computer technician who had perfected the plan. As one of those responsible for maintaining the school's substantial array of servers and computer labs, he had nearly unlimited access to every university-owned computer on campus. Personal computers were another matter, but since nearly every student connected to the university network, why not use it to their advantage? The worm was his brainchild. Once embedded, it mined the target computer and sent the results to a very secure server in the heart of Washington, DC. Access to the server was limited to the worm's creator, Cat, the director, the server's administrator, and later, only a scant handful of other analysts.

One of the most basic rules for uncovering illegal activity is to follow the money. It's always about money—who has it, who wants it, where it came from, and where it went. Anyone who's spent any time at a university knows that students generally don't have a great deal of disposable income. Unless a kid were born with a silver spoon in his mouth, he would have a bank account consistently bordering on overdrawn and would subsist on a steady diet of pizza, beer, and ramen noodles. Students who didn't fit that pattern were subjected to deeper scrutiny. A little over three months ago, the team had struck the mother lode.

Smith, however, wasn't a member of the Harvard team. While it was certainly possible that, like Cat, Smith was on a simple errand, it seemed out of character for him to be spending time in the area of Harvard Square. Her curiosity piqued, she'd slipped downstairs and pretended to browse while she waited for him to exit the coffeehouse. He'd emerged carrying three cups and set off down the street. Maintaining a discreet distance, she had pulled up the collar of her coat and followed him.

When Smith turned the corner at Hilliard Street, Cat's antennae began to bristle. When he entered the squat little building with the stone façade and red shutters, she'd gone into full alert. She ducked into a real estate office that offered an unimpeded view of the building's front door and cornered an agent whose desk fronted the window. After a few questions, the agent eagerly turned to her computer and ran a search for properties that would meet the walk-in client's need. Cat studied the resulting list, and while asking for an endless number of details, maintained her watch on the building across the street.

Thirty minutes later, Cat was completely taken aback when Roger Pulaski, her boss, stepped out of the building. He was followed in short order by Serita, the young woman posing as Cat's "daughter," who was in turn trailed by Smith. Cat intentionally dropped her purse to the floor, spilling the contents in a noisy cascade onto the hardwood floor, and ducked to retrieve them just as the threesome passed by the window.

That Roger was in Boston was a matter of curiosity. That he was with Smith at the apartment, and without her knowledge, was cause for real concern. In the months since the new unit was formed, Cat and Paul Marshfield had assembled the Harvard team, wooed two analysts from the NSA into the fold, and recruited Jones as a player. Jones's knowledge of the day-to-day operations of the Harvard team, however, was limited. It had been generally conceded that while his size and demeanor worked to his advantage in the more seedy corners of Boston, he'd stand out like a sore thumb across the river in Cambridge.

Smith and Roger, while potentially having some peripheral knowledge about the unit's mandate, were not involved at all.

As the person in charge of her agency's New England

operations, Cat was responsible for coordinating the activities of the operatives in the region and disseminating the intelligence they gathered. She was, in effect, the hub of the area network. As the person leading operations for the newly formed unit, she was intimately familiar with its day-to-day activities. But she had been cut out of this meeting and had no idea why or at what level the decision had been made.

Cat mumbled her thanks to the realtor and, after offering a fictitious name and phone number, promised to be back in touch. She scrambled outside in time to watch the agents round the corner a block away, headed in the direction of the subway. After taking a few steps in that direction, she hesitated, unable to decide on the best course of action. She briefly debated shadowing them, but uncertain about which of the three to follow and being on foot, she abandoned the idea completely. After waiting another five minutes, she stepped to the curb and hailed a cab.

By the time she found Tom, she was in a state of barely controlled panic. She slid into the intimate booth at the rear of the restaurant and, ignoring the uncorked bottle of her favorite wine positioned in the center of the table, immediately requested an espresso.

Tom gave her a quizzical look. "No wine?"

"No." She accepted the cup from the waiter and noticed with dismay that her hands were shaking. Tom noticed, too.

"What's wrong, Cat?"

"Not here. I apologize, but would you mind if we skipped dinner?"

Alarm spread over his face. He'd rarely seen Cat so rattled. He signaled for the check and waited for her to finish the espresso, then gently took her elbow and led her out the door. "What happened?"

They walked the streets of the North End as she outlined the event that had transpired. When it involved her work, Cat almost never sought counsel from her husband. This was a rare exception; she needed to hear his analysis. They found a quiet bench in the park across from the Old North Church and sat while Tom contributed his thoughts.

"There might be a perfectly plausible explanation. Perhaps it's a disciplinary matter that Roger preferred to handle himself."

"It's possible, but doubtful. If that were the case, why involve other agents?"

"Point taken. Look, why don't you just call him? You can surely find some excuse. Let it drop that you have dinner reservations. If he tells you he's in town, invite him along. See how it plays out from there."

She chewed her lip and thought about Roger. They had known each other for just over two decades and had a mostly civil, occasionally tempestuous, professional relationship. They had been equals in the Agency until nine years ago, when their boss had retired and Cat was tapped for the position. But after four months of riding a desk and dealing with the daily mountain of bureaucracy, she'd thrown in the towel, and Roger was ultimately given the job. For months afterward, however, she'd sensed his resentment at having been second choice.

Twice-divorced and estranged from his two grown children, he lived and breathed work. He was dedicated and persistent, and the word "fun" was not in the man's vocabulary. While Cat rated Roger as a mediocre agent, his skills as a bureaucrat were incomparable. He was politically astute, knew everyone's personal secrets, and was a master at avoiding fallout from operations gone awry. Roger thrived on power, and the bump up the ladder had been a perfect boost to his career aspirations.

Cat generally regarded Roger's transparent ambition with mild amusement. But he was also known to resent any operation of which he wasn't made immediately aware, and careers had been known to suffer because of it. As a result, he was read into nearly every operation within his purview.

Per the director's instructions, however, Roger hadn't been told about the worm file until a month ago, several months after its release. While Roger was technically Cat's superior in the agency, he held no authority in the new unit. And while he served his country well, in this business trust was like vapor: hard to hold onto.

Cat turned toward Tom and responded agreeably to the suggestion. "It's a thought. If I'm overreacting, there's nothing lost by calling him. If I'm not, maybe I'll learn something." She didn't vocalize her next thought. *As surely as the sun will rise tomorrow, Roger's going to lie.*

Cat dialed the mobile number from memory, one of several that she didn't store in the phone. Roger answered almost instantly.

"Cat! What's up?"

She tried to sound relaxed. "Hi! Just wanted to check and see if you got the report I sent in this morning. There were a couple items of interest, and I didn't have a chance to review them with you."

"I was just going over it. I've been stuck in meetings all day. It's been a bit hectic."

Undoubtedly. "Sounds like you've been as busy as I have. We're still trying to track down the reason for all this chatter we've picked up lately. In fact, I'm just now getting ready to meet Tom for a late dinner. There's a wonderful little restaurant in the North End that he's found."

"I think all the restaurants there are wonderful—you're making me envious. Here I am, stuck in a hotel in New York ordering room service."

Her heart pounded, and she coughed to disguise the catch in her voice. "Sorry to hear that. Would it be better if I gave you a chance to review the material and called you in the morning?"

"That would be best. Let's make it early, say seven?"

"I'll call you then."

"Good. Enjoy your dinner, and give my best to Tom."

She clicked off and looked up at Tom. "He says he's in New York."

Tom emitted a low whistle. "Then I'd say you're right to be worried." He placed a hand gently on Cat's cheek, tilting her face toward his. "Look, I know you keep a lot of secrets, but I can't help if I don't know anything."

She took his hand from her face and held it tightly. "I wish I could tell you more, but I swore an oath. And honestly, I can't find out what I need to know and have to worry about you at the same time."

His jaw tightened, but she knew he wouldn't argue. They'd had too many discussions about the issue.

"All right," he conceded. "I'll drop it for now. But if you've been compromised from the inside, then you might want to consider involving someone from the outside. Just keep that in mind."

Cat had taken Tom's advice. Knowing that Paul Marshfield was in Washington, she'd called and suggested dinner, then took a flight to DC late the following afternoon. Her hopes for a quiet conversation were dashed, however, when a senator and his wife joined them at the table. With a rumored Cabinet position in the works, even Paul wasn't above schmoozing with those who would cast the final vote. She'd caught the last flight back to Boston, returning no wiser than when she'd left.

The next day she pleaded a case of the flu and sent out an e-mail advising that she would be working from home. She spent most of that time examining the data on the server, sensing that the key to the mysterious meeting lay somewhere within its files. There would be a record of her access, of course, but it wasn't unusual for her to browse the content in hopes of learning what the "students" and their associates were planning. More unusual was the amount of time that she devoted to the task that day. She meticulously noted each of the bank accounts that the worm had uncovered and to whom the accounts were assigned. What she discovered made her blood run cold. There were three offshore accounts that had been opened in the name of one of her employer-managed identities, and two in another. Someone, somehow, had set her up.

She was tempted to run. Instead, she spent the next two days scouring the North Shore, seeking a place to hide if it became absolutely necessary. When she spotted the room in Gloucester, with the Grimes-Babcock Funeral Home directly across the street, it sparked an idea, and the plan was born.

Chapter 33

When she wasn't taken into custody on the second day, or the third or fourth, Cat became increasingly convinced that they were waiting for her to make a move. Perhaps they thought she would lead them to the source of the money, and with it, some clue about the reason for the payoff. What they didn't know, however, was that Cat was pursuing exactly the same course. The primary difference between the two investigations was that their sights were focused squarely on her, while she was still trying to determine who, exactly, *they* were.

She toyed with the possibilities, eliminating none. The offshore accounts had obviously been created to cast suspicion on her. Whether they were intended to be discovered now or later was a question to which she had no answer. If someone wanted to discredit her now, it stood to reason that the culprit had inside knowledge about the worm, although it was always possible that someone in the inner circle had inadvertently let slip something about its existence. In addition to the original four, that group had expanded to include her boss, Roger, the Harvard team, a few additional analysts in DC, Jones, and now—by inference—Smith. If the accounts had been set up for discovery later, however, then the field was more wide-open. But there was no question that the person had considerable access to information—only an insider would have known of her other identities.

The other factor that initially puzzled her was that she'd been unable to detect anyone shadowing her. While any person assigned to such a task would be exceptionally adept, Cat could generally spot a tail. She had a distinct advantage in that no one was aware that she'd become more vigilant as a result of having seen the group in Cambridge. The absence of surveillance suggested to her that they were more interested in monitoring her activities on the computer and phone than in following her around the city. They would pay dearly for the lack of foresight.

Trusting no one within her own agency, she had ultimately decided to take Tom's advice seriously and—contrary to all her instincts—contacted the FBI. She'd read hundreds of the Bureau's reports over the years, and more recently she and Paul Marshfield had reviewed the records to assemble a short list of candidates for the new unit. To set the wheels in motion, she needed someone with a reputation for uncompromising integrity and who could be counted on to follow up on what could be perceived—by less-inquiring minds—as the delusional ravings of a lunatic. Adrian Santori fit the bill perfectly.

She had caught an early flight to DC and taken a taxi to Union Station. She'd slipped into one of the restrooms as Cat

Powell and emerged as a bag lady. After shuffling the five blocks to the FBI building, she had insisted on speaking to Agent Santori personally. Unwilling to reveal her true identity or any other details that might compromise her position, she'd laid out the problem. While he had appeared to listen earnestly, she sensed his skepticism and left with little reassurance that he would pursue the matter. Regardless, Cat had gone as far as she was willing to go with the Bureau.

On the flight back to Boston, she leaned back into the seat and evaluated her situation. If they wanted to question her, they would send a select team to her home or office and escort her quietly to Washington for interrogation. If they wanted her out of the way permanently, they'd simply arrange an assassination. That course of action, however, might arouse unwanted suspicion. Another option was to leak a few tantalizing pieces of information, such as Cat's link to a couple of offshore accounts, to an agency such as the DEA or ATF. If the new unit weren't involved, a very public arrest would leave them somewhat hamstrung—unable to acknowledge or question her without jeopardizing the secrecy of their existence. If Cat were calling the shots, she knew exactly what she would do.

At home that evening, she'd taken Tom's hand and led him to the swings in the park across the street. Gently swaying back and forth in the canvas sling, she told him what she'd discovered. She then outlined her strategy. The first step would be to copy some of the files from the DC server. Somewhere in those files there must be information that would hold the key to the entire mystery, and it was crucial to gather the data before someone "sanitized" it. It was equally important to have a backup, and Lindsey's computer business would provide an ideal storage facility. The second order of business was to work out the details for the disappearance of Cat and Tom Powell. When both those tasks were accomplished, she would take the room in Gloucester and establish a second life there.

Tom was aghast. "Cat, are you out of your mind? First of all, involving Lindsey puts her at extreme risk. I think you should leave her out of it completely."

"She's not going to know. I'll tell her that my computer is acting up. I know how she operates; before doing anything, she'll make a backup of my hard drive. The copy will just sit somewhere in their office, no one will be the wiser, and I can retrieve it later if I have to."

"They'll find it, you know."

"Why would they even look? From their standpoint, it would be completely out of character for me to make a copy and store it anywhere other than a bank vault. Don't you see?"

Tom wasn't convinced. "And if they actually kill you ..." He winced at the thought. "I don't know how you can be so damn pragmatic about this." He hesitated, and then continued, "So, if they kill you, then what? Lindsey would be sitting on a time bomb."

She responded lightly, "Well, then, I guess it would be up to you to defuse it, wouldn't it?" Her tone became serious. "If I'm not here, it might be up to you to try to find whoever did this and bring them to justice. I can't bear the thought of everyone thinking I was a traitor."

"Cat, you know I'd never just sit idly by—I'd go to the ends of the earth for you—but honestly, I don't even want to think about that happening. So let's just skip over that, okay? How are you going to accomplish this other scheme of yours?"

"I've thought it through as much as I can. If they arrest me at the office, it's all over. I'll never be able to figure out who's behind this. But if they come to the house, we stand a good chance of getting away."

"And you think that you can just disappear?"

"We are both going to disappear," she corrected. "But you're leaving town. I'm staying nearby."

"Cat, I love you more than I can say, and I know you're good at what you do, but—"

She interrupted before he finished the thought. "Tom, I am more than good at this; it's what I do. It's primarily a matter of planning. I just hope that I have enough time to firm it up before the roof caves in."

Tom stared at his feet. "All right. You've obviously made up your mind, and I know that whatever I say will fall on deaf ears. So, tell me what the plan is."

Cat hesitated. "Well, we're not just going to disappear. We're going to die."

His head jerked up, and he turned to face her, bewildered. "What are you talking about?"

"I made a couple of phone calls from the airport. Tomorrow, we're going to have a few new appliances delivered: a dishwasher, cooktop, refrigerator, and a nice big freezer chest. I won't be home. Have them put the freezer in the garage."

"A freezer?"

"A temporary resting place for our doubles."

His eyes were as big as saucers. "You're going to kill

somebody?"

She laughed. "Of course not. I called an old, shall we say"—she coughed—"friend? He runs an antique shop down in Providence, but has an interesting little business on the side. His prices are exorbitant, but then again, he's very discreet, and his services are rather unique. He supplies bodies."

Tom's mouth was hanging open. "You are kidding, right?"

She looked at him levelly. "No, I'm not kidding. You give him the race, sex, approximate height and weight, and he finds them. Un-autopsied, un-embalmed, and complete with dental records. Delivers them wherever you want."

Tom stood up and ran his fingers through his hair. "This is crazy. You want to put a couple of dead people in a freezer in our house? And you want me to just pretend they're not there?" He shuddered. "The whole idea gives me the willies. How does he find them?"

"The bodies? I've never really wanted to know. If I were to hazard a guess, I'd say that he has an arrangement with a crematory or two. An urn full of ashes is an urn full of ashes. Who would ever know the difference?"

"Jesus, Cat. So we disappear and leave a couple of frozen corpses behind? You care to tell me how we're going to defrost them in time, and how anybody is going to believe they're you and me?"

"Tom, we know how they operate. They will never act without examining the possibilities from every possible angle. They'll look for lies in the truth and truth in the lies, and it will take them days to commit to any direct action. We'll have a window of opportunity—maybe a small one, but something."

Cat's firm belief that she would have some subtle warning of an imminent action against her was based on many years of experience and firsthand knowledge of the general operational mind-set. There was a fine balance between spending enough time to build a solid case and waiting so long that the bad guys' mission was accomplished. But in dealing with one of their own, particularly at her level, they would proceed with utmost care. There were humiliating and career-ending repercussions when the wrong people were accused.

She lowered her eyes and toyed with her watch. This was the difficult part—their home on Harboredge Way had been a labor of love. "We'll position the bodies, and then I'm going to burn the house."

Tom's expression was first stupefied, then angry. "Cat, you've cooked up some schemes in your life, but this one defies reason. Find another way."

"I've looked at this every way from Sunday. It raises the fewest questions and buys more time than any other option. We'll rent a storage unit for the important art and anything else we can't replace. The antiques are tougher, but we could send some out for restoration and appraisal. It's not like anyone will realize things are missing."

Tom threw up his hands. "This is your world and I accepted that when I married you, but it doesn't mean I have to like it. I think this is a terrible idea." He paused and shook his head in resignation. "You knew that would be my reaction, yet you pursued it anyhow. Is there really no other way?"

"Not that I can figure out. I'm sorry, Tom."

He pursed his lips and blew out a long breath. "I am too."

He met her eyes. "It's at times like this that I wish we could lead a normal life like all the other couples in the universe. But you would be bored."

"Understatement. I'd hate it."

Chapter 34

I n the following days, Cat had awakened each morning with conflicting emotions: dread that this might be the day when her world came to an end, and relief that she'd survived another night and had additional time to prepare.

Copying the files from the server was problematic. While she was one of only a dozen people on the planet with sufficient authority to access and read the data on the server, she could do so only from the desktop computer that the agency had issued for her home use. If she were to attempt to enter the system from her personal laptop, it would lock her out and create a record of the denied entry.

To further complicate the issue, her machine was specifically designed to prohibit its user from doing what she was trying to do: produce copies of the material. There was no DVD drive, no USB port, and no *Print Scrn* button for capturing screen content. More than one hapless agent had attempted to install a DVD drive or attach a different keyboard on machines like this, only to discover that the computer's operating system had been modified to prevent the installation of devices other than what was authorized.

She clearly recalled the day when she'd listened as Lindsey discussed computer security with a client. "Where there's a will, there's a way," she'd said. "Can you see the screen?" The client had nodded, unsure where the conversation was headed. "Then so can this," she'd continued. With dramatic flair, Lindsey had pulled a digital camera from her briefcase and snapped a picture of the screen. The client was stunned, but Cat had tucked the revelation away. It had proved to be a very useful tidbit of information—laborious and tedious, but useful. Over the past several days, Cat had systematically captured several thousand images.

She reasoned that if they were monitoring her online activity, it followed that they had probably infected all of her computers with the worm file. Taking no chances, she'd disabled the Internet connection before transferring the images to her personal laptop—into an innocuous folder she'd named "Whale Watch."

The following day, Cat had stopped by Lindsey's office and dropped off the supposedly malfunctioning machine. Admitting that she was less than fastidious about backing up and caring for her machine and expressing distrust of the cloud, she'd asked the technician, Jason, to keep a backup copy of her data as a precautionary measure. When she retrieved the laptop several days later, she'd swapped out the hard drive with a clone she'd made previously, minus the "whale watch" folder, and incinerated the original to eliminate the evidence of her activities.

She'd been less than forthright with Tom about involving Lindsey. She was certain that Lindsey, like Tom, wouldn't sit idly by. Lindsey was smart as a whip—and a control freak to boot—and would demand to know exactly what had happened and how. And if she did not get answers, she would begin to dig, eventually leading her to the backup copy of the hard drive. Contrary to what she'd told Tom, Cat knew that she would never be able to retrieve the data personally, disguised or not. The only reasonable alternative was to have Lindsey deliver it to her.

Cat had subsequently made arrangements with the Grimes & Babcock funeral home and finalized her will. The Dunkin' Donuts box clause in the will was an inspiration born of desperation—she'd simply run out of ideas. It was a tenuous thread at best; she only hoped that Lindsey would grasp it.

Following her bout with "the flu," Cat resumed her normal work routine. If there was any doubt that she'd been ill for a week, her appearance dissuaded the notion. Dark shadows had developed under her eyes, she'd lost weight, and her face held an unhealthy pallor. That the underlying cause was actually a combination of stress and sleepless nights was irrelevant; her obviously deteriorated condition bolstered the lie. When she attacked her work with a renewed vengeance, no one was particularly surprised. She'd been sidelined for days, after all, and there was a mountain of work to be done. In Cat's mind, the fact that she was under suspicion was merely secondary to helping protect her country from those who wished to destroy it.

It was a given that there was something big in the pipeline. The sharp increase in the volume of seemingly banal e-mails and cell phone calls over the last few months had caught everyone's attention. That they'd been unable to ascertain the exact nature of the threat had left her analysts and agents feeling frustrated and ineffectual. Even the worm file had initially yielded little, other than identifying a few suspicious accounts and names that would otherwise have gone unnoticed. It wasn't until an obscure undergrad named Naji sent an e-mail, casually mentioning an upcoming research project, that the worm proved its worth. Naji had stated that he was excited at the prospect of working so closely with one of his esteemed professors and that the project was very well-funded. He had even thoughtfully attached a picture of the Boston skyline so the recipient could fully appreciate the grandeur of the city.

The worm installed in Naji's computer obligingly copied the e-mail and a number of Naji's personal files to the agency's server in DC before returning to its hiding place. The server compared the recipient to its current database and, after flagging the name as suspect, assembled a list of possible IP addresses to which it might be assigned. When Naji reconnected to the Internet later that evening, the worm dutifully connected to the server and received its instructions. Following its programmed routine, it then attempted to connect to each address designated by the server. When it found the computer whose stored e-mail address matched, it replicated itself to the machine.

With the thousands of files being sent, it was simply impossible for the analysts to review all of the information personally. Thus, every five minutes, the server replicated its contents to another server, which in turn analyzed the files it received. The very sophisticated program pegged Naji's e-mail as an item of interest and flagged it for human review. The woman who read the message brought it to Cat's attention, and Cat directed the Harvard team to investigate.

When the administrative assistant and associate professor determined that Naji was a mediocre student at best and could find no documentation linking him to a research project, the team raised a collective eyebrow and set out to learn more about the young man's activities.

When the worm on the e-mail recipient's computer started sending its data, the team redoubled their efforts. Cat began a nightly routine of snapping photos of new data that had come in during the day and transferring the images to a flash drive. She kept the camera and the flash drive in a plastic bag in an airtight plastic container, beneath a dusting of dirt and leaves in a shallow depression of earth beside the back driveway.

Chapter 35

Friday
Boston, Massachusetts

C at never expected that it would take them so long to come after her, although in retrospect she should have anticipated the strategy. In the waiting game, the quarry, sensing no danger, tends to eventually relax and go back to business as usual, inevitably making a mistake. Cat was no exception, although the lapse was more a result of fatigue than any feeling of security.

The Harvard team had called her about nine thirty that morning, requesting an urgent afternoon meeting at the apartment in Harvard Square. If she had been thinking clearly, she would have walked around the block and approached the building from a different direction. Instead, she took her customary route and walked directly in front of the realtor's window before crossing the street to the apartment. Just as Cat was turning the knob to enter the building, the agent had flown out of her office, a sheaf of papers in hand.

"Mrs. Mitchell, Mrs. Mitchell!"

Cat released the doorknob and slowly turned to face the agitated woman trotting across the street toward her.

"Mrs. Mitchell, I've been trying to call you! I must have copied down the wrong number. Anyhow, I think I've found the perfect property for you!"

Cat groaned inwardly and forced a smile. "Oh my! I'm so sorry—I meant to get back with you. We've had a change in plan. I don't think we're going to purchase anything just yet."

The woman wasn't about to let a potential commission just slip away. "Well, we do have a number of other properties that have listed over the past few days. A couple of them are being offered below market value; one in particular is hoping for a quick sale."

It took all of Cat's effort to be polite. "I really am sorry, but we changed our minds."

The woman was clearly disappointed, but handed Cat her business card. "Well, if you change your mind again, please contact me. I'm sure I can find just what you're looking for."

Cat turned back to the door and was startled to see her "daughter," Serita, standing in the doorway. Her deep purple ski jacket was unzipped, as if she'd just rushed outside, and her gaze was firmly fixed on the realtor's retreating back.

"Hi, honey!" Cat greeted the young woman warmly, embracing her in a motherly hug. *Damn. How long had she been standing there?*

"Hi, Mom," she replied, returning the embrace. "What's with the 'Mrs. Mitchell' bit?"

Cat wrapped her arm around Serita's waist and steered her

through the door. The lie came easily. "I was wandering around a few weeks ago, doing some shopping, and started thinking that maybe I should look into some investment property in the area. I noticed that real estate office and just stopped in to get an idea of what was on the market. You know how they are—they'll bug you to death—so I invented a name. It doesn't matter, since it's all out of my price range." It was a bit flimsy; if she had truly been interested in such a transaction, she would have contacted one of several brokers whom she knew personally. But the story should hold water if they decided to check, unless the pushy agent had noted the date of the visit. It was time to redirect the conversation. "So how's school, honey?"

Serita twirled a lock of brunette hair between her fingers, curled her lips upward in a cryptic smile, and arched an eyebrow. "Learning something new every day."

Cat looked at her quizzically and managed to offer a suitably cheery response while she processed the words. She couldn't determine if the remark was intended to broadcast a hidden message, a mundane comment about a class, or a tantalizing hint about some new discovery from the worm's probing. The encounter with the real estate agent had unnerved her, and the warning sirens were shrieking in her brain. She'd made a potentially costly mistake.

She entered the apartment and was surprised to find the remainder of the team already assembled—she was normally the first to arrive. The apartment was inexpensively furnished, as befitted a student's budget, and appropriately untidy. She shook off her coat and draped it over the tiny café-style breakfast table, then poured herself a cup of coffee. She wrapped her hands tightly around the mug as if to warm them and, slowly inhaling the coffee's steamy aroma, stretched out the moment in an effort to regain her calm. They looked at her expectantly, and she forced her feet to move, settling into her customary seat on the well-worn sofa.

She turned toward Serita. "So, what have you found?"

"Several things, actually. All quite disturbing."

Cat's nerves jangled again. The young woman was obviously excited; she couldn't sit still. "And?" she prompted.

"Seems that Naji's research project has a backer."

"The research project that doesn't exist?"

"Right. Not at the university, anyway."

"Explain."

"There's a group, called 'Prayers for Peace,' that forwards its donations to several supposedly humanitarian organizations."

"Such as?"

"Like 'Physicians Without Borders.'"

"Isn't it 'Doctors Without Borders'?"

"That's exactly the point. The names are similar enough that—"

"I get it. It's a scam. Where is it?"

Serita gestured toward the computer technician, Terry, signaling him to field the question. He leaned forward eagerly. "Their website gives an address in Newark, but it's a mail-forwarding operation. The checks actually go to a bank in St. Vincent, in the Grenadines, but—"

Isn't that interesting? That's where one of my supposed

accounts is held. What are the odds? Cat pushed the thought aside. "Let me guess," she interrupted. "Nobody knows the name of the actual signatory on the account, and once the money gets there, it's transferred somewhere else in about a millisecond.

He nodded. "Right, as best as we can tell. I, uh, have a friend in the DEA. There's a lot of crap going on down there—drug smuggling, money laundering, black market weaponry ..."

"So, what's the tie-in to Naji?"

"Well, our little worm has been very busy lately, as you know. That account showed up on one of the files it snagged, and the file came from the computer where Naji sent that original e-mail."

"We still haven't figured out who it is?"

"No, he—or it could be a she, I guess—is exceedingly careful. We've got a bunch of first names and a bunch of e-mail handles, but no last names yet."

"Keep digging. He'll make a mistake ... they always do." *As I well know.* Cat scanned the other faces in the room. "Now, what about this research project?"

Serita opened and closed her right fist rapidly as she spoke. "That's the thing that's making us really jiggy. Our little friend got a check yesterday from the American Education Foundation, made out to him personally—for thirty K."

Cat's head jerked up and she set the mug down hard, sloshing the liquid onto the scarred end table. "Excuse me? Thirty thousand dollars? Are you shitting me?"

"No, ma'am."

She squeezed the bridge of her nose tightly between her thumb and forefinger, trying to make sense of the information. "Do I want to know how you discovered this?"

Serita averted her eyes and glanced at the others in a silent plea for help. The other team members eyed one another, hesitant to respond. The other student, Vijay, took a deep breath and reluctantly made the plunge. "Uh ... we were ... uh ... watching him when he picked up his mail yesterday. When he kissed one of the envelopes, we ... uh ... sorta got curious about what was in it."

Cat stared at him and bit her tongue, waiting for him to finish, already sure what was coming.

"When he left for the library last night, I ... uh ... snuck into his room. I found the check."

The urge to reach out and strangle him was tempered only by her recollection of having taken similarly idiotic actions as an impulsive and naive young agent. The room was profoundly quiet as Cat pondered the best way of handling the situation without decimating the young man's zeal.

When she finally spoke, her voice was steely. "On your own, without my authorization."

She could barely hear his whispered response. "Yes, ma'am."

"You were all involved?" She shifted her eyes to each one in turn, cowing them under the intensity of her glare.

They all nodded reluctantly.

"All right. Let's forget that you've violated every established protocol for this operation. Forget that we'll never be able to present the check as evidence in a court of law. Forget that everything we discover as a result will be tainted as fruit of the poisoned tree. Forget all that. But," she continued, her voice rising, "did it not occur to you that you might have jeopardized the entire operation? That you might have been seen? That Naji might have rigged some trap to let him know if anyone had been in his room? Did you even consider any of those minor, insignificant little details?"

They studied their feet, their hands, the dust bunnies on the floor. No one dared to answer.

She shook her head in resignation. "What's done is done. We'll just have to deal with any repercussions later. With that said, I applaud the initiative. But next time, you might want to discuss it with me first. So, what have you found out about the foundation?"

The professor raised his head. "We obtained a copy of the articles of incorporation this morning; they were filed a little over a month ago. The analysts are looking into the names of the officers, but only one jumps out immediately: Reza Badakhshanian."

Cat heard her own sharp intake of breath as the neurons in her brain fired in shock.

The professor looked at her intently and kept talking. "You know him, right?"

She gave a tentative nod, trying to sort it out. Know him? Hell, yes, I know him. What in God's name is going on?

The computer technician, Terry, looked at her warily. "There's one more thing."

She stared at him. "What?" The question was clipped, sharper than she'd intended.

"The foundation received an electronic deposit three days ago. One hundred thousand dollars. From a bank in St. Vincent."

Cat's hands shook noticeably as she reached for the now-tepid mug of coffee. "Can you trace the originating account?"

"We're still working on that."

Come on, Cat, pull it together. She sat up straighter. "Okay. Let's make sure we've got the dots connected." She paused, then put the pieces in order.

"First, Naji sends the e-mail claiming he's on some well-funded research project, only we can't find the project. It's a bit odd, so we deploy the worm to whoever was on the other end of that e-mail.

"Second, the worm sends files from that unknown target computer, and you find some account numbers in St. Vincent.

"Third, one of those accounts turns out to be Prayers for Peace, and they've got a scam going.

"Fourth, the American Education Foundation gets an infusion of a hundred thousand from a bank in St. Vincent.

"Fifth, one of the principals in the American Education Foundation is Dr. Badakhshanian.

"Sixth, the foundation sends Naji a check for thirty thou. Does that about sum it up?"

There were nods of assent from around the room.

"What happened to the rest of the money?"

Terry leveled his gaze at her. "The other 70K was wired out of the account within seconds and jumped to three other banks before I lost it."

Cat, now fully alert, delivered her words rapid-fire. "It's

not airtight, but it's entirely too coincidental, and I don't believe in coincidences. Ladies and gentlemen, 'jiggy' doesn't even begin to describe how I'm feeling about this. I think we have a real problem. I'm calling DC to pull some additional resources in on this. We need to know everything there is to know about this guy Naji, and we need that information yesterday. Equally important, and perhaps more so, we need to take a very close look at my old friend Dr. Badakhshanian."

Chapter 36

Cat laid out the instructions for the team to keep Naji under constant surveillance, with the proviso that under no circumstance should any of them get close enough to draw attention.

"Stay far enough away that he doesn't see you. If he even turns your way, take off. I don't have to tell you not to do a 180; it's too noticeable. If at all possible, veer off at forty-five degrees. To his left, if you can, since human eyes generally track more to the right. If you lose him, you lose him. Better that he's gone for a few hours than to have him notice you, because we can always try to trace his movements later. If he's up to no good—and the evidence is certainly pointing in that direction—he's going to be more alert. If he suspects anything, and I mean anything, he'll bolt, and then we're really screwed."

Over the years, Cat had acquired a reputation for knowing how to manage people. It was simple, really. Instill confidence, encourage independent thinking, support their decisions, praise publicly, chastise privately, and most important, set an example that they would want to follow. But she was also a realist. In truth, she had little confidence in their ability to manage an unobtrusive twenty-four-hour watch.

No one in the little group was an experienced field operative. Most of their work at Harvard was of the electronic variety, and while they were marvels at intercepting cell phone calls and hacking into computers, at the core they were still young, eager, and naive. With only five people, it was going to be particularly dicey. If she couldn't pull in reinforcements quickly, one of her stars would surely make a costly mistake. There were significant obstacles, however, to finding people with the right qualifications. She studied the youthful faces gathered in the room. Therein lay the quandary. To fit in, the operatives would have to be young. But they would also need to be experts in the art of active surveillance, a craft that few mastered quickly and most took years to learn. To further complicate the issue, the best of them were abroad, where their skills were being tested daily in harrowing places she'd once known well and would now prefer to forget. These young pups had no idea.

Masking her concern, she doled out the assignments. Their excitement was palpable, each of them practically slavering at the opportunity to get in on some "real" action. She could warn them of the pitfalls, of course, but the message would fall on deaf ears. New agents are notoriously arrogant and unmindful of their mortality.

She was reminded of the day she received notification of her first field posting—the ego boost she felt at being rewarded for her hard work in training, the perceived pat on the back for being more skilled than her peers. She'd been cocky as hell until a subject she was tailing had somehow given her the slip and ended up behind her, shoving a Sig Sauer into her ribs. The agent with whom she'd been paired had saved her bacon, and thus it wasn't her blood that had seeped into the hard-packed dirt that night. He'd never reported her failing and had eventually become her mentor. She'd always wondered why he'd covered for her. Was it because he'd thought she had potential, or because he, too, had acted foolishly at the onset of his career? She'd always meant to ask, and now would never know. He'd been ambushed in Iraq in 2003, his tortured and decapitated body found weeks later in a muddy ditch beside some godforsaken road near Tikrit. She pushed the thoughts aside and prayed inwardly that the team could pull it off.

Cat slipped into the tiny bathroom to make the call, felt the resistance as the door seal flexed into position, and wondered briefly how a casual visitor would regard the heavy door. There would be no embarrassing sounds of expelled gas or urine hitting the water in this apartment, the room having been equipped with the latest in soundproofing materials.

She punched in the number on the satellite phone, made the appeal, and—surprisingly—was off in less than thirty seconds. She tucked the phone in her pocket and waited another five minutes before opening the door. Requests like these almost always required at least that much time for the back and forth discussion while you defended your position. On this occasion, however, she simply needed the time to think. Roger had accepted her assessment on its face. This was both a novelty and a dead giveaway that he'd already been informed of the situation.

With sudden clarity, she knew she'd just been tested. What did he think? That she'd gather her hidden millions and skip the country? Or that she'd panic and run to some unknown handler? In the end, it didn't matter. Any course of action she recommended would be suspect. They would assume she was leading them in other directions, would think she had a hidden agenda. Her chest filled with a cold dread. She was now on the outside.

Chapter 37

Pulling the apartment door closed behind her, Cat descended the stairs and strode purposefully down the street, the mask of professionalism firmly stamped on her every gesture. Turning the corner, she slowed her pace, finally giving way to the inner turmoil that had gripped her from the moment that pesky real estate agent had unwittingly given her away.

Her brain was churning with the implications of the encounter, the subsequent revelations from the team, and the abbreviated phone call. Serita now knew that she'd used a false name. The girl was smart as a whip—it would nag at her and eventually she'd pick it apart, would probably mention it to the others. From there, it wasn't a giant leap to assume that it would find its way to the ear of Cat's boss, Roger. In short order the hapless real estate agent would be confronted, and they would discover exactly when Cat had been in that office. Roger would remember her phone call, would clearly recall that he'd told her he was in New York. And then he'd know that she'd stumbled onto his surreptitious visit to Boston, would know that she'd put two and two together. This would surely escalate his timetable.

How much time? Twenty-four hours? Less? Probably. Cat shuddered. There were simply too many unknowns and not enough time to sort it out. She'd made preparations. Now she knew that the plan would be put into play and that the deadline for acting on that plan was imminent. She experienced a moment of self-pity, the reality of the situation setting in and the hurt immeasurable. After all she'd done for her country, that it would come down to this. From this moment, she'd be on her own to try and sort out the connections to the St. Vincent accounts, on her own to determine Dr. Badakhshanian's role, on her own to discover the truth. She tasted the bile in her throat and forced it back. *Stop it. Focus on what has to be done. If you don't trust me, so be it. I don't trust you either. One of you set me up, and for that you will pay dearly. I will find out what's going on, and I will find you, you traitorous pig.*

She turned onto the side street and spied her car in the middle of the block, nestled between the same two cars that had been there when she left. She scanned the surrounding buildings, the cars, the pedestrians, spotted the young couple necking on the stoop of the townhouse in the dead of winter, eyed the old woman with the grocery sack crooked in her left arm, noted the legally parked UPS van. In this part of the city, delivery trucks that stopped in the middle of the street were an accepted inconvenience. Her antennae were bristling now. Either it was the driver's first day on the job, or ...

She left the sidewalk, approaching her car from the driver's side, and glanced at the side mirror of the SUV just behind. She caught a brief glimpse of a spot of purple, a flash of brunette hair. Serita. The girl may have been sharp, but was obviously disinclined to part with her favorite winter jacket. She had the fleeting thought that she should turn around, offer the girl some helpful guidance. *No, they asked for it. Let the games begin.*

She reached in her bag, fished out her wallet, and did precisely what she'd told the team never to do. She turned on her heel and headed back the way she'd come. No one she worked with would ever see it as an evasive move—it was so contrary to everything she preached.

She deliberately fumbled with the wallet, extracting a five dollar bill, and pretended not to notice Serita, now desperately seeking an escape into the nearest storefront. Shoving the money into her coat pocket, she blindly oriented her fingertips on the phone, pressed the key programmed to dial Tom's cell, then touched another key and held it down. After mentally counting off twenty seconds, she disconnected. Tom would hear the single tone and would recognize the signal: *Ready, Set, Run.*

Cat headed straight for the building known as "The Garage," home to myriad shops and eateries, and most importantly, Starbucks. Her penchant for lattes was well-known, and she was betting the farm that her trackers would simply assume that she was seeking caffeine. They would follow her, of course, but with no sense of urgency; the line for coffee was always long. She joined the crowd surging through the doors and pushed into the building.

Pulling the coat off as she wove through the throng gathered in front of the Ben & Jerry's, she swept past the Starbucks and headed for the opposite door. The coat went back on, now reversed from camel color to black, and she twisted her hair up under the black hat she kept in her bag. She pulled out the foldup nylon tote she always carried for shopping, stuffed the purse inside, and pulled out the glasses with the thick black frames. Forty-five seconds later, she was outside again, a different person than the one who had entered the building. The shoes could be a problem, but there was nothing that could be done about it. "Always look at the shoes," her mentor had advised. "You can change many things about your appearance in an instant, but nobody carries an extra pair of shoes." Neither did she.

She estimated that she had about two minutes before they realized she hadn't stopped for coffee, wasn't happily ensconced at a table thumbing through e-mails, wasn't anywhere. They would think she'd head for the subway, where she could blend in with the crowd. They would calculate that she wouldn't go back to the car. They would be wrong.

Three minutes later, she saw the UPS van swerve around a corner, headed toward the Harvard Square T station. She turned the opposite corner. The lovers were gone, as was the woman with the groceries. Seconds later, she slipped her key into the ignition and quickly pulled away from the curb.

Cat had no idea who'd been in the van and, wasn't certain whether or not the others on the street had been parties in the operation. Still, it would be unusual to limit a team to a vehicle. Of one thing she was sure: she'd never seen them before.

That would work to her disadvantage. They would have studied her file, would have expectations about her methodologies and behavior. She allowed herself a slight smile. If they depended on that information, it would be their undoing. She figured the odds were tipped ever so slightly in her favor.

Her mind raced over the possibilities. If they were experienced, they would have attached a tracking device to the car; she certainly would have. She considered the possibility that one of the kids had planted a device on her while she was in the apartment, but deemed it unlikely. It wasn't common knowledge, but she knew that the satellite phone also had a GPS tracking device, one that operated independently of the phone's battery. While its original purpose had probably been cast as a safeguard for agents operating in hostile environments, it was reasonable to assume that it would also be useful for tracking anyone they suspected of having turned to the dark side. She would dump the phone, but later. For now, she needed it.

So, first things first. She felt behind her seat for the small umbrella stowed there. It was rarely used for rain, although it would certainly function in that capacity. This one was a bit out of the ordinary, a gift from a South Korean associate at the conclusion of a successful mission. Who would ever notice that one of the spokes was actually two? With a simple twist, she activated the jamming device embedded in the handle. She navigated three quick turns, twisting through the narrow streets of Cambridge, before entering a quiet side street. Checking her rearview mirror to ensure there was no car behind her, she touched the tiny recessed button under the steering column. She heard the whir and felt the clunk as the Massachusetts license plate disappeared into the recess and the New Hampshire plate slipped into its place.

Her colleagues had frequently razzed her about her attachment to the car, jokingly referring to her as a soccer-mom wannabe. Most of them had encouraged her to check out the vehicles that could be purchased through the company, complete with all the little extras that befitted her status as a superspy. She'd laughed with them, inwardly enjoying a very private joke. They would have been stunned to learn of the secrets her SUV held.

Cat weighed the options before steering north, out of the city, and up I-93 toward New Hampshire. For all appearances, she was just another border-state commuter.

Chapter 38

Cat left the interstate up near Lawrence, taking the smaller roads east, then south, entering the town of Beverly with night setting in.

The choice for a roundabout route was a risky one, allowing them additional time to plan their strategy, position resources in key locations on the roads into town, and establish surveillance on her house if they hadn't already done so. While she treasured Marblehead's quaint little homes and spirit of community, they had been minor considerations when she and Tom bought the property on Harboredge. That it was bordered on three sides by water, had meager road access onto the peninsula, and was noted for its nosy neighbors were the factors that had carried the greatest weight in the decision. Thirty-five years of covert operations equated to thirty-five years' worth of paranoia, and she had no intention of making herself an easy target. The flip side of that choice was maddeningly clear: she'd have a devil of a time returning to the house.

She killed the lights as she turned into the small lot off Water Street, found a spot away from the lights, and took several minutes to adjust to the feel of the place. The marina was deserted, with nearly all of the boats in dry dock for the harsh winter and their owners nestled in some warm refuge for the night. Even the seagulls were quiet, the only sounds coming from the buoys and gentle slap of the waves against the docks.

Cat appraised the water with a sailor's eye, noted the overcast skies, calm air, and absence of chop in the water, and grimly thought that at least one thing was actually going in her favor. The stacks of the power plant on the east side of Salem Neck were clearly visible across the water, a mile and a half as the crow flies, closer to four to navigate around the Neck by water. The power plant would be her North Star, the beacon that would guide her to the mouth of Salem Harbor. From there, it was a bit less than a mile across the harbor to Harboredge Way. Five miles. It was a long way in the dead of winter in a small boat.

When she first mentioned the possibility of returning to the house by water, Tom had been vehemently opposed. They'd argued for the better part of an hour, she insisting that they needed a backup plan, he insisting that it was entirely too dangerous. In the end, he reluctantly assented and purchased the eleven-foot Boston Whaler for $6,000 cash, from a local who'd posted a note on the bulletin board at a Beverly market. The owner had been delighted to receive his asking price, but appalled when Tom insisted the boat be removed from its winter cradle and returned to the water. He'd given the guy an extra $3,000 to start it up every day and keep it fueled. There'd been questions, glimmers of suspicion, but in the end, the money won out. If the boat was ever needed, the guy would know. Even if he couldn't actually connect the dots, people in the Boston area had been very squiggly since the bombing at the marathon; they were suspicious of everything. Ultimately, it wouldn't matter. By the time he reported it and someone listened to the story, it would be too late.

Cat killed the interior lights, walked around to the trunk, and pulled the foul-weather gear out of the spare-tire compartment. She pushed the backseats down, climbed back in through the passenger door, and laid out flat and struggled into the thermals, then the overalls. It took ten minutes of wriggling in the confined space to don all the gear, fumbling in the dark with the assorted fasteners and hoping she got it right, dreading the result if she didn't. Cold, water, and the human body were a bad mix.

The Whaler was tied fast to the cleats on the dock, the ropes stiff and unyielding. She pulled off the gloves to work the lines, her hands numb by the time she pushed off and put the gloves back on. She slipped the oars into the locks and stroked for about a hundred yards before trying the motor, felt a burst of panic when it didn't start, and exhaled a long sigh of relief when it finally caught. She thought, *God, it's cold.* Then, *Five miles, oh God, help me.*

Chapter 39

As the boat hummed across the water, Cat considered the action she was taking. If Tom and Cat were to simply disappear, it would fan the investigatory flames and severely hamper Cat's ability to discover and pursue the traitor. Her plan required actual bodies. However, while freezing preserves the body and allows it to be stored for a long period of time without bacteria growth, it also meant that even a cursory glance at the faces would promptly reject the Cat and Tom identities. Cat had no illusions that the subterfuge would hold up to prolonged or intensive scrutiny; there were simply too many uncontrollable factors and too many modern tests that could be performed. No, all she hoped was to delay the result by staging as many obstacles as possible.

A body subjected to freezing becomes a very large block of ice. Even if the corpse were warmed sufficiently to prevent handlers from recognizing its prior frozen-solid state, any competent medical examiner would discover ice crystals in the tissues faster than Cat could say "freezer burn." Bribery was out of the question, not because the local coroners were above the occasional monetary supplement, but because the high-profile autopsy would be well-attended by others in the law enforcement and medical community. Having been exposed to all manner of death, someone would surely notice and bring the issue into question.

The solution, of course, would be to thaw the bodies. However, anyone who's pulled a twenty-pound turkey from the freezer on Thanksgiving morning can testify that thawing is far from instantaneous. Given that the male corpse was two hundred pounds and that decay and its putrid odor would quickly become a problem, thawing at room temperature wasn't an option. Added to the challenge was that water represents about 60 percent of the weight of the human body. As water freezes, it expands and destroys cellular structure, another oddity that would be immediately recognized and questioned by the pathologist.

There is a reason why fire is a favored tool of murderers and assassins who want to delay or thwart identity verification or cause of death: it destroys human tissue. Charred human remains necessitate the use of dental records or DNA testing to establish identity. It would, however, be unlikely that a frozen body would melt and burn sufficiently to ensure total tissue destruction.

Since the day when the freezer's contents were delivered, the rule in force was that unless she and Tom were together, one of them had to be home at all times. One of them had to set the stage when the signal was given. Her earlier call to Tom had been that signal, and he would have immediately dragged the bodies from the freezer and positioned them in the hot tub.

Cat's plan required that the bodies remain frozen until needed, be quickly thawed, and then burn to a crisp. A million things could go wrong.

Chapter 40

As the boat neared the power plant, Cat steered the Whaler east, toward the Marblehead side of the harbor. She could just make out the tiny patches of light along the far shore and aimed for a large dark notch that should be the cemetery located just south of her home. From there, it would be a very short run to the small beach at the foot of Harboredge Way.

Six minutes later, Cat pulled the throttle back and finally cut the motor, letting the boat's momentum propel it toward the shoreline. Retrieving the oars, she guided the boat toward the small beach, a short scrap of coarse sand abutted at both ends by a rocky ledge. The large stone outcropping at the south end provided not only cleats on which to tie the boat, but also a foothold by which she could get onto dry land without wading through the icy water.

With her hands and feet numbed by the cold, she struggled

to stand and loop the ropes over the cleats, stumbling as she climbed up the rock. Once firmly ashore, she headed for the obscurity of the trees. Even in winter, with the branches barren of leaves, the growth was dense enough that one could get through the area without being noticed, particularly at night. In her boating attire, she would have immediately drawn suspicion if she were spotted. She'd studied every streetlight and other obvious lighting and had practiced the route several times to ensure she could get by undetected. Thus, she now knew that, on one street, two neighbors had sophisticated motion detectors on their properties that threw broad beams of light across the pavement. She'd fleetingly wondered if they were up to some illegal mischief.

Within five minutes she'd traversed the line of homes and the thick woods bordering the cemetery. Plucking the cigarette lighter from her pocket, she flicked it twice and was relieved to see the set of headlight beams wink back.

Settling into the passenger seat of Tom's car, she quickly set the heat on full blast and took a moment to relish the car's warmth before turning to the driver.

"Tom's okay?" she whispered.

"Right as rain. Went off without a hitch. He's probably making his way through my liquor cabinet as we speak."

Cat looked at the giant black man and nodded her gratitude. "Thank you."

"Nothing that you wouldn't do for me if the situation were reversed, and you're welcome. Now, not that it hasn't been interesting sitting here wondering what some cop on patrol would think if he found a black man trespassing in a white man's cemetery, but let's get the hell out of here."

A few minutes later, they pulled into the drive next to her house, positioning the car tightly against the covered entryway. The dense shrubbery would make it more difficult for prying eyes to recognize that the person in the heavy winter garb was someone other than Tom. Cat pulled two parcels from the backseat and followed Jones into the house.

Once over the threshold, all verbal communication between them ceased. Cat opened one of the bags and retrieved the MP3 player, flipped the switch, activated the Bluetooth, and glanced at Jones. The voices of Tom and Cat, engaged in a normal just-home conversation, sounded from the speakers.

She heard herself say, "I'm so ready for the hot tub and a glass of wine. Let's try a bottle of that lovely Pinot you bought last week."

And she heard Tom say, "I was in the tub a bit earlier so it should still be warm. Why don't you get it running, and maybe light a fire while I pour."

On cue, she unlocked the French doors to the enclosed privacy deck, lit the kindling under the logs in the fireplace, and watched Jones prepare the wine.

Taking care to leave none of his own fingerprints, Jones wrapped a towel around the neck of the half-full wine bottle and pried out the cork. He plucked the small envelope of ketamine from his pocket and carefully poured the powder into the wine, then rapidly canted the bottle back and forth to dissolve it. He poured a small measure of the Pinot into each glass, swirling the wine to ensure that there would be some of the drug's residue for the investigators to discover. Finally, he positioned the glasses and bottle on the tub's shelf.

Cat plucked a set of wedding rings from her pocket, and as she did every time she stepped into the tub, positioned them on the shelf beside her wineglass. She pulled the clothes from the other bag and dumped them haphazardly on the floor, as if she'd stripped right there before stepping into the tub.

Jones mashed his huge fist into the chest of the male corpse, judging its thaw. He gave a thumbs-up signal, and she nodded. Cat passed him the man's ring, and he slipped it on the corpse's left hand. The drivel of everyday conversation continued to drift from the speakers.

She waved Jones over to the bar and pushed her finger on the corner of one panel to reveal a hollow space. Tucked inside was a brick-sized, orange-yellow block. His eyes grew huge as Cat withdrew the block—which had a consistency similar to clay—and began kneading it with her hands. She rolled the substance into a short rope that she tucked onto the hearth of the fireplace, before plunging a blasting cap squarely in the middle. She glanced at Jones and saw that he was visibly sweating.

Tom's voice rang out from the speaker. "Mozart or Queen tonight?"

"Queen!" she heard herself exclaim.

Moments later, the room was filled with the unmistakable strains of *Bohemian Rhapsody* and Freddie Mercury blasting from the speakers. The loud rock opera would cover any noise Cat and Jones made during the next few minutes.

Working quickly now, Cat retrieved the two gas masks from the supply bag. She and Jones pulled them over their heads, each checking the other for a tight fit. Jones dragged the bodies from the tub and positioned them on the floor, giving the sprawled appearance of two people who had simply collapsed. Cat unscrewed the connection to the propane tank and removed the gasket before threading the two pipes back together.

Signaling Jones, she rotated the knob to start the gas flow. Starting the fire would be the trickiest, and most dangerous, part of the deception. Contrary to what television would have one believe, a propane tank won't arbitrarily explode. The gas inside has to be under more pressure than the tank can withstand. The way to increase the pressure is to heat the gas so it expands, and the best way to do that is to expose the tank itself to fire.

For the ruse to be successful, they needed a big, all-consuming fire that would incinerate the two bodies. There had to be enough gas present to establish a good burn, eventually producing enough heat to blow the propane tank and enough fire to spread to the fuse detonator in the Semtex on the hearth of the fireplace.

It would take a few crucial minutes for the fire to become well-established before any alarms were raised. Cat's few neighbors were tucked into bed. Any watchers would be focused on the front of the house and wouldn't immediately spot a problem. Once the fire was reported, it would take local firefighters a minimum of five minutes to reach the house from the station on Pleasant Street. If all went well, the fire would be well under way and the explosions would occur before the firefighters arrived at the scene. The ensuing uncertainty about other possible explosions would keep the firefighters at bay long enough for the blaze to accomplish its task.

Jones and Cat signaled each other. Cat gathered the bags of equipment and the MP3 player, and sped to the side door. Jones carried a crystal dish with a small votive candle into the adjoining sunroom and waited for the relaxed lull in the taped conversation between Tom and Cat. Placing the dish on a waist-high divider separating the two rooms, he mouthed a silent prayer that the gas hadn't yet permeated the space in which he stood. He struck the match and lit the candle, then bolted for the door. They inched the door open and silently descended into the blackness of the backyard.

Cat stopped briefly at the side of the back driveway, bending down to scoop up the plastic container with the camera and flash drive before scurrying away from the house. Moments later, they glanced back and were gratified to see an orange flare as the gas came into contact with the flame.

They swiftly covered the distance to the cove, and while Cat readied the boat, Jones struggled into foul-weather gear. He made quick work of paddling to the middle of the harbor, where they started the engine just as the sound of the first explosion boomed across the water. They were abeam of the Salem power plant when they heard the first faint wail of a siren, followed by the second explosion and the blaring cacophony of emergency responders.

Chapter 41

C at had often lamented the dearth of security cameras in the metropolitan Boston area, because their value as an investigatory tool was second to none. In a matter of minutes, one could fast-forward to the hours or moments before an incident, the incident itself, and the aftermath. On this night, however, as she lay prone on the SUV's backseat, she was grateful that she and Jones would leave little in the way of visual evidence regarding their whereabouts. Even if the feds managed to find a recording, they would be looking for a lone white woman in an SUV from Massachusetts. This vehicle, with New Hampshire plates and a black man at the wheel, wouldn't warrant a second glance.

As Cat wiggled out of the nautical gear and slipped on the wig and prosthetics, Jones steered the car through the streets of Beverly.

"Seriously, Cat, Semtex? What in the hell were you

thinking?"

"Think of the props, Jones. There's ketamine, so maybe we were drugged; a missing propane gasket, so maybe someone wanted us dead; Semtex, so maybe there was someone from Eastern Europe involved. The explosions happened before anyone responded, and two blasts would cause the firemen to be very cautious and give the fire even more time to burn. And the Semtex was long expired. I wasn't even sure it would detonate. In any event, it doesn't have to make sense; it's all about muddying the waters. If they chase their tails for a few days, the end result is that it buys me time."

Jones pulled to the curb a block from the train station, turned around to face the backseat, and posed the question. "Where is this going?"

She hesitated before answering. "I don't know. Who wants to bring me down, and why? And who knows my other identities? The identity part is a very small circle."

"I'm in that circle."

"I know you are. So, is it you?"

Cat detected a wince, a small glint of hurt in Jones's otherwise stoic expression.

"You know me better than that."

"Yes, I do. We've known each other a long time, and I've trusted you with my life. Nothing's changed. I know it's not you." She silently prayed it was true.

"If you need me, you know how to reach me. There's also a burner phone in the bag if it's urgent. I programmed the number."

Cat laid her hand gently on his. "Thank you. And tell

Tom that I'm okay and that I love him." She opened the door and, transformed into Elizabeth, walked briskly toward the train station. Jones watched her safely start the old Ford and point east toward Gloucester before he turned the SUV south into Boston.

Pulling into the parking lot, Jones parked the SUV and walked over to the car he'd positioned several hours before. Retrieving the earlier parking stub, he placed it in Cat's glove box and locked the doors. Using the new stub, he paid a minimal fee and drove his own car out of the lot.

The SUV would be found several days later, minus the New Hampshire plates and boating gear, in the small private lot in the North End. The parking stub in the glove box would indicate that the car was admitted to the lot at 3:46 p.m., about five hours before Cat, her husband, and their house were incinerated in a fire and subsequent explosion at their home in Marblehead.

Speculation held that, since Cat and her husband had been seen entering the house on Harboredge Way together, they had met for dinner in the North End, a place they were known to frequent. It was widely assumed that after enjoying an intimate meal and drinks at one of the myriad Italian restaurants dotting the community, they had left Cat's car in the lot with the intention to pick it up the following day.

For most who were tasked to scour the North End and pinpoint the couple's whereabouts that night, the lack of evidence was frustrating but not worrisome. However, for a few more well-informed persons who were closely following the investigation, the missing hours were much more than a passing annoyance; they were an anomaly and a gaping hole in the time line. The woman was, after all, a damn spy. What the hell had she been up to? One such suit, surveying the lot where the car had been found, was overheard ranting to the parking attendant, "What is the matter with you people around here? Doesn't anyone in this city use cameras?"

Chapter 42

On the day following the fire, Cat left her apartment in Gloucester and was on the road before the sun peeked over the horizon. The previous day, when the Harvard team revealed that Dr. Reza Badakhshanian's name was associated with the group that had sent the check to Naji, she'd felt as if she'd been sucker punched. Reza was a good and honorable man. If he was involved in any way, she felt sure that he was being coerced. The only way to make that determination was with a face-to-face meeting.

She was certain that the Badakhshanians and their homes, offices, and cars would be under surveillance and that their phones and other electronics would be tapped, so it was imperative to choose a place where they would be least likely to be observed. An encounter at Reza's office on the campus of MIT would be difficult and would require extensive planning. There were too many people and, in that hub of science and technology, far too many cameras. His wife's psychology practice, however, was housed in a small office building on Highway 1A in South Hamilton, just a few miles to the west of Gloucester, and accommodated scheduled appointments on Saturdays.

Cat had been to Simin's office only once, three or four years ago, and could recall little about its layout. What she did remember, however, was that Simin's office was equipped with a private bathroom and had doors opening to the office area for the convenience of staff, and to the hall for the convenience of cleaning crews. Patients were expected to use the building's facilities adjacent to the central stairwell. While the offices might be bugged, it was doubtful that watchers would have seen any need to plant listening devices or cameras in the more-public ladies' restroom.

Cat pulled into an open space on a side street a block from the office, with a good view of the building's main entry. Small, quiet towns like Hamilton, with their neighborly personas and relaxed attitudes, are notoriously lax about security. Aside from the occasional act of vandalism or petty theft, crime is perceived as something that happens elsewhere. Yes, the citizens might lock their doors at night and most offices had alarm systems, but all in all, security was of little concern.

At six forty-five, an early-riser keyed the lock on the front door and entered the building. While Cat couldn't see where the man had gone, she couldn't detect any movement that would indicate the man had touched an alarm panel or re-locked the main door. She pulled a woolen scarf over her head and mouth, walked casually down the street, and yanked the door open.

Inside, she quickly surveyed the first floor. There was a light under the door of suite 107, and she noted the inscription on the door: "Judson Nelson, CPA." *Of course*, she thought. *Tax season.* Accountants started work early and finished late.

She rushed up the stairs and toward the last office on the second floor. While the doors leading from Simin's office area into the bathroom would surely be alarmed, Cat doubted that the hall door would be protected. Pulling the set of picks from her bag, and with a cautious eye down the hall, she had the door open in less than fifteen seconds.

She lifted the ceramic lid from the toilet tank and, using the corkscrew tool on her knife, tore a hole in the flapper. Water rushed from the tank into the toilet bowl, and when the float dropped, the system made a futile effort to refill the tank. With no standing water in the tank and only a stream of water from the refill running into the bowl, flushing wasn't possible. This toilet was out of commission.

She slipped into the public ladies' room and evaluated the four stalls, finally selecting the stall nearest the door. This position would allow her to peek through the gap between the door and its frame and easily see anyone who entered the room. Now it was just a matter of waiting. In the morning, Cat would typically grab a cup of coffee, take a quick look at e-mail, and use the bathroom before getting down to the day's business. Most women she knew followed a similar routine, and she hoped that Simin wasn't an exception.

Shortly after eight, two women, in the midst of a conversation about a leaking toilet, entered the ladies' room. Confirming that Simin was one of the two, Cat watched her enter the third stall, while the other staffer entered the second. *Damn*, Cat thought. Cat had engaged in a bit of wishful thinking, that Simin would be alone. Cat couldn't allow anyone but Simin to see her in this building.

She heard the toilets flush and the doors open, and peered at the two women washing their hands. The second woman was blonde with blue eyes—not a likely candidate for understanding Simin's native language. Cat took a deep breath and started singing a tune in Farsi, interjecting the words, "It's Catherine, and I need to talk with you." She saw Simin's startled expression and continued to sing, repeating the refrain, hoping that Simin would grasp the meaning.

She heard Simin tell the other woman that her stomach was suddenly upset, that she shouldn't have had coffee without something to eat, and that she would be a few more minutes. The blonde didn't appear to register any surprise or undue concern and left the bathroom to return to the office.

The moment the door to the room banged closed, Simin whirled around as Cat opened the stall door. Cat stepped toward Simin, opening her arms to embrace her old friend. Simin's vehement hiss shocked her to the core.

"What are you doing here? Are you insane? Do you think that disguise is going to prevent them from finding you? I hope you rot in hell after what you have done. This is my son, my only son. You have betrayed us, and they will kill him. You are a lying whore, and I hope they chop you into a thousand pieces and feed you to the fish."

Simin raised her hand to strike, and Cat grabbed her, twisting her into an armlock and covering the smaller woman's mouth before she could scream.

Cat whispered forcefully, "Listen to me. I don't know what you think you know, or what you are talking about, but we go back over thirty years, and I would never do anything to harm you or your family."

"You lied to us! Our son is alive!"

Cat was stunned that Simin possessed this knowledge. Fewer than a dozen people in the world knew the truth about Jalil. She recovered quickly and whispered urgently, "Simin, your son joined the clandestine intelligence service of the United States. What in the world did you expect? An open invitation to their secrets? That he would be able to talk openly about his life? Don't be naive. People in this business die, are injured, or disappear, and their families never know how or why. It's ugly and unfair, but necessary. Your son knew and accepted those terms."

"You let us believe he was dead. How could you do that? We were friends. I trusted you."

"I'm not going to apologize for doing what was in the best interests of the country and for taking the steps that were necessary to protect Jalil. It is an unfortunate downside of this business that families and loved ones can't always be told the truth. While I understand your anger, it's not going to help the situation."

Simin spat out her response. "The situation? Is that what you're calling it? Why are you here?"

"Simin, I don't have time for word games or your indignation. Right now, there is something major in the pipeline. I don't know what it is, but it is big. I discovered a money trail that points to Reza and accounts that point to me. I know the accounts aren't mine, and I have a hard time accepting that Reza is participating voluntarily. And if Jalil is somehow involved, that adds another dimension. If we're going to figure this out, you have to talk to me."

Simin opened her mouth to vent more anger, then closed it abruptly. Tears spilled from her eyes as her posture collapsed and she fell against Cat.

Cat embraced her friend, holding her close and stroking her hair to calm her. "Tell me what has happened."

Simin spluttered, "They showed us a video. They are going to kill him."

Cat's brain was racing. "We can't talk here. We don't have enough time. And I'm sure you're being watched, so your office is out of the question." She pursed her lips, her brow furrowed in thought. "Do you know the accountant on the first floor? The sign had the name Nelson on it."

"Jud? Of course. He does our taxes, and we play tennis and socialize occasionally."

"What does your schedule look like today?"

"My first appointment is at nine, and I'm booked solid until three."

Cat looked at her watch: 8:11. "It's tight. Quickly, tell me about the accountant's office. Does he have more than one room? Does he have a receptionist?"

"Two offices and a small waiting area. The second office is more like a storage room, but I remember a small table and chairs in there, too. I don't know if he has a secretary right now. I think he hires a temp during tax season."

"Okay. At eight twenty-five, tell your staff that you have an appointment downstairs and should be back before your nine o'clock. Go to Mr. Nelson's office and walk right in. It doesn't matter what he might be doing—demand his attention. Whisper that you'd like to borrow his other room for a short session. You can tell him you have a client who refuses to be seen in your office." Cat looked pointedly at her friend. "It's even the truth. Can you do it?"

Simin hesitated, then nodded. "Yes."

"There's one more thing. You cannot breathe a word about this—not to anyone, not even Reza. If you are in as much trouble as I suspect, you have no real way of knowing who might be listening or watching, or whom you can really trust. I know it sounds ridiculous for me to say that, and in the same breath, ask you to trust me. I'll say it anyhow. Trust me."

Simin looked deep into Cat's eyes, seeking some reason, some reassurance, for making the commitment. After a long pause, Simin swallowed hard. "I'm not sure I will ever trust you again. But I will talk with you," she murmured.

Chapter 43

C at stepped back into the stall and sagged against the wall, her thoughts turning to the impending encounter with Simin. The woman had mentioned a video, and in the same breath, Jalil. Clearly, she was tortured with worry about the well-being of her son, and Cat felt a stab of sadness in having asked for the woman's trust. The vitriolic attack about Cat being a lying whore wasn't so far off the mark.

Jalil. All of Boston believed that Jalil had been carrying a vial of anthrax spores and had been killed in a shootout with police just outside of Logan airport. The truth was a bit more complicated.

Yes, Jalil had arrived in Boston on a flight from Frankfurt. Yes, Jalil was carrying a vial. Yes, it was anthrax. But no, he wasn't really a terrorist, and no, he hadn't been shot. Smoke and mirrors, secrets and lies, and families betrayed and broken—such was life in the clandestine service of the United States of America. Cat knew all too well that when lives hung in the balance, there was no trust for anyone outside the circle of need-to-know. She had no illusions about whether or not her meeting with Simin would end well; with the genie out of the bottle about Jalil, Cat would say and do whatever was necessary for damage control.

Jalil was, like his father and his father's father, a young man of integrity. He had developed a passion for his adopted country that transcended the ordinary lust for American music, blue jeans, fast cars, and other material goods. Shortly after graduating from Harvard, he had hopped a train to Salem, caught a bus into Marblehead, and was perched on a step at the back door when Tom and Cat came home. "I want to help," he'd said.

There was little point in feigning ignorance. Obviously his parents had let slip that Cat's professional career was something more than what was revealed on the surface. She listened intently as Jalil described his motivation, wanting to serve his adopted country, while at the same time doing whatever he could to educate and enlighten the people in the land of his birth.

After Cat consulted with several of her peers in the intelligence community, they brought Jalil in for a formal interview, rounds of testing, multiple polygraphs, and deep background investigation. While his Iranian origins and fluency in Farsi could be of considerable value, there was always the danger that his professed loyalties and motivations might be something else entirely. His candidacy was reviewed more extensively than most. Six months later, he was in training.

Jalil was initially tasked to London, followed by two years in Germany, to monitor the activities of persons thought to be actively engaged in, or providing support for, anti-Western activities. He gained a reputation for his skills in building relationships, and for identification of several cells and key players in the jihad against the enemies of Islam in the West.

Jalil's parents, Simin and Reza, were told only that he was working for the government. Given their considerable intellect, it was safe to assume that they had reached reasonably accurate assumptions about which sector of the government was paying his salary. But as to the true nature of his work, Cat was sure they'd never been informed. They had likely inferred that he was conducting analysis and providing translations, and would not have suspected that he was headed down the shadowy path of an operative.

While Jalil's postings were in the moderate range on the security risk scale, the classification changed abruptly with the anthrax incident. Some very nasty people had assigned Jalil to commit an act of terrorism. It had been a classic no-win situation. If he performed the act, hundreds or thousands would die. If he refused or otherwise failed to accomplish his mission, they would know he was a fraud. At the end, the world needed to believe that Jalil was dead. From an operations standpoint, the death needed to be revealed in such a way that there could be no doubt as to Jalil's participation in acts against the United States, thus supporting and preserving the truth of every lie Jalil had told to his militant "friends."

His supposed death had also opened up other opportunities that were both important to national security and inherently dangerous. The thought that he'd been compromised sent chills down Cat's spine.

At 8:21 a.m., she pulled the scarf over her face and exited the bathroom. She knew that she must be in position before Simin left her office. After that, the watchers would have eyes on Simin's destination and would take note of anyone else who entered the accountant's office.

She descended the stairs to the first floor and suite 107, and quietly pushed open the outer door. Cat spent a moment studying the suite. The waiting area was tastefully appointed, but lacked warmth or personalization. One of the interior doors was slightly ajar, and there were muffled sounds as papers were moved about. She deduced that the room beyond was Mr. Nelson's primary space. The other door was fully closed. She stepped to a position against the wall and willed herself to be invisible.

Chapter 44

Simin opened the outer door at precisely 8:27 a.m., and after a quick glance in Cat's direction, strode across the reception area. She rapped briskly on the accountant's office door and, without pausing, marched into his office.

Cat held her breath and heard a muted exclamation of surprise, followed by a muffled conversation. Moments later, Simin beckoned from the doorway. Cat hesitated only slightly before joining her friend in the spacious room.

Jud Nelson, a bespectacled, graying, and slightly stooped man, was wearing a somewhat befuddled expression as he stood behind his desk and greeted Cat. "Good morning. Dr. Badakhshanian explained your predicament. Please feel free to use my office. Unfortunately, I do have a rather important audit that I have to finish, so I'll just be over here at my desk."

When Cat's eyes widened, he explained further. "Oh, don't worry. I have these earplugs from when they were doing construction next door. I won't hear a thing."

He waggled the orange plugs at her and exaggerated the

motion of pushing them into his ears. Offering a slight smile and a nod, he sat down and went back to his work.

Cat wasn't sure whether she was shocked or amused at the man's naïveté. Perhaps, she admitted to herself, it was a bit of both. She whispered to Simin, who nodded and locked the door.

They sat across from one another at a small worktable at the back of the office. The situation dictated a challenging juxtaposition of their actual roles, with Simin straining to adopt the interested posture of the therapist, and Cat attempting to assume the part of the troubled patient.

"Tell me exactly what happened," Cat demanded.

"First, you tell me why you lied to me. You tell me why you allowed me to believe that my son was dead—and that he was a traitor to his country."

I am going to hell, Cat thought. She composed her face and pressed her lips into a thin line before responding. The fiction slipped easily from her tongue. "Jalil hooked up with some very nasty people. We don't know exactly when, or why, he began to view the world from their perspective. Jalil was intent on performing an act that would kill hundreds of people. We found out about it and cornered him at Logan. Against all odds, he escaped. We suspect that one of the cops was instrumental in that. You have to understand that we just couldn't let the world think that he was on the loose; there would have been a panic. We've been looking for him ever since. Now, tell me about the video."

Simin stared at her in shock. "I don't believe you."

"I have no reason to lie to you now. You're a psychologist.

You were in Iran during the revolution. You've seen firsthand how seemingly intelligent people can be swayed by demagogues and mob mentality. It's profoundly difficult to stay true to yourself when surrounded by powerful influences. If Jalil is alive, then the wisest and best thing we can do is to attempt to exfiltrate him and get him the help he needs. Now, tell me about the video." She uttered the last sentence with such urgency that Simin's head jerked back as if she'd been slapped.

"Promise me that if you find him, you will not hurt him—that you will bring him back to me alive."

"Simin, I cannot, and will not, promise such a thing. What I can promise is to do everything in my power to protect him." *At least that much is true.*

Without another word, Simin opened her purse and pulled out her phone. After locating the video, she passed the phone and earbud across the table. As she did so, there was a knock on the office door. Alarm instantly spread over Simin's face as she looked to Cat for direction.

Pointing at the accountant, who was blissfully unaware of the noise, Cat whispered, "Get him to answer the door. You go sit in the chair in front of his desk. Take these papers." She thrust a stack of paperwork at Simin and shoved her toward the accountant's desk before crouching behind a stack of file boxes in the corner of the room.

She heard the annoyance in Jud Nelson's voice as he finally opened the door. "What is it?" The question was followed by an indistinct response before Mr. Nelson dismissed the intruder. "My hours are by appointment only. Please call the office phone, and my receptionist will attempt to find a time.

Frankly, at this time of year, there are very few openings available. I can recommend another CPA whose firm is somewhat larger than mine." There was another pause, and the sound of a drawer opening and closing. "Here's a business card. I hope they can assist you."

There was more unintelligible mumbling before the door closed.

"Unbelievable!" he railed before returning to his desk. Oblivious to the tension in the room, he reinserted the earplugs and resumed his work.

Simin's eyes were wide as she gestured to Cat and whispered, "I don't think that was a client, because he didn't have any papers with him. He looked and sounded Hispanic."

DEA, Cat thought. She nodded and directed her attention to Simin's phone. There was an e-mail on the screen, with a link and the ominous text, "Your son is alive, for the moment. Follow our instructions and he will live." She scribbled the web address on a scrap of paper and clicked the link.

A moment later, the video lurched to life. A young man, bound at his arms and legs to a straight-back chair, sat in the center of a drab gray room that appeared to be constructed of cinder block. The room was devoid of any descriptive value that might help define the location, and could have been anywhere. The young man stared at the camera. Cat was expecting the hollow-eyed look that was so often the expression of Westerners kidnapped in Pakistan and Afghanistan, and was shaken by the tight line of his lips and the upward tilt to his chin. Instead of appearing cowed by his captors, he appeared angry and belligerent. A fist shot out from the right side of the field of view, striking his left temple and causing the chair to rock precariously. The subject's eyes appeared to lose focus, and his head lolled to the side.

Cat frowned in puzzlement as the video jumped to a frame showing the subject's erect head. The fire was gone from the young man's now-unfocused eyes, and his demeanor portrayed a conquered man. When he spoke, he had the same disembodied voice that always sent chills down her spine. The cadence and monotone were characteristic of other captives forced to speak on camera after being tortured and threatened with execution. It was a voice of hopeless resignation and acceptance that death was imminent.

"My name is Jalil Badakhshanian. I work for the United States government. I am a spy. I have forsaken my homeland in Iran to serve my American master. My mission was to wipe Islam from the nations of the Middle East, and to replace those in positions of power with men and women who are puppets of the United States."

Cat listened to the entire three minutes of prepared monologue, hoping that there would be an odd turn of phrase that could offer a clue about the subject's location or his captors. The words themselves, while somewhat stilted, indicated that they were written by someone with a good command of the English language. But she could detect no other audible indicators.

She turned off the volume and froze a frame of the video, studying the man's appearance. She then replayed the video from the beginning, concentrating on the man's hands and face, looking for any subtle movements that might communicate a separate message. Again, she found nothing.

Operatives were extensively trained on methods by which they could communicate messages when appearing on camera. In circumstances where the hostile party didn't appear to be sophisticated about clandestine communication, the operative could employ an effective signaling system by blinking his eyes, flaring his nostrils, twitching or pursing the lips, or a combination of these methods. When the hostile parties were more attuned to movements of this nature, operatives could employ other signals, such as where the hair was parted, whether the index finger touched the middle finger, whether the thumb was touching the palm or held perpendicular, whether cheeks were puffed prior to a sentence or not, and whether the corners of the lips curved up or down.

This video was so bland in its absence of signals that Cat's first instinct was to question its validity. The subject certainly looked and sounded like Jalil, but only an expert could confirm a match to his facial structure and voice. She thought back to the jump in the frames at the beginning of the video and at the difference in the subject's comportment. Clearly, the video had been edited. What could have happened in those missing frames that would warrant their removal? She contemplated other such videos that she had seen and couldn't recall even one that had been edited. They were always the same: camera on, subject looks at camera, subject reads message, camera off. There was never anything more than that.

Tugging the thread a little further, she considered the blow to the subject's head, the way his head had rolled back, and the sudden shift in his demeanor. It was possible that the blow had injured the man, and they had neglected to stop the camera while someone attended to him. The missing frames might have shown the captors, leading to their identification. But the blow, in her estimation, didn't appear strong enough to inflict serious damage. She replayed the scene, pausing the action at the moment of the strike. *Whoa.* Perhaps his peripheral vision had detected movement or there had been a sound, but he had anticipated the blow. His head was already canted away from the impact. And was that a smirk on his face? Or a grimace?

Cat would have given anything for a high-resolution screen and playback that would allow her to view the clip frame by frame. Instead, she glued her eyes to those of the young man as he began to speak. She watched as his eyes crossed. Twice. She played it again. She had previously assumed that the lack of focus in his eyes was a result of the hit or torture that had taken place after the opening frames. What she now saw were two deliberate occurrences of the subject crossing his eyes, and it took her breath away. *Double cross.*

Fighting an urge to throw the phone across the room, she instead turned to Simin and asked what had transpired after the video had been received.

"They wanted Reza to set up a corporation. I don't remember the name, but it sounded innocent, like a foundation for educating kids. He was supposed to get a corporate account and credit cards to go with it, and they wanted him to start putting money in the account. They gave us lists of things to buy with the credit cards. We did everything they asked."

"Were there any other videos?"

"Only one. It was terrible, worse than this. They cut his neck. It wasn't deep, but there was blood streaming down his chest, and they kept the knife there while Jalil spoke. He said that if we didn't comply with their wishes, they would behead him."

Simin broke into tears and turned her head away so that her face couldn't be seen by the accountant, who was still at his desk shuffling through sheets of paper.

Cat prompted her to continue. "What did they want after that video?"

"Money. They told us to send one hundred thousand dollars to an offshore account. In the Grenadines, I think, St. Vincent. We wanted to call the FBI, but we wanted our son safe." She choked back a sob. "He's probably dead anyhow."

The mental battle between empathy and revulsion raging within, Cat admonished Simin. "What's done is done. But don't let anyone know, including Reza, that we have talked. One wrong word, one minor slip, and we could fail. Now, I need your e-mail address and password. And I'll need to keep your phone for a bit."

———

Simin offered a grateful smile, thanking Jud Nelson for the use of his office, before returning to her own. The accountant was a perfectly accommodating and unperturbed host, suggesting that Cat could stay as long as she liked and even offering to check the halls for any lingering paparazzi. Bemused, Cat briefly wondered what story Simin had concocted for the accountant.

Cat lingered for thirty-two minutes, inspecting Simin's

phone and deciding the next course of action. It was suspicious that the video of Jalil was still online. The longer it remained on the web, the greater the chance that it could be traced to the hosting server. After that, one could, with the right tools, determine the IP address of the machine used to upload the file and, hopefully, the owner of said machine.

She sat quietly, twisting a strand of hair around her index finger as she considered the possibilities. Here again was an odd departure from the normal sequence of events for videos of this nature. After releasing the video, the standard procedure was to publicize. In the black-humor jargon of Cat's profession, they referred to these videos as "killer marketing," or, more profanely, "candid captive."

Her hands involuntarily balled into fists when the realization struck her. The video was still online so that "they," whoever "they" were, could track visits to the site. It was a lure for the Badakhshanians and a trip wire for everyone else. The truth of the matter was that if the Badakhshanians had contacted the authorities, a terrorist cell would have almost no way of knowing. An out-of-place IP or GPS location accessing the site could, however, certainly alert them to the possibility. The methodologies associated with the delivery of this video were unprecedented. And when she thought about the implication of Jalil's crossed eyes, an icy hand gripped her heart.

Cat needed another set of eyes on the video, both to confirm her suspicions and as a backstop for any other clues or signals she had missed. To avoid setting off any alarms or trip wires, she suspected that they would need to spoof Simin's phone. She wasn't sure how much information would be needed, but having spent time in the company of some very adept hackers, she did know that more was better than less.

Every smartphone has a jumble of hardware, software, and identifiers that are used to send and receive calls, texts, e-mail, and data from the Internet. From cellular tower connections, Wi-Fi, Bluetooth, and near field communications, to satellite transmission, a smartphone is a people tracker's amusement park. She found the MAC ID for Simin's phone, navigated to a browser site to find the IP address it was currently using, and jotted down any other system details that seemed important.

Cat asked the accountant to return the "forgotten" phone to Simin and thanked him graciously for his forbearance. Five minutes later, she was behind the wheel of the old car and speeding toward Boston.

Chapter 45

After pulling into a parking space just off Washington Street in the South End of Boston, Cat locked the car and wound her way north to West Newton Street. When she'd last walked through the area about twenty years ago, it was essentially a slum in the early stages of urban renewal. Preservation and restoration efforts had saved the largest area of Victorian row homes in the nation, and the South End is now on the National Register of Historic Places. She was pleasantly surprised to see the changes that had taken place in the neighborhood's dynamic. There were galleries, restaurants, retail shops, and parks at every turn. The South End had actually become a pleasant place.

While the red brick bowfronts gave the neighborhood a unified appearance, their sameness made it difficult to differentiate one from another. She paused on the sidewalk and examined the exteriors of three homes before deciding which was correct. She spotted the camera mounted in the eaves of the home to the right, scampered up the seven steps to the arched portico, and silently prayed that the occupant was home.

Less than a minute after she pressed the buzzer, the heavy door opened, and Cat looked into the suspicious eyes of a man she hadn't seen in ten years. The shots of gray at his temples, and the occasional shimmer of silver in his curly dark hair, gave him a distinguished appearance. He was still a handsome man and seemed to have aged well.

"Arnie," she said stiffly, "I assume you've heard."

"Heard? It's all over the news. I even left a message on Lindsey's phone—not that she'd remember me after all this time."

"Please don't start, Arnie. We're way past recriminations."

He glared at her. "Well, it's nice to see that you're still alive. Not so nice to see that you're still a bitch."

"I need your help. Please. May I come in?"

Arnie studied Cat intently before waving her inside. He led her up the stairs to the study on the second floor, closed and locked the study door, and drew the heavy curtains across the windows.

He turned around and faced her. "State-of-the-art sound-proofing," he muttered, "a fitting complement to my paranoia."

"Don't start."

"Whatever." He flipped his hand in dismissal.

Cat sank into an overstuffed chair and leaned forward, her index fingers forming a steeple over her lips. After leaving Tehran, Arnie had become interested in computer technology and, by his fellow Pan Am employees, was regarded as the resident expert. Unbeknown to most, he was also an expert in cryptology and an occasional conduit of information for the intelligence community. Following Pan Am's demise in 1991, Arnie had parlayed those skills and stepped into the world of contractor services for the federal government. He was brilliant, his analysis was superb, and his honesty and integrity were above reproach—until ten years ago.

Cat tried to relax and keep her posture and tone nonthreatening. "Ten years ago, I found a trail of missing money that led straight to your lovely South End doorstep. All the evidence was there."

Daggers leapt from Arnie's eyes. "Yeah. All that evidence. Disregarding, of course, the fact that I never took a fucking dime. You almost ruined me."

"Where did you get the money to buy this place?"

"You're asking now? It took you ten years to ask me that? You are unbelievable."

"Arnie, we can kick the shit out of each other later. Right now, stop whining. This is important. Where did you get the money?"

He sat heavily on the sofa across from her and let out a hard *pfff* sound before he spoke. "I helped get several Iranians, and a lot of their gold—quite a lot, actually—out of the country."

"You took bribes?" Cat's voice went up an octave.

Arnie shook his head in disgust. "Of course you would think that I took bribes. After all, you think I stole government money. Any other false accusations you'd like to make before I boot your ass out of my house?"

Cat took a deep breath and held up her hand, palm out. "I'm sorry. Just explain it to me."

Arnie considered for a moment before speaking. "They were good people. They were kind, intelligent people, and they were friends. They could foresee what was coming, and they were frightened, as we all were. Iran was headed straight back to the Middle Ages. You were there; you remember. For people who weren't willing to drink the Ayatollah's flavor of Kool-Aid, it wasn't a good place to be. I wanted to help some of them and I did, and it was nothing more than that. About five years later, I got a handwritten note in the mail, hand-signed by almost all of them. It choked me up, that they had gone to all that effort to have each person sign the card and that I had helped make such a difference in the lives of a few people. Hell, maybe I even saved some of their lives. I felt so damn proud."

A wistful smile played across Cat's face. "I know that feeling. So what else was in the note?"

"Instructions on how to access a safety deposit box at a bank in Geneva."

"Now there's an interesting display of gratitude. Did you consider sending it back?"

"There was no return address on the envelope. I had no idea where they were. Remember, Cat, this was way before you could run your finger over your smartphone and have it do magic."

"There are moments when I could live quite contently without that magic, but unfortunately I've resigned myself to the knowledge that I will die with my mobile glued to my hand. But a Swiss account begs the question—and I have to ask—did you report the income?"

"You think I didn't?"

Cat tensed and snapped, "I wasn't making an accusation."

"But it certainly wouldn't be out of character. I'm quite used to that from you."

Cat pressed her face into her cupped hands. "I'm sure you are."

Arnie raised his eyebrows. "So, what do you want from me? You must want something; otherwise you wouldn't be here."

"You seem to be under the misconception that I had something to do with your investigation. I made the initial discovery about the money, but my relationship with you meant that I was cut completely out of the loop. I wasn't permitted any direct access to the investigation, and the few reports the team leader deigned to share with me were pretty damning." She took a deep breath to control her impatience. "Look. That was then, and this is now. I don't have the time or energy to rehash what I should have done, or should not have done, ten years ago. I cannot make that disappear. But what I can do is examine it now, today, here, if you will just put a cork in that anger of yours and tell me all that you remember about the missing money."

Arnie sat back, hiked his right leg over his left knee, crossed his arms over his chest, and silently fumed. After a few minutes, he seemed to reach some acceptance of the situation, and his posture relaxed. He sprawled his arm across the cushions.

"There isn't much to tell. There were two accounts. They were both under bogus names that matched my initials, and the signature card for each matched my handwriting. They told me that money from the agency was traveling through those accounts and disappearing. Or, shall I say, *most* of it was disappearing.

"Shortly after I contracted to buy this house, there were three separate infusions of cash into my account. Remember that everything was pretty much paper and snail mail at the time, and I wasn't exactly fastidious about reviewing the statements. I mean, really, if you can't trust a Swiss bank, what *can* you trust? When I discovered the deposits, I just figured that my Iranian fairy godmother friends had learned I was buying a place and wanted to throw some additional moola into the pot. What else was I supposed to think?

"The prevailing theory, of course, was that I had funneled money from those two agency accounts into my Swiss account, and then to my bank back here. It didn't make sense then, and it still doesn't. What kind of idiot would do that?"

Cat rummaged through the tale, trying to find a flaw other than simple naïveté. She frowned and shook her head. "Someone needed a fall guy."

"Oh, absolutely. But your bosses weren't buying my version of the story. They couldn't prove their own version conclusively, not enough to take to trial, but they damn sure made my life miserable."

"Let's narrow this down. Who would have known you? And known enough to even set you up? Who could possibly have known about the Swiss account?"

Arnie had obviously spent ten years considering the possibilities, because the answer was quick and caustic: "Smith or Jones."

Cat tilted her head and looked at him inquiringly. "Seriously? That's an interesting speculation."

Arnie eyed her carefully. "But you're not surprised at all, are you?"

"Not really," she sighed, "because I'm beginning to think that the same thing has happened again. But this time, I'm the nominated fall guy."

Chapter 46

Arnie busied himself by making coffee while Cat laid out the details about the accounts the worm code had found.

"This situation is different, because the accounts I found are under two of my covert identities, but the similarities to your experience are striking. As in your case, there's a very compelling trail of breadcrumbs. It would certainly warrant enough conjecture on their part to discredit me, but it's not enough proof to stand up in court. The worst part is knowing what will happen if I go in and subject myself to a formal investigation. It would derail my team and everything we've been working on. There is something very big going on, and we can't afford the distraction. I have a terrible tickle in my brain telling me that the money and my current operation are related. Someone wants me out of the way."

Arnie's persistent frown deepened. "What does that have to do with what happened ten years ago?"

Cat pointed at the laptop on the counter. "I don't like coincidences. I can't help but wonder if what happened ten years ago wasn't about you at all, but was about me somehow. Let's go play on Google."

A quick search brought up lists of events that occurred in 2003. Eliminating the disaster of the space shuttle *Columbia* and the drivel of celebrity divorces and winners of various entertainment awards, two relevant events stood out. The United States had invaded Iraq, and the Department of Homeland Security had begun operations.

Arnie cupped his chin in his hands and let his mind focus on the past. "There was a mountain of money flying around over in Iraq, and swarms of people trying to snag it. There were thousands of contractors betting their lives that they'd come back in one piece—with a nice pot of gold for their efforts—and those were the honest ones. There was so much theft and corruption that the United States still can't account for some five or six billion dollars that was spent in that hellhole."

Cat considered the logic. "And DHS got its big-ass boots in the door, too. A lot of people in DC were trying to protect their turf—and their butts. With the mandate to share intelligence with other agencies, there had to be people who were sweating. Maybe someone was worried about what might be uncovered."

Arnie finished the thought, "Someone with a nice stash of cash to supplement his pension."

Cat, who had been clicking links with abandon, froze. "You were doing some computer work for us, right? Was there anything unusual or memorable?"

He nodded and described an operation in which he planted

spyware on several computers at MIT.

"Which department, Arnie, do you remember?"

"Biological engineering."

Holy shit, she thought. Vague references had surfaced back then about research and development on a bioweapon that would incapacitate but not kill. She had spent several weeks trying to track down more information, but the source of the intel had been elusive, and there was no indication about where the research was being conducted or for whom. The involvement might have been US or foreign interests; she wouldn't have been surprised either way. The Geneva Convention aside, anyone who thought the United States would stand idly by while others amassed such weapons was either mentally deficient or sadly naive. Her gut had told her that there was something substantive, but the mission was like chasing air. With nothing concrete to show for the work, she'd been pulled off the hunt and re-tasked.

She struggled to recall the meeting when they'd pulled the plug. There had been two other people already in the room when she took her seat at the conference table. Her boss at that time, Jeff Keely, had been there. Her present boss, Roger Pulaski, was there as well.

She closed her eyes and played the scene in her mind: Roger nodding to Jeff, Jeff opening the folder on the table, Jeff announcing that the investigation would be turned over to DHS, her angry retort, the ensuing heated argument, a door opening behind her, and a second folder passed over her shoulder toward Jeff's outstretched fingers. She blinked at the sudden recollection of that folder, with its distinctive orange top-secret markings, and the owner of the hand that held it: Smith.

Cat's eyes narrowed as she looked up at Arnie. "Pack a bag, and throw in a suit for good measure, because we need to get out of here, right now. And you're going to a funeral Tuesday, up in Gloucester. Have you ever driven a limousine?"

Chapter 47

Cat and Arnie spent the remainder of Saturday shopping for supplies along Route 1, north of the city. To avoid drawing attention from the patrons and cashiers, they established a limit of three items per store. Using cash, Arnie made the purchases, while Cat waited anxiously in her car. Six disposable cell phones, a package of twelve legal pads, four pens, a package of assorted-color Post-its, one 64GB flash drive, one inexpensive laptop, a twenty-seven-inch monitor, and one software download later, they finally stopped for takeout and drove to Cat's room in Gloucester.

Arnie plumped a couple of pillows and propped himself up on the bed while Cat told the story of the backup at Lindsey's company and the more current data on the flash drive she'd retrieved from her backyard. She finished with, "I think the key will be in one of those images I took—there is a trail there somewhere."

"I know that Lindsey's smart, but what makes you think that she'll figure out that she's supposed to put those files on a flash drive and stick it in the doughnut box? You are delusional."

The corners of Cat's lips hinted at a smile as she responded, "She's smart, yes, but more than that, she's suspicious and curious. She doesn't like things that aren't firmly embedded in logic. When she considers the explosion, a funeral in Gloucester, and a doughnut box as a parting gift for my corpse, the sum of all those odd things is going to nag at her. None of it is logical, and she's going to start digging for answers. She'll remember the computer backup, and she'll discover the whale-watch files. I have no doubt at all."

Arnie shook his head resignedly and shot his gaze upward. "I hope you're right. Otherwise, we're toast." He looked at Cat questioningly. "But I don't get it. Why didn't you just keep the copy of the files yourself?"

Cat plunged her fingers into her hair and took a deep breath. "My reasons seemed sound at the time. I didn't want to keep anything with me, in case I was taken in. I didn't want to leave it at the house, in case it was searched. I wanted someone to have it in case my plan went to hell and I ended up dead or shipped off to no-man's-land for the rest of my days. It's a major flaw in my plan, really, that I didn't make a copy that I could get to easily. I can't imagine what I was thinking. But we do have the images I've taken since then, and one of them will surely lead us to the Harvard kid, Naji. From there, I am betting the farm that we'll find a few breadcrumbs to lead us in the right direction." She shrugged her shoulders. "Sorry; it's all I've got."

Arnie spread his hands in a "whaddya gonna do" gesture and tried to soothe her. "We'll find it. Let's get some sleep and start digging in the morning.

"Agreed. My head feels like someone is pounding it with a jackhammer." She dry-swallowed an aspirin, grabbed a blanket and two chair cushions, and crawled into a makeshift bed on the floor. When Arnie switched off the light, she whispered into the darkness, "I know that none of this is easy for you, Arnie. Thank you for helping. You're a good man and we're going to prove it."

Arnie woke with the first hint of the daylight on Sunday and took an ice-cold shower to jump-start his brain. Cat took her turn, favoring the hottest water that she could bear, while he rummaged for coffee. After dosing themselves with caffeine, they connected the monitor and flash drive to his laptop and began reviewing the images, a task that was both tedious and difficult. When Cat first told Arnie about the images, he had immediately proposed using OCR software to convert them to text. It was the only way they'd be able to effectively search the data. During their shopping spree, they'd parked outside a local office supply store, connected the new laptop to the free Wi-Fi hot spot, and downloaded a free version.

The ability of an Optical Character Recognition program, or OCR, to read text depends on a number of factors, including the sharpness of the characters in the image. They tested several settings and bumbled through several minutes of chaos before devising a system to divide the work. For the first hour, they both performed conversions. Then, armed with a stockpile of text files, Cat began searching while Arnie continued the conversions.

Sophisticated programs on the server had already performed an initial evaluation of the data and had flagged many files to indicate that human review was warranted. Cat set about tackling those first. She filled pages of yellow legal paper with notes, drew flowcharts to indicate communications, and implemented her own five-star review system.

At two thirty the following morning, she shut down her computer and stretched out on the floor. "I'm suffering from eyeball coma. Let's call it a night."

Arnie kept working.

Chapter 48

Monday
Gloucester and Boston, Massachusetts

Under Cat's direction, Arnie called Evelyn Wainwright's office first thing on Monday morning. Feigning fright and desperation, he appealed to the voice on the other end of the phone as he rattled off a scattered story about how he'd been threatened with a federal indictment. Evelyn's soft spot was ordinary people who were caught in the extraordinary threshing machine of the US Department of Justice. As she had stated to Cat on more than one occasion, "We don't have a justice system. We have a legal system, with laws written by politicians who are lawyers, interpreted by judges who are lawyers, and defended on both sides by lawyers. If you're not a scholar of jurisprudence, you don't stand an ice cube's chance in hell of winning that game."

Before leaving, Arnie handed Cat the flash drive with the files he'd converted during the night. He appeared exhausted, and Cat felt a moment of regret that she'd allowed fatigue to overcome her. She gently took the drive, and embraced him in a brief hug. "Thank you," she whispered.

Arnie caught the next train into Boston and made his appearance at the appointed hour. He was promptly escorted into Evelyn's outer office, where he spent the next ten minutes impatiently drumming his fingers on the armrest of a very comfortable and very costly leather chair.

"Mr. Ford," a voice beckoned.

With a start, he remembered the name he had given when making the appointment, and nodded. He entered the office and shook hands with the rather dowdy and unkempt woman who introduced herself as Evelyn Wainwright.

"Arnold Ford. Thank you for seeing me." He shook her outstretched hand before reaching into his pocket and withdrawing a small card and one of the disposable phones. He extended them to her.

Initially puzzled at the gesture, Evelyn's eyes widened as she read the text penciled on the card: Cat's name and phone number. Arnie stared beseechingly at her, willing her to comprehend.

Evelyn arched her eyebrows and sat back in her chair, waiting for an explanation.

Arnie pulled out his federal ID card, discreetly positioning his index finger over the last name, and displayed it to her. At the Pentagon or any other federal building, the green bar across the card would have been readily recognized as belonging to a contractor, but few civilians would be aware of the color's significance. Without actually stating that he was on official business, he was providing her with just enough information to respond truthfully to questions that would surely come later.

"I need for you to arrange a loaner of one of the limos you use. Actually, I need to drive the limo, pick up Lindsey, get her to the funeral, and take her back home. And I'll need a uniform, too."

When Arnie later related the story, he described Evelyn's reaction as "someone having bitten into a lemon." Cat had doubled over in laughter and enjoyed a brief moment of reprieve.

Evelyn had phoned the limo company and instructed them to deliver the car and a package to her associate, who would be waiting at the Salem Waterfront Hotel at 7:00 a.m. sharp the next morning. Whoever drove the car to Salem was invited to enjoy the hospitality of a suite at the hotel until the limo was returned in the early afternoon. While the operators of the limo service were accustomed to odd requests, they had balked. Evelyn, a longtime and well-paying client, had proceeded to assure them that her new associate did indeed have a license. Although she intentionally omitted *chauffeur* as the license type, the implication was otherwise. The deal was struck.

In the morning, Evelyn would call the funeral home to advise them of the new arrangements. "A security precaution," she would tell them.

Chapter 49

During Arnie's absence, Cat remained in Gloucester and continued to review the files. She was convinced that the key was to be found in data related to Naji. He was a kid, and he was receiving his orders from someone higher in the pecking order. She recalled Naji's e-mail from the team's initial discussions about him and was certain that she would recognize the destination e-mail address if she saw it—*Conrad*-something.

After uploading the most recent batches of converted files, Cat found the target e-mail address among the myriad e-mails that Naji had sent in the past two weeks. The message was addressed to *conrad27.barrymore@gmail.com*, and read, "Boat next week. Looking forward to journey." She located the time stamp, 4:03 a.m. on Friday, and felt her heartbeat accelerate.

She searched for further correspondence between the two addresses, but found nothing, so she switched tactics and began to look for emails sent *from* Conrad27. There were several, and while most seemed innocuous, seemingly harmless content is no guarantee that the sender is pure of heart. About halfway through the list, she found a message that gave her pause. As with the previous e-mails, the banal content of this one raised no alarms. But the address to which it had been sent was another matter. She stared hard at the monitor, trying to wrap her brain around the address displayed on the screen and its implications. *Arthur.tobiason@aliasops.com* stared back at her.

AliasOps was a domain that she, Smith, and Jones had purchased, on a whim, twenty years earlier. E-mail and the Internet were in their infancy at the time, and it had seemed a good idea to explore the capabilities of the emerging technologies. Originally, Cat set up a server in the basement of her old house and purchased various software products for purposes of experimentation. One of the purchases had included e-mail server software, so the three of them began using it to send and receive e-mails off the grid. Later, after she and Tom had built the home on Harboredge, she'd purchased a new server and housed it at Lindsey's office. Even with the vast number of free and virtually anonymous accounts now available out in the ether, they'd held onto the domain. Most e-mail providers servicing the general population will snoop, scrape, and gather personal data, and can be compelled by the US government to share that data. The handful of people using the AliasOps server appreciated its aversion to the intrusive tactics used by other providers, but at the same time recognized that there was no expectation of anonymity. Cat recognized the e-mail immediately. Arthur Tobiason was an identity that Jones used.

There were a few additional messages sent *to* the Tobiason e-mail address, including confirmation of a very large money transfer into the account in St. Vincent's. But to her consternation, she couldn't locate a single outgoing e-mail *from* the account. Her scalp tingled. Something wasn't right.

Cat desperately wanted to access the administrative tools of the AliasOps server and trawl the logs for information. She itched to discover if Jones had read that e-mail, when he had last logged in, whether there were messages in his Drafts folder, and where the e-mail to him had actually originated. The looming question was whether he was the actual recipient, or instead, another pawn being sacrificed. Reluctantly, she closed the program that would have given her access to the server. The risk of exposure was too great. If there were electronic eyes on the AliasOps server, they would be able to trace her to Gloucester in a matter of seconds.

She raised her fingers from the keyboard and tried to focus. The information that she'd uncovered held national security implications, and entrusting that information to the wrong person could have catastrophic consequences. She considered the FBI agent to whom she'd reached out in Washington, Adrian Santori. Her research on Adrian had led her to believe he'd be sharp, and Cat shook her head ruefully as she recalled the encounter. He had been polite, but ultimately disbelieving and dismissive. She ran a mental tally of persons who might show up at the funeral and who could be counted on to take action. She could think of only three: Paul Marshfield, Evelyn Wainwright, and Jones.

After Arnie's return to Gloucester, Cat showed him the e-mails that she'd found, and together they diagrammed the trail of money and communication.

Cat commented, "I'm really spooked by the mention of Naji and a boat. What's he doing with a boat? They are planning something, and I've no idea what it is. We need that data from Lindsey." She hunched over and hugged her knees. "God, I hope we can pull this off tomorrow."

Arnie was troubled. "Even if I stick to Lindsey like glue, I'll never be alone with that doughnut box. We need a distraction."

She sat up. "I have an idea." In their entire history, Cat had never contacted Jones directly. If she wanted to reach him, there was a list of numbers she would call, and the message would always be relayed. Tonight, however, she retrieved the phone Jones had given her and pressed the pre-programmed number.

A deep voice answered, "Alias."

"I could use an actor tomorrow."

"I'm interested. What's the play?"

"Grimes and Babcock; get there before 11:00 a.m. Bring a date, someone who could resemble me from a distance. Drive around the block a couple of times. We need a distraction."

"And you need my considerable talent because I blend in so well with all those white folks on the North Shore."

"Exactly. Your date will be the real bait, so choose her wisely. We wouldn't want her to panic if someone points a muzzle in her direction."

"I might know someone who fits the bill. It's not exactly any sane person's notion of a first date, but it will surely test her mettle," he chuckled.

"And Jones," she added, "be careful. I may have found something."

"Anything you care to share?"

"Not yet. Whoever's behind this is very clever. I've got to get a look at those other files. I need to be sure that my conclusions are solid before I start making accusations." She could sense Arnie's eyes boring into her back as she spoke.

***

Cat and Arnie worked through the remainder of the afternoon and into the early evening, reviewing more images, until an unexpected call from Evelyn trilled against the tedium. Arnie activated the speaker, and Cat mimed that she would remain silent—although she had almost cried out when Evelyn spoke of the attack on Lindsey. The framework of the plan with the limo would remain intact, although Arnold would now be staged as part of Lindsey's personal protection detail. Michelle would follow in another car to provide actual protection, should it be needed.

"I'm assuming that these skills aren't listed on your resume," sniped Evelyn. "Can you get to the Westin tonight? I think it's best if you become acquainted with Michelle and partake of some of her wisdom before tomorrow."

Cat nodded emphatically, and Arnie agreed to drive into the city and meet with Michelle. When he disconnected, Cat gave him instructions to first stop by Walgreens and pick up four small flash drives.

He looked at her quizzically. "What do you have in mind?"

"Think of yourself as a Paul Revere cum Johnny Appleseed hybrid. Tomorrow you're going to initiate the warning for Boston, but you can't start yelling, 'the terrorists are coming.' Instead, you'll drop a few seeds of information into fertile soil."

Arnie followed her instructions to the letter, stopping at Walgreens before speeding into the city. He found Michelle waiting impatiently in the lobby of the Westin. He endured a half-hour lecture about the fundamental procedures for personal protection that, in the end, left no doubt about who would truly be in charge tomorrow. Finally, he'd been introduced to the torn and bruised Lindsey, and had blinked back tears as he realized she didn't recognize him at all.

Cat spent every available minute assembling all of the evidence available. She gathered all of the supporting files into a single folder, and composed a document detailing what she had discovered about the student Naji, her friends Reza and Simin Badakhshanian and their son Jalil, the trail of communications, money, and extortion, and the similarities to the case against Arnie ten years earlier. She pointed out the St. Vincent bank accounts that had been opened under her identities, and surmised that further investigation would reveal similar accounts for Jones. She revealed the whereabouts of the AliasOps server and provided instructions for accessing the IDs and administrative passwords that would allow access to the actual e-mail accounts. She issued a plea for tasking resources to find and intercept Naji before he accomplished his mission, and to locate and rescue Jalil.

The final page summarized her assessment of who was

orchestrating the plot and possible motivation. Lastly, she explained her next course of action. "I'm counting on you to stop whatever Naji has planned. You have access to data and resources that are now beyond my reach. Nevertheless, I'm several steps ahead of you and may find myself in a situation from which I cannot back down. While you may have terrible concerns about my loyalties, I can only assure you of my innocence. I am, first and foremost, a patriot to my country and will do whatever it takes to protect her. I know that the same holds true for you, and I trust that you will take whatever measures are necessary. If we reach the endgame at the same time, I hope we will find clarity there. Godspeed."

Chapter 50

Tuesday
Gloucester, Massachusetts

On Arnie's return from his unscheduled drive to the Westin, Cat insisted that he take the bed and try to get some shut-eye. He argued halfheartedly and finally relented after admitting that he was dog-tired.

He had fared well with sleep, Cat thought, judging by his soft snoring during the night. He was at peace, she realized, and smiled wistfully at the idea. He had been wrongfully accused and had suffered with that dishonor for ten years. Now that Cat had accepted that he'd been framed, it was as if a tremendous weight had been lifted from his soul. *Amazing*, she thought, *what a difference a little trust makes.*

She positioned an overstuffed armchair near the window and curled into a ball as she tried to get a little rest before dawn.

At four thirty, Arnie crept out of the apartment to catch the train to Salem. Cat positioned the armchair nearer to the window and sat in the darkened room, waiting for the drama to unfold. At about five thirty, two black SUVs pulled to the curb in front of the funeral home and disgorged a swarm of bodies. The agents scattered quickly and silently, taking positions with a sight line to the building. The moonlight reflected a glint from a rooftop across the way, confirming the presence of at least one sniper. She scrunched deeper into the cushions and tried to ignore the unsettling sensation of watching one's own funeral.

Shortly before nine, a limo pulled to the entrance, and she saw Arnie step out of the driver's side and open the rear door. Seconds later, she saw Lindsey emerge, dressed in black and carrying a pink and white box, followed by Lindsey's Uncle Peter and Aunt Holly. Cat's brow furrowed as she pondered what might be going through Peter's head. She'd investigated him, and many others related to Lindsey's mother, when her dad had married the woman. Peter had been in military intelligence for twenty years. The man was no fool.

Another limo arrived an hour later, and as the occupants exited the vehicle, Cat realized that a second funeral was taking place that morning. She briefly wondered if the second service would help or hinder the plans she'd made, and ultimately shrugged the thought away. They would simply have to play the hand they'd been dealt and manage any consequences as they arose.

At about ten fifteen, she spotted a white van, made more noticeable by the huge black arm draped over the track of the open driver's window. Her eyes followed the van until it turned the corner behind the funeral home, and reacquired it as it began another pass. Just as it was again moving away from the building, she spied Lindsey stagger onto the porch, one hand over her mouth as if she were about to be sick. A moment later, a swarm of men in tactical gear materialized from seemingly nowhere and gave chase to the van.

The text was ready, and she instantly pressed the Send button on the phone. If Arnie hadn't already managed to grab the flash drive from the doughnut box, there would be no better opportunity.

The next phase was to deliver the flash drives that she had prepared for Jones, Paul Marshfield, and Evelyn Wainwright. They had agreed that it would be easiest to reach the ambassador before the service started. Afterward, as Paul became recognized, it might be impossible to capture a moment alone with him. Evelyn, however, could be counted on to linger and look after Lindsey's interests until the mourners had dispersed. Arnie would have to pick his own moment for passing the data to Jones. Cat tried to remain calm and ignored the acid building in her stomach as she observed the scene across the street.

Arnie was positioned at the side of the building, pacing the smokers' zone and feigning the anxiety of a man suffering from nicotine addiction. Cars pulled into the parking area at a steady rate, and while it was difficult to distinguish one occupant from another until the driver exited the vehicle, there were certain characteristics that could be expected. The Ambassador's rental would be a late-model midsize and relatively free of the snow sludge that had built up on many of the resident autos in the area.

She and Arnie spotted the silver Nissan at about the same time. Arnie stepped toward the parking lot, adjusting his pace so that he reached the car just as Paul Marshfield cracked open his door. Arnie reached for the handle and pulled the door fully open. Paul, who was accustomed to an escort when traveling abroad, initially took no notice of the man holding the door. She detected Paul's brief startle as recognition dawned, and silently applauded his quick recovery.

Arnie, playing his part beautifully, bowed his head slightly and pointed to the entrance as he closed the car door and turned back to the smoking area. Paul's face remained placid as he strode toward the building, but Cat could imagine that he was fighting mightily against curiosity about the contents of the envelope that Arnie had dropped into the car.

She watched the parade of faces, some that she knew well and others not at all. A few of Lindsey's coworkers had come, and a few of her own, and some of her friends. Of more interest were those who were not in attendance, and she made mental notes to follow up on them later. She caught a glimpse of a young man who appeared to be issuing instructions to a number of people who, while unobtrusive, were certainly not present to mourn her departure from this earth. She finally associated the face with the agent she had visited in Washington, Adrian Santori. His presence was intriguing, and she wondered if she had underestimated him.

The next hour passed uneventfully before the scene erupted in chaos. Uniformed and tactical officers surrounded the building, and Cat concluded that they were searching for someone—or something—and that no one was allowed to leave. She experienced a momentary surge of panic at the thought that they might have discovered that Lindsey's "present" was missing from the doughnut box, and chided herself for worrying about something that no one even knew about.

After what seemed an interminable length of time, groups of people began to trickle out of the funeral home. At long last Lindsey, with Evelyn by her side, stepped into view. Arnie herded the family into the limo and drove away, leaving Evelyn standing on the sidewalk. Had Arnie managed to slip the envelope to her? Cat tried to read the expression on Evelyn's face and—not for the first time—wished that she'd had the foresight to buy binoculars.

Chapter 51

C at snatched the flash drive from Arnie's outstretched hand and bunched her fist around it. "With this," she said emphatically, "we have all the marbles, or we have nothing, and—"

Arnie interrupted. "What are you hoping to find?"

"A mistake."

He tilted his head. "Come again?"

"I have a very strong hunch. At the beginning, when we turned the worm loose, there were only four people on earth who knew about it: me, the kid who programmed it, the server administrator who set up the server, and the director himself. That's it."

"How does that help?"

"I think that, originally, whoever's behind this believed that they were completely under the radar. That's why these files are so damn important now, because they are the only evidence of their treachery. I think that once they learned about the worm, they started to worry, and planted so-called evidence to lead everyone in the wrong direction. And they've been successful in their efforts—just look at the maelstrom around us. I'm sure, as well, that they would have tried to get rid of anything that might point to them directly. I'd stake a year's wages that the server's been sanitized by now. But what they can't possibly know is that I took all of those pictures of the data. Some of the images I saved go back several months, before anyone would have known of the worm's existence."

"Holy smoke."

"Yep. Let's get cracking."

Three hours later, she located the very first e-mail from Naji detected by the worm. She added the name to her diagram and inked in the additional details. An hour later, she'd added twenty-nine names. The diagram had begun to resemble a web, and Cat tapped her pen on the name of the spider at the center. All the threads that Cat followed had one thing in common: they had all communicated, at one time or another, with *conrad27.barrymore@gmail.com.*

Cat concentrated on Conrad27 and saw the pattern begin to emerge. Naji, and others presumably like him, reported their status to this e-mail address. They did so regularly, with banal messages about schoolwork, health issues, or sightseeing. On an equally regular basis, Conrad27 sent an e-mail to *cetustrak@yahoo.com.* That message spoke about the family, and about their schoolwork, health issues, and sightseeing.

The final e-mail to cetustrak had been in mid-January, when all communication with that address abruptly ceased.

Thereafter, communiques were sent to an offshore domain that Cat knew to offer ghost e-mail accounts and, equally important, encryption.

She pumped her fist in the air and smothered the yell that threatened to leap from her throat. "Got him!" she cheered.

Arnie slapped a high five with her. "Who is it?"

"cetustrak@yahoo.com."

"Another whale guy?"

Cat froze. "What do you mean?"

"Cetus. It's a constellation. You know, the Whale."

Cat blinked rapidly as she mentally ticked off dates from the past month. The last e-mail to Conrad27 had been on the same day that she had seen Smith and Roger at the Cambridge apartment.

"Smith," she breathed. "It's Smith."

PART THREE

Lindsey and Cat

February, five months ago
Wednesday through Tuesday

Chapter 52

Adrian laced his fingers behind his head and arched his chin upward, trying to relieve the tension in his neck as he puzzled over the mystery of the limo driver. His phone trilled, and he looked at the caller ID quizzically before answering. "Mr. Ambassador?"

When she heard him address the caller, Lindsey immediately concluded that the conversation would involve watching out for her well-being. She moved toward the kitchen to afford him some privacy, but he held up his hand and signaled for her to stop.

"Yes, sir," he said quickly, "this is a secure phone, and Lindsey is here."

Lindsey watched, fascinated, as Adrian's posture stiffened and his jaw tightened; his expression changed from curious to solemn.

"Yes, sir. I understand." He disconnected the call, and was

still as a statue for several moments.

"Adrian?"

The question seemed to pull him out of his reverie, and he stepped toward Lindsey and began barking orders. "Throw a few things into an overnight bag, enough for two nights, and bring your laptop. Do it now. Where are Gabe and Jason?"

She took a step back, suddenly wary. "Excuse me?"

"Where are Gabe and Jason?"

"Probably at Jason's place. What's wrong?"

"Not now. Please don't argue. For once, just do as I say. And hurry."

Lindsey was suddenly frightened. Something the Ambassador said during the call had really spooked Adrian. She yanked an overnight tote from the closet and threw in sneakers and casual attire for three days. As someone who traveled with some frequency, she kept a cosmetic bag ready, along with the ridiculous one-quart plastic bag for liquids, and added those to the tote. She tugged on a pair of boots, grabbed a parka and hat, and presented herself in just over four minutes.

"Set your voice mail. You're going out of town for a few days to have some time with close friends and to get away from the media circus. Don't talk too fast, because you don't want to sound nervous. Try to sound subdued. Remember that you're in mourning."

Lindsey's nerves were fraying, and her fingers trembled as she pressed buttons to record a new message on the phone. It took three tries before she calmed enough to speak steadily.

Adrian instructed her to pick up Jason and Gabe and drive to the North Shore Mall. He would follow in his car and would provide further information once there.

Lindsey pointed to the Mercedes parked out on the street. "What about Michelle?"

"She'll follow, too."

Convincing Gabe and Jason to drop everything turned out to be easier than Lindsey expected. Jason actually seemed excited, and while Gabe was more circumspect, neither raised any objections to being whisked away to parts unknown.

Lindsey pulled into the parking lot adjacent to the Sears store and noticed Adrian flash his headlights before turning into one of the parking aisles. Lindsey took the next aisle and parked nose-to-nose with his car. Ten minutes later, she was shocked to see the limo driver, Arnold, park in the next space. The rear window of his car slid down, revealing Evelyn in the backseat. Responding to Evelyn's urgent beckoning, Lindsey joined her.

Evelyn studied Lindsey intently before speaking. "There are a number of things that I need to share with you. You'll have questions, but please allow me to finish first."

Acknowledging Lindsey's nod of agreement, she continued, "The Ambassador and I both received information from Cat yesterday afternoon, which confirms that she was very much alive during her funeral. Arnold delivered your flash drive to her, and my understanding is that she spent most of last night analyzing the data. Arnold brought the results to me this morning. There are some very disturbing assessments that she's made as a result, and a number of questions that are urgently in need of answers. Agent Santori will provide you with more details. For your safety, and for other reasons that will later be made clear, you and Gabe and Jason are being temporarily moved to a more secure location. I will not be told where that is."

The gravity of her expression indicated that she was not entirely happy with the arrangement.

"Are we in danger?" Lindsey asked.

"There is certainly that possibility. You've already been attacked once. As your legal counsel, I have to advise you that I am not completely comfortable with not knowing where you are. With that said, however, this might very well be an instance where lack of knowledge is the safest course."

"Will I be able to reach you if I need your advice?"

"I've been told that some sort of communication can be arranged, but I don't yet know any of the details."

"Who else knows about this?"

"Very few. Our little group here in the parking lot, of course, Ambassador Marshfield, and a few others. I've been assured that this entire operation is being tightly held at the highest level, and that any others will be personally vetted by the Ambassador."

Lindsey's eyebrows shot upward at the implication. "Paul Marshfield. Wow! He's a bit more involved than I'd expect from an ambassador. Really. Wow."

"You'll have to draw your own conclusions about that. I won't speculate. But I feel some confidence in saying that I believe you to be in good hands."

Lindsey wasn't sure if Evelyn's assurances made her feel

any more secure. She reluctantly left Evelyn's car, opened the door to Adrian's, and was overcome by a surge of anger. She demanded to know where she was being taken and what was happening to her car.

Adrian spoke in the calmest voice he could muster. Lindsey's car, he explained, was taking a little journey, with Arnie as the driver and Michelle following. Arnie would leave the car at the destination and ride back with Michelle. Evelyn was returning to her office. Adrian would drive Jason, Gabe, and Lindsey to their destination, with additional details to be provided on arrival.

Guantanamo? Lindsey wondered, biting her tongue.

Adrian then ordered the group to relinquish all cell phones and laptops. There was an immediate uproar as his passengers protested, but the objections were firmly denied and he refused to allow any further discussion. "I can assure you that you will have state-of-the-art equipment to work with. If there is anything that you need, we will arrange to provide it. But we cannot have you actively accessing the Internet with your own devices or with any of your own screen names. In fact, those devices will be on and functional, but they will be far away from your actual location. For a few days, you will not access your own e-mail or other sites that you frequent, and any online activities will be under a name that we assign to you. Is that clear?"

The trio from Marblehead looked at each other, stunned and wondering how they had become the puppets in this drama. Without another word, Adrian started the car and drove away from the mall.

Chapter 53

Adrian followed I-95 south for several miles, the silence broken only by the hum of the engine and the occasional tink-ah-tink-ah of the turn signal. He was fully alert, the tension evident in his every movement.

Lindsey finally summoned the courage to inquire about lunch, and received nods of appreciation from her fellow captives. Without so much as a sideways glance, Adrian informed the trio that there would be food at the destination. *Bread and water?* she wondered. Being deprived of information has an odd way of making one question the motives of others, Lindsey reflected. She was beginning to have doubts about the faith she had placed in Adrian, and by extension, the government he worked for. She was seriously considering methods of escape when he exited the interstate near Foxborough.

Signs pointed to Gillette Stadium to the west, but Adrian drove south and, after several turns, pulled onto a narrow rural road somewhere near Lake Cocasset. The area was sparsely populated, with the few houses distant from one another and set back from the road. Some of the drives simply led into the woods, and any buildings were invisible to passersby. He turned into a long narrow drive, and the car was engulfed by forest for a few moments before emerging at the edge of a broad clearing. The center of the expansive lawn was occupied by a large two-story house. Lindsey twisted in her seat to look around and, although it was winter and the trees were bare, found that no other structures were visible.

Adrian parked beside a black SUV, nose facing outward, and pointed to a door tucked at the side of the house near the garage. Lindsey unfolded herself from the car and stretched, scanning the house and wondering what other surprises were in store. She followed Gabe and Jason through the proffered door, which led into a breakfast room off the kitchen. Her stomach growled in immediate response to the aroma of barbeque filling her nostrils. Relief flooded over her when Jones thudded into the kitchen.

Adrian noticed her face relax. "We thought a friendly hulk would be in order."

Lindsey wondered fleetingly if her uneasiness during the ride had disturbed him. They had begun to develop something of a friendship, and her inability to cope with the unknown was translating into distrust. Admitting to herself that she was allowing her discomfort to rule her thinking, she made a mental reminder to try viewing the situation from a less emotional point of view.

Famished, they piled their plates high with pulled pork

and coleslaw. Jones, they learned, loved to cook and claimed to have won awards from barbeque competitions across the South.

Adrian started to speak, but Jones stopped him. "Eat first."

They found places at the table, and conversation ceased as they sloppily and noisily shoveled the food into their mouths. Finally sated, Lindsey sat attentively with Gabe and Jason as the rules were laid down.

Jones spoke first. "There are security systems here that you can't see. From now on, the doors and windows will be alarmed at all times. You shouldn't need to go outside, so don't. If for whatever reason you do need to go outside, tell us first. The lawn is off-limits, and beyond that elm by the driveway is no-man's-land." He pointed to a large tree just beyond the garage.

Adrian chimed in, "No calls out. Don't answer any phone. Don't go to the door; stay away from the windows. Your best protection is not being seen."

If Adrian and Jones were trying to scare her, Lindsey realized, they were succeeding, as evidenced by the goose bumps that had risen on her arms. Trying to absorb the serious nature of the place, she was only now coming to grips with the fact that they might actually be in jeopardy. She found herself wondering how people actually chose careers necessitating the use of safe houses and lawns studded with devices one could only imagine. How did they manage it?

As if reading her mind, Adrian interjected, "Now that I've scared you to death, I hope you appreciate how serious this is. We are not kidding, and your safety is paramount. But let's get to the underlying reason why we brought you here."

Before anything further was said, he produced documents for each of the three to sign. Lindsey had seen and signed one before, at the FBI office in Boston, but found this one to be even more detailed. She read it carefully, trying to absorb the legal mumbo jumbo and the implications of signing. Finally she caved to the pressure and inked her signature. Jason followed suit immediately. Gabe took longer, reading some sections of the document several times, before signing his name.

Jones excused himself as Adrian collected the documents and looked into each of our faces.

"While you're guests here, let's establish who you can trust. First, there's me." He winked and grinned.

There was an uncomfortable silence before Adrian realized that his attempt at humor had fallen flat, and he coughed into his fist to cover his embarrassment.

"Everyone at this table has been vetted, as have Evelyn Wainwright, her bodyguard Michelle, and the man you know as Arnold. His friends, by the way, call him Arnie, and his last name is Powell. He is a cousin of Tom Powell. There are three people who must approve any other person who might join our circle: Ambassador Marshfield, the Agency director, and Catherine Powell."

The room was uncommonly still as the group from Marblehead struggled with the revelations. Lindsey let out an audible gasp as the shoe dropped and she realized that Arnold was a man whom she had, in her youth, referred to as Uncle Arnie. She was mortified at not having made the connection.

Gabe's mouth was agape as he croaked, "Cat?"

"Yes."

As if on cue, Jones stepped into the room with Tom Powell close on his heels.

Tears sprang from Lindsey's eyes as she jumped up and wrapped her arms tight around Tom's neck.

"I knew it. I just knew it," she cried.

Tom patted her head gently. "Thank you for all you've done, Lindsey. To be truthful, I wasn't sure you'd figure it out, but Cat had every confidence in you. It turns out she was right. She was always the smart one in our marriage."

Adrian refocused their attention. "Let's talk about why you're here."

Chapter 54

Adrian escorted the group back to a large office with multiple computers and an enormous display monitor on the far wall. He turned on the monitor, and the faces of Ambassador Marshfield and a younger man and woman materialized in the bottom right corner. They waited expectantly.

Paul Marshfield performed the introductions. "Melodie and Trent work in an organization that I'm presently not at liberty to name. It operates at a level far out of the realm of most people on this planet. They are two of the best intelligence and threat analysts in the nation. Gabe and Jason, joining us today for this mission, are from the private sector. They bring formidable programming and hacking talent to the table.

"We are taking the very unusual step of bringing all of you together because we have a major problem and little time to solve it. The data that Gabe found on Cat's computer, which was originally transferred to the flash drive, as well as more recent data provided by Cat, suggest a high probability of an imminent terrorist action in Boston.

"Under ordinary circumstances, we would involve other agencies and have a very large team working night and day on this. But what Cat also discovered is that it appears at least one of our own people may be funding or otherwise helping to orchestrate this plot. We have only suspicions, but trust is a delicate thing. We simply cannot take the risk.

"We will share with you what we know with certainty. We want you to collectively use your considerable intellectual skills to try and determine where, when, and how the attack will occur. If we are successful, we believe we'll also uncover whoever is betraying us."

Gabe and Jason looked shell-shocked. Lindsey sat numbly, overwhelmed by the enormity of what Paul Marshfield was now revealing and what she and her friends were expected to accomplish.

Gabe was the first to recover. "Let's get to it. Tell us what you know."

For the next hour, Paul Marshfield and Adrian laid out the entire chain of events, the data, the implications, and the facts known thus far. There was a great deal of information to absorb.

Melodie was all business as she opened a whiteboard program and entered the salient points in the briefing. She had sharply defined cheekbones and a stern countenance, her short natural twists were tautly pulled back from her face by a woven blue headband, her dark eyes were sharply attentive, and she was perfectly typecast for Lindsey's perception of an intelligence analyst.

Tom Powell contributed his own observations about the events of the past month and the reasons for Cat's decision to fabricate her own death. While Cat had refused to share any sensitive details with him, his perceptions offered perspective to her actions.

Like Melodie, Trent was conservatively dressed, but his spiky blond hair and the tattoo snaking down his arm spoke of a person who didn't always toe the line. He offered an initial assessment. "Let's first come to some agreement about what we might expect. Cat's documents suggest explosives. What about biologics?"

Paul Marshfield spoke up. "I don't want to dismiss biologics completely, but they are exceedingly difficult to acquire through any channel, legal or otherwise. They are also subject to environmental vagaries, must be handled with extreme caution, and are difficult to disperse to a sizable population with any degree of success. I agree with Cat. It's much more likely that we are looking at explosives of some sort.

"With that said, there is the possibility of some involvement of nuclear material, given the connection with Dr. Badakhshanian. The man is, after all, a nuclear physicist. But let me emphasize that we view that possibility as remote. He has been under intense scrutiny since last Thursday night, and there has been no indication of any involvement except for the money."

"Why did he contribute the money?" Tom asked.

"I'm not at liberty to divulge that information. Suffice it to say that Cat discovered the true nature of the payment and included that in her documentation. We are presently satisfied that Dr. Badakhshanian was under extreme duress and has no other involvement."

Trent took that as his cue to continue. "If we're looking at explosives, our first task is to consider where this might happen. From there, we'll have a better chance of coming up with the how and when."

There was general agreement, and Trent prodded them for more information. "We have to start somewhere. There was the message about a boat. We have no context, so we don't know if he was buying or renting or simply had a ticket for a cruise. Let's narrow it down."

Jones jumped in. "A cruise isn't feasible. No cruise ships go out of Boston at this time of year."

Trent nodded. "Buying or renting, then. Would that be important?"

"Renting," Lindsey said. "There's paperwork associated with purchasing a boat. I had a sailboat for a few years. It's like a car. There's a title and registration, Coast Guard sticker, and other requirements. That's assuming, of course, that you're going about this legally, which he might not be." Tom nodded his agreement.

"All right," Trent conceded, "but why would anyone rent a boat in Boston in the middle of winter? Wouldn't it arouse some curiosity?"

Melodie countered, "Maybe that depends on the type of boat."

"Wait a minute." Tom held his hands out, fingers splayed, and seemed to be playing a movie in his head. Finally, he closed his eyes and pinched his fingers into his forehead. "In Charlestown, there are a couple of piers that have houseboats, I think. Some of them are rentals."

Trent immediately warmed to the idea. "Sure. He could come and go, carry stuff aboard, and wouldn't raise any suspicions at all."

Melodie frowned. "But houseboats aren't very mobile. What would you do with one? It doesn't seem like a recreational pier would make a particularly valuable target. Even if you load the boat with explosives, it seems a lot of trouble for little reward."

Adrian, who had been listening quietly, observed, "I had friends who lived on a houseboat out in Sausalito. They kept a dinghy tied to the side for their excursions around the Bay."

"Bingo." Melodie's eyes gleamed.

Trent nodded and added, "Before we start chasing our tails, let's figure out where he might go with a boatload of explosives in Charlestown."

Jones laced his fingers behind his head and leaned back in his chair. "It could be anywhere. Boston is what you might call a target-rich environment."

Gabe and Jason suddenly looked at one another. "Can you pull up a satellite image of the harbor area?" Gabe asked.

Melodie gave a toothy smile, and seconds later they were looking at some very high-resolution imagery of Boston Harbor.

"Impressive," Jason admitted. "How close can you zoom in?"

"Close enough to read the headline of the newspaper in that man's hand."

Gabe was fully engaged now. "Zoom out just a bit. Where would he go in a dinghy? Not out to sea. Maybe to the financial district or the Seaport area, but that doesn't feel right." He paused and tapped his index finger against his cheek. "Hmm ... you know ... if I wanted to make a big statement, I'd hit the tank farms."

Lindsey was carefully watching Paul Marshfield during the exchange and saw his eyes pop wide with comprehension. Fuel tank farms dotted Chelsea Creek and the Mystic River, both of which flowed through the metropolitan area before emptying into Boston Harbor.

Jones summed it up for everyone. "Holy Mother of God."

Chapter 55

Naji was euphoric as he heaved the duffel over his shoulder. Thus far, everything had gone according to plan, and there was no reason to think that he would encounter any problems in completing his mission.

The concept of using an American group to fund the operation had been brilliant. The group's name, the American Education Foundation, had been an added inspiration. With so many suspicious eyes on large transfers of money, staging the money as funding for a university research project was the perfect subterfuge. The check for $30,000 had purchased basic supplies and provided the deposit and first month's rent on the boat. It had also covered the final payment for delivery of the explosives.

The blocks had come in ten satchel charges, with sixteen blocks of explosive per satchel. Over the past week, he'd been able to position all but the one satchel currently in his duffel. It

was, he admitted to himself, a relief to get the last of the bricks out of his dorm room. While he knew intellectually that C-4 requires very specific conditions to detonate, stretching out on top of a hollowed-out mattress containing two hundred pounds of the high explosive had not contributed to restful slumber.

He took a final look around the room he'd occupied since arriving at the university so many months ago, then stepped into the hall and closed the door tightly behind him.

Naji bounded down the steps at the Harvard Square T station and leaped into the last car just as its doors were beginning to close. He found a seat in the back of the last car and nestled the duffel behind his legs. Leaning his head back against the window, he dreamily wondered what the explosion would be like. Would it, as he'd been told, rain fire over a huge area? Would it truly produce the level of destruction they'd promised? And would he escape?

He'd been given timing devices that, once activated, promised to allow him four minutes to be clear of the blast zone. If he managed to survive, insha'Allah, he would have to be very careful to act normally and do nothing that would arouse suspicion. After the bombing at the marathon, he'd seen firsthand how the city had lusted for revenge. He and his brethren, however, had learned from that event and knew that cameras had been the undoing of the brothers responsible for the carnage. But pictures held value only if the image showed some of the person's features. This time, it would be night, and he would be wearing a balaclava to cover his head and face.

Chapter 56

P aul Marshfield scanned the faces in the room. "Assessment?"

Fingers pounded on keyboards to access both public and classified projections of damage, injuries and fatalities, and economic impact.

Melodie's face was grim. "Casualty assessment is directly tied to the type of fuel. Liquid natural gas presents the greatest threat for loss of human life, since a tank explosion at the LNG facility could level everything within a half-mile of the site and cause injuries as far as two miles away. A comparable amount of explosive at one of the petroleum fuel farms has far less potential for casualties."

"Which is most likely?"

This was a subject Jones knew well. "The LNG port is pretty well-secured. It attracts a lot of media and political attention, so security measures there have been beefed up in response. Anything's possible, of course, but one guy in a dinghy? Very unlikely that he could get close to the facility, much less cause any damage."

"Tell me about the tank farms, then."

In comparing notes, the group generally agreed that the rupture of a single tank at one of the farms could cause a serious fire, but minimal casualties, and had relatively low environmental impact. If the fire wasn't quickly suppressed, however, the heat could expand the fuel in nearby tanks, causing them to rupture. Fuel from the fractured tanks would spill out, ignite, and further spread the fire.

Some tank farms were closer to residential areas than others, and casualty and damage figures would be higher at those locations. The tank farms had earthen berms around them, acting as secondary containment to hold the tank contents in the event of a leak. But if explosives were used to breach the berm, all bets were off. The fuel would spill into the waterway and flow into Boston Harbor.

Trent somberly explained the impact. "You're looking at up to 50 million gallons at a single facility. That's more than the Exxon Valdez spill in Alaska. It could be an environmental catastrophe."

Paul Marshfield thanked the group and reviewed his notes before commenting. "The conclusions that you have all reached are logical, but there is also a great deal of supposition. Find me some evidence that Naji has been on, or near, one of the piers in Charlestown. I can't sit on this for very long, but everyone will swallow it a lot easier if we have something concrete to back us up." He glanced at his watch. "It's almost five thirty now. I'll initiate a warning in two hours. Get me something before I make the call."

Melodie quickly framed the approach we would use. Because there was no time to attempt retrieval of video or camera images from private businesses, our sole recourse was to access footage from government-owned sources.

"How would he get to the pier?" she asked.

Gabe spoke up. "On the T. Red Line from Harvard to Park Station, Green Line to North Station or, maybe, Haymarket. From there, you walk or take a bus."

She posted an MBTA map on the screen. "Point it out to us."

Gabe showed them the route. "It's probably a mile and a half from North Station to the pier. It's winter. I'd take the bus."

Adrian agreed with him. "Bus, or maybe a taxi."

"Would he take a taxi?" asked Melodie.

"Maybe. He's got money, and lots of it. But he'd be easy to remember in a taxi. On a bus, you're just a face in the crowd."

"I disagree," piped in Jason. "The bus is up close and personal, and people watch you. It's creepy. I'd want the backseat of a taxi."

"Okay, so which? Haymarket or North Station?"

"North Station," Jason answered.

"I'd choose North Station, too." agreed Gabe.

"Perfect. Trent, get access to the feed for the Green Line tracks in North Station and the exits he might use."

Jones had worked transactions like this before. "Maybe we can narrow this down. If I'm renting some boat, you'd better believe I'm going to check it out first. And if I'm the owner, the keys are staying all cozy in my pocket until I have the moola in my fist. What do you want to bet that Naji went to the pier carrying a nice wad of cash?"

"Excellent thinking." Melodie's fingers flew across the keyboard. "Our guy sent an e-mail almost every day. Then one day, out of the blue, he mentions a boat. There is nothing before, and nothing after, about a boat. My assessment is that he sent the message as confirmation of having made an arrangement. Let's concentrate on the time frame between the e-mail mentioning the boat and the one immediately prior, because that's when he probably made the deal. I've loaded all of Cat's files to drive N-J, November-Juliett. Jason or Gabe, find the dates."

"I'm on it," Jason replied.

Melodie continued, "Once we get the feed, we'll look at it together. Subways present difficulties because there are multiple cars and hundreds of people entering and exiting at the same time. We have facial recognition software we can apply and it will speed things along, but it's not perfect. We'll divide it up so that each of us has an area of focus. Let's assume we find this guy. How do we figure out which boat?"

Jones was quick to respond. "He heard about it somewhere. Kids today do everything online. I'd start there."

Melodie's head was bobbing up and down in agreement. "Gabe, we might need your razzle-dazzle. If we find out how he learned about the rental, we'll find the owner."

For several minutes, the only sounds were the soft thwacks of fingers on keyboards, until Jason broke in with a shout.

"Got it. Our guy sent the boat e-mail on Friday at 4:03 a.m."

All eyes were glued to the monitor as Trent accessed the archives and selected the first video recorded on Thursday at the Green Line tracks in North Station. Gabe performed a quick calculation and determined that, on a weekday, there would be approximately 120 trains arriving at the station on the outbound tracks of the Green Line. Lindsey evoked a silent prayer to the subway gods that Naji had taken a morning train, coupling it with a bigger prayer that he'd actually taken the train at all.

After exactly eighty-three minutes of watching the slow-motion drag of passengers exiting the trains and the fast-forward between arrivals, Adrian found Naji. Lindsey, whose eyes were glazing over after watching people and subways come and go, admitted to herself that she would not have spotted him.

Trent was on his game, watching the direction that Naji took and extrapolating an exit. The team watched as Naji emerged from the station and hailed a taxi.

"What's the number?" Melodie's voice was clipped.

The first two digits were visible, but the third and fourth digits were obscured by traffic. Trent pulled the feed from another camera and watched the same cab cruise by. "Got him. I'll see if I can find out where the taxi dropped our guy."

"He had a duffel bag," Jason observed.

"Yep," chorused five other voices.

Lindsey found herself battling mixed emotions at how readily they had tracked the suspected bomber. She was, on the one hand, horrified because she'd just experienced the reality of how much Big Brother is watching. On the other hand, she was fascinated by the amount of information to be found with a few keystrokes and the speed with which it became available. And, she realized, she'd felt quite a thrill at having their adversary within their grasp.

Jason found the online ad for the boat rental by accessing the cached version of the previous week's *craigslist* ads on Google. On the screen were two entries for houseboat rentals at a pier in Charlestown. A quick comparison with the current ad showed that only one was still being advertised. Our guy had rented the other, and now our search became easier. The ad provided a phone number. *You can't hide anything anymore,* Lindsey thought. *Once you put something out on the Internet, it's there forever.*

Adrian handed a phone to Lindsey and prompted her to dial. The device looked harmless and quite ordinary, but she held it warily. It was easy to imagine that the phone boasted all manner of security mechanisms and could probably encrypt, store, and transmit every breath she took. As she dialed, she shuddered to think of the consequences if she pressed the wrong key.

A pleasant male voice answered on the third ring, and Lindsey inquired about the boat. He was sorry, he told her, but the boat had been rented at the end of last week. She hurriedly explained that she had just moved to Boston from San Francisco, and casually mentioned that she'd once lived on a houseboat in Sausalito. He warmed to her story and suggested that she try calling the owner of the boat in the second ad.

"It's in pristine condition," he assured her. "My friend Beth invested a lot of money in it last year. I've been aboard several times."

"That sounds perfect! Where is it? And where is yours? If I take it, I'd like to stop by and say thanks." Lindsey paused for a fraction of a second. "Oh, I guess you won't be there, will you? Do you think I'll like my new neighbor?"

The voice at the other end of the line chuckled. "Beth's boat is at the end. It's the one with pink trim; you can't miss it. Mine is just three down, charcoal gray with white trim. The guy seems nice. He's the serious type and said he just wants a place away from the college crowd so he can study. He's a student. Harvard, I think," he said.

"Bingo," Melodie chirped.

Adrian shuffled everyone out of the conference room and into the kitchen, then returned and closed the door for a private call with Paul Marshfield.

"How confident are you?" queried the Ambassador.

"Very. I think it's solid," Adrian responded. "I'm heading up there now. Jones will be here to watch after Lindsey and her friends."

"Don't let them kill the guy. He didn't set all this in motion by himself. If he dies, we have a dead end. We need him."

"I know. The people up here are good; they'll appreciate the consequences if they toast the guy. But you never know what the subject is going to do. Public safety has to come first."

Chapter 57

L indsey paced the kitchen floor impatiently as they waited for some word about Naji and the explosives that were presumed to be on the houseboat, fully aware that they were all going to feel very foolish if Naji was merely an innocent student seeking a little peace and quiet. *Innocent?* She shivered and hugged herself. She knew intuitively that they had tracked the right guy and that he'd soon be in jail—or he'd be dead. She didn't really care one way or the other, as long as he was prevented from detonating a bomb and incinerating half the city.

Shortly after nine o'clock, Jones hurried into the kitchen. "Trent's got the tactical feed up on the screen if you want to watch. They've located the houseboat and are getting ready to board. I'd like to stick around and watch the action, but I got an urgent text. Duty calls; there's someone I've got to meet. With both Adrian and me gone, be careful. Don't touch anything; don't go anywhere. Just stay put. I should be back before midnight."

Chairs scraped noisily on the floor as the group jumped to their feet and sprinted back to the conference room. The screen glowed in mottled shades of gray and green, and it took a moment for Lindsey's eyes to comprehend what she was seeing.

"Night vision," Jason whispered.

"Can they hear us?" she whispered back.

"No," Trent laughed, "but it's a common reaction. Just about everyone dials the volume level down during these operations. We're on the team leader."

They listened to the one-way audio feed, and Lindsey could hear the heavy breathing of the man wearing the headset and the rustle of fabric as he moved. There were several verbal exchanges, but she found it difficult to decipher what was being said or what it meant.

Finally she heard, very clearly, "I've got eyes on the back of the boat. Negative on the dinghy. Repeat, negative on the dinghy."

The camera bobbed up and down as its wearer ran alongside the boat. The screen was filled with two men using a ram to break down the door, and a minute later, a swarm of people in tactical gear streamed into the boat's interior. Shouts echoed through the conference room as the squad cleared the boat.

"Boat is secure. Target is *not* aboard and dinghy is *not* here. Repeat, target and dinghy are at large."

Lindsey's heart was in her throat. If the dinghy wasn't there, Naji was already on the move. She glanced at Jason, Gabe, and Tom Powell. All three were ashen, a sheen of perspiration evident on their foreheads.

The audio feed was interrupted by the distinct sound of a helicopter's rotors. "This is Air3. Mystic River is clear. No unusual small craft movement. Continuing search pattern."

Another voice jumped in, "This is Air5. We have visual on a small craft on the east side of the Inner Harbor, approaching Chelsea Creek."

"This is HU-1. Confirm your visual and go camera live."

"That's the Harbor Police," Tom whispered.

"Air5. Camera is live."

The screen in the conference room re-sectioned to show the live feed from the helicopter designated as Air5. The spotlight shone on a small dinghy speeding away from the chopper.

"HU-1 is two minutes out. Keep him herded in the inner harbor. You have your instructions. Dead men tell no tales, so we want him alive. But if he makes a move to detonate, splash him."

The image on the screen spiraled sickeningly as the helicopter dove in pursuit of the dinghy. The second helicopter joined the chase, beaming its own image of the attacker to the screen.

"This is HU-1. Keep him out of the creek."

A different voice, this one from a loudspeaker on the chopper, spoke forcefully. "This is the Boston Police. Stop the boat immediately, or you will be fired upon."

The dinghy kept going.

The voice spoke urgently, "This is your final warning. Stop the boat immediately, or you will be fired upon."

Lindsey nearly jumped out of her skin at the sound of gunfire.

The dinghy slowed.

Another voice, rising above the cacophony of rotor blades and boat engines, shouted, "Federal agents! Do not move! Put your hands behind your head!"

The helicopter camera careened around to face the front of the dinghy and reveal a full view of the suspect. His head was bowed, and his hands were out to his sides instead of behind his head. Lindsey's breath caught in her chest. The man's hand wasn't empty. He was holding a rectangular block about the size of a brick.

The Harbor Patrol boat was perhaps seventy-five feet to starboard of the dinghy. Adrian's disembodied voice sounded from one of the loudspeakers. "If you move a muscle, we'll blow your head off."

The man, wearing a balaclava so that only his eyes were visible, raised his head and looked squarely into the helicopter's camera. An instant later, there was a distinct twitch of Naji's thumb against the brick he held. The man's body jumped spasmodically as a volley of gunfire ripped into him, and he tumbled backward into the water.

A voice yelled, "Back off, back off! He armed a bomb! Back off!"

The watchers in Foxborough watched, mesmerized, as the armada of helicopters and boats hastily retreated from the dinghy. Several minutes went by as they waited for an explosion. Helicopter Air5 was just settling into a hover when a plume of water erupted, thrusting the dinghy a good fifty feet in the air before spilling it back into the water.

Chapter 58

H e checked his watch for the third time in ten minutes and anxiously toyed with his napkin. *Calm down and stop fidgeting,* he told himself. *It's all under control.* Having very limited exposure to fieldwork over the last decade, he knew that his skills were rusty. Admittedly, he was a good operative, but not a star, and was much more adept at playing a supporting role in an operation than starring in it. Strategy and planning were his forte, and he had used them in good measure for tonight's operation. The devil was in the details. He had repeatedly refined and honed the plan until he could no longer detect any faults. He could not afford the slightest deviation; it had to be perfect.

None of this would have been necessary, he thought, if it hadn't been for Cat Powell. He would have quietly stashed the money in one of his offshore accounts while the blame for the explosion of the fuel tanks fell squarely on some crazy radical

Islamists. No one would have been the wiser. He'd used similar methods over the years to skim from black ops accounts, always careful to leave a trail of breadcrumbs pointing to someone else as the guilty party. In every case but one, the diversion of money had gone undetected.

In that single failed instance, he'd chosen Tom Powell's cousin, Arnie, as the patsy. Everyone knew Arnie was a computer geek, so sampling some of Uncle Sam's bankroll wasn't beyond the man's capabilities. Arnie was a nobody and would never have been able to prove he hadn't dipped his fingers in the cookie jar. The timing and circumstances had dovetailed exquisitely. There was Arnie, buying a house with funds straight out of a Swiss bank account, at precisely the time that he was eyeing a big, loose account that appeared to have little oversight. When the account unexpectedly became the target of a random audit, the investigators followed a path that led straight to Arnie's newly purchased doorstep. That Arnie had a close relationship with Cat Powell made it even more delicious.

He stood when Serita returned, and graciously held the chair as she resumed her seat at the table. "Would you care for another coffee?"

"I would, thank you. Dinner was exquisite. Thank you so much for inviting me."

"It's a well-deserved reward for your hard work."

He'd first met the young woman on an impromptu visit to the Harvard Square apartment, the day after learning about the existence of the worm file. Serita had been circumspect and initially reluctant to share information about how the worm functioned or the type of information it was revealing. Over the course of an hour, and facing a barrage of questions from three senior employees of the agency, she had weakened. She was smart and she was loyal, but she was hopelessly naive when it came to the political infrastructure of the intelligence community. The poor girl actually believed that they were all on the same team.

When she had described the type of data being mined by the worm, he had mustered all of his strength to maintain his composure. He knew, beyond any doubt, that somewhere in those files was a thread that could lead back to him. That very night, he began taking steps to remove any traces of his involvement. Now, with Cat an urn of ashes on a mantel and the server having been purged of incriminating files, he merely needed to tie up a few loose ends. It was a shame, really, but at least Serita had enjoyed an elegant dinner as her last meal.

He mimed to the waiter to bring the bill and a coffee refill. He mentally calculated the total, added a hefty tip, and laid a pile of cash on the table. He checked his watch once again. Nine ten. He offered Serita an apologetic smile.

"May I borrow your phone this evening? Mine seems to have died for no apparent reason, and I won't be able to have it looked at until tomorrow."

She hesitated only a moment before returning the smile and extracting the phone from her purse. "Of course. I charged it earlier this evening; it should be good to go."

He took the phone and stepped to the back of the restaurant. Cradling the phone, he sent the first text.

Need you here. Saw Smith at
restaurant. Overheard phone
call re payment. He is meeting
contact named Jalil re c4. Suspect Jalil is member of terrorist
cell. Seaport, parking lot A St,
trailer in lot. I am following.

The replies from Jones came in almost instantly.

Wed 9:14 PM

On my way. 30 min. You are
NOT cleared.

Wed 9:14 PM

DO NOT FOLLOW. STAND
DOWN.

He smiled. The mention of Jalil had done the trick. He dialed a number from memory and waited for the man to answer.

"Yeah."

"Don't talk—there's no time—just listen. I've got word
that JB is in trouble. He's being held at the Seaport." He heard
a sharp intake of breath as the listener mentally translated *JB*
to *Jalil Badakhshanian*. This is a need-to-know situation, and
you're the only one in position. You're on your own." Roger
rattled off the location. "He's too important to lose. Get him

out of there and call me when you have him."

Roger disconnected without waiting for a response and lingered at the rear of the restaurant for another ten minutes. At nine twenty-five he pasted a mask of urgency on his face and hurried back to the table.

He whispered urgently in Serita's ear, "We have a problem. Are you armed?"

Her eyes grew wide, and she nodded, "Yes."

"You need to get in your car right now and go to the Seaport. I've got word that Jones is meeting up with a terrorist to buy explosives. We've had our eyes on him for some time, and now we have him."

He shuffled her out of the restaurant and gave her the location. "I'm going to call for a tactical team. Keep an eye on the place, but if Jones gets there before we do, try to stop the meeting."

Serita ran for her car.

Chapter 59

Cat had found Smith easily enough. For an operative, he was infuriatingly predictable when it came to food and drink. When in town and not engaged in an active operation, he frequented an upscale pub on Beacon Street. Cat found a space close to the entrance and settled in for what she expected to be a long wait. She was taken by surprise when he bolted from the bar a few minutes later—clutching his phone and pecking feverishly at its screen—and ran to his automobile.

She was now three cars behind Smith and headed over the Congress Street Bridge into the Seaport District. The route didn't give her any comfort. While the northern part of the Seaport was undergoing a massive renovation effort, the southern area was still rundown and crime was rampant. At A Street, Smith abruptly pulled into the right lane and turned south. The two cars ahead of her went straight, and Cat fought the instinct to swerve after him. She continued straight, took a left at the next corner and looped back around. She turned onto A Street just in time to see the flare of brake lights as a car in the distance turned right.

The road was deserted; it threaded through an area of dilapidated buildings before spilling into a flattened wasteland of massive parking lots on the right and left. She spotted the lights of Smith's car diagonally across the lot to the right, about three hundred feet away. She was exposed and made a snap decision to ease into a space on the street and kill the car's lights. If Smith was watching, and she assumed he would be attentive to anyone nearby, he would expect a flash of light as the occupant exited the car. She obliged and walked a few steps, in the opposite direction from the lot, until she was out of view.

She tucked herself into the building's entryway and leaned against the cold rough brick of the building while composing her thoughts. Obviously Smith was headed into the lot, but why? She briefly contemplated trying to reach out to Paul Marshfield, but quashed the idea. Maybe, she thought, when she knew more. She took a deep breath and scurried around the corner toward the lot.

The parking area appeared to be rectangular, and Smith had driven his car down the street opposite to where she now stood. This side of the lot had trees evenly spaced beside the brick walkway lining the fence, and she crept slowly from tree to tree. The fence ended with an entry to the lot, a replica of the one Smith had used on the other side. She positioned herself against the last tree and gave silent thanks that she had worn dark brown tonight.

Cat studied the landscape in front of her. The lot was poorly illuminated and nearly empty, save an old construction trailer standing forlornly near the middle. On the alert for any sound or movement, she heard Smith's car before she saw it, lights off and slowly crunching across the broken pavement toward the trailer. She was momentarily startled by the squeal of tires behind her and flattened herself against the tree as a black SUV raced down the street toward her. The vehicle rocketed past, burst through the barrier, and screamed to a stop a few yards from the trailer.

The SUV's door flew open, and Cat watched, mesmerized, as the huge figure of Jones launched himself at the door to the trailer. She fleetingly wondered if Smith had lured him to this place. In the same instant, Smith flicked on his headlights, leaped out of his car, and sprinted toward Jones.

She was mentally trying to put the pieces together and make some sense of the two of them rushing to a meeting in a parking lot in South Boston, when she heard footsteps pounding the pavement toward the trailer. She was shocked to see a young woman run by, not ten feet away, with her gun drawn. The woman was screaming, "Freeze! Federal agent! Drop your weapon!"

Cat was dumbfounded. The woman looked and sounded like Serita, but Serita was a novice. What in the world would she be doing here? She felt the blood rush from her head as the sickening realization washed over her. Smith hadn't lured Jones here; someone else had baited both Smith and Jones into coming to this desolate place. This wasn't a meeting—Jones and Smith were targets.

Cat registered Jones running out of the trailer—cradling a bundle in his arms—and managed only to scream a single frantic

"Noooo" before the blast shook the earth. The shock wave knocked her down and blew out windows in the building behind her, raining shards of glass and other debris on the street below. Performing a quick self-assessment before trying to move, she touched her face and realized it was wet with blood.

Dazed and unsteady, she staggered to her feet and stumbled toward the crater that had once been the trailer. She spotted a mound, and upon drawing closer, realized it was Serita. She winced at what remained of the beautiful and intelligent young woman whose life had held so much promise. Struck by shrapnel, Serita had a gaping wound in her chest, and her eyes were lifeless. Of Smith, she saw no sign, save the remnant of what appeared to be a severed appendage.

She discovered Jones, facedown, thirty feet away. Beneath him lay Jalil. She checked each for a pulse and choked with emotion when she determined that both were still alive. Jones had a hole in his thigh, pulsing blood. She pulled the long wool scarf off her neck and shoved it into the wound, using the ends to tie it in place. She must have been talking or screaming, because Jones opened his eyes, focused unevenly on her face, and forced out the words, "Get out of here."

She heard sirens in the distance and knew there was nothing more she could do here. She raced back to her car and sped toward the highway.

Chapter 60

C at fled to Gloucester, donned the wig, and in the middle of the night, rapped on her landlady's door. With her damaged face lending credence to the narrative, Cat explained that her drunken husband had found her at work and that she had barely managed to escape. She thanked the older woman for her kindness and discretion, but told her that she was afraid to stay any longer and was moving out of state. As soon as the older woman retreated to her bedroom, Cat gathered her few belongings and the computer equipment and loaded them into the car.

She knew she was taking a risk driving the car. Certainly the authorities would be mounting an extensive investigation into the explosion at the Seaport. It was possible, even probable, that a camera mounted on one of the newer buildings in the district had captured the image of her car. But the flip side of simply disappearing without a trace was that her landlady would surely submit a missing person report. Any resulting probe into the whereabouts of one Elizabeth McCarthy would eventually point to Catherine Powell. Most of the world thought Cat dead, and it needed to stay that way for the moment.

She wound her way south, to Lynn, and parked two blocks from the church. She checked her watch: 4:30 a.m. The door to the rectory was locked, as she expected it would be, and she quickly worked the lock to gain entry. She had been in the rectory only once before and, given the location in which she found herself, murmured a quick prayer. Cat crept up the stairs to the second floor and knocked softly on the door. The disheveled and disgruntled man who answered couldn't conceal his shock. "Catherine?"

"I need help and a place to stay where no one will see me. I've nowhere else to go."

He opened the door and beckoned her inside.

Father Claudio Poratti and Cat had been casual friends for many years—he frequently attempting to cajole her into attending services, she always finding excuses. But despite the differences in their beliefs, never once had he berated her or threatened her with eternal damnation. He was, quite simply, a kind and caring human being.

She explained the situation as succinctly as possible. She was in the employ of an agency of the federal government, there had been a horrible incident, she was being set up by unknown persons, and she needed a place to stay for just a few days and a place to hide her car.

He didn't hesitate. "The room down the hall has fresh

sheets."

He invited her into a sitting room and turned on the television, channel surfing until he found a report in progress related to an explosion at the Seaport.

"... where he is in serious condition. While initial reports from the Boston PD stated that there were four victims, that figure has been revised, one of the victims apparently having been counted twice in the confusion. Again, two people have died, and one is in the hospital in serious condition, after an explosion in the A Street parking lot in the Seaport District. It is believed that all of the victims were homeless, and that the explosion occurred when they were trying to siphon gasoline from a car to use as fuel for a fire. Authorities have advised that they do not believe the incident had any connection to terrorism. This is Cassandra Sanders, reporting live from the Seaport."

Cat breathed a sigh of relief. Jalil's presence was being kept under wraps, but the questions remained about who had extricated him and whether he was truly safe.

Chapter 61

Thursday
Foxborough, Massachusetts

At 6:00 a.m. Lindsey was awakened from a deep, dreamless sleep by the pounding on the door, and stumbled to open it. Adrian's face was taut.

"Get dressed. We have a briefing in three minutes."

She threw on a pair of jeans and scurried to the bathroom, trying to remember the events of the previous evening. Her last recollections were of Naji's body being tossed about like a rag doll and Jason handing her two pills. She had no memory of getting into bed.

She found the others already gathered in the conference room, their faces haggard and their motions slow and sleep-deprived. She looked questioningly at Jason, who shook his head slightly. He had not slept. With the group assembled, Adrian activated the wall screen and turned up the speaker volume.

Ambassador Marshfield walked into view and tiredly faced

the camera. "Adrian, what's the latest on the attempted bombing at the tank farm?"

"Techs have finished processing the houseboat, the subject's room at the dorm, and what remained of the dinghy. The FBI is in possession of his computer and is interviewing anyone they know to have been acquainted with him. Our best estimate is that he had about two hundred pounds of plastic explosive, C-4 we believe. We're basing the amount on the dimensions of a hollowed-out space in the subject's mattress. We know that at least one block was detonated. Divers will be in the water at first light to attempt recovery of the remaining blocks. The channel is about forty feet deep, visibility is minimal, the current is strong, and the water temperature is only thirty-four degrees. It will be a long day."

"Is there any danger of the C-4 exploding if a vessel were to strike it?"

"The explosive itself is very stable. You can put a match to it or shoot it with a gun, and it doesn't explode. It needs a primary explosive, like a blasting cap or det cord, to set it off. The problem is that we don't know if the fool inserted the blasting caps in advance. We're working under the assumption that he did, because he would be in a hurry. We also don't know with certainty how they were to be activated. We suspect a timing device. After reviewing the video feed, we believe he activated a timer with his thumb. The explosion occurred four minutes later. But he may have used a different method for the remaining blocks."

"What do we know about him?"

"He was born in Dubai, of all places. His mother was

originally from Iran, and her family escaped the country in 1978. His father is a diplomat. They married in 1990 and had four children. Naji was the second, born in 1992. They spent almost fifteen years in the Indian subcontinent, with the first half in Islamabad and the last half in Delhi. He was issued a student visa by the US Embassy in Delhi and arrived in New York last June. Initial reports have it that he spent the summer with relatives in New York before moving up to Boston in August. We're digging through every aspect of his life."

Paul Marshfield ruffled through a stack of papers and drummed his fingers for a moment before speaking. "There was a second incident last night. The agent whom you know as Smith and a young female operative, whose name was Serita, were killed in an explosion in the Seaport District. Jones is in the hospital, in serious condition, but his injuries aren't believed to be life-threatening."

Lindsey's face crumpled as she tried to process what Ambassador Marshfield was saying. She swiveled to face Adrian. "Jones got a text last night. It was after nine. He had to meet someone. He said it was important, and that's why he left us."

Adrian nodded. "Gabe mentioned it. Melodie and Trent are pulling the records. We'll have them soon."

"This is a terrible situation. Cat, Jones, Smith, Serita, and—"Melodie caught herself before mentioning Jalil—"and I'm just glad there weren't others who were hurt. At least the leadership is still standing."

Jason rubbed his eyes and tried to concentrate. "Um. What caused that explosion?"

Adrian sat down heavily. "The explosive experts are telling

us it was also C-4. We should know soon enough if it was from the same source as that from the dinghy. Most C-4 has taggants that can be used to identify the source. It's probably premature to say, but my gut tells me we'll find a match."

Lindsey's intuitive sense was tingling. "So if the C-4 is from the same source, these bombings may be related. But what ties Smith and Jones to Naji?"

Adrian's eyes narrowed. "Cat."

Lindsey frowned and turned back to face the Ambassador. "So this is about what you said before, that someone set Cat up?"

"We think so, yes. And I don't want to muddy the waters, but you should be aware that, about ten years ago, a similar financial incident took place. Though the case was never proven, some of the evidence pointed to Arnie. It severely damaged his reputation."

"Are you saying that if we pull on the thread to Cat, we'll find that it's the same person who tried to set up Arnie?"

Paul Marshfield's gaze bored into her. "That's a leap at this early stage, but it's an avenue worth exploring. There are similarities, and I don't like coincidences. Let's see what the evidence says."

Melodie's eyes glittered as she turned to face Paul. "If both are the work of one person, it's unlikely that he, or she, would lay idle for ten years."

"Indeed."

She arched her eyebrows and clicked her mouse. "We'll just keep that in mind, won't we?" She directed her eyes back to the camera. "In the interim, we have the transcript between

Jones and Serita. I'm downloading it for you now. We have redacted certain information for which you are not cleared. But I think that this exchange sufficiently reveals the nature of the events leading to Jones and Serita being together at the Seaport."

The file appeared on the screen.

[Serita] Wed 9:13 PM

Need you here. Saw Smith at restaurant. Overheard phone call re payment. He is meeting contact named ██████ re c4. Suspect ██████ is member of terrorist cell. Seaport, parking lot A St, trailer in lot. I am following.

[Jones] Wed 9:14 PM

On my way. 30 min. You are NOT cleared.

[Jones] Wed 9:14 PM

DO NOT FOLLOW. STAND DOWN.

[Jones] Wed 9:16 PM

Ack prev STAND DOWN.

[Serita] Wed 9:23 PM

Where r u

[Jones] Wed 9:28 PM

95N Ack prev
STAND DOWN

Adrian interpreted the content. "From the files she gave us, we know that Cat suspected Smith, but she was lacking any solid proof. I don't know if this agent Serita followed Smith to the restaurant or saw him by coincidence; perhaps she had her own suspicions about him. In any event, as you can read from the transcript, at some point she overheard a suspicious conversation and decided to follow him. She did this despite her lack of training and despite being told to stand down. We will probably never know why she didn't acknowledge Jones. It's a terrible loss that she followed Smith and lost her life because of it.

"We will, of course, interview Jones, and we are beginning a formal investigation. We would like for you to participate, at least to some degree, to bring fresh eyes and an external perspective to the data we have. We are going to inspect every minute detail of Smith's life: his activities, his whereabouts, his acquaintances, his reading habits, and what he ate for breakfast. Until we answer the questions of why he did it and who was helping him, this case will remain open, and the investigation will continue."

Tom Powell, who hadn't uttered a single word, rested his elbows on the table and perched his head on his folded hands. "Well, that's wrapped up very nicely, then. So why isn't Cat here?"

Paul gazed at him steadily. "Cat has gone dark. Arnie tried the cell number she's been using, and it goes straight to the default voice mail. We can't locate a signal for it on any tower in the metro area. I think she tossed it. Arnie knew where she'd been staying and drove up there early this morning. She's gone, along with her belongings, and at this point we don't know why. Of course, we find this disturbing. I'm hoping that she'll surface when she feels safe or when she has information to share, but you know her better than I. Until she tells us otherwise, the story remains that Catherine and Tom Powell died in an explosion at their home last Friday."

Chapter 62

Adrian returned to Boston to assist with evidence processing and analysis of the two explosions. The other members of the team worked for three days and were still unable to identify the middleman between Smith and Naji, the elusive figure with the e-mail account linked to *conrad27.barrymore@gmail.com*. Whoever he was, he was exceptionally stealthy. Similar to the methods by which Cat had tracked e-mails leading back to Smith, the team was seeking any clue that would lead to Conrad27. Even with the advanced capabilities of the server and the availability of the actual files, as opposed to the images Cat had used, it was painstaking and discouraging work.

Particularly frustrating was that the only evidence supporting the theory of Smith's treachery was contained in the files that Cat had supplied.

A credit card charge put Smith at his favorite pub on Beacon

Street before the explosion, and he had paid his bill at 9:16 p.m. Adrian and a team from the FBI ripped through Smith's townhome and found nothing to spark interest, aside from a small collection of soft-porn DVDs tucked into a well-worn tote bag in the master closet. The Bureau confiscated Smith's personal computer and other electronics and shipped them to its laboratory in Quantico, Virginia. Within twenty-four hours, an exact duplicate of each device, including the software and data, was in the hands of Jason and Gabe.

The computer's files revealed little aside from Smith's obsession with whales. The browser history showed that he had recently visited a number of sites about India, including several related to the attack on the Taj Hotel in Mumbai in 2008. Millions of people visit random sites every day when some random event stimulates their interest or sparks curiosity. The website visits were probably exactly that—a case of random access—but Melodie dutifully logged into the central database and recorded the links as a curious anomaly in the Smith investigation.

Smith's bank accounts likewise showed no suspicious activity, and his assets and credit balances were squarely on par with a civil servant who had invested moderately but wisely.

Most problematic was that, despite Serita's text saying that she overheard a call from Smith, they could find no log of a call placed from Smith's phone that night. This led to speculation that Smith had used a burner phone. They pulled recordings of all the calls received by nearby cell towers and ran them through a highly accurate voice recognition program. But when they tried to find a voice match, first for Smith and then for Serita, the program came up empty.

Jason, his countenance strained, posted a time line on the screen. "We missed something that's staring us right in the face. What do you see here?" he asked.

(9:10?) Serita overhears Smith
9:13 Serita texts Jones
9:14 Jones texts Serita (twice)
9:15 Serita calls Smith
9:16 Jones texts Serita
9:23 Serita texts Jones
9:28 Jones texts Serita

Melodie noticed the anomaly first. "Serita called Smith *after* overhearing his call about the C4—and *after* she texted Jones. Why would she do that?"

"I've been asking myself the same thing. We've been so focused on the texts between Serita and Jones that we overlooked the timing of the one actual voice call. It's the one entry that makes no sense; something isn't right."

Melodie was quick to respond. "I concur. And,"—she paused thoughtfully—"the entire series of communications is very suspect. To further stir the pot, I'm very disturbed about the offshore accounts. It's my assessment that they were too easily discovered, given Smith's credentials. It's almost as if someone wanted us to discover the accounts. I don't like it. I'm beginning to wonder if the evidence pointing to Smith is completely manufactured.

"I've been operating under the premise that Smith was the

guilty party, and I focused my efforts on locating evidence to substantiate that conclusion. I screwed up. I'm now of the opinion that we should start over and approach the problem from a different direction." Melodie's expression was stony, and it was evident how much the admission had cost her.

"Everyone has been working under that same assumption," Lindsey countered. "Don't beat yourself up for following the evidence down a logical path."

"But it's my job to analyze and find those facets that aren't expected."

"And you will. So shrug it off and look at it from a fresh perspective. We should all do the same."

Melodie smiled good-naturedly. "Thank you for the encouragement. I freely admit when I'm wrong; I just don't like it. Let's discuss this with the Ambassador. He's on a flight to Boston as we speak."

Chapter 63

Sunday
Boston, Massachusetts

Paul Marshfield pulled the wool watch cap over his hair and turned up the collar of his parka before pushing on the revolving door at the main entrance of the sprawling facility that was Massachusetts General Hospital. Eschewing his contact lenses and usual suit and tie, he'd chosen casual dress and a pair of heavy framed glasses in an effort to avoid recognition. The press would be decidedly unwelcome today. He lowered his head and squeezed into the crowded elevator, pressing the button for the fifth floor.

The door to Jones's private room was ajar, and Paul slipped into the room unnoticed by the squad of nurses hovering around the central desk down the hall. He pushed the door closed and stepped toward the bed. Jones lay amid a sea of plastic tubing and blinking monitors. Paul expected that Jones would be asleep, and was surprised to find Jones's eyes open and following his movements. "I would ask how you're feeling, but it's a rather stupid question."

Jones smiled wanly and, with some effort, muttered, "Better than the alternative."

"Indeed. I got the call last night that you were awake. I can't tell you how relieved we all are. You lost a lot of blood. It was touch and go there for a while."

"The docs took good care of me, I guess. They say that after some rehab for my leg and arm, I should be as good as new."

"What do you remember?"

"I got that text from Serita. She said she was following Smith and that she'd overheard him mention Jalil. No way. I knew something was wrong. Smith wouldn't have spoken about Jalil in any place where someone might have overheard."

"What else?"

"I drove hell-bent ... right up to the steps of the trailer. Smith was at the corner of the trailer, and I saw his face in my headlights. He looked totally befuddled, like he didn't know what either of us was doing there. I just reacted, I guess. Bashed in the door and found Jalil unconscious on the floor. The whole situation smelled. But I grabbed him and took a leap out the door. That's all I remember until I woke up here. How's the kid?"

"From what I've been told, Jalil was badly beaten and tortured. Roger managed to keep his presence at the explosion under wraps, so nobody knows Jalil was there. Roger got him into a top-grade psychiatric care hospital under a different name."

"Roger is nothing if not resourceful."

"It's a good place, but the shrinks don't know if he'll ever recover. We sent a couple of people to try and interview him, but he's drugged and unresponsive. Is there anything else that you remember about that night? Was anyone else there?"

"I don't think so, except I thought I remembered Cat being there. Speaking of Cat, I've got a message from that priest friend of hers."

"The one from the funeral?"

"The same. He came late yesterday evening. For a moment I thought he was here to give me last rites. Why else would some Catholic priest be in my room? I have to tell you, that was an interesting moment."

Jones pulled the sheet aside and pointed to one of the ties on his hospital gown. "He said it was an important message from Cat, and wanted me to safeguard it until you got here."

Paul was stymied for a minute, until he saw that the tie was wrapped around a rolled-up piece of paper. He unwound the paper from its cocoon. "You've read it?"

"Of course."

Paul read the note. "So Cat *was* there. She tried to use her scarf to stanch the bleeding in your leg."

"Yeah, I owe her one. Who do you think is behind all this?"

Paul grimaced and shook his head. "Initially, everything seemed to point to Smith. But we've found no solid evidence, and from what Cat said in this message, she's rethinking it, too."

Jones shifted his bulk, trying to find a more comfortable position. "She was convinced someone had painted a target on her back. Her instincts are usually spot-on."

"I think she's right. You have any thoughts?"

"You mean her enemies? Pfft. I can't count that high."

Chapter 64

Paul Marshfield arrived at the Foxborough house midafternoon and eagerly shared news from the hospital. "Jones woke up yesterday. He's groggy, but responsive. He'll need recovery time, and rehab, but the doctors don't expect any permanent impairment. He was exceptionally fortunate."

Murmurs of relief swept through the room.

The Ambassador continued, "Unfortunately, he remembers little about the explosion, so there's no help from that quarter. But we have an interesting development. It seems that a priest stopped by to see Jones last night, bearing a gift—a note from Cat."

Tom pumped his fist into the air. Remembering the priest from Cat's funeral, Lindsey wondered about a connection. "Who was he?"

"I'm not sure, but you can ask her when she arrives. The

note contained instructions for contacting her, which I did. It took some convincing, but she'll be joining us here later today. I've dispatched Arnie to drive her. Before we discuss what she shared with me, tell me what you've found."

Melodie spoke for us. "We've found, or not found, enough to suspect that Smith may not have been the party behind these events." She quickly recited the inconsistencies in the narrative that had labeled Smith as a traitor.

The Ambassador's face betrayed no emotion as he digested Melodie's words. Finally, he nodded and sat down. "Cat subscribes to your point of view. She now believes that both Smith and Jones were lured there. According to Cat, Serita is a huge question mark because she followed Smith without authorization and ignored Jones's order to stand down. She believes that Serita's actions were out of character. Her working theory is that Serita was somehow coerced into driving to the Seaport and was unknowingly the bait for Smith and Jones."

The implications were shocking, and the room grew somber as the group absorbed the ramifications. Melodie's eyes were huge, leading Paul Marshfield to ask, "What are you thinking?"

"That would mean that whoever is responsible ..."

Paul finished the thought. "... would have an awareness of Smith and Jones and Serita. Indeed."

Chapter 65

Sunday night
Foxborough, Massachusetts

C at arrived in Foxborough in the early evening to a chorus of enthusiastic welcomes. The celebration was short-lived, as the Ambassador quickly dismissed everyone from the conference room and sequestered himself with Cat.

"Before I bring in Trent and Melodie, I'd like an explanation about why you decided to drop off the face of the earth."

If he was expecting that Cat would be chagrined, he was mistaken. "I couldn't trust anyone associated with this business."

Paul's eyebrows shot up. "You can't be serious."

"Very. You're one of the very few people I trust completely. But you're also surrounded by eyes and ears that I don't know. Someone with deep access went to great lengths to set me up and, I now believe, set up Smith as well. By staging my death, I removed myself as a potential target. It also wiped out any concern that I might interfere with whatever was planned and gave me time to investigate. I gave you all of that information as soon as was practical."

"But your assessment pointed the finger at Smith."

"It did, yes, but think about it. Whoever staged this has an incredible reach. Very few people have the depth of access and knowledge that would be required to set up both Smith and me and—perhaps more revealing—make me believe that Smith had turned."

"All of that may be true, but I would argue that you have some responsibility to share your concerns with those who have chosen you as the operational leader of this unit."

Cat shifted uncomfortably, then straightened and asked defiantly, "And if I had shared my concerns with you, would you have shared them with others? And after you knew I was still alive, did you share that information with anyone?"

Paul Marshfield didn't blink. "To the first question, not without running it by you first. To the second, no."

Cat looked at him quizzically. "I did what I felt was right—and we still don't know who's pulling the strings. Do you really think I was wrong?"

"Honestly? I'm not sure. Your instincts are remarkable and you've spent your career keeping information buttoned-up tight. But our new unit operates under a different paradigm. It's imperative that we keep each other informed and openly discuss our intended actions. We'll fail otherwise."

"Point taken. You're right."

"I need to tell you that Adrian Santori from the FBI is now onboard. I know that we hadn't finalized him, but he rose to the top when he called me after your visit to DC. The day before you disappeared, his director and I agreed to bring him to Boston to meet with you. He'd only been in the city for about three hours before you died. It was quite the initiation."

"What about Lindsey and her friends? They're here at the safe house. They've obviously become involved."

"One of the directives in our mandate was to use civilian personnel to add perspective and diverse points of view. They've performed exceptionally well. I'd like to keep them on to help us determine who was behind the plot to attack the tank farm and the explosion that killed Smith and Serita. After that, we could discuss keeping them on retainer, to provide services as the need arises. What do you think?"

"As analysts, correct? No field operations?"

"Correct."

"Agreed. Do they know about Jalil?"

"Not yet. I'm not sure that we should take that step right now."

"That feels right, although there may come a time when they need to be told."

He smiled. "You might also be interested to know that Lindsey and Adrian have begun to develop something of a friendship. I overheard him asking her to go out to dinner once this is over. I didn't hear the response, but I suspect she said yes."

"That could be a complicating factor."

"Maybe, but it could also work to the unit's advantage. Let's see how it plays out."

"Agreed."

Chapter 66

C at sat down with the team to pick apart the events leading up to the explosion. She related how when Serita ran into the lot, yelling at Smith and Jones to freeze, she had immediately sensed a trap. She'd screamed a warning, but too late.

"I keep coming back to Serita. I can't imagine what she was doing there. She had no real operational experience, and she disregarded Jones's direct orders to stand down. She was eager, yes, but she wasn't stupid. I have no evidence to support it, but I strongly feel that the three of them were the target of an assassination."

Gabe strummed his fingers on the table. "Melodie, you made a statement earlier that piqued my curiosity. You said something to the effect that the leadership was still standing."

Melodie's head bobbed up and down. "That's right. Roger came out of this unscathed."

"So where was he that night?"

Trent and Melodie glanced at one another, then at Paul

Marshfield.

"Pull his phone logs," Paul ordered.

They had the answer within minutes. At 9:13 p.m., when Serita had supposedly sent the text to Jones, Roger's phone had been within two feet of her location. In fact, Roger's phone had been in close proximity to hers for the better part of the evening.

Lindsey stared at the GPS logs for both phones. "So, this establishes that Serita and Roger were together almost the entire evening."

"No," interjected Melodie. "It only proves that the two phones were close together. What if Serita didn't actually have her phone with her? What if, instead, Roger had it?"

Cat gasped in astonishment. "That would certainly explain why she didn't respond to Jones."

Melodie had another thought. "After the explosion, where was Serita's phone? Did they find it?"

Trent keyed in a query for evidence gathered from the scene. "Yes. It was in the parking lot, about three hundred feet from the center of the explosion."

Cat's eyes narrowed. "I want Adrian to concentrate on that phone. Was there other debris in the area? If so, did any of that debris belong to Serita? What kind of damage did the phone sustain? Did she have a belt clip or some other holder for the phone? Because when I last saw her, she was running into the lot with both hands on her gun. If the phone is in her pocket or purse, how does it end up all by itself three hundred feet away?"

Trent typed rapidly, recording Cat's questions to send to

Adrian.

Jason stood and began to pace. "There's more. If we think that Roger had Serita's phone, that means he was there, at the scene. He probably witnessed the entire thing. Let's find out if he had a car, and if so, where it was. We can use map overlays to plot the time and location of each phone and each car before and after the event. If our theory is correct, the data will support it."

Chapter 67

I t took two days for the team to accurately reconstruct the whereabouts of the phones and automobiles belonging to Smith, Jones, Serita, and Roger. What they discovered made them nauseous.

Roger had flown to Boston on the afternoon of the explosion and had rented a car at Logan airport before driving into the city. At 7:45 p.m., the cars of Serita and Roger had been parked within a half block of one another, and they both had begun to move in the direction of the Seaport at 9:29 p.m. Serita's car crossed the Summer Street Bridge and stopped on a narrow street just north of the parking lot at 9:41 p.m. Roger's car, however, had stopped on A Street at 9:42 p.m. and was stationary for seven minutes. The phones of both Roger and Serita were in the same location as Roger's car.

Adrian determined that none of the other debris near the phone had originated from Serita's belongings. Her torn clothing and other possessions had largely dispersed in a cone that extended about seventy-five feet to the west of where the trailer had once stood. Her phone, however, had been found well to the east of the trailer.

Adrian visited the site and streamed video from the geo position where Roger's car had been parked. From that vantage point, there was a clear view of the trailer and the entire lot. Adrian parked in the same spot, rolled down his window, and heaved an old phone in the direction of the trailer. It flew across the street, over the fence, and into the lot, bouncing twice before coming to rest within ten feet of the spot where Serita's phone had been found. While it wasn't scientific proof, it substantially bolstered their belief that Roger had thrown Serita's phone into the parking area immediately after the explosion. When combined with the fact that Roger had never reported meeting or speaking with Serita that evening, and had never mentioned witnessing the explosion, the evidence was substantial.

Smith had driven to the Seaport from his favorite pub in Back Bay and had been nowhere near Serita or her car at any time during the evening until converging at the parking lot. There was a record of a two-minute call from Serita's phone to Smith at 9:15 p.m., just after the text was sent to Jones.

Once the team pulled the first thread, the remaining fabric of lies unraveled. Trent and Melodie compared time stamps and IP routing paths from e-mail, cell tower hits for mobiles, and archived GPS logs for the cars. Smith could not possibly have sent all the e-mails and made all the calls attributed to him. But one person certainly could have. In each case, Roger's location matched precisely.

Chapter 68

Over the next weeks, the team documented every detail related to Naji's thwarted attack on the tank farm and the events surrounding the explosion in the Seaport District.

They had been stumped by the lack of a voice match to the call that was placed from Serita to Smith at 9:15 p.m. But after identifying Roger as the most likely person of interest, they ran another search for Roger's voice. Smith's single-word response upon answering the phone, *Yeah,* had not been enough to trigger recognition. Now, the program captured Roger's voice and they heard him directing Smith to the Seaport. A shiver of anger ripped down Cat's spine as she listened to the man sending Smith to his death.

Agency personnel installed microphones and tiny cameras at strategic positions in Roger's office at the agency, capturing every action. The FBI obtained sealed warrants allowing them to search his residence, properties, cars, and storage units. They tapped his phones, tracked his credit card and bank transactions, inserted themselves into the computer network and monitoring cameras in his home, and assigned eight agents to watch and record his every move when away from the office.

It was during one such recording that they discovered the metal box embedded in the fifth step of the stairway to the second floor. From the fourth step, Roger reached for the fifth baluster in the railing and gave it a sharp twist. The tread of the fifth step released, and he lifted it out of the way to reveal a small metal box. He sat on the fourth step and opened the box. They watched as he withdrew a photograph and caressed it lovingly, before setting it aside and retrieving a bundle of letters. Ten minutes later, he carefully placed the items back in the box and returned the step to its original position.

Cat was about to issue an order when Adrian spoke. "We're on it. As soon as he leaves for work tomorrow, I'll have a team get photos of everything in that box, put everything back exactly as they found it, and send us the files. They'll be back by eleven."

If Adrian expected to find bank statements, ledgers, receipts, or other evidence regarding the offshore accounts and materials purchased for the harbor bombing, he was disappointed. "They're telling me there's not much of interest—photographs of a girl, a bunch of letters, and a journal—nothing that immediately stands out as damning evidence. But I guess we'd better read the letters."

Cat nodded in agreement and waited as the tech in DC sent the images from the camera to the printer in Foxborough. She poured a cup of coffee and reached for the first stack of papers that emerged. The handwriting on the first page was feminine, addressed to *My darling Roger*, and signed *Your one and only love, Anoo.*

She read the first two paragraphs. *What the hell?* Speeding through the remainder of the first letter, she reached for the second. Halfway through, she yelled at the tech, "Where is that picture of the girl?"

The tech found the photograph, fed it to the printer, and Adrian pulled it from the tray. Cat yanked it from his hand and looked at the face; a wave of nausea engulfed her. "Damning enough."

For the next thirty minutes, Cat listened as Adrian urged her to tell him about the letters and the photographs. He finally threw up his hands in defeat and phoned Paul Marshfield, who was on a plane to Boston within the hour. Cat curled into a chair and was silent until Paul Marshfield arrived. She stood and steered him back out the door. "Let's take a walk." She refused to talk with anyone else.

The amassed evidence would see Roger facing lethal injection or confinement to a maximum-security federal facility for the remainder of his days. Cat freely admitted that his fate didn't much matter to her one way or the other, but before they stuck a needle in his arm, she wanted answers. On the other hand, she thought, Roger was far too arrogant to be cooperative. They might never learn the extent of his betrayal.

There were grave concerns about the identity of the middleman between Naji and Roger: the person using the email *conrad27.barrymore@gmail.com*. At a minimum, they now knew that Conrad27 had supplied the C-4 intended for the tank farm attack and had been instrumental in plotting Jalil Badakhshanian's abduction. The how and why of Jalil's captivity were still unknown, as was whether or not his cover had been fully penetrated.

Initially, they hoped that Jalil would be able to shed some light on the people behind his abduction. The team that had been sent to interview him came back empty-handed and distressed about Jalil's mental condition. After discovering that Roger was behind the explosion, Cat and Paul became extremely concerned about the nature of Jalil's confinement. Their level of concern became greatly elevated when they learned that Roger placed a call to the hospital every day to inquire after Jalil's health.

Cat was horrified that they couldn't take any steps to extract or evaluate Jalil without endangering the investigation and would have to wait until Roger was removed from circulation. There were dark moments when Cat was supremely tempted to knock on the front door of the Badakhshanian home and lead them to the bedside of their heroic son. Cat buried those thoughts in the deepest recesses of her mind and focused on Roger. His time as a free man was becoming shorter. *Soon*, she thought, *soon*.

Epilogue

June, present day
Fairfax, Virginia

Cat selected a table at the far end of the Hyatt's reception area and ordered from the hostess, paying cash when the small coffeepot was placed on the table. Ten minutes later, Paul Marshfield emerged from the elevator and scanned the faces in the vicinity before selecting a seat midway across the room. He placed an order with the hostess, sipped his coffee, and toyed with the scrambled eggs before pushing them aside. He poured a second cup of coffee and relaxed in his seat, habitually folding the *Washington Post* into quarters. Assuming a preoccupied air, he absently tapped his index finger against the back of the paper. Once. Twice. After several minutes, he arched his back in an exaggerated stretch and signaled the hostess for the bill.

Cat rose and walked toward the door leading to the rear courtyard. She stepped to the curb and leaned casually against a small tree, cigarette and lighter at the ready should anyone question why she was there.

Paul's car swept around the corner of the building and came to a stop beside her. She opened the back door and slid in, swiftly pulling the door closed behind her as Paul accelerated away from the hotel.

Thirty minutes later, he pulled into a gas station, and as he pumped a few gallons into the tank, urged Cat into the front passenger seat.

He looked at her with concern. "Are you ready?"

"Oh yes. Let's go nail this bastard," she replied.

The guard at the gate accepted their identification to compare with the admission list scheduled for that day, while cameras dutifully examined and recorded the car, its occupants, and its undercarriage. By now, the identification and facial recognition software were sending alarms to the guard's workstation, although, to his credit, he didn't flinch. The instructions accompanying the authorization, and signed by the director, were clear: admit and do not detain.

The first barrier was lowered, and they moved into the box, where additional electronic examination was conducted on the car. As requested, Paul popped open both the hood and the trunk for further inspection. Once cleared, the second barrier was lowered, and they were directed to a visitors' parking area not far from the entry.

They presented their credentials and passed through the building's security checkpoint without incident, although there were a few raised eyebrows among the guards and a rising buzz of whispering as they stepped toward the officer waiting beside the open elevator. The officer keyed his access to the seventh floor. They ascended in silence, and when the doors opened, the officer escorted them to the door of the conference room. He was quickly joined by three men wearing sidearms.

He pressed his ID against the screen and waited for the electronic lock to be deactivated from the inside. Cat waited as Paul entered the room. She heard murmured greetings from the director, and another man chimed in similarly. Cat felt her skin crawl upon hearing the voice she'd known for so long.

She stepped into the room.

Roger Pulaski's face paled, but he maintained his composure. "Catherine. It appears that the reports of your death were greatly exaggerated. You're looking well. Dare I ask where you've been?"

"Looking for you." Cat waited and could sense the electricity as his brain struggled to process an appropriate response.

"Looking for me? Well, I've been right here, wondering if you might have somehow staged your demise. Really, Cat, a propane explosion? I would have expected something less mundane. What a waste of a beautiful home. But then, you probably thought that your finances could sustain the hit. That is, until we prevailed upon our friendly Caribbean neighbors to freeze your funds. I must admit, I'm both surprised and delighted to see you here." He turned to the guards. "Please place Ms. Powell under arrest."

Watching him now, it was easy to see how his treachery had gone undetected and how he'd passed every polygraph for all these years. The man was a gifted actor and consummate liar. She almost had to admire his talent.

"The guards aren't here for me, Roger."

His eyes narrowed slightly, but he seemed otherwise unperturbed. "What is your point, Catherine?"

"You can stop lying. We all know what you did. You've been funneling money from Agency accounts for the last twelve years, and you set me up to take the fall, just as you did to Arnie a decade ago. The theft itself is despicable. But that you had knowledge of the planned bombing in Boston Harbor and orchestrated the deaths of Smith and Serita—and almost killed Jones and Jalil—well, that is unforgivable."

His eyes narrowed, and his tone was icy. "You have nothing."

"Oh, but we do. We have proof, Roger, proof that will stand in a court of law. The auditors are estimating that you skimmed about five million dollars. It would seem a nice chunk of change for your retirement."

"The accounts are under aliases that you use, Ms. Powell. Not me. You can't twist this."

"Well, Roger, there might have been reasonable doubt if you were just stockpiling the money. But you weren't, were you? This was never solely about the money, was it?"

He continued to stare haughtily, certain that Cat was bluffing.

"This was about revenge. This was about revenge on the US government, and me. You used the money to fund acts against Americans, first abroad, and then here, in your own country."

"Now you're being preposterous. What possible reason would I have for revenge?"

"Anoosheh Naziri. You called her Anoo."

Roger blanched, then spat, "You don't have the right to even speak her name."

Cat spoke quietly. "You were both at Princeton. You fell in love. Let me guess ... when she went back to Iran to see her family, you were worried, but not terribly concerned. You probably encouraged her to go. Of course, at that time, you weren't as well-versed in international affairs as you are today. It should have been a quick trip, over and back. But neither of you appreciated the danger. When they confiscated her passport, you thought it would be cleared up in a few days, but days stretched into weeks. What you didn't know until later was that she was pregnant. During the wait for a new passport and visa, she began to show."

Roger glared at Cat with pure hatred and picked up the tale. "She wrote that she talked to an American woman, someone who was still in Iran in October 1979 and who had helped others out of the country. She asked for help, but the woman turned her away. There weren't many Americans still there at that time. I did a little research and figured it had to be someone who worked for the government. Do you want to know why I joined the CIA? To find the woman who killed Anoo. To find you, Cat Powell."

"Roger, I have tremendous regret about what happened to Anoosheh, but there was nothing I could do. Her death haunted me for a long time, but whenever I considered what I might have done differently, I had no answers."

"You got other people out. They hanged her. She was nineteen years old and pregnant with my child, and they hanged her. You could have helped her."

Cat took a deep breath. "I did help people to get out, but that was months earlier. Anoosheh flew into Tehran on October 22, the same day that the shah was admitted to the United States for cancer treatment. The timing could not have been worse. The country erupted in a firestorm; she got caught in it. I'm sorry, Roger, but what happened to Anoosheh was something I could not prevent; it can't possibly excuse what you've done."

The director turned toward the door and called, "Agent Santori?"

Adrian Santori entered the room, his voice heavy. "Roger Pulaski, on behalf of the United States government, you're under arrest for treason, attempted sabotage, murder, attempted murder, and whatever additional charges the Justice Department decides to bring against you."

Cat could no longer contain her anger. "What happened to Anoosheh was abhorrent, but you are despicable. I hope you rot in hell." The pounding in her head was so loud that she barely heard Roger's protestations as he was searched, handcuffed, and Mirandized. She turned on her heel and walked back to the elevator as Paul and the director called after her. She glared at the escorting officer, who hesitated only a moment before activating the elevator's descent to the first floor.

She strode through the lobby and stopped to face the Memorial Wall. The two new stars, freshly carved and still black, were like two eyes, unblinking and unseeing, boring a hole into her soul. She raised her right hand to the wall and touched each star, then closed her eyes and whispered a solemn oath.

She turned to find Paul standing behind her, sorrow etched on his face. "What will you do?"

"Well, I can't go back to Marblehead without a lot of questions being raised by the townsfolk. Some enterprising reporter would get a whiff, and our entire New England operation would be in jeopardy. I'm blown there. The DEA has the house, and we can't share our secrets with them. One of Uncle Sam's black accounts will compensate me for the financial loss, but it's more than that; we were happy there. Lindsey is fighting the seizure, but it's going to be a tough battle. With Evelyn Wainwright at the helm, though, one never knows. She's quite formidable."

"Indeed, she is. And your work? We need you."

"Tom and I are looking for a place to hang our hats. Once we're settled, I'll be back to continue the good fight. But I have to tell you that as long as Conrad27 is still out there, I won't let that go; I will keep looking. Sooner or later he'll make a mistake. When he does, I will find him."

Acknowledgments

Spies in our Midst is a work of fiction. First-person accounts of events occurring in Iran in 1978 and 1979 provided inspiration for the novel's Tehran setting, although the characters and their circumstances and interactions are a product of my imagination. Any errors or inaccuracies in the narrative are solely mine.

This novel was started a number of years ago, and set aside while I was implementing a new software product. At the conclusion of that effort, friends encouraged me to return to writing. The bulk of my writing is a product of a lifetime of learning and observation, and an insatiable appetite for reading. While I was growing up, our house was filled with a wide variety of publications and books. To this day, I will read almost anything that crosses my field of vision, from the label on the ketchup bottle to the discarded medical journal in the airplane seat pocket. Like the person who climbs the mountain because it's there, I read the written word because it's there. Thanks,

Mom and Dad, for being advocates of education and believing that one's learning is the sum of many sources.

My husband has an encyclopedic memory that continually astounds all who know him. He is my first source for confirming the obscure details that lend credence to a story. Our shared life of global adventures provides a deep well from which to draw inspiration and paint the story's canvas.

The Internet is a fabulous place to wallow in information, provided that one doesn't just automatically accept as fact whatever happens to be posted online. I am continually awed that I can now find in seconds what previously entailed a drive to the Library of Congress. Thank you, Merriam-Webster, for a site that helps me to ensure that I've chosen the word with the correct meaning. Thank you, Wikipedia, for providing a fountain of content. The editors do a laudable job of policing what is a monumental amount of data, and the effort is appreciated. Thank you, Google Earth and Google Maps—with Street View—for helping to confirm my recollections of places I've lived and visited; you've given me many trips down memory lane.

I owe an enormous debt of gratitude to a circle of close friends who have provided encouragement and support through life's every turn. Karen Thrasher, thank you for your persistence and confidence. Without your voice in my head, this novel would be gathering dust. To Scott, thank you for being my go-to person for honest assessment, critique, and the plausibility check. I remember our first discussion about this book, in which you worried about how you would tell me if I'd produced something worthy only of a landfill, and ultimately decided that you would be honest. Your stamp of approval meant the world to me. To MM, your nod made my day.

Susan Reynolds's insightful comments were immensely valuable and led to subtle, yet important, enhancements in the narrative. Sallie Pecora-Saipe, educator and fellow traveler, lent her critical eye and attention to detail and helped ensure that the staging of people, events, places, and times were accurately constructed. Annita Stokes-Thomas, former Pan Am-er and current host of a weekly Atlanta-area radio show, provided great insight in shaping the characters of African Americans who make an initial appearance in this novel and will return in future stories.

Other fellow Pan Am'ers Susan Kendall Mayer and Cindy Pritchard, longtime writers and editors of aviation manuals and talent contributors to the League of Women Voters and therapeutic riding centers, respectively, provided sharp eyes for content and structure. Chris Cinkoske, former special ops USAF, filled the many gaps in my knowledge about weapons and explosives. Ben Shelfer selflessly spent time with me to educate me on the intricacies of the publishing world labyrinth.

My editor, Cheri Madison, has an amazing eye for detail. Thank you, Cheri, for your invaluable guidance.

Thank you, as well, to other early readers of the book: Bob Butler, Morgan Pecora-Saipe, Brian Reynolds, Fawn Choate, Joy Farenden, Gary Eichhorn, and Marilyn Crockett.

And to all who read this novel, thank you. I hope you find it enjoyable.

About the Author

LM Reynolds is an IT consultant and Pan Am veteran. An inveterate traveler, she has visited over 125 countries on six continents and continues to seek adventure in new destinations. She currently resides with her husband in Florida.

Author photograph by Brooke Vande Zande

LMReynolds.com
Facebook.com/LM.Reynolds.author
@LMReynoldsBooks

Made in the USA
Columbia, SC
25 February 2019